A NIGHT MADE OF LOVE

"This wasn't the way I wanted it to be for you," Mick said. "Not in some godforsaken cave in the middle of nowhere, with Freddy Halliday hot on our tails."

"I don't care."

The simple declaration caught Mick off guard. "You don't know what you're saying. You may not care tonight. But tomorrow . . . we have no future, Julia. You have no future, not with a man with a price on his head. There isn't a tomorrow for us."

"Then we have only tonight." Reaching over her head, Julia pulled a pin from her hair and smoothed the liberated curl over her shoulder. "I want you to love me, Mick."

He coiled the loosened curl around his finger. "Do you know what you're asking? Do you know what it's like when—"

"You can teach me," Julia whispered.

Diamond Books by Constance Laux

TWILIGHT SECRETS
MOONLIGHT WHISPERS

Moonlight Whispers

CONSTANCE LAUX

DIAMOND BOOKS, NEW YORK

This book is a Diamond original edition, and has never been previously published.

MOONLIGHT WHISPERS

A Diamond Book / published by arrangement with the author

PRINTING HISTORY
Diamond edition / January 1993

ISBN: 1-55773-844-0

Diamond Books are published by The Berkley Publishing Group, 200 Madison Avenue, New York, New York 10016. The name "DIAMOND" and its logo are trademarks belonging to Charter Communications, Inc.

PRINTED IN THE UNITED STATES OF AMERICA

10 9 8 7 6 5 4 3 2 1

For my parents, Stan and Milly Deka, with love. Thanks for giving me a place to write this book, something to write it on, and, most of all, thanks for the babysitting.

County Mayo, Ireland
1882

HE was a dead man for certain.

Eyes narrowed against an unrelenting rain, Patrick stared down at the muddy road which twisted past the hillock where he lay concealed and confronted the indisputable truth—he was a dead man for certain.

He settled himself further into the sopping bracken and his honey-gold brows drew together in a frown. What little he could see beyond the steady curtain of rain confirmed his worst suspicions. A long column of English soldiers was heading directly toward him, materializing like wraiths from a mist as thick as a blacksmith's bootlace. Patrick tried to calculate their numbers, but the swirling fog made any accurate count impossible. He knew only one thing: there were too many of them, at least a dozen more than his informer had promised.

"The devil's own luck," he mumbled under his breath, more annoyed than frightened. It wasn't that he objected to dying. In the eight years since he'd pledged himself to the Fenian cause, he had flirted with death not one, but one hundred times. No, the cause of Irish independence was well worth dying for.

But why did it have to be today?

Patrick pulled his soggy tweed cap further down on his head and let his thoughts drift to the small comforts awaiting him at the farm cottage where he'd been in hiding these past few days. Though his empty stomach protested noisily, he couldn't help but picture the slabs of fresh brown bread the farmer's wife had assured him would be ready when he returned. The farmer had pledged tankards of his delicious, bitter ale to go with it. And the farmer's fetching red-headed daughter? She had not promised anything. Not in words. But Patrick had not failed to notice the tantalizing looks she gave him with those catlike green eyes of hers, and he knew as well as any man of twenty-four years what looks like those implied.

Now, instead of spending a contented night wrapped in the warmth of those pink, freckled arms, he would be lucky if his body was buried by nightfall. More likely it would be left for the crows or dragged to the nearest town and hung on display, a grisly lesson in the inherent evils of Irish nationalism.

Patrick shrugged off the decidedly unpleasant picture. Better to be dead along the side of the road than abroaded to Australia, he told himself, or to go off with the leaf on the end of a British hangman's noose.

The English patrol neared, horses picking their way over the slippery ground, and Patrick swore under his breath. He could see the wagon that contained the Irish prisoners he'd been sent to rescue. It was directly in the center of the troop, protected on all sides by the burliest of the infantrymen. His initial diversion would work well enough on the horsemen up front, but the sturdy-looking guards would be a problem. Damn these Saxons for being so bloody patriotic! Why didn't they keep their strapping young sons at home instead of sending them out to protect the Empire from radicals like himself?

Perhaps he should have listened when one of his superiors suggested he take along a handful of local lads spoiling for a fight. Patrick shook his head and brushed an errant raindrop out of his eye. They couldn't risk an open act of aggression, especially with Connacht boys who might later be identified. This escape attempt had to look, not like terrorism, but like the random act of a madman. His mouth curled into a cheerless smile. At least they had chosen the right man for the job.

Wiping a ribbon of moisture from his forehead, Patrick offered himself false comfort by pretending it was no more than rainwater. As he did before every skirmish, he closed his eyes and whispered the words of the Fenian oath, the sacred pledge which bound him to the secret Irish society.

"I, Patrick O'Flaherty Fitzgerald, in the presence of Almighty God, do solemnly swear allegiance to the Irish republic now virtually established, and that I will do my utmost, at every risk, while life lasts, to defend its independence and integrity, and finally, that I will yield implicit obedience in all things not contrary to the laws of God, to the commands of my superior officers. So help me God! Amen."

He signed himself with a cross, more out of habit than religion, and hoisted his rifle out of the bracken. When the first sounds of disquiet told him the soldiers had found his roadblock, he was ready.

"May as well kick up the devil's delight," he muttered and setting his mouth in a thin, dangerous line, he leapt out of the underbrush and charged down the hill.

Patrick pulled himself to a stop at the bottom and cautiously glanced to his left where the rocks and tree limbs he'd scattered across the road effectively obstructed all movement. His mouth curved into a disbelieving smile.

In a sloppy display of discipline and an infuriating show of arrogance, the British commander had ordered all of his men up front to help clear away the debris. Patrick snickered quietly, unable to control a rush of unequivocal relief. It would serve the English bastards right when they came back and found their prisoners gone.

He slipped out from the trees and crept to the prison wagon. He heard voices from inside, low and secretive, voices that stopped the moment he began to grapple with the lock. It opened easily enough, thanks to the key his informer had provided. Patrick swung the door open and peered into the darkness.

He'd been told nothing more than that there would be two prisoners, both being sent to Dublin to be executed for the crime of treason. Patrick came face to face with the captives and stopped, stunned into immobility. One was a wizened old man who stared past him with a vacant, questioning expression which left no doubt in Patrick's mind that the man was blind. The other was a lad of no more than thirteen, with the downy face of a corpulent cherub and the frightened eyes of a rabbit trapped in a poacher's snare.

Damn! He had expected more capable allies. Patrick shook off his initial surprise and attacked their bonds. He ignored their mumbled thanks, signing them to be quiet and shoving them out of the wagon ahead of him. The youngster wasted no time. He headed for the undergrowth on the other side of the road as fast as his chubby legs could carry him. The old man was another problem altogether. He stopped just outside the wagon door, turning this way and that, his empty eyes searching for the help he so badly needed.

Patrick jumped from the wagon and tugged at the old man's sleeve, urging him to follow into the safety of the nearby woods. The old man started to run, slipped on the rain-soaked ground, and fell to his knees. It took only a second for Patrick to haul him back to his feet, but it was one second too long. Someone sounded the alarm.

Patrick looked up to find the entire patrol heading for them, rifles raised, bayonets at the ready.

Secrecy was useless. "Arrah!" Patrick cursed the fates which had saddled him with this helpless old man and resorted to the only diversion he could think of. He called for the boy to stop and pushed the ancient gentleman toward the trees with a firm, quick command to run straight on and keep on running.

"Well, boyo, you always had more guts than brains," he told himself. And he turned to face the British.

The soldiers were astounded, so much so that for a split second they stopped their attack. Patrick was sure it wasn't the escape attempt itself which surprised them as much as it was the unmitigated audacity of the lone fool who stood between them and their prisoners, daring them to advance on him while his two confederates stumbled their way to freedom.

They didn't stay astonished for long.

Patrick fought them off as long as he could, even managing a shot or two before they got too near. As they closed in, he used the butt end of his rifle as a club. But there were too many of them and they came on too fast.

A second later, he heard the ominous crack of rifle fire and felt a searing pain shoot through his forehead. He collapsed into the muddy ruts alongside the prison wagon, only one thought making its way past the devastating pain in his head.

He was a dead man for certain.

Chapter 1

Yorkshire, England
1886

"Let's ask the spirits something about you, Julia. Let's ask them who you're going to marry."

Julia tossed her long, dark hair over her shoulder and bit back a sharp response to the ridiculous suggestion. Was marriage the only thing Harriet ever thought of? All afternoon, Harriet had peppered the spirits with questions about herself and her own prospects for marriage. Now she wanted to do the same for Julia.

Julia wrinkled her nose and made a face at her friend. But before she could protest further and move her hand away from the small heart-shaped planchette poised in the center of the table, something curious happened.

The planchette began to stir.

Though neither girl touched it with more than her fingertips, the planchette rolled back and forth between them as if it were, indeed, guided by the spirits who were said to communicate through it. Its tiny wheels carried it slowly and noiselessly toward the top of the sheet of heavy vellum writing paper placed in the center of the table. There it stopped.

For a second, Julia took her eyes off the spirit-contacting

planchette and glanced at Harriet. In the dim glow of the gaslights, she saw that Harriet was staring down at the table, a mixture of wonder and renewed amazement in her wide blue eyes. Harriet really believed they had contacted the spirit world! Julia suppressed a chuckle of skepticism and studied Harriet with the cunning of a doctor diagnosing a particularly difficult patient.

There was a fine mist of perspiration around Harriet's mouth. She shuddered and licked her lips, her tongue flicking in and out nervously. Harriet was afraid, Julia decided, but not so afraid that she would dare break off contact with the spirits. She sat dutifully straight in her high-backed chair, her right hand barely touching the planchette and a look of decided concentration on her dainty, beautiful face.

Julia was not as surprised as she was interested, both in what was happening with the planchette and with Harriet's reaction to it. For all afternoon, Julia herself had been using small, undetectable hand movements to guide the planchette in replying to each of Harriet's questions with exactly the answers Harriet wanted to hear.

Until now.

Now, the planchette was moving on its own. Julia dismissed the fleeting and altogether improbable idea that Harriet had anything to do with directing its movements. Harriet was neither clever nor cunning. She believed in the powers of the planchette as surely as she believed in what she called Julia's "special gifts."

"Julia!" The planchette began to move again and Harriet's voice, raised an octave above its usual high-pitched tones, pleaded with Julia to pay attention. Julia looked down at the table. This time, the planchette's movements were smooth and quick. It danced across the paper, and the pencil Julia had carefully sharpened and inserted, point down, in one corner of it, left a clear message.

"P-A-T . . ."

Harriet read the letters as they were formed, her voice hushed and reverent.

"R-I-C-K."

That was enough. Julia pulled her hand away and buried it in the folds of her gown.

"Julia!" Harriet's eyes sparkled with vexation. "Don't you want to know more? The spirits say you're going to marry someone named Patrick. Don't you want to know Patrick Who?"

"Don't be such a dolt." Julia tossed her head. "It's tommy-rot! We don't know any Patricks, do we? And I doubt Grandmother is going to allow me to marry someone from a family she doesn't know well."

"Please, Julia. Do let's try again." Harriet gave Julia a beseeching look.

Julia sighed with annoyance. "Is that all you care about? Getting married? There has to be more to life than that, don't you think, Harriet?"

Harriet's perfectly shaped eyebrows came together in a scowl. For a long, silent moment, she considered Julia's words.

"No," she finally said, shaking her head with uncommon conviction. "I don't. And you'd be wise to think the same. What are you afraid of, Julia? You're twenty-one tomorrow. It's time you started thinking about marriage. I'm certain that's what your grandmother wants to see you about tonight. What did you say she called it? A special dinner? Just the two of you? Of course you'll talk about marriage. You're a woman now and it's time you started thinking about settling down with a home. And a family."

"And someone named Patrick? Tommy-rot!"

"Well, it's true. We don't know any Patricks." Eyes closed, forehead puckered with the effort of concentration, Harriet considered this small complication. "Maybe Patrick isn't his Christian name, maybe it's his middle name," she announced, her eyes flying open with the excitement of discovery. "Or a family name. Have you met anyone named Patrick?"

"I have not." Julia pushed away from the table.

Harriet caught her hand and held her in place. "Please," she begged. "Let's find out if Patrick is the man's Christian name or his family name."

"Oh, very well." Julia conceded defeat. She perched on the edge of her chair and placed the fingers of her right hand on the planchette.

Harriet followed her lead. When they were settled, she whispered her request. "Oh spirits! Tell us the full name of the man Julia is destined to marry."

Instantly, the planchette shifted beneath their fingers. Julia closed her eyes. The mystery of how the planchette was working without her careful direction was baffling. She would give it some thought later, after Harriet was gone. For now, she sat in silence and waited while the instrument finished its message. When it jerked to a stop, Julia opened her eyes and read the words printed on the page.

"Patrick O'Flaherty Fitzgerald." Julia read the message aloud along with Harriet. "Now you know it's nonsense," she said. "Grandmother would never let an Irishman within five hundred feet of the house!"

Harriet's response was interrupted by the opening of the parlor door.

"Not talking with the spirits again, are you?"

Even from across the room, Julia clearly detected the edge of exasperation in Mrs. Dean's voice. Her grandmother's housekeeper marched into the room, a flurry of jingling keys and rustling bombazine. She turned up the gas jets along the wall as she went, then stopped next to the table, one fist propped on each substantial hip.

"Your father's carriage is here to collect you, lass," she informed Harriet, looking at the girl down the full length of a nose so wide and large, it was a wonder she could see around it at all. Harriet's face paled noticeably.

Julia laughed to herself. She reached for a piece of toffee from the bowl at her elbow, discarded the wrapping and popped the confection into her mouth. Poor Harriet, she thought, chewing the sweet. She was intimidated too easily. Mrs. Dean's bark had always been worse than her bite, especially when she pretended to be angry.

At times like these, Mrs. Dean's deep Scottish burr thickened almost beyond understanding. Her already ruddy complexion turned two shades darker and she invariably brandished her finger in warning. It was enough to scare anyone. Anyone but Julia. Julia knew Mrs. Dean was really as gentle as a lamb, and as easily placated as a cat with its whiskers in a bowl of cream.

"And as for you my bonnie, sweet lass." Mrs. Dean turned on Julia, wagging her index finger. "If the mistress finds out about this, she'll have your head first and then mine, just for extra measure. You know she'd not take to the idea of fortune-telling under her roof."

"But she'll never find out, will she?" Julia smiled and hopped out of her chair to wrap one arm around Mrs. Dean's stout shoulders. "You know we're only having fun, Nanny Dean," she cooed. "Whatever else is there to do on an afternoon as frightfully cold and gloomy as this?"

As if to make sure no one was listening, Mrs. Dean glanced over her shoulder toward the door. She pointed at the planchette. "Get that thing put away for one. Before the mistress sees it," Mrs. Dean said. "And show your guest out, for another."

Julia scooped the planchette into her pocket and unwrapped another toffee while Mrs. Dean shooed Harriet to the door. She joined them in the foyer, chatting to Harriet while the footman brought the girl's coat and hat. After she'd gone, Julia turned to Mrs. Dean.

"You won't tell Grandmother, will you? We were only having fun."

"Fun?" Mrs. Dean tipped her head toward the door and

the now departed Harriet. "She's a right fair lass, is that Harriet Lloyd, but she's as simple as oats. You call it fun to fill her silly head with your spiritualist gibberish?"

Julia dropped onto the second step of the stairway and propped her elbows on her knees. "I wasn't saying anything to hurt her," she said. "I'd never do such an awful thing to Harriet. All she ever wants to know about is sweethearts and marriage and babies. It's easy to answer questions like that. I only told her what she wanted to hear and I haven't told her anything that isn't true."

Mrs. Dean's eyebrows shot up almost to her hairline. "You mean to say that not only do you have that poor, wee lass believing in your psychic nonsense, but you're misleading her as well? That you're making that . . . that—what is it you call it?—give Harriet the answers you want her to have?"

There was a mixture of amusement and begrudging admiration on Mrs. Dean's face. Julia found it hard to suppress a smile. "I've only told her the truth," she admitted. "That she's going to marry Reggie Atwalter."

"And how would you be knowing that bit of information?"

"It doesn't take a visit from the spirits or even a fortune-teller to know that," Julia laughed. "Anyone with half a brain could tell. Reggie's been courting her for months. Besides, Harriet's family is one of the richest in this part of England, isn't it? And for years, they've been dying, just dying, to marry into the nobility. Now here comes Reggie, titled, handsome—and very, very poor. Harriet's absolutely mad for him. And Reggie . . ." A momentary feeling of pity for Harriet flooded through Julia and the words caught in her throat. "Reggie will treat her well enough," she finished in a quieter voice.

Julia shrugged off her feelings of apprehension and winked conspiratorially at Mrs. Dean. "Besides," she said, "we were at Harriet's for tea last week and I overheard her father discussing the betrothal arrangements with his secretary. If Harriet paid more attention, she'd know about it, too."

"You're not a fortune-teller," Mrs. Dean said. "You're a witch! You'll come to no good, Julia Barrie, you can take my word for that." Mrs. Dean shook her head, but it was impossible to miss the gleam of delight in her eyes that belied her dire prediction.

"Then you won't say anything to Grandmother?"

"Ach, no, I won't tell. Just you be careful."

Julia rose and smacked a kiss on Mrs. Dean's cheek. "You're a paragon among women, Nanny Dean."

"Yes, that I am. Now get yourself upstairs and get ready for dinner. Your grandmother's due home soon and I've been told she's got something special planned. Don't you dare be late."

"I won't." Julia scurried up the wide staircase. At the first landing, she stopped and turned to Mrs. Dean. "Only . . . Nanny Dean? Do you know what it is Grandmother's planning for tonight? I mean, is it . . . is she . . . has she said anything about my getting married?"

"Married!" Mrs. Dean's chuckle echoed against the polished oak floors and reverberated off the portraits of Julia's ancestors that lined the stairway. "She'd be hard-pressed to find a man to take a troublemaker the likes of you, lass," Mrs. Dean laughed. "Now hurry! I hear her carriage."

Less than two hours later, Julia stood outside the door of the formal dining room. She smoothed the skirt of her newest evening gown and patted her freshly coiffed hair, making sure each dark curl was exactly in place. She raised her hand, ready to knock.

Something made her hesitate.

Silently, she chided herself for her misgivings. Tonight should be like any other night, she told herself. It would be. She would join her grandmother for dinner and polite conversation. They would sip coffee afterward while the servants hovered in the shadows, anxious to tidy up and get to their own meals. Then they would retire to the drawing room where she would entertain Grandmother with a selection of her favorite Schubert waltzes on the piano.

Yet, somehow, tonight felt different. Julia shook her shoulders to rid herself of the uncomfortable feeling of impending trouble. Grandmother had something special planned, she reminded herself. Something special for her twenty-first birthday.

If only she could be sure it was something nice.

Julia scolded herself for the uncharitable thoughts that made their way into her head. For the thousandth time, she found herself wishing Grandmother could be more like Mrs. Dean. No, that was impossible. Mrs. Dean was a warm, affectionate, loving woman. And Grandmother?

Grandmother was Grandmother, the fabulously wealthy head of a mining and milling conglomerate which spanned the Empire from Scotland to India, Australia to South Africa. It was her own private realm and she ruled it with an iron fist and a will to match.

Julia pushed the bad feelings out of her mind. Grandmother was Grandmother, she told herself again, and as kind as she was able to be in her own way. She was certainly generous. Julia had never lacked for a thing: dresses, jewelry, horses to ride, friends to visit and entertain, an education in Paris, a Season in London, another in Egypt. Grandmother's money had bought her everything money could buy a young woman.

If only it could buy her affection.

Julia sighed and knocked on the dining room door. It swung open silently on well-oiled hinges and the footman who opened it stood back to allow her to enter.

Grandmother was seated at the head of the table. As was her custom, she was dressed in black from head to toe, each item of clothing designed and impeccably tailored to enhance her figure and make the most of what remained of her beauty. Her silver-gray hair was expertly piled atop her head and diamonds glittered at her ears and throat. The neckline of her gown was cut low over her bosom, as was the fashion, and even for all her years, she looked remarkably beautiful in the revealing dress.

Her eyes, as light and unemotional as Julia's were dark and expressive, directed Julia to take her seat.

Dinner was a formal, and mostly silent, affair. It wasn't until Grant, the butler, had instructed the staff to clear away all but the wine glasses that Grandmother spoke with anything more than cordial indifference.

"You are twenty-one tomorrow, are you not, Julia?" She didn't expect a reply. She waved her hand toward Grant, waited while he deposited a silver coffer on the table in front of her, and motioned him away. He hesitated near the door, unsure if she would need him further, but she inclined her head in a firm and very regal gesture that told him his services would, indeed, be unnecessary for the rest of the evening. She watched him back out of the room, her gaze as intent as a hawk's on a newly hatched chick.

For a long time after he'd gone, Grandmother sat with her eyes vacant. Her long, thin fingers, each adorned with at least one ring of inestimable worth, lay against the surface of the silver box. She did not caress it, as Julia knew she herself would have done if something that beautiful had been placed before her.

Instead, Grandmother rested her hands on the box as if she were drawing strength from it. Her eyes flickered closed for a second, then snapped open, and she turned to Julia with a look even more unnerving than the one she had given Grant.

"You have seen your father's portrait." It was a statement more than a question. The portrait of Julia's father was enshrined in a place of honor in Grandmother's private rooms, hanging next to the portrait of her grandfather.

Donald Barrie had been Grandmother's only child and he had died nearly twenty-one years ago, shortly after Julia's mother died giving birth to her.

Of course, Julia had seen his portrait hundreds of times. The painting showed Donald to be a handsome young man, magnificent in his gray suit. His thick, dark hair shone splendidly in the light and his deep blue eyes glittered out from the painting, as vibrant and intense as they must have been in life. She had seen other pictures of him over the years. He was invariably in the foreground, always laughing, even in those horribly staged photographs where everyone else looked as if they'd been stuffed and mounted.

Julia couldn't remember a time when she hadn't been in love with him.

"But you've never seen this." The sound of Grandmother's voice, strangely grating, brought Julia back to reality. The old woman lifted the lid of the silver box and withdrew a time-worn photograph. She handed it to Julia, then sat back in her chair, watching the girl's reaction.

It was a photograph Julia had never seen. The woman in it was posed in front of a vase of exotic-looking flowers, her left arm draped dramatically across the back of a settee. She wore a long, flower-printed skirt and a billowing, light-colored blouse with sleeves that flowed out from her shoulders and were gathered tight around her wrists. Her long, dark hair was pulled back from her face and held in place by a patterned scarf and there was a huge, golden hoop in each of her ears.

But it was neither the strange surroundings nor the woman's peculiar clothing that riveted Julia's attention. It was her face.

There was nothing weak or fragile about that face. Though it was supremely feminine, it was not beautiful. Her expression was solemn, yet there was a spark of mystery—or perhaps mischief— in her wide, dark eyes. Her cheekbones were clearly defined, high and exotic, and her lips were full and rounded, parted slightly over even teeth. There was more than just a hint of mettle in her well-molded chin, and the confident way she held her head spoke of both tenacity and determination.

It was a handsome face.

It was Julia's face.

Julia stared down at the faded photograph. She was too stunned to speak, and even if she could think of the proper words to say, she knew she could never get them out. Her throat was dry, her fingers, trembling. She drew in a deep breath and raised her eyes to meet her grandmother's.

"I see you know who it is." Grandmother's voice crackled with emotion.

The first, tongue-tied moments of astonishment evaporated into excitement and Julia found her voice. She could not contain her smile. "It's my mother!" In all the years she had lived with Grandmother, she had never before seen either a portrait or photograph of her mother. When she was a child she had asked about pictures, but she had been told, firmly, that none existed. "She looks like me. I look . . . I look like her!" Julia laughed, studying the picture with renewed interest.

"Yes."

The single word from Grandmother contained more than an acknowledgment. In all her life, Julia had never heard any word, prayer or insult, spoken with more feeling. Her head snapped up and she looked across the table at her grandmother.

The old woman stared back at her, her eyes dangerously dark. Even in the brightly lit dining room, her face was shadowed, as if a cloud had settled over her, turning her features into ruthless silhouettes of themselves.

"You do look like her." She did not raise her voice, but Grandmother's words were no gentler than her look. She inclined her head in the direction of the photograph.

"She was a Gypsy. A Gypsy and an actress." Grandmother spit the words out as if they were obscenities.

"You never told me—"

"Now I will. You need to know about her." Grandmother jabbed her finger at the photograph and Julia found herself clutching it tighter, instinctively sheltering it from the fire in the old woman's eyes. "You need to know about her and what she did to my dear Donald. Yes. She did it to him. You didn't know that, did you?"

Uncomfortable beneath the burning indictment in Grandmother's eyes, Julia squirmed in her chair and pulled the photograph into her lap.

"Hide it if you like," Grandmother murmured, her voice hardening with each word she spoke. "It won't change anything. It won't change the fact that she killed your father."

"No!"

Without knowing or caring why, Julia refused to believe her. Her mother would never do such a thing, she was as certain of that as she was of the next day's sunrise. Not her mother. Not the enchanting girl with the flashing eyes and the dark, mysterious look. Julia clasped the photograph to her chest protectively. Her mood veered sharply from disbelief to anger. She raised her eyes to her grandmother's, blazing her resentment.

Grandmother was not used to being challenged, not by Julia or by anyone else. The old lady flinched, obviously just as surprised by Julia's sudden, stubborn courage as she was appalled by the girl's lack of common sense and respect for her elders. Her face lost all traces of composure, and when she spoke, her voice quavered with emotion.

"Just as obstinate and stupid . . ." Grandmother sputtered. She leveled a withering look at Julia. "Pretend it isn't true, if you must, but you'll hear me out. Donald met her while he was in London on business," Grandmother said, raising her voice and pronouncing each word with unmistakable precision so that Julia could not fail to hear and understand. "She must have enchanted him with her sinful Gypsy magic, it's the only reason a boy of such fine parentage could possibly fall in love with such a . . . such as that. It was a whirlwind romance at best, more likely lust than love." Grandmother snorted with derision.

"Less than six months later, they were married. Donald never consulted me, nor did he ask my blessing. They came here soon after the wedding. That's when I learned she was with child. You. The strumpet tricked Donald into believing the baby was his. Well, maybe it was. But he didn't need to marry her. They came here and expected me to welcome them with open arms.

"I welcomed Donald. And desperately pleaded with him to get rid of the Gypsy and her bastard. But he was so bewitched by the creature he refused to listen. He even threatened to leave. Told me to take his inheritance and the very generous allowance I gave him and burn in Perdition with it."

Twenty-one years later, the pain of that quarrel still transformed her face. Grandmother's cheeks darkened, her eyes narrowed with revulsion and the sting of remembrance.

"They would have left, too," she continued, her voice choked with hate, "but for you. You decided to be born a month too soon. It was only by a stroke of very good fortune that the Gypsy died giving birth to you."

Julia sprang from her chair, too disgusted to listen to any more of the old lady's bile. Grandmother's hand came down on her arm. Like a claw, her fingers twisted around Julia's arm and forced her back into her chair.

"Shocked?" Grandmother asked, her voice as smooth as a well-honed knife. "You shouldn't be. I was elated. It saved me the trouble of arranging a very difficult divorce. I had Donald back. All to myself. There would be an appropriate time of mourning, then a suitable, acceptable marriage. If I was lucky, I might even be able to convince him to get rid of you, send you to some girls' school where you'd be neatly tucked away for years on end. Except . . .''

While Julia had seen only hate in her grandmother's eyes before, now she saw sorrow, an anguish so deep and warped from feeding on itself that it ate away at the old woman's self-control as surely as it had eaten away at her sanity. Her eyes filled with unshed tears and her grip tightened on Julia's arm.

"Except," she whispered, "the day your mother was buried, Donald took a hunting rifle from the lodge and shot himself in the head.''

Julia squeezed her eyes shut and turned her head away. A sickening feeling of nausea filled her and she grasped the arm of the chair with her free hand and willed herself to display a calm she did not feel.

"You said he died of a fever. You never told me.'' She meant it to sound like an accusation, but Grandmother seemed not to notice.

"Of course I never told you! I've been saving it all. Saving it all for tonight. Donald left this.'' Loosening her hold on Julia's arm, Grandmother pulled a ragged envelope from the silver box and placed it on the table in front of Julia. "You may read it once," she told her, "but it is mine to keep.''

The edges of the envelope were worn smooth from constant handling. Julia reached for it, then jerked her hand away. Along one side of it, there were dark spots that might have been ink stains. They might have been ink stains. Or something else.

Grandmother seemed to be reading her mind. "I found it when the blood was fresh,'' she said. "I had to burn the clothes I was wearing. Go ahead. It won't hurt you to touch it now.''

Carefully avoiding the dark stains, Julia pulled the letter from its envelope and smoothed it open.

"'My darling Julia,'" the letter began.

"It's for me." Julia's voice rose with indignation. "It's addressed to me and you've never shown it to me."

"I'm showing it to you now. It is my letter. Read it, or give it back." Grandmother's hand shot across the table, her fingers, like talons, stretched toward the fragile paper.

For a moment, Julia met the challenge, dark eyes sparking against cold, pale blue. But the letter was too precious, the stakes too high. Julia mastered her anger. Sliding the letter along the tabletop out of Grandmother's reach, she read it aloud.

"'My darling Julia, I trust Mother will save this and give it to you when the time is right. I'm sorry to leave you, my precious heart. I know it will be years before you are able to understand. Your dear mother is dead and I am neither strong enough nor brave enough to live without her. She is my life, my soul. I give you into the care of my mother who will give you all you need. I leave you nothing more, or less, than my love.'"

Julia choked back a sob and stared down at the paper. It was some minutes before she realized Grandmother had her hand out, reaching, waiting.

For a second longer, Julia rested her fingertips against the letter, struggling to read it one last time before it was taken from her, fighting to see the words through the veil of tears that clouded her eyes. She might not remember the words, she told herself, stroking the edge of the letter one last time, but the emotion that flowed from Donald Barrie's pen would be imprinted on her heart. It would be safe there, safe from Grandmother's bitterness.

Julia lifted the letter and placed it in her grandmother's hand. "Why?" she asked. "Why are you telling me all this now?"

Only when the letter was safe inside the silver box did Grandmother answer. "Don't you see?" the old woman said. "You need to know all of these things so that you'll understand what's to happen. After all, tomorrow you're twenty-one. I've waited for this day for a very long time."

Grandmother rose from her chair and crossed the room to the rosewood and marble sideboard where Grant had left a decanter of brandy. She poured herself a glassful, threw her head back, and finished it in one swallow.

Turning, she studied the blank, dazed look on Julia's face. "You still don't understand, do you?" The amusement in her voice was more bone-chilling even than her malice. Her words were like ice, echoing in the vastness of the dining room and freezing Julia with the cold dread of foreboding.

"I've nurtured you and given you everything money could buy," Grandmother said, inching ever closer to Julia. "At first I did it only because Donald asked me to. Without that letter from him, I would have deposited you in the nearest orphanage." She dropped her empty glass onto the table as neatly as she would have discarded Julia.

"But after a while, I realized you could be the instrument of my revenge. You're right. You do look like your mother. Every minute of every day, I have been reminded of her through you. You talk like her and act like her, you look like her and think like her. I hate you for it.

"Everything I did, I did in preparation for this day. If I would have left you at the door of an orphan home, I daresay you'd be coping well enough with life by now. You'd be a servant, perhaps, or a girl in a shop. Instead, you've had it all—a fine home, clothes, money, jewels. But what are you good for, Julia?" The old woman leaned her palms against the table and stared down at her granddaughter, her eyes filled with loathing.

"Think about it. What are you good for? You spend hours and hours playing your foolish fortune-telling games. You sit in the library with your nose in a book, dreaming about ridiculous adventures, searching for some foolish romance." Grandmother grunted and tossed her head.

"I should have had those books burned years ago. Then

perhaps you'd be more attentive to practical concerns. You've never bothered to cultivate the social graces that will assure you of an advantageous marriage. If you had, perhaps I'd be lucky enough to be rid of you by now." The old woman shook her head and clicked her tongue. "You are certainly not the girl I hoped you would be."

"You mean I'm not you." Julia faced her, her eyes ablaze. "You mean because no matter how hard you tried, you couldn't turn me into a woman like you, a cold-hearted machine who thinks about money every minute of every day—"

"Oh, you'll think about money." Grandmother's voice dropped until it was no more than a noise that rumbled in her throat like the purr of some predatory cat. "I guarantee you'll think about money soon enough. You want adventure? Then you shall have it. You shall have it beginning tonight."

The terror of slow realization filled Julia. She rose from her seat and backed away from Grandmother, the photograph of her mother still clutched in her fingers. "Whatever are you talking about?"

"You're twenty-one tomorrow," her grandmother said. "And I want you out of this house. I never want to see you again."

Chapter 2

"My poor, dear girl." The man seated across the train carriage from Julia clicked his tongue in sympathy. "What a dreadful story. How awful for you! Imagine anyone being so heartless." The elderly clergyman, who had introduced himself as Vicar Weems, shook his head in silent wonder as if trying to understand the unfathomable complexities of human nature.

"Did you try asking your grandmother's forgiveness?"

Julia gave the idea careful consideration. "I think perhaps if I had begged her for mercy, promised I'd change my ways . . ."

Mr. Weems's forehead puckered with astonishment. "Then my dearest girl, what are you doing here? You should be on your way home to apologize. Back to your grandmother's arms!"

Julia hesitated before she said more. Mr. Weems had proven himself a delightfully old-fashioned and chivalrous traveling companion, not the kind of man who could easily understand either Grandmother's banishment or Julia's reaction to it.

She shook her head. "You don't understand. Grandmother would have loved to hear me plead, but it wouldn't have changed her mind. No. Her plan was fixed twenty-one years ago. Nothing I said or did could make a difference.

Besides''—she smiled at the elderly vicar—''once I knew the truth, I had to leave. It would have been disloyal to my parents not to.''

''Disloyal to people who have been dead all these years?'' This was clearly not a notion Vicar Weems understood. His brow furrowed and he tugged at his left earlobe. As if embarrassed to offer advice, he flicked his gaze to Julia and away again. ''You have yourself to think about, my dear,'' he said. ''That is where your chief loyalty must lie.''

For the first time since the dreadful confrontation with Grandmother, Julia allowed herself to laugh. ''But that's just it, don't you see? I am thinking of myself. I know I shall miss Mrs. Dean and all my childhood friends terribly, but this is my chance to be away from it all.'' She made a gesture of dismissal toward the countryside hurtling by outside the train window.

''It's my chance to do all the things I've only dreamed of. To see the world without Grandmother hovering over me like a spiteful guardian angel. To meet people, and go places and see things.'' Julia settled herself more comfortably into the plush train seat and leaned toward the vicar.

''Do you know, Mr. Weems, we visited Egypt last winter and I never once saw the pyramids. It's not that we weren't given the opportunity. Scads of people invited us to go exploring with them. It was just that Grandmother decided the desert is not an appropriate place for a young lady of breeding. Tommy-rot! That's what I say. It's dreadful, don't you think? To go all that way and not see the one thing you can't see at home.''

Mr. Weems's face reddened. ''But my dear, to be so alone. A young lady, all by herself, with no means of support . . .'' He fanned himself with one hand, too overcome to follow where his train of thought was leading.

''Oh, that's no problem!'' Relieved that the vicar had not been too mortified by her progressive and slightly scandalous thinking, Julia smiled. "I'm a bright girl and I was much more clever than Grandmother thought I would be. She gave me only enough money for my train fare to London." Julia patted her handbag. "But I managed to bring along enough of my own money and jewelry to keep myself quite well for a good long while. In the meantime, I'm convinced a young lady of sufficient means will be welcomed anywhere. Perhaps I'll contact some of the people I met in London last year, or locate my mother's people. Someone will help me."

"Admirable." Mr. Weems beamed at her and his face, as rumpled as a well-used blanket, folded into a million congenial wrinkles. "You are a strong-willed young lady. But you must be very careful, my dear. Very careful indeed. London is full of charlatans, ne'er-do-wells who will pick your purse or your pocket before you know what's happened. Perhaps you'd be more comfortable if someone guarded your savings for you?" He held out his hand, an eager look of saintly concern on his pleasant, red-cheeked face.

Julia hesitated, but only for a moment. "I think not," she said, and added apologetically, "although I do appreciate your concern. But if I'm to learn to live on my own, I'd best start now."

"Admirable," Mr. Weems said again. "I can't tell you how much I admire . . . I say!" The old man's voice rose with excitement. "I've just had the most splendid revelation. Why don't you . . . ? What I mean is, would you . . . ? Would you consider coming home with me?"

Julia's face must have registered her astonishment. A second later, the vicar's broad face broke into an embarrassed grin. "Oh dear," he mumbled. "I seem to have phrased that quite badly. I most certainly did not mean to impugn your character. What I meant, my dear, is that my wife, my dear Mrs. Weems, and I have quite a lot more room at the vicarage than we could ever fill. You could stay with us, at least until you've decided what to do."

"Mr. Weems!" Julia's voice trembled with emotion. To receive such kindness from a stranger when only hours ago her own grandmother had turned her out of the house! "That is most kind of you, Mr. Weems, but I would not dream of putting either you or your wife to such inconvenience."

"Nonsense! If we are not put on this earth to help each other in our times of need, what are we here for? I won't hear another word of dissension. We'll be in London inside two hours. At that time, you'll come with me. Between your own commendable spirit and the help of the good Lord, we'll find a solution to your problem."

Julia's eyes filled with tears.

"There now." Mr. Weems leaned across the compartment and handed Julia his handkerchief. "It's very early. Why don't you relax, perhaps get some sleep? You've had a very difficult few hours."

Mr. Weems was right, she would benefit from a few hours' rest. Julia dabbed at her eyes and leaned her head back. For a moment, the horrible confrontation with Grandmother intruded on her thoughts. She expelled it as quickly as she could, refusing to dwell on the memory lest it eat away at the edges of her excitement.

She could not dismiss thoughts of Mrs. Dean as easily as she did those of her grandmother. What terrible lie would Grandmother tell Mrs. Dean to explain Julia's disappearance? Certainly, the housekeeper would never be satisfied with the truth. And just as certainly, Grandmother would never tell it. No, there would be some more logical story. A lover, perhaps, who had whisked Julia away in the middle of the night? An urgent message from some imaginary relative? Whatever the story, Grandmother would make it believable.

Grandmother.

For a moment, Julia gave in to the anger that eddied through her composure like a dangerous current beneath the surface of a tranquil lake. She clenched her jaw and buried her fingernails into the upholstery of the train seat.

Her life had been a lie orchestrated by a bitter old woman who wanted nothing less than Julia's soul in exchange for her patronage. No matter how bright the promise of the exciting days ahead, nothing could erase that thought. Nothing could make her forget.

Julia forced herself to calm down by concentrating on the steady swaying of the train. Minute by minute, it swept her closer to London, closer to a life free from the shackles of Grandmother's menacing bonds, closer to adventures the likes of which she had read about, and talked about, and dreamed about, but never dared to wish she could live.

"London, miss!"

A gentle tap on her shoulder roused Julia from a sound sleep. She stared at her surroundings, unsure of where she was or what she was doing there. A second later, the memories came flooding back. She thanked the porter for waking her, stretched and looked around the compartment.

Something was very wrong. Mr. Weems was gone. And so was Julia's handbag.

A sinking realization filled her and she called into the corridor.

"Porter! That man, the one who shared my compartment. Where is he?"

"The old gentleman?" The porter scratched his head and considered her question. "Got off at a station back aways," he finally said. "About an hour ago."

An hour! The shock of understanding hit Julia as distinctly as a slap. Her eyes clouded with tears, her breath caught in her throat. How could she have been so stupid! She had trusted the old man. She'd even told him where her money and jewelry were kept. Now he and the money were gone. It was probably no use even reporting the theft to the police. Mr. Weems had an hour's head start.

And when the authorities found out she was alone and destitute, what would they do with her? Julia felt the nauseating sinking of despair. She tried not to think of the horrible things she'd heard about London's workhouses, its sweatshops and common lodging houses where the poor were huddled together, five and six families in one squalid room. But even to sleep in a common lodging house, you needed money. And Julia Barrie had not a penny.

As if in a trance, Julia disembarked from the train and walked though the station. She bit back a sob and forced the first, terrifying feelings of panic to the back of her mind. There was nothing to be gained by causing a scene in public, she told herself, pressing her lips together and forbidding herself to dwell on the problem. She would manage. Somehow she would get by.

"Ho! Here you go! Fresh this morning!"

A thunderous voice called out, and Julia stopped to glance around. Across the platform stood a street vendor. She was a shabby old woman dressed in an odd assortment of cast-off clothing. Green plaid sleeves, yellow striped bodice, faded velvet skirt; pieces of scraps and discarded garments clattered and clashed across the lady's portly body. But it wasn't her eccentric clothing that riveted Julia's attention. It was the huge basket of apples braced against her hip.

Hunger drove every other thought from Julia's mind. Her mouth watered, and she licked her lips and eyed the apples. Automatically, she felt in her pocket for the pieces of toffee she always carried with her. She remembered, too late, that they were gone. She had eaten them on the train in the small hours of the morning, more to calm and console herself than because she was hungry.

Julia dropped onto a bench and buried her face in her hands. She admonished herself for giving in to her despair.

It won't help, she told herself over and over again. It won't help to cry. But it proved impossible to control the tears. They splashed over her eyelashes and flooded down her cheeks. Julia rocked back and forth, her arms wound tightly around her body.

How the sounds of the whispering penetrated through the horrible, sobbing noises she was making, Julia never knew. But somehow, she realized someone was talking about her. She sniffed loudly and pulled Mr. Weems's handkerchief from her pocket. She blew into it, wiped her eyes, and looked up.

Standing not four feet away were two girls, one short and plump, the other tall. Neither was any older than Julia herself and they were both looking directly at her.

"She might do," muttered the shorter girl, nodding her head as if she were a farmer studying a prize sow at a fair. The girl came closer, peering nearsightedly into Julia's face. "She just might do for Annie's place."

"I dunno." The other girl, thinner and far homelier, was not convinced. "Ain't up to just us, after all, Daisy. It's up to the rest of 'em, including Mick. And I'm sure I don't like to be tellin' Mick his business. Scares me to death, that one does. You know how he is, partic'lar like."

"Aye, partic'lar like." The girl called Daisy took a step back, her head to one side. Her hair tumbled over her shoulder like a golden waterfall. "But if he do like her, there might be something in it for us, what? And if he don't . . ."

"If he don't he'll tell her to shove off and maybe us with her."

"Won't neither, Rose, and you know it," Daisy replied, obviously convinced of the logic of her argument. "Ain't time for him to find three more girls. He's having enough trouble fillin' Annie's place."

"Annie's place doing what?"

The two girls flinched and stepped back, as if Julia's

question had surprised them. They gave each other a long, silent look before Daisy, apparently the spokeswoman, stepped forward.

"Annie's place at being a lady's maid," she said. "We're on our way to a country home. You know, the type what's all the go with the swells. We've got to leave this afternoon and we've lost one of our maids. Annie Leathers. Run off with the butcher's boy, she did, not three hours ago. We need to fill her place. You look to be about the right height." Daisy studied Julia from head to toe. "And your coloring's the same what's described in Annie's references. Do you know anything about waitin' on a lady?"

"Don't be ridiculous!" Julia sat up straight and threw a withering look at the two impertinent girls. "I am a lady."

Daisy sucked her teeth. "Well, you look enough like one, but I ain't never seen no lady sittin' in the middle of Euston Station crying," she said matter-of-factly. Rose nodded furiously in agreement.

The simple truth of the statement brought Julia up short. "I'm sorry," she stammered. "You're absolutely right. If I was a lady I wouldn't be sitting here talking to you, would I?" Embarrassed by her anger, Julia laughed through her tears. Yesterday, she might have found this whole conversation mad and entirely impossible. Today, it seemed like a solution to her problems.

"Did you say there's a position open?" she inquired. "With wages? And a place to live?"

"That's right," Daisy said. "Though it ain't much pay, of course." Rose and Daisy exchanged knowing looks. "But Mick, he'll take care you get what's coming to you. He's a devil when it suits him, but I never knowed him to be nothing but fair."

"Well, it just so happens I know all about waiting on ladies," Julia explained, warming to the idea. "I know when they want their tea and which dresses they like to wear, what hairstyles compliment them most and how to lay out their night clothes. Would I . . . ? Do you think I'd do?''

''Can't really say,'' Daisy replied. ''Ain't up to us alone to decide. Mick, he's the butler, he has a say and so does the rest of 'em. We can take you to 'em if you like. And if they does decide they like you, you'll tell 'em how we found you, won't you?''

''Yes. I'll tell them it was your idea.''

Julia followed the girls out of the station. They emerged onto a street choked with crowds of people hurrying through a fine, drizzling rain. Daisy and Rose walked quickly, sure of where they were going in the maze of winding, narrow streets. With each step, they led Julia farther from the station and from any section of London she had ever visited.

The thought that they were robbers like Mr. Weems crossed Julia's mind, but only briefly. She had nothing left to take, she noted sourly, and Daisy and Rose seemed nice enough. They were certainly serving girls. Julia had seen enough upstairs maids, downstairs maids, and tweenies in her life to recognize a servant when she saw one. They both had the fresh-scrubbed appearance demanded by every employer, and their clothes, though certainly not fine, were clean and presentable.

Julia tugged at her own coat self-consciously. It obviously branded her a class above these girls. That might work to her advantage. Perhaps this Mick, whom the girls discussed with so much apprehension and respect, could be convinced that she really was a lady's maid, between positions right now and looking for work. Certainly Julia had observed her own maid enough to know the routine by heart: set out the clothes, run the bath, make the tea. It really couldn't be that difficult. After all, didn't Grandmother spend countless hours complaining about how little the servants did?

As Julia considered her situation, the two girls led her through a warren of run-down shops and shabby pubs. After a while, what little daylight was able to filter through the dull, gray sky was blotted out altogether by buildings that overhung the streets and stood piled one atop the other like tinned sardines. The constant belch from smoking chimneys was trapped in the airless labyrinth of tangled streets, coating buildings and people alike with a dismal layer of gray-black grime.

The soot gritted between Julia's teeth and clouded her eyes. She pulled her coat tighter around herself, not daring to stare at the people they were passing. Most of them were huddled in doorways or sprawled in the gutter; ragged, dirty people with a look of hunger and despair in their eyes. This was the London of the poor, Julia reminded herself, and she was destined to become a part of it if she wasn't shrewd enough to secure this situation as a lady's maid.

Daisy and Rose stopped suddenly and disappeared into the doorway of a pub. Julia followed. The smell inside nearly took her breath away. It was far worse than Grandmother's stables. Julia clutched at the doorjamb for support, swallowed the bitter taste rising in her throat, and forced herself to look around.

The pub was even darker than the street outside. Julia hesitated, allowing her eyes to become accustomed to the pallid light thrown by tallow candles set around the room. The candles guttered in the gush of air from the door, sending weird shadows skipping up the walls. Their feeble light gave little illumination. Perhaps, Julia thought, it was just as well; what she could see was incredibly filthy.

Even at this early hour, the pub was crowded with men in work clothes. As she continued to look around, they turned as one. Their eyes, glazed by drink and lack of light, were firmly on Julia.

Disregarding the pointed stares, Julia searched the crowd for Rose and Daisy. She found them seated at a table along the far wall. She squeezed through the crowded room, markedly ignoring both the outstretched hands of a few, bold patrons and the lewd remarks of others.

Daisy had lost no time. She had a glass of ale in front of her and another ordered for Julia. Julia wiped the edge of the glass with her gloved fingers and sipped gingerly. The ale was as foul as the rest of the pub, but she was thirsty. She took another sip.

Daisy pointed to a man seated in the corner. "I've told him a bit about you."

Julia could see why the girls had spoken so cautiously of Mick. He was a short, thin man and very dark. His eyebrows met above the bridge of a long, angular nose and framed a pair of dark slit eyes that looked no friendlier than the rest of his face. He was not dressed as well as either Rose or Daisy. His shirt must have been white at one time, but now, even in the feeble light, she could tell it was yellow and stained. His shirt sleeves were pushed above his elbows to reveal two very hairy arms and his collar was open and hanging askew.

Julia disliked him instantly, not so much for his appearance as for the look he was giving her. She had seen low-class men look at women that way before, as if they were so many bolts of fabric in a shop window, but she was not used to being examined quite so blatantly herself.

Curbing the sharp remark she was tempted to hurl at the man, Julia extended her hand. "How do you do? My name is Julia Barrie. I'm looking for a post as a lady's maid."

The man did not stand or give her his hand. He inclined his head in her direction, spat on the floor and smiled, his thin lips spreading over a set of blackened teeth.

"Name's Ben Jessup," he said.

"Oh. I assumed . . ."

Jessup jabbed one finger toward the stairway across the room. "If it's Mick O'Donnell you're wanting, that's him there."

The man coming down the staircase was as different from

Ben Jessup as night from day. While Jessup was slight, Mick was tall, so tall he needed to bow his head to avoid the open beams of the low ceiling.

Jessup was slovenly; his clothes, his hair, even his skin encrusted with what looked to be a permanent layer of dirt. Mick's clothes, though they were simply cut, were clean and well-pressed. Dark tweed trousers emphasized his long legs, a pair of brown braces skimmed along the front of his shirt, accentuating his broad shoulders.

His hair was neither blond nor brown, but some indeterminate shade in between. In better light it may have been honey-colored, Julia noted, but it was impossible to tell in here. It was long for a man's, and it fell over his collar and was combed back from his forehead to reveal a wicked scar just below his hairline.

The scar did nothing to diminish the man's undeniable good looks. He had handsome, even features; a well-shaped mouth, a strong, slightly squared jaw that gave his entire face a look of rugged appeal.

Mick's manner was as charming as his appearance. He strolled through the crowded pub, heading in their direction, and stopped occasionally to exchange friendly greetings with the other patrons. After a moment, something in the darkest corner of the room seemed to catch his eye. He fished into his pocket and came up with a coin. Julia watched as he tossed it to a ragged man who sat alone near the fireplace. The old fellow moved faster than would seem possible for a man of his years. Snatching the copper penny while it was still in the air, he smiled a toothless grin and called to the barmaid for a drink. The room rang with Mick's laughter.

Julia forgot the stench of the pub, the still bitter aftertaste of the cheap ale, the frightening reality of her own singular situation. Beneath the curious warmth of Mick O'Donnell's smile, her troubles seemed to melt like snow before the spring sun. She stepped forward, her hand extended, eager to make her presence known.

She didn't need to. Mick's engaging blue gaze swept the crowd and stopped full on Julia. The smile faded from his face.

"By the holy poker and tumbling Tom! What's this, then?" Mick asked no one in particular. His voice was strongly accented, musical, yet not as pleasant as it was insolent.

An Irishman. Dropping her hand to her side, Julia pulled herself up to her full height. "My name is Julia Barrie," she said. "I've come about the post as a lady's maid."

"You've come about the post?" Mick looked her up and down, his golden eyebrows rising even as his gaze dropped.

She was a pretty enough girl, he decided, dark-haired and exotic looking. She had skin like cream tinted with roses and dusky eyelashes that fluttered onto her cheeks like a butterfly kissing a flower. She looked curved and rounded in all the right places, too, even if she was too tall for most men's taste.

Mick stepped back, his head to one side. The girl had no trace of an accent, though her eyes made her look foreign. They were slanted like a cat's, and like a cat's, there was a spark of devilment in them. That could prove interesting.

He cursed himself even as the thought came to his mind. This was hardly the time to be entertaining thoughts of women, especially women who looked and talked like this one.

When he had examined Julia from the top of her head to the tips of her well-polished boots and back again, Mick let out a long, low whistle.

"And who in the name of the saints and angels ever brought us the likes of you?"

Julia clutched her hands at her waist. "How I found you isn't important," she said. "What is important is that you need a lady's maid. I'm qualified and I'm willing to work. That's what's important."

"Saints preserve us!" Mick shook his head, too stunned to decide if he should laugh or scream. This was all he needed, some pretty, young thing fresh from the nursery, tagging along and mucking up his plans.

He tossed Julia a scathing look. "You don't look like a lady's maid."

"You don't look like a butler."

For a moment, Julia thought she had gone too far. Mick's eyes sparked, his fingers tensed and curled into fists. The next second, the absurdity of the situation seemed to dawn on him. His mouth tipped into a lopsided, skeptical smile. "And what would the likes of you be knowing about butlers?" he asked.

Ignoring the glimmer of wry amusement in his eyes, Julia raised her chin. "I am a lady's maid, after all," she said, keeping her gaze firmly fastened to his. "I've worked with butlers for years."

Mick looked down at her, still smiling. "You, my fine and fancy lady, are no more a lady's maid than I am. And I can prove it. Give me your hands."

Julia hesitated, instinctively pulling her hands tighter to her sides.

Mick seemed to enjoy her discomfort. A slow smile spread across his face and he took one step closer. "Oh, come now," he said, his voice shimmery and low. "I'm not going to toss you down onto the floor and have my way with you. I only want to look at your hands." He stepped nearer and ran his hands down the length of her arms, drawing off her gloves.

His touch was as staggering as a jolt of electricity. Julia started and backed out of his grasp. "I can do that quite well myself." She slapped Mick's hands away and tossed him a look of contempt.

"There," she said, sliding off her gloves. She flipped her

hands palm up, then down, but kept them safely from Mick's reach. "You've seen my hands. Are you satisfied?"

"Satisfied you've never done a day's work in your life."

"Not recently. I'll admit that." Julia scrambled for any credible explanation and grabbed at the first that presented itself. "I've been . . . traveling." Where the word came from she never knew, but she seized the idea and held on. "Traveling with a theatrical company. I worked as a dresser and a dresser does much the same as a lady's maid, doesn't she?"

Mick did not reply. He stood before her, his arms folded across his chest, doing nothing to disguise a look so brazen it sent Julia's temper soaring at the same time it caused an uncomfortable tingling in the pit of her stomach.

"I was a lady's maid before that," Julia continued. Even to herself, the story sounded too hurried, too desperate. Mick wasn't believing a word of it, she could tell that from the look in his eyes. They were twinkling, curse him! Even in this murky light, she could see they were twinkling. But whether it was with amusement or with mockery, she couldn't tell.

She swallowed the light-headed feeling of hysteria rising within her and continued. "Prior to that, I had a position with a lady in Kent. If you doubt me, I'd be happy to provide references." What was wrong with her? She didn't know a soul in Kent. Julia held her breath, waiting for certain dismissal.

It came without a second's hesitation.

Mick leveled an exasperated look at Daisy. "Get her out of my sight!"

"Now wait a moment, Mick."

To Julia's surprise, it was Ben Jessup who had spoken. He rose from his chair and scurried around the table to face Mick. "If you let this one go, who'll take Annie's place? That's what I should like to know. If we show up at that there fine country house without a lady's maid"—he tossed a look over his shoulder at Julia—"any lady's maid, them rich folks, they'll be askin' questions for sure."

"Ben's right, Mick. Askin' questions. That's what they'll be doin'." This time, it was Daisy who spoke.

Julia gave her a small, gratified smile.

Mick ran one hand through his hair and rolled his eyes. "Are you all daft?" He puffed out his displeasure and looked at the others. They stared back at him, silently imploring him to listen.

Mick threw his hands in the air. "Very well. I can't fight all of you. We'll talk about it." He turned to Julia. "If you'll excuse us one minute?" He bobbed his head, directing her toward the bar.

Julia looked over Mick's shoulder to the dirty, crowded room beyond. "I will certainly not go stand across the room alone. It isn't proper."

"Not proper?" Mick's surprise was clearly etched on his face. The next second, his incredulity dissolved into an enormous grin. "Very well, my fine and fancy lady," he said, bowing from the waist. "You stay here. We'll go to the bar and talk." With that, he motioned to the others and they crossed the room.

Mick leaned against the bar, his hands stuffed into his pockets, his legs crossed at the ankles. Jessup, Daisy, and Rose began voicing their opinions, all of them talking at once, competing for his attention, but Mick only grunted, half listening.

He cocked his head to one side, amazed and more than a little annoyed, his thoughts not on the lively argument that swirled around him, but on the girl standing as stiff and as tall as a statue on the other side of the room.

Why was it every stray seemed to find its way to his door? he asked himself. For a stray she undoubtedly was. But this one was different from most of the other drifters he'd seen. Perhaps that was why she disturbed him so. This one talked like a lady and was dressed as fine as a duchess. This one was trouble, to be sure.

No woman so well dressed was a servant. Mick was certain of that. No woman who spoke the way this one did had ever been a maid. He was sure of that, too. That should have been enough to make him send her away.

But no woman as pretty and obviously inexperienced as this one had any chance if she was turned away and sent, alone, onto the streets of London. The thought nagged at Mick's mind.

Was it charity that made him so vulnerable to the girl's petition?

Charity had never been one of Pat Fitzgerald's weaknesses, he reminded himself. No matter how desperate the situation, Patrick O'Flaherty Fitzgerald would have never risked involving a stranger in his business. He would have been too suspicious, too distrustful, too afraid of the peculiar tug of emotion he felt each time he looked at this curious English girl.

But Pat Fitzgerald was as good as dead. Not for the first time, Mick smiled at the thought, genuinely pleased he had abandoned Pat Fitzgerald to rot in his Fenian hell.

But while Mick O'Donnell might not be as heartless as Pat Fitzgerald, he was still not a charitable institution, he told himself again and again. He had not been sent to London to take in wide-eyed innocents and keep them safe from the harsh realities of life on the streets. He had not been sent to London to take in strays, no matter how pretty they were. He had more important things to do than play nursemaid to a Saxon brat, especially one who was stubborn, willful, and spoiled.

"We need her, Mick." Daisy's voice broke into his reverie. "We need her right bad or there'll be hell to pay from the nobs."

Mick shook off his preoccupation long enough to remind her, "Servant girls never say hell."

"Well?" Now that they had his attention, Ben Jessup looked at Mick, a question in his eyes. "We all vote to let the girl come with us. What about you, Mick?"

What did he want to do about this mysterious girl? Mick took one more look at Julia. He was making her nervous, he thought, though she was plucky enough not to show it as most women would. From across the room, she kept her gaze on him, her hands clenching and unclenching at her sides. Nervous? Perhaps not. There was a spark of impatience in her dark eyes and her lips were pressed closed as if to force her silence. Nervous, hell! She was angry. Damn these Saxons for their haughtiness!

At the thought, a flash of resentment shot through Mick. He was keeping her waiting. And Julia Barrie was clearly not used to waiting.

Without replying to Jessup's question, Mick stalked across the pub. He stopped only inches from Julia, his eyes narrowed, his mouth pulled into a scowl.

"What are you running from?"

The question caught Julia completely by surprise.

"I asked you, what are you running from?" Mick took another step closer and glared down at her. "Are you hiding from someone?"

Standing this close, he towered over her. The light coming from behind him created a fiery aura around his head, a light that was reflected in the flash of blue lightning in his eyes. Julia pushed a nearly uncontrollable feeling of alarm from her mind and forced herself to look up into Mick's face. She could not answer him.

He took her silence for obstinacy.

"I won't take you on without knowing the whole truth about you," Mick told her.

Julia swallowed the taste of panic in her throat. This was her chance. Her only chance. She would not lose it because of some hardheaded, ill-mannered Irishman. "And if you don't, who will you find to take Annie's place?" she demanded, desperate enough to confront him. "You've only got a few hours, haven't you? And not a ghost of a chance of finding someone to match Annie's references. I'm the right height, aren't I? You'll be hard-pressed to find another woman so tall. And the right coloring? Dark, just like Annie. If you let me leave, you won't find another."

Charity or no charity, the woman was boiling his blood. Mick swore softly to himself and spoke, a barely controlled anger in his voice.

"Saint Brendan and Saint Joseph! It seems we have another Joan of Arc on our hands. Enjoy fighting, do you? Then you've come to the right place. But before you go and say too much and get yourself tossed out onto the street, there's something you should know. I won't be risking my own reputation for someone who isn't quick, or clever, or obedient. If you come with us, you agree to work by my rules. I won't tolerate—"

"You won't tolerate . . ." The absurdity of the remark nearly caused Julia to laugh out loud. She forgot her apprehension in a rush of righteous outrage. "You may be the butler, Mr. O'Donnell, but let me remind you that as a lady's maid, I would have a certain rank of my own quite equal to yours."

"As far as our employers are concerned, perhaps," he conceded. "But I'd best make myself clear to you now. I am in charge of this operation. Make no mistake about that. I may agree to take you to Cornwall with us. I may not. But if I do, it won't be because I feel sorry for you. I'll be expecting you to work and to work hard. You won't be Julia Barrie, the fine and fancy lady. You'll be known as Annie Leathers, the maid, and you'll work from sunup until sundown." He grabbed her right hand and held it tight in one of his.

"You won't weep or carry on because your perfect little white hands have become red and rough," he said. As quickly as he had seized it, he dropped her hand. "You won't complain or cry because your pretty face has been spoiled by the dark circles under your eyes." He brought one finger up to her face and stroked it across her cheek, not gently, but swiftly, as if the feel of her skin against his burned through him.

"I won't see things jeopardized by your stubbornness," he said, his voice edged with unspoken challenge. "If you can't or won't abide by our agreement, you'd best be leaving right now. I'll not be tolerating someone who won't work, and I'll not be risking the success of this little venture on someone who isn't bright enough—"

"Someone who isn't bright enough?" Julia's fury choked her. "Why, you insolent—"

"Insolent what? Irishman? Is that what you were about to call me?" In an instant, Mick's anger dissolved. He threw his head back and laughed, genuine amusement in his eyes. "Go ahead, my fine and fancy lady. Call me an Irishman. That's one insult I wear like a badge of honor."

If nothing else, his boisterous, good-natured laugh served to diminish their animosity. Julia relaxed. In spite of herself, she returned his smile.

In that one brief second, the harmony between them seemed absolute. The spark in Mick's eyes softened to a brilliance that Julia responded to immediately, instinctively. Like sun after a spring rain, his smile warmed her, inside and out.

But as he watched her, the smile faded from Mick's face. This one was trouble, his conscience reminded him none too gently. This one was too young, too innocent, too vulnerable.

"If you're wise you'll leave here now, while you can," he told her, his voice lower, gentler than she'd heard it before.

Julia shrugged. "I can't. I've nowhere else to go."

Mick nodded his understanding. "Then the position is yours," he said simply.

Julia breathed a sigh of relief. Before she had a chance to thank Mick or to assure him she would not disappoint him, Jessup and the other servants joined them. When they approached, Mick pasted the bold, slightly cynical smile back on his face.

"I've told her she's to have the position if she wants it," he told them. "But I'm holding those who brought her here responsible for her behavior." He threw a knowing look at Daisy and Rose. "They'd best see she don't bungle things."

That settled, he turned back to Julia.

"I'll have to take your clothes."

Julia bristled at his statement. "I beg your pardon?"

Mick grinned almost sheepishly and his cheeks reddened. "What I mean," he said, "is you can't go into service dressed like that. I know a priest who'll be happy to take your clothes for the needy. The girls will take you for more proper attire."

"I haven't any money."

Mick paused for a moment, thinking. "No. Of course not. I'll loan you the money," he finally said. "You can pay me back from your wages."

Their business concluded, Julia moved toward Rose and Daisy. Mick's voice stopped her.

"There's one other thing," he said.

"Yes?" Julia turned to find him watching her carefully.

"You said I don't look like a butler."

Julia smiled. "It's your hair," she said. "It's far too long."

Mick waved away her objection. "I'll be as clean cut as the Prince of Wales before we're anywhere near Cornwall."

"And it's the way you look at people," Julia said quickly, before she could convince herself to say nothing at all.

This criticism was apparently not as easy for Mick to take. He lifted his chin and pinned her with a look so bold and insolent it made her tremble. "And what, exactly, is wrong with the way I look at people?"

Julia straightened her shoulders. "You're a butler. Butlers never look their betters in the eye."

"Is that all?" Mick's eyes glinted with mischief. "I know that now, don't I? And I'll be sure to pay it some mind, as soon as ever I meet someone better than me."

bundle on the dry-cleaning table. "And how are you this lovely morning, Joan of Arc?"

His congenial manner did little to improve her mood. Too tired and miserable to care what he thought, Julia snapped at him. "I'm awful, that's how I am, as if it's any of your concern."

She elbowed past him and grabbed for Miss Regina's gown. With one fluid movement, Mick pushed the gown out of her reach and stepped in front of her, blocking her way.

"What's this?" He tilted his head, trying to get a look at her face.

Julia refused to meet his eyes. She stepped away. Mick countered perfectly. He was between her and the stairway. And he wasn't about to move.

He folded his arms across his chest. "What's wrong?"

"What's wrong!" The man's callousness was equaled only by his bullheaded stupidity. Julia's mood veered from depression to anger with a swiftness that surprised even her. She propped one fist on each hip and glared at Mick, her voice sharp with rage.

"What's wrong? I'll tell you what's wrong, Mr. O'Donnell. I hate this place! I hate Miss Regina and I hate Miss Louise. They're hard to please, inconsiderate and nearly as rude as you. I hate working from before the sun comes up until well past when it goes down while Mrs. Beecher watches over my shoulder just waiting for me to make a mistake so she can criticize me."

Barely controlling a smile, Mick listened to Julia complain. She looked more like a hellion than a pampered lady, more like one of the witches that were said to haunt the surrounding moors than a lady's maid. Ringlets of hair fell from the knot at the back of her head and her eyes sparked with fury. There were copper-colored flecks in her dark eyes that he had never noticed before and a curious catch in her voice. She was not telling the complete truth. Mick was sure of that. She was holding something back, something that made her uncomfortable.

A satisfied smile spread across Mick's face. He suspected he knew what was really bothering her, but it would be delectable to hear it from her. He turned his brilliant smile full on her, his blue eyes glittering with delight.

"And what else is it that you hate, Joan of Arc?" he asked, his voice as sweet as honey, goading her on.

It wasn't the question, it was the way he said it. He was maddening, almost as maddening as the tiny, thrilling thread of excitement that flowed through Julia each time he looked at her that way.

Forcing herself to ignore the glimmer in Mick's eyes, she concentrated on the frustrations and miseries of the past four weeks. "I hate pressing and I hate cleaning," she said, giving her workbasket a shove. "I hate petrol. But most of all, I hate you, Mick O'Donnell. You're too bold, too familiar, and altogether too pleased with your Irish self. I hate you for letting me come to this place!"

"You hate me!" Mick threw back his head and roared with laughter.

With every second, Julia felt her annoyance grow. Mick was laughing at her and the thought rankled more than she cared to admit. She turned away and went to stand near the windows, her arms wrapped defensively across her chest, her lips clamped together, determined to contain her tears of humiliation. It was no use. With one hand, she dashed the tears from her eyes while with the other, she frantically searched through her pockets for a handkerchief.

She felt Mick approach before she heard him. Suddenly, the temperature in the small room shot up and the air thickened until it was too close to breathe. Julia fumbled through her pockets. But as Mick closed the distance between them, even the simple search for her handkerchief became impossible. Her fingers were stiff and unresponsive, her heart thumped against her ribs so violently, she was sure he could hear it.

"There, there, *acushla*. Now you really are going to cry, aren't you?" Mick's voice, hushed to a whisper, was soft against her ear. Gently, he placed both his hands on Julia's shoulders and turned her to face him.

All remnants of amusement were gone from his face, replaced by a look of understanding so poignant, it caused Julia's breath to catch in her throat. It escaped in a slow sigh, then caught again and she hiccuped loudly.

Mick chuckled and smoothed a stray wisp of hair from her face. He tucked the curl behind her ear, his fingers lingering there for just a moment before he slid his hand down to take hers.

The warmth of personal contact was too much to bear.

Julia wound her fingers through Mick's and leaned closer. When he wrapped one arm around her, she did not move away. She buried her face in his shoulder and cried.

All too aware of the feel of Julia's body pressed against his, Mick smiled to himself, content for the moment. He dipped his chin to rest it atop her hair. It was soft and warm and it glowed with blue-black highlights in the sunshine. Ignoring the odor of petrol that clung to her, he concentrated instead on the subtle, more pleasing fragrance of heliotrope that perfumed her clothes and hair, and on the small vibrations that fluttered through her as she cried. She trembled against him, her movements as delicious as the touch of sunshine that warmed his hand where it lay flat against her back.

A month ago, Mick would have sworn he'd never be foolish enough to jeopardize a job by getting involved with one of his subordinates. But a month ago, he hadn't met this rare girl, so elegant he might have thought hugging her this close would break her. So tenacious, she had not succumbed to the unending demands of life as a servant, even though he had tried his damnedest to see that she did.

She was his enemy, an old, unpleasant voice inside his head interrupted his fancies to remind him. The girl in his arms represented everything he had ever struggled against: class differences, the privileges of the wealthy, the obscene system of land distribution that kept his people slaves in their own country.

The enemy? Mick banished the voice to the back of his mind where it belonged. How could any feeling this marvelous be caused by an enemy?

He loosened his hold and reached into his pocket. "I'm sorry. I never meant to make you cry." He dabbed Julia's face with the corner of his handkerchief. "Just look at you. You've gone and got yourself all red. Your hair looks like a broom in a fit and your eyes are as swollen as a landlord's pocketbook. Here." He reached for the high collar of her gown and began unfastening the buttons. "You need some air."

Surrounded by the heavy warmth of the attic, dazzled by the tender concern in Mick's voice, Julia closed her eyes and gave herself to the shivery sensation of his touch. Her buttons popped open, one after another, until she felt a breath of cooler air, first on her neck, then against the moist skin just above the top of her lace-edged corset.

Mick moved back one step, forcing his hands to his sides and commanding them to stay there though they seemed to have a mind of their own. They longed to flick aside the bodice of Julia's gown so he could gaze at the smooth expanse of skin beneath the stiff black cloth. They tingled, eager to spread the fabric wider so he could watch the play of light and shadow against the delicious swell of her breasts.

With more self-restraint than he knew he possessed, Mick kept himself from doing either. Instead, he brought only one finger to Julia's neck, allowing himself the small pleasure of gliding it from her ear to her collar. He meant to slip inside her open collar for a second before he retraced his path back to her ear, but Julia did not give him the chance.

She stiffened at his touch. Her eyes flew open and she swatted Mick's hand away.

"What on earth do you think you're doing?" she demanded. "If you think you can take advantage of a lady just because she is not in possession of her emotions—"

"I was trying to get you some air, that's what I was doing." Mick held up his hands in a gesture of surrender. "What's wrong with you, girl? You act like you've never been with a man before."

Julia glared at him and grappled with her buttons. Her fingers refused to cooperate. With each try, her cheeks grew redder, her movements more agitated.

Mick watched Julia struggle to regain her composure. Any other time, the scene would have appealed to his imagination. What better way to spend a spring morning than watching a beautiful woman fumble with her clothes? The truth behind Julia's embarrassment dawned on him gradually, erasing his pleasure.

"It's a guffoon I am, to be sure. You haven't been with a man, have you?"

Julia's fingers froze and her gaze snapped to Mick's, her eyes burning with indignation and embarrassment.

It was the only answer he needed. Damn! First he'd made her cry and now he'd nearly caused her to lose what little pride she had left.

Mick turned his back. "Then what of the story that says you were turned out of your grandmother's house because of a love affair?"

"My grandmother!" Julia tensed, her buttons forgotten in her astonishment. "What do you know about my grandmother?"

"I know you're Julia Marie Victoria Eloise Barrie," Mick said simply, wrapping his accent around the words until they were more of a song than a name. He dared one quick look over his shoulder and smiled.

His brief, all-too-interested glance was enough to spur Julia into action. She compelled herself to keep silent until she was finished fastening her buttons. When she was done, she asked, "And my grandmother?"

Mick turned back to her, his expression thoughtful. "I know she's one of the richest women in all of England. I know she's Margaret Barrie." He did not speak Grandmother's name as delicately as he had spoken hers. He hurled the words across the distance between them, as if keeping them too long in his mouth would scald his tongue.

"Yes." Julia looked Mick in the eye. "She is my grandmother. How did you find out?"

"It's my business to know things. You don't think I'd have let you get this far if I didn't know all about you, now do you?"

"How long have you known?"

Mick crossed his arms over his chest, looking very pleased with himself. "Since the second week we were here. You told me your name, finding out the rest was simple."

"And you heard . . . ?"

"The entire story. How you had a falling out with the old woman. How you were sent from your home because of a scandal involving a man."

"Do you believe it?"

"It doesn't make no never-mind what I believe, does it? It's nothing to be ashamed of. You're not the first girl who's been taken in by a fast-talking lover, if it is true."

"And if it isn't?"

Mick pursed his lips. "If it isn't . . ." He paused and considered her, an expression something like relief sweeping across his face. "If it isn't, I've thought wrong of you all this time and I'm sorry."

Julia nodded, accepting his simple apology in silence.

Mick cocked his head. "Then what of the rumor that says Margaret Barrie's granddaughter ran off with a rather unsavory gentleman?"

"It's tommy-rot, that's what it is," Julia said, anger simmering in her voice. She dropped to the floor and leaned back against the wall, her gaze focused firmly on the ceiling. "It's all tommy-rot. A pack of lies fabricated by my grandmother."

"And why would a lady like Margaret Barrie tell that kind of story about her own granddaughter?"

Julia sighed. "Because she hates me."

"What?" Mick settled himself on the floor next to her and rested his chin on his knees. "I can't believe she'd disgrace her own flesh and blood because—"

"Believe it, Mr. O'Donnell. She's been planning this for years, at least that's what she told me. When I turned twenty-one . . ." Julia's voice caught in her throat and she sat quietly for a moment, willing her errant emotions to obey her reason. When she spoke again, she sounded calmer than she felt. "When I turned twenty-one, she told me I was no longer welcome in her home. She sent me away."

"Well, if that don't beat Banaghan!" Mick shook his head, his golden brows lowered. "Alone? With nothing but the clothes on your back?"

Julia laughed, cheered by the look of absolute bewilderment on Mick's face. "It wasn't as bad as all that. I thought I was off on some marvelous adventure. I even had the sense to bring along enough money to keep myself." She felt her face flame at the memory of her naïveté and her blind trust of the dishonest Mr. Weems. "The money was stolen before I ever got to London," she admitted. "So you see, I took this position because I had no choice. It was the only thing I could think of at the time. It was obviously a mistake, but . . . well . . . even making a mistake is better than starving."

Mick shifted his weight, turning to face her. She was a

brave one. He should have known that from the first. He saw it in the set of her chin, the fire in her eyes, the firm, unwavering way she held her shoulders, whether she knew it or not, that told those around her she was not one to be trifled with.

Reaching for Julia, he delicately brushed a tendril of hair from her eyes. A small smile tugged at the corners of his mouth. "And are you staying here now because you have no choice?" he asked.

For a moment, Julia was too dazed by the concern in his voice to answer. She swallowed hard, battling a surge of emotion that was frightening at the same time it was breathtaking. "That's right," she finally answered. "I'm staying here because I have no choice." Eager to escape Mick's disturbing nearness, she gathered her skirts, preparing to stand. The feel of his hand against hers stopped her.

Julia dropped back to the floor, trying to deny the implausible comfort of his touch though her tired spirit cried out for more. She should draw her hand away, a proper voice inside her said. But another voice, another self, longed for human nearness, for the warmth of communication and, perhaps, the hope of understanding. Julia raised her eyes to Mick's and her defenses melted beneath the appeal of the smile that greeted her.

"Are you that unhappy?" Mick was laughing before he even finished the question. "Of course you're unhappy. I suppose you've told me that and more, haven't you?" He gave Julia's hand a friendly pat. "You tell me what I can do to make things easier for you and I'll see about helping you out."

"You'd do that? For me?" Julia felt the gloom that surrounded her lifting.

Mick chuckled. "What would you like?"

"What would I like?" Julia tilted her head back, her eyes closed. "I'd like a new pair of shoes. These are pinching my toes. And I'd love some toffee." A second later, the harsh realities of her position overshadowed her. She sat up straight, the smile fading from her face. "I'm sorry," she said. "Neither of us can afford those things on our wages."

"I can and I will." Mick hopped to his feet, pulling Julia up with him.

There seemed to be nothing more to say. Julia smiled her gratitude and moved to pull her hand away, but Mick would not allow it. He folded his fingers over hers, tighter, warmer than before. For a minute, he did not speak but only stared down at her, sunlight glinting off his hair, reflecting in eyes as blue as the sky outside.

There was danger in this man, a voice of logic inside Julia's head told her; danger in his eyes, danger in his lips, a danger that terrified her even as it sent a ribbon of desire curling through her. Though her body ached for his touch, her reason warned against it.

If Mick saw the hesitation in her eyes, he did not acknowledge it. He leaned nearer, his mouth perilously close to hers. "And what else is it you'll be wanting, Julia Barrie?" he asked.

In an instant, Julia made up her mind. When she spoke, her voice was almost as low as Mick's. "What I'd really like," she said, "is some printer's ink."

"Some . . ." Mick took a step back and dropped her hand. After a second's uncertainty, his eyes mirrored her amusement. "What in the name of the Holy Mother are you going to do with printer's ink?"

"Tell fortunes." Julia laughed at the astonished look on Mick's face. "For Daisy and Rose. They want their palms read and it's easier to do if I can make a print of their hands. With a gelatin roller, I can roll the printer's ink over their palms"—she demonstrated with her own hand—"press them on paper and read their palm prints. So, you see, what I really need is some—"

"—printer's ink," they finished in unison.

He looked at her doubtfully. "If Mrs. Beecher finds out,

up goes McGinty's goat! And that means all hell will break loose.''

''She won't find out. It's just for fun. We'll only do it in our rooms when all our work is finished. Please. I promised Rose and Daisy, and they've been so good to me. Without them, I never would have gotten through this past month.''

Mick cupped his chin in one hand and rubbed it thoughtfully. ''How is it a fine and fancy lady like yourself knows about fortune-telling?''

Julia smiled. She went to the window and stood looking out, and when she spoke, her voice was distant.

''When I was a girl, there was a lady in our village. Mrs. Tooley. Grandmother said Mrs. Tooley was a witch. A filthy, evil witch. She absolutely forbade me to visit her. Of course after that, I made a point to call on Mrs. Tooley every chance I could.'' Julia laughed and traced an invisible pattern on the window glass with the tip of her finger.

''Mrs. Tooley was the one who taught me card reading and palmistry.'' She turned to Mick. ''It was such a marvelous game, I never told her I knew it was tommy-rot.''

''Then you can't really do it? You can't really see what's in a person's future by looking at his hand?''

From the sparkle in Mick's eyes and the smile he could barely contain, Julia knew he was having her on. He was teasing her, gently, playfully, but teasing still. She found herself returning his smile and joining in the game. ''Well, that all depends.''

''On what?''

''On how good a subject I have. On how cooperative the person is while I'm reading. On if he really believes.''

''All right, then.'' Mick crossed the room to stand in front of her. He opened his right hand, palm up. ''Tell my future.''

''Here?'' Julia looked at him, surprised and more than a bit disconcerted. Palm reading could be emotional and intensely personal. The thought of getting that close to Mick

O'Donnell caused her heart to begin thudding uncomfortably again.

"Here." He took another step toward her, his hand out.

Julia stepped back and countered with the only excuse that came to mind. "I should be getting back to work."

Mick's smile widened, his voice took on the smooth, mocking tones of a dare. "You can't do it, can you?"

Julia bristled at the challenge. "Of course I can."

Before she could stop herself, she grabbed for Mick's hand and pulled him closer. His skin felt warm and supple in the light of a sunbeam that flowed like a shaft of liquid gold through the window. She gazed down at it and tried to convince herself it was a hand like any other hand. He was a palm-reading subject, nothing more. The small shiver that tickled its way from the pit of her stomach to the top of her head warned her she was wrong. Julia swallowed hard and spoke with as much composure as she could manage.

"The first thing we look at is the shape of your hand," she explained, driving the emotion from her voice. "You have a philosopher's hand. That means you're one of those people who search for the truth. You are a great advocate of justice and social freedom. The next thing we examine are the fingers. You have a strong Jupiter finger." She pointed to his index finger, barely daring to touch it with the tip of her own.

"That, coupled with your strong thumb, show that you are overbearing. Your Line of Mars confirms this." She pointed to a vertical line near his thumb. "People who have a Line of Mars quarrel easily and are often swaggering, overbearing, and truculent." She looked up at him, a sweet smile on her face.

"That, at least, we can attest to being true. However, on the positive side, the line does equate with bravery. Your Mount of Mars Positive shows this, too. It shows you possess great courage, strength, vigor, and the capacity to cope with the hardships of life."

She pointed again, being sure to keep her finger just above his palm. "This is your life line. It shows that many of your actions are undertaken on impulse, uncontrolled by practical considerations. Your hand also shows you want success. Success at all costs. Of course, we'll have to take into account all the other indications on your hand to determine if this means success in business, or monetary success, or—"

"What about success in love?"

Julia felt her throat go dry. She wiped the palm of her left hand against the skirt of her gown and prayed Mick couldn't feel her right hand trembling. "Love means so many things," she said, her voice wavering more than she liked. "We must read your heart line in conjunction with your head line to see how your mentality and emotions balance. Now your head line—"

"Damn my head line. What's this about a heart line? What does it tell me about love?"

There was no use trying to distract a man who was so obstinate. Recognizing she had lost this round, Julia cleared her throat and continued. "I can tell just by looking at your Mount of Venus that you have a warm and sympathetic nature," she said. "Your heart line . . ." She took a close look at the horizontal line near the top of his palm. "Your heart line begins close to the Mount of Saturn." Julia stopped and swallowed hard, feeling the color rise in her face.

"The heart line doesn't really tell us much," she said briskly, folding Mick's fingers over his palm and backing away. "Not until we check it against the indications—"

"What does it tell us?" Mick's smile widened. He took a step nearer and opened his hand, holding it flat for her to see.

What had started as a game had obviously turned into more of an ambush. Julia rose to the challenge, her temper and some other, less clearly definable emotion pricking her on in spite of herself. It took less than a moment for her to fix upon a plan. A counterstrike was in order.

She took a deep breath and looked up at Mick, not examining his hand at all, but keeping her dark gaze locked on his. "Your heart line tells us you have very strong sexual . . ." In spite of her resolve, she stumbled over the word. She paused and started again, deliberately speaking slowly, her voice very low. "It tells us you have a very passionate nature."

Saints and angels! The woman had guts. Mick opened his mouth to tell her as much, then snapped it shut again. She had guts, right enough, and lips so moist and pink, just looking at them caused everything he was about to say to fly out of his head.

Mick knew he was not one to go out and borrow trouble. But he also knew as sure as he was standing here that this girl could make a fool of him. She would make a fool of him, and he would follow gladly, smiling all the while.

His heart filled with regret at the same time his head reminded him there was only one thing to do. He had no choice. His safety—and hers—hung in the balance. He had to rid himself of her.

Mick grabbed for Julia's right hand. "I'll wager a week's pay I can read your palm."

Julia stood perfectly still, too surprised to object, too overwhelmed by the staggering feel of his hand on hers to do more than watch as he nudged her fingers apart.

Her hand was dry and red, her skin chapped and cracked from countless hours in water and strong lye soap. Mick didn't seem to care. He ran his index finger down the center of her palm. "This line shows you'll be going on a short journey very soon."

"A journey? Does it?" Julia felt her breath catch in her throat. His finger brushed up and down her palm, causing a dizzy feeling inside her head.

"That it does." Mick nodded his head solemnly and

leaned nearer. "It shows that you'll be in St. Ives on Sunday next. It shows that you'll be at the Red Lion Inn in Pudding Bag Lane no later than four." He traced another line across her palm with his thumb.

"And once you get there," Mick said, his voice like velvet, "it shows you'll meet a man." He closed her fingers over her palm and gave her hand a squeeze. "That man is me."

With that, Mick turned, bundled Mr. Beecher's clothes under his arm, and was gone.

Julia stared down at her hand. She brushed it against the skirt of her gown, but the strange, mesmerizing magic of Mick's touch did not evaporate once he was out of the room.

"You're a dangerous man, Mick O'Donnell," she mumbled, echoing his Irish brogue. Imagine, wanting to meet her in St. Ives on her free afternoon!

There was no question what he wanted. The only question was, would she go?

Chapter 4

THE muffled sounds of crying reached Julia's ears outside the kitchen door. She tilted her head, listening, but there was little she could distinguish other than an occasional moan and a few choked sobs.

Her hand on the door, she paused, and wondered briefly if she should involve herself in whatever minor crisis had reduced the nameless voice to tears. It was Sunday, her free afternoon, and if she was delayed, she would miss the choral concert at St. John's church in Redruth.

"Mick's the only one what can take care of somethin' this serious." This time she recognized the voice raised in pitiful lament. It was Daisy's.

If it had been anyone else, Julia would not have given it another thought. But it was Daisy, and Daisy had been kind to her. Sighing, Julia pushed open the kitchen door.

The sight that met her eyes was nearly as pathetic as the pitiful wailing that had brought her here. Daisy's eyes were as big as teacups, her nose was raw and red from wiping.

"God a'mercy! There you be!" At the sight of Julia, Daisy's face brightened. "Maybe you can figure what's to be done. If she shows her face, we'll be out of here before you can say Jack Robinson. And without no references."

Before Julia could ask for an explanation, Daisy grabbed her hands. "Mick just has to get to her a'fore she talks to

Mrs. Beecher, don't you see? And I've looked all over for Mick. In the larder. In the wine cellar. I even had the cheek to go into Mr. Beecher's room seeing as the mistress and the master are out and I didn't think I'd ever be found out by no one but you and you wouldn't be tellin' on account of it's an emergency and all, would you?'' Daisy's question was punctuated by a sob.

"What on earth are you babbling about?" Julia demanded.

Daisy blinked at her and sucked in a long, unsteady breath. "Mick's not here," she said simply. "What are we going to do?"

Exasperated, Julia pulled her hands from Daisy's and turned to Rose, who was standing near the massive cooker twisting the skirt of her best Sunday gown into unsightly knots. "What is she talking about?"

"It's . . . it's Annie Leathers, don't you see." Rose's usually quiet voice was lowered even further. She looked to her right, her left, then glanced over her shoulder. "Daisy's heard from her," she said, her voice quavering. "Had a falling out with the butcher's boy, she did. He's tossed her out and she's got no place to go. She's on her way here to take up her position."

Frozen by shock and alarm, Julia stared at the two girls. The same panic she saw in their faces seized her. "Annie Leathers is coming? Here? But if she does—"

"If she does," Daisy moaned, "the Beechers are sure to find out you ain't who you say you are, and then there'll be hell to pay."

"Hell." Julia repeated the word, not as a curse, but with the certainty of someone who could see into the future.

It would, undoubtedly, be hell.

Obliged to face the genuine Annie Leathers, Julia would have to explain who she really was. She would be forced to admit she was an imposter. Worse than an imposter, she was a sham, a fraud without any qualifications, who had made it through the past weeks only by sheer luck, the help of Rose and Daisy, and her own quick wits. She might even be coerced into confessing that there were those within the household who knew of her deception.

What would happen to Daisy and Rose? When their treachery was discovered, these two young girls would be turned out on the streets without references. And a maid without references was worthless.

A quick, disturbing thought invaded Julia's mind. What would happen to her? The Beechers would surely call the police. And then . . . ?

Julia swallowed hard. "What can we do?"

"We've got to find Mick," Daisy said, her voice stronger. "I've checked Mrs. Beecher's ledger—the good Lord forgive me for pokin' into her private papers—and Mick signed out right enough, just like we're supposed to do when we're leavin' the house. But it don't say where he went. I've talked to some of the others, but they've been no help."

The answer struck Julia like a thunderbolt.

"St. Ives."

"What?" Daisy looked at her as if she'd lost her senses.

"St. Ives. St. Ives." Julia twirled around and clapped her hands. "He said he'd be in St. Ives today."

"He did?" Daisy studied her uncertainly. "He didn't tell anyone else that. How is it you know Mick's whereabouts?"

Though she told herself she had no cause to be ashamed, Julia felt her cheeks get hot. She looked away. "He invited me to meet him there. He said to be at the Red Lion Inn at four."

Daisy hugged Julia and laughed. "Then if you hurry, you'll still have time to find him!"

"Oh, no." The thought of meeting Mick sent a prickly sensation skittering up Julia's spine. As it had so many times since that day in the attic dry-cleaning room, the memory of his touch ate away at the edges of her composure. She could still feel his hand against her skin, still remember the warmth of his fingers as he traced the shape of her ear and caressed her neck.

Julia fought to form the words that would keep her from St. Ives and save her from herself. It was the only safe, the only wise, thing to do. She shrugged helplessly. "Send someone else."

"Can't do that." Daisy shook her head. "Not anyone's free afternoon but yours and Mick's. You're the only one what can go for him. You have to, don't you see? You have to, for all of us."

"I can't." Julia looked from Daisy to Rose and back to Daisy again. "If I do—"

"If you don't, you may as well just walk out the door and keep walking," Daisy said. "On account of 'cause once the Beechers find out about the real Annie Leathers, you won't have a place to go anyway besides maybe the local gaol."

"But—"

"And he invited you, didn't he?" Daisy breezed on, completely ignoring Julia. "It's not like you're throwing yourself at the man. He asked you to meet him."

If logic could not save her, perhaps a show of propriety could. Julia sniffed decorously, her back rigid. "He asked me, I didn't say I intended to go. I am not the kind of girl who meets men at inns."

"Of course you ain't." Daisy patted her hand sympathetically. "Unless it were a gentleman, of course."

"Mick O'Donnell is no gentleman." Even Julia was surprised to hear the tartness in her voice. She turned from Daisy and paced to the other side of the kitchen, as much to hide her embarrassment as to calm the peculiar flutter of exhilaration that curled through her at the thought.

Mick O'Donnell was no gentleman. Was that why, a hundred times since he'd asked her to meet him in St. Ives, she'd actually considered going?

Grateful her back was turned and Rose and Daisy could not see the spark of awareness that must surely have betrayed her feelings, Julia pulled herself to a stop.

Mick O'Donnell was no gentleman. Perhaps, she admitted to herself, that was why he fascinated her so.

MICK was not here.

As if someone had opened the run-away to draw all the water from a kitchen sink, the excitement that had been growing inside Julia churned, eddied, and drained away, leaving an empty, puzzled feeling behind.

She knocked at the hotel room door again, but this brought no more results than her first, unsuccessful tries.

For just a moment, Julia was convinced the pang she felt was nothing more than relief. Mick was not here. She was saved from whatever temptation awaited her on the other side of that door.

Before the thought had a chance to form, she recognized it as a lie. There was more to this feeling wrenching her insides than simply relief. Even worry over the arrival of Annie Leathers was not enough to explain the cold, disheartening sensation that had filled the spaces left by her evaporating excitement.

Sighing, Julia turned and headed toward the stairs that would take her back to the ground floor of the Red Lion Inn. At the top of the stairway, she pulled herself to a stop and threw a look over her shoulder toward the still closed door. If Mick wasn't here, where was he?

Why had he asked her to come if he hadn't planned on being here? Had Mick invited her, not because he wanted to be with her, but merely to see how susceptible she was to his charms?

Julia fought to contain a shriek of aggravation. "Of all the impertinent, vulgar . . ." She marched back to the closed door and pounded on it with her fists, stopping only long enough to listen for sounds of movement from inside.

Though she heard nothing, a moment later, the door swung open.

Julia peered through the open doorway. The curtains were drawn on all the windows and there were no lamps lit. The only light in the room came from a fire in the grate. In front of the fire was a table set for tea and two chairs. A bare writing desk stood against the wall, and across the room, and looking as if it had been used recently, was an enormous canopied bed.

There didn't appear to be anyone about.

Julia took one tentative step over the threshold.

"Mr. O'Donnell?" She called Mick's name hesitantly and took another step into the room.

"Good afternoon, my fine and fancy lady."

Startled by the sudden sound of Mick's voice, Julia whirled around in time to see him step from behind the open door and sweep her a low, ostentatious bow.

His hair was tousled, and he smoothed it back with one hand and snapped the door shut with the other. He threw a quick glance over his shoulder at her before he turned the key in the lock.

"I fell asleep," Mick smiled and dropped the key into his pocket, his eyes lighting with an emotion more genuine and unassuming than any she'd seen in them before. Behind her, the fire crackled and flared, sending up an odd, bright flash of orange that accentuated the angry-looking scar at Mick's hairline.

Somewhere in the back of Julia's mind, she knew she should protest the locked door and the key, so conveniently tucked away where she could not get at it. But it was neither the problem of the key nor the smile on Mick's face that set her heart pounding and made her breathing quick and irregular.

Her gaze slid from Mick's face to his neck and down to where his white shirt was open, baring a good portion of a chest that was broad and powerful. His shirtsleeves were pushed above his elbows, and as he moved, the muscles of his arms, like corded ropes, rippled with suppressed strength. His skin glistened in the light of the flickering fire, burnished and golden, like those statues of the ancient pagan gods Julia had seen sketched in history books.

Pictures were one thing, reality was another altogether.

There was a quivering in the pit of Julia's stomach, a ripple that danced its way to the top of her head and back down to her toes. She tried to swallow, but her throat was too dry. She tried to speak, but the words refused to come. Instead, she merely stared.

Following her gaze, Mick looked down at his bare chest. A shaky, flustered grin tightened the corners of his mouth and an unexpected flush darkened his face. Instantly, he did up the buttons along the front of his shirt. Finishing as fast as he could and folding his arms across his chest, Mick breathed a sigh of relief, at ease again. "I was beginning to think you might not come," he said. "But then, I should have known you'd not be able to resist the charms of Mick O'Donnell."

The sound of his voice, as cool and self-assured as ever, broke the spell that held her. "Don't flatter yourself." Julia folded her arms across her chest in a perfect mirror to his action and looked at him, shaking her head. "I hate to disappoint you, but I'm not here because of your invitation. We have an emergency at the house."

"An emergency, do you say?" Mick sauntered to the table, picked up a slice of bread and mounted it on the toasting fork that lay nearby. He dangled it idly over the fire, examining the bread every few seconds to be sure it was not burning. After a minute, he removed the fork from the fire and gingerly slipped the bread from fork to plate. A dollop of butter, a knifeful of jam and the feast was prepared.

He sliced the bread in two and brought one piece to his mouth. "Oh, would you like some?" he asked, his eyes wide and innocent, as if he'd just remembered Julia's presence.

With each second, Julia felt her annoyance grow. She hadn't realized she'd been holding her breath during his culinary performance, but now it rushed out in an aggravated puff. She spun from him, exasperated, and paced from one end of the room to the other.

"I've come all this way to tell you something important and the only thing you can do is offer me toast?"

"Ah, and it's a simpleton I am," Mick said, his brogue more exaggerated than usual. "A fine and fancy lady like yourself isn't used to being treated no better than a street wench." He took a bite of the toast and carefully finished chewing before he spoke again.

"It's colder than a virgin's bed outside. And you've come a long way. Would you like some wine?" He picked up a bottle from the table and poured a glass for himself and another for her. He took a long drink. "It's a very good vintage. Try it and see." He held a glass out to her. "Not at all like that swill the Beechers drink."

Julia stepped up to him, her hands on her hips, and faced him, her dark eyes blazing into his cool blue ones. "How can you stand there discoursing about the pleasures of fine wine when I've just told you there's trouble at the house?" she demanded. "Daisy and Rose sent me to find you. Don't you care? They said you're the only one who can help."

"Did they now?" Mick seemed pleased. "They said that about me? God bless 'em. They're good girls in a pinch, that's for certain. I didn't tell them that part. Only told them to tell you Annie Leathers was on her way."

"What!" Julia's mouth dropped open in surprise. She clenched her hands into tight fists and shoved them into her pockets, certain that if she didn't, she would surely try to pummel the self-satisfied smile from Mick's face.

He pretended not to notice. Instead, he raised his glass. "To Daisy and Rose," he said. "My eternal gratitude for bringing this little rendezvous to completion." Mick smiled. "Even though you were reluctant."

Whatever disappointment Julia had felt outside in the corridor dissolved beneath the bold assurance of Mick's smile.

"Reluctant!" The word caught in her throat and when she spoke, her voice was shrill. "Not reluctant. Far from reluctant. Unwilling. Indisposed. Opposed." With each word, her voice rose, more angry than before. "I had no intention of coming here to meet you for tea"—she looked from Mick to the rumpled bed—"or for anything else. How dare you make up that nonsense about Annie Leathers just to get me here."

Mick threw back his head and laughed. The firelight glinted off his even white teeth and added a sparkle to his eyes. "It seems to have worked a charm."

Julia stamped to the table and dropped into a chair. "I thought Daisy and Rose were my friends," she mumbled, half to herself.

"And that they are." Mick sat in the chair opposite hers and lowered his voice, tilting his head to get a look at her down-turned face. "They didn't mean you any harm. They wanted to see you have a bit of fun for yourself. Besides"—he snatched up her hand and held it in his own for a minute, turning it over and stroking her palm through her glove—"hands never lie. You said so yourself. And yours said you were coming to St. Ives. Now, take off your coat and—"

"Why?"

"Why? You're as stubborn as an old woman. Because it's warm in here."

"That's not what I meant and you know it. Why? Why me? Why here? If you were looking for . . . for entertainment, you might have asked one of the other girls to meet you. I've heard the way some of them talk about you." Too late, Julia remembered herself. Her face flooding with color, she swallowed her next sharp remark.

Mick seemed to enjoy her discomfort. He propped his chin on one hand and watched her fidget in her seat.

Julia disregarded the strange rushing noises inside her head caused by his steady, unnerving look. She avoided his eyes by looking at everything in the room except Mick. She heard his chair squeak and assumed he had leaned back in it, his hands clasped behind his head, his long legs out in front of him, relaxing the way she had seen him relax so many times after dinner at the Beechers'. She was certain he was wearing the same, disturbing look he wore when he watched her there, that arrogant smile that was so annoying and, at the same time, so strangely inviting.

Julia picked at a loose thread hanging from the sleeve of her coat. "I had no intention of meeting you here today," she said, as calmly as she could.

"I knew that the day I asked you," he said. "I knew you would never come without a little persuasion."

"But—"

"But I knew you wanted to."

Julia's head shot up and Mick chuckled as she winced and blinked at him in surprise. "You can't keep any secrets from me. Now, take off your coat," he instructed, "and I just might tell you why I wanted you here."

Julia gave him a long, hard look. "Oh, very well," she grumbled, standing to remove her coat and gloves, but making it very clear the idea was her own and not influenced by his invitation. She deposited her coat on the back of the nearest chair. "There. Now please explain what all this is about."

Mick's gaze wandered from her hair to her throat, then slowly slipped down the length of her body. The smile on his lips faded until there was no amusement left on his face, only a stark longing reflected in his eyes, an intense yearning for . . . what?

Try as she might, Julia could not face the expression in his eyes and remain composed. She made a great show of refolding her coat and straightening it on the chair. To give herself something to do, she sat down and reached for the wine glass he'd offered earlier. She sipped at the wine, her gaze firmly on its burgundy depths, and waited for him to speak.

"You look awful in black."

It was not the comment she expected. Julia's head snapped up and she forced herself to meet Mick's eyes. They were smiling again, the momentary longing she'd seen in them effectively hidden by the usual layer of nonchalance he wore like a second skin. Or a suit of armor.

Her voice softened. "If it's companionship you're after, Mr. O'Donnell, or friendship, conversation or sympathy, there are easier ways to obtain it than by luring me here with some absurd story." She glanced at the table. "You might start by offering me tea," she suggested. "I'm famished!"

Mick smiled back, sincerely and without a hint of impertinence, and reached for the toasting fork.

It was an unspoken truce, but, Julia knew, a truce nonetheless. She relaxed against the back of her chair and watched him circumspectly from beneath her lashes while he toasted the last of the bread and slid it from the fork. He spread it with jam, cut it for her, and looked on with real satisfaction while she ate. How odd, Julia mused, licking the bramble preserves from her lips, Mick didn't seem at all like a butler.

He looked enough like one. She had seen him erase the bold arrogance from his face, throw his shoulders back and walk with the uncanny, inherent grace valued in every butler. But his mind was too astute, his hands too large and strong, his body too lean and athletic to belong to a butler. He had the quick mind of an Oxford don and the sinewy body of a stablehand.

Although the very thought set off warning bells inside her

head, Julia couldn't help but wonder what the rest of his body was like; if his legs were as muscular as his arms, if his lips were as persuasive as the look she sometimes saw in his eyes.

"I asked if it was good."

Mick's question snapped her out of her trance. Julia blushed, caught in her traitorous thoughts. She gulped down the rest of her meal dutifully, and poured the tea which was steeping in the pot.

"There, you see," she said, brushing crumbs from her skirt, "I ate my entire meal and didn't try to run away once. You can unlock the door now." The moment the words left her mouth, Julia regretted them. Mick stiffened ever so slightly and she felt, rather than saw, the shadow that darkened his handsome features. She watched the easy camaraderie they'd established disintegrate beneath the onslaught of that shadow, as if a cloud had raced across the sun.

Mick ignored the cup of tea she set before his plate and reached for his wine glass.

"Does it bother a fine and fancy English lady like you to be locked in here with an Irishman?" he asked, his voice husky, irritated.

The fire in the grate did little to warm the sudden chill. Julia pushed back from the table and moved to the window. She was angry at herself for upsetting the fragile, friendly balance between them; angry at him for being so temperamental.

"What is it you're afraid of?" she asked over her shoulder. "Is there a reason you keep the door locked and the windows covered?" She yanked open the curtains on each of the room's three windows. "Are you trying to keep me in, or are you trying to keep something else out?"

Without a word, Mick rose from his chair and walked to the windows. His face was an impassive mask, as indecipherable as stone and just as cold. He came nearer and Julia could not help but notice the quick, deliberate glance he shot up and down the seafront outside.

"You're as canny a wench as the best of them when it serves your purpose," he said lightly. Though he carefully contained it, Julia saw the effort his indifference caused him. The hand he put up to hold back the edge of the curtain was white-knuckled. With his other hand, he crooked one finger under her chin and lifted her face to his. "You come here acting as innocent as a spring lamb, pretending you don't know what it is I really want from you. You will not let me bare my heart to you and yet you ask me to bare my soul."

"It's neither your heart nor your soul I want." Julia's move to step away was blocked by Mick's arm. "I merely asked a question, why you keep yourself wrapped in a layer of darkness, behind locked doors. If it's none of my concern—"

"It isn't."

"Then tell me so and be done."

"It isn't any of your concern." He looked down at her, his eyes flaming. There was unspoken pain deep within those eyes, and a spark of some indefinable emotion which cautioned Julia that she was treading on dangerous ground.

"It isn't any of your concern," Mick repeated, his voice and his look softening. "But I would tell you if you would listen, and be glad for the chance to talk."

Julia sat on the window seat, her eyes on Mick. She nodded her acquiescence, words refusing to form in her mouth. She was not at all sure Mick noticed. His gaze was fastened far out over the churning sea.

To the west, a bright band of yellow glimmered close upon the water. The sun sent its last, golden rays streaking into the room, changing their surroundings from drab to brilliant. Its color hung in the air for one glorious moment, firing Mick's hair into a red-gold crown. A second later, it slipped below the water and, like a candle, went out.

"I keep the curtains pulled so I can't see home," Mick said, his voice no louder than a murmur.

"Ireland?" Julia laughed. "It's impossible to see Ireland from here," she said. She turned in her seat and squinted out the window, following Mick's intent gaze, but saw nothing more than the expanse of icy ocean, its surface broken only by the granite outcroppings that reared out of the water like pebbles thrown from a giant's hand.

"Eire." Mick whispered the word like a prayer, his voice so low she could barely hear it.

Julia turned from the window to study him. Mick's eyes reflected the gray water, turning their usual cornflower color to smoke. His forehead was creased in thought, his hand still toyed idly with the edge of the curtain.

"If you miss it so much," she asked, "why don't you go back?"

"There are those who can go back and those who cannot."

"And you?"

"Cannot."

Like the pieces of a puzzle falling into place, something clicked in Julia's mind. "You're hiding from the law, aren't you?"

"Ah, now that all depends on what you might be considering the law." Mick tore his gaze from the churning water and looked down at Julia. "If it's the law of justice and truth you're talking about, no I'm not hiding from that. I've never done nothing but what's right in the eyes of that law. But if it's Saxon law you're meaning, well, that's another story altogether."

Julia's eyes widened in surprise. Though politics was a sordid subject not fit for a lady's ears, she had overheard enough male conversation to know the British ruled the world because they were the most powerful, the most efficient empire since the time of the Caesars. There were those who disagreed with British policy, even those who openly opposed it, but they were no better than rabble who cared more for nationalistic pride than the good of the Empire. They were dangerous and fanatical. They were revolutionaries.

Her body stiffened with shock and fear. "You're a Fenian." The words escaped her lips before she could stop them.

To her surprise, her accusation was met with a glimmer of amusement from Mick's eyes. "Is that what you think? Well, even if I was, I couldn't say. The Irish Republican Brotherhood is a secret society—so I've heard told—and those who are its followers are bound by oaths that can never be revealed to the outside world."

She accepted the ambiguity of his answer without question. Somehow, before she had ever spoken the dreaded word *Fenian,* she knew he would equivocate. She decided on a more direct approach. "Why did you leave Ireland?"

"That I can't tell you." Mick dropped to the window seat beside her and shook his head, whether with regret or dismissal, she did not know. For a few long, quiet minutes, there was silence between them. Julia stared down at her hands, clenched together on her lap, confident he would talk to her if she had the patience to wait. After a while, she glanced to her left, and watched him.

Mick had his elbows on his knees. He stared at the fire across the room, his eyes distant, vacant. For a long time, he seemed to be struggling with his thoughts. The turbulence of his mind was clearly reflected on his face. Julia watched each emotion steal across his countenance. There was frustration, anger, even pride, but they were all underpinned with another, deeper emotion.

Mick blinked suddenly as if woken from a long, nightmare-filled sleep. In that moment, Julia knew what the emotion was. It was grief, pure and absolute. It transformed his handsome features, tightening his mouth and adding lines of fatigue around his eyes. A second later, it was gone, hidden beneath a mantle of hatred.

"Have you ever heard of Charles Stewart Parnell?"

After such a long silence, Mick's question sounded thunderous.

The tension relieved, Julia sat back and gave him a smug look. "Whatever do you take me for? Of course I've heard of Parnell. He's that trouble-making Irishman. Even though he's one of the gentry, he's thrown his lot in with those insurrectionists who believe in Home Rule. He's a—"

"Patriot." Mick sighed and shook his head in disgust. "I can see there's a lot you need to learn about politics, miss. You may have had a fine and fancy education, but I'll stake my next month's wages they never taught you more than polite French phrases and singing arias around the piano."

Mick leaned back, more at ease now. He gave her an indulgent look.

"Charles Stewart Parnell is a landowner, as you say, and a member of Parliament. He's one of the few with the moral fiber to stand up for what he knows is right. For years, my countrymen have struggled against unjust land laws. We can live on the land. We can work it. But we can never own it. We are tenants in our own country. Tenants who can be evicted when the rent is late, our homes demolished, our lives destroyed.

"Parnell knows that owning the land is the only solution to Ireland's problems. He's a remarkable fellow. He's united the Home Rule party and come to terms with the Fenians. He's close." Mick balled his left hand into a fist and drew in a deep breath.

"He's so close, Julia. So close to making us a free people. Not through violence and murder. That's the way of Captain Moonlight, the secret societies, and that way will never succeed. Parnell knows our only road to success lies straight through the heart of Parliament and he's well on his way to taking us there."

"And you are one of his supporters?" It was a foolish question. Julia needed only to hear the passion in Mick's voice to know how important the issue was to him.

"A local organizer." Mick shrugged off the importance of his involvement. "Just one of the lads who helps get the word out."

"But if what you say is true, if Parnell is working within the law, then what you're doing isn't wrong. Why are you hiding?"

"There's an old Irish saying: 'You'll wake up one of these fine mornings and find yourself dead.'" Turning to Julia, Mick reached for her left hand and held it tight in both of his. He stroked each of her fingers in turn, not softly, but firmly, his anguish and loneliness telegraphed to her through every pore.

"There was a time," he said, capturing her gaze with his own, "a time before Parnell, a time when I was young and rash and foolish. I woke up one morning. And I found myself dead."

The pain in his eyes was absolute. Julia brought her right hand up and eased a wayward strand of hair from his face, smoothing it over his forehead. She grazed the wicked scar and inspected it closely. It was dreadful, wide and jagged, beginning at his hairline and disappearing into his lush thatch of golden hair.

"And now you're in hiding." She turned the thought over in her mind, not comprehending all of what he'd said, but understanding the intensity of his beliefs. "But why here? Why in England? Aren't you afraid they'll find you?"

"What better place for the fox to hide than under the hounds' noses!" Mick stood and shook his shoulders, as if to rid himself of the bad memories. He pulled Julia up from the window seat and they stood facing each other, their hands entwined.

"Mr. O'Donnell, I . . ." Another thought struck her and

she stopped short and studied him for a moment. "Is your name really O'Donnell?"

"O'Donnell is as good a name as any. Besides, the name is Mick," he said, pulling her closer. "And I don't want your sympathy or your pity. I only told you all that so you'd understand why I keep the doors locked and the curtains drawn. There are some people I want to keep out," he said. He dipped his head, his mouth so close that she felt rather than heard his words. "And there are some people I want to keep in."

Julia responded to his breath against hers. She closed her eyes and leaned forward, the sound of her heart drumming wildly in her ears. Mick moved his mouth closer, brushing his lips against hers rather than kissing them.

"There's something I need from you, Julia." He whispered the words close to her ear.

Reluctantly, Julia opened her eyes and looked up at him, her blood pounding anticipation through her veins. "If you tell me what it is, I—"

"No." With one finger, Mick held the words on her lips. "I need your promise. No explanations. No excuses. I want you to promise you'll do as I ask."

Julia took one step back, out of his arms. "If this is some sort of game you're playing—"

"It's no game."

"Am I supposed to beg you to kiss me, is that what this is all about?"

"Saint and angels!" Mick spun from her and moved a few paces across the room. "I didn't mean to mislead you." He turned back to her. "I don't want . . . that is, I do want . . . that is . . . Holy Mary, you've got me muddled, woman! What I do want I'll tell you straightaway. I want you to leave. Now. Today. I want you to leave the Beechers and never come back."

Mistaking her silence for interest, he rushed on. "There's no need for you to worry about money. I've enough to get you to London and then some. I know people there, I'll give you their names. There's a train at seven. You'll be halfway across Cornwall before anyone knows you've gone.''

The first numbing moments of shock melted into white-hot anger. Julia backed away, her eyes wide with disbelief. "I was right. The only reason you asked me here was to see if I'd really come. You've had that satisfaction. Apparently that's enough for you. Now you want to cast me aside.''

Mick stalked across the room. He took her shoulders between his hands and brought his face down level with hers. "I'm not casting you aside. If I could tell you more, I would,'' he said, his eyes ablaze. "I can't. You need to be gone from here. That's all you can know. I—''

As if Mick sensed some sound beyond Julia's hearing, he stiffened and stepped back. There was a knock on the door.

"Damn!'' The oath exploded from him. "Is it that late already?'' He turned and went to the door.

Still dazed by the humiliation of being dismissed so effortlessly, Julia stared at the door in stunned bewilderment. She could see little beyond the wide expanse of Mick's back outlined against the light flowing in from the outside corridor. She heard Mick speak, his voice low and muffled. Even from this distance, she could detect the edge of irritation in his words. He was answered by another voice, a man's voice, but she could understand none of what was said.

Mick stepped aside and Julia gasped. Ben Jessup was standing outside the door holding a battered wooden chest.

Ever since the day she had met Jessup at the shabby pub in London, Julia had disliked and mistrusted him. He had a thin, artificial smile that never quite reached into his eyes, and the quick, furtive gestures of a rodent on the hunt for food. He was the Beechers' outside watchman, and, until this moment, she had assumed he and Mick had no contact other than that required by house business.

Now Mick let Jessup into the room and moved to stand in

front of the door, his face devoid of all the exquisite emotion she had seen in it only a short while earlier. Whatever bond they had forged in their time alone was broken. He was a stranger, cold and aloof.

Julia forced herself to sound calmer than she felt. "I didn't expect company," she said. She spoke to Jessup as nonchalantly as she could manage. "I'm sure you and Mr. O'Donnell have a great deal to discuss that does not concern me."

She moved toward the door and found Mick blocking it. It was difficult to face him with the taste of him still on her lips, but she lifted her chin and spoke with all the authority she could muster.

"Would you mind telling me what's going on?"

Mick looked away, pointedly ignoring her question. Without a word, he walked past her and went to the windows, snapping closed the curtains one at a time.

"Come on. Come on." Jessup tapped his foot against the bare wooden floor. "Ain't got all bleedin' night. Let's get to work."

Julia turned to Mick. When he paid her no mind, she asked Jessup, "What are you talking about? What kind of work?"

"Ain't Mick told you nothin'?" Jessup sidled up behind Julia, his breath hot and foul against her cheek. "I comed all this way to help you be ready and you don't even know what I'm talkin' about." He threw a sly look from Julia, to Mick, to the rumpled bed. "Maybe you ain't had a chance to explain, eh Mick?"

Mick's face darkened, but he did not move or speak. He merely stared at Jessup, the look in his eyes so forceful, the smaller man instantly backed down.

"Ain't none of my business what you been doin'." Jessup's top lip curled over his teeth and Julia was sure, if they had been outside, he would have spit. He cleared his throat. "Let's get this girl down to something so she'll be ready when the time comes."

Julia's breath solidified in her throat. "Be ready for what?"

Jessup laughed, the sound of it like tearing paper. "Ready for what!" He hauled in a great breath of air and coughed heavily. "Ready for the Beechers. We're gonna burgle them, gonna rob them as blind as a dead man's eyes. And you, my girl, you are goin' to help."

Chapter 5

MICK turned and chanced a look at Julia.

All the color had drained from her face, leaving her ashen, her hair an inky frame for her alabaster skin. Her arms stiff at her sides, she watched silently as Ben Jessup dragged the heavy wooden box nearer the fire and hoisted it onto the table.

After a moment, she blinked and turned to Mick, her head high, her dark eyes sparking with accusation.

Damnation! Mick looked away, unable to face the searing condemnation in her eyes. He had never meant for things to get this out of hand. He had meant for her to be gone, long gone, before Ben Jessup arrived. Why had he been careless enough to go on prattling about Parnell and the Irish when he should have been shooing her out the door?

Why? Mick mumbled an oath, disgusted with himself. The answer was as plain as a yard of pump water. All he need do was look at the girl. There was his answer—there in her hair, the color of an autumn midnight, there in her lips, as moist and red as summer apples, there in her luscious woman's body, so soft and warm and willing when he drew her near.

He'd been distracted by her. No. Mick shook his head, sure the indictment wasn't nearly strong enough. He'd been befuddled and overwhelmed by her unpretentious beauty, dazzled by her wit, her charm, her courage. It was a mistake. A serious mistake. And now Julia was being made to pay for his foolishness.

"You at least started explainin' about them special locks on Mrs. Beecher's jewel cases, didn't you, Mick?" Jessup asked over his shoulder while he unlocked the chest.

Mick disposed of the question with a quick wave of his hand. "There wasn't time."

Wasn't time? The corner of Mick's mouth twisted with annoyance. There would have been time enough if he hadn't been so damned reckless. Now it would be impossible to shield Julia from the terrible truth.

Her faith in him had already been shattered. One look at the stunned, betrayed expression on Julia's face told him that much. What Ben Jessup was about to do would successfully complete the demolition, grinding what was left of her trust into fine shards and trampling it underfoot.

But if he sent Julia away now, if he made up some excuse to dismiss her, Jessup would surely become suspicious that Mick was trying to protect her. Mick discarded the idea. As much as he wanted to spare her the pain and humiliation, he could not jeopardize his own mission, not even for the sake of this woman he'd come to care for.

Countless times Mick had pledged his loyalty to the cause of Irish independence. Countless times he had faced danger with a smile on his lips, eager and willing to sacrifice all it took to free his people. He had given his home, his family. He would gladly give his life. He never thought the cause would demand his heart.

Mick drew in a deep breath and forced a cheerfulness he didn't feel into his voice. "Right this way, my fine and fancy lady." Grabbing Julia's elbow, he steered her to the table. "A few hours with Ben, and you'll know all there is to know about—"

"About what?" Julia yanked her arm from his, giving him a sidelong look. Without waiting for his reply, she seated herself on the edge of one of the chairs, her hands clasped in front of her on the table.

It was no use trying to explain. Not here, not now, with Ben Jessup looking at them both expectantly, eager to be started.

Mick backed away and busied himself turning up the three gas jets in the room. The light sprang around them, harsh and glaring.

"Well, we're ready then." Jessup cleared his throat and went to the table. "Pay attention, girl. You're about to learn a valuable lesson what will keep you in good stead for the rest of your days. I'm best at what I does, you see." He drew back his angular shoulders, a shallow, superior smile fixed on his face.

"If I weren't, Mick here wouldn't let me be in with him. 'Cause, you see, Mick, he's the best at what he does, too." Jessup beamed an oily grin in Mick's direction, obviously currying favor. "And you—" he looked down at Julia— "are about to share some of my secrets." As if he were an artist unveiling a masterpiece, Jessup unsnapped the latches on the box and threw open the lid.

Julia craned her neck to see inside and blinked in surprise. She looked from Jessup to Mick, her eyes wide with questioning.

"They're locks."

"Yes, they're locks." Jessup clicked his tongue. "And you are about to learn to pick them."

It wasn't just the idea of being a thief that caused a heavy, sick feeling to settle in Julia's stomach, it was the thought that she had been deceived, brought here by Mick not for romance or friendship, but merely to learn his criminal ways.

Julia dashed her hand across her face, banishing the tears that threatened to betray her true feelings. She swiveled in her chair and faced Mick, her voice trembling more than she liked.

"It's impossible. You can't be . . . can't be thieves. You all have references, just like mine."

"Just like yours!" Jessup cackled with delight. "But yours is the same as them what belonged to Annie Leathers. And Annie Leathers is the best little lock picker this side o' the Channel. Just what you need in the mistress's room to get at them things what Mick and me would never have a chance to."

"I don't understand." Julia looked to Mick for an explanation.

For a moment, she did not think he would answer. He rubbed his chin pensively and studied her, the expression in his eyes hollow, detached. Finally, he nodded, as if agreeing she had the right to know.

"Have you never heard of screevers?" he asked.

His voice was distant, unemotional, and Julia could not find the strength to make her tone match his. She shook her head.

"Screevers are forgers," Mick explained. "For the right price, you can find a screever to provide references for any position." He dipped his head in Julia's direction. "Lady's maid." He indicated Jessup with another tip of his head. "Outside watchman, and even," he said, pointing to himself, "butler."

"Then Annie's references were—"

"Bought and paid for, like all the others."

"And none of you is what you say you are," Julia whispered, almost to herself, and did not care if Mick answered. The thought that he had lied hurt more than the realization that she had fallen in with a band of thieves.

All that balderdash about being committed to the cause of Irish independence, all that foolishness about how he missed his home, all that nonsense about Charles Stewart Parnell. She'd been so easily deceived by his story and so eager to console him.

Julia felt her cheeks redden. She had gone as far as letting

Mick take her in his arms, and, she admitted to herself, she'd been willing—even anxious—to let him go even further. How could she have been so foolish? She blinked back a tear and stared at Mick in stunned disbelief.

He paid her no mind. Seating himself in the chair across from Julia, Mick looked at Jessup. "Let's get to work," he said.

Jessup pulled a lock from the box and held it up for Julia's inspection. "Look here. There's nothing much to these things. The barrel"— he pointed—"and the spring. That's it. Nothing more than that. It ain't difficult to pop." Jessup dug into the box on the table and came up holding a thin metal rod. "All you need do is get this in here," he said, concentrating with all his might. He fiddled with the rod for less than ten seconds when, with a quiet snap, the lock popped open. Jessup smirked. "Easy as taking milk from a babe."

Julia had watched Jessup's demonstration, but now, shaken and dismayed, she turned to Mick. "You want me to do that?"

Jessup answered before Mick could. "Ain't nothing to it," he assured her. "The only hard part is when the lock's in place. Then you can't see it with your eyes. You've got to use your ears and your fingers to do your seeing for you. Look." He drew another lock from the box, selected a wire rod with a hook on the end of it, closed his eyes, and got to work. Moments later, there was a soft clicking sound. "Like milk from a babe," Jessup purred again.

Though Julia's eyes were on Jessup, she comprehended only bits and pieces of what he said. Her mind raced with a myriad of thoughts, each more frightening than the last. Her first thought was flight, but she knew that was impossible. Mick was far larger and quicker than her; she would be no match for him. She was sure to be stopped and even if she wasn't, where would she go?

Her only hope seemed to be in cooperating. With an

effort, she turned her full attention on Ben Jessup. The sooner she learned how to pick locks, the sooner they would be finished with her, and the sooner she could leave.

Jessup droned on. ". . . it tries your knowledge, you see, as well as your skill. Any bloody bastard with enough time and a little brains could force a lock. But from what Mick tells me, we ain't going to have the time. And we ain't going to want everybody and his brother to know what we've been up to, not right away, anyhow. That means you work quick, you work quiet, and you don't leave no telltale marks. Here." He shoved a lock at Julia.

In spite of the warmth radiating from the fireplace, the metal was cold against her skin. The lock was heavier than she expected. She weighed it in her hand. With her other hand, she accepted the pick Jessup handed her. It was long and thin and had a pointed, zigzagged tip.

"That there's called a rake," Jessup explained, pointing to the pick. "Take it in your fingers like you're holding a pencil. That's right. Now slip it in there until you feel the spring. No, no. Not like that. Not with your wrist. Let your fingers do the work. There. Steady your hand with your little finger. Like this." He leaned over and took Julia's hand in his, showing her how to manipulate the pick.

Mick sat back, pretending to be interested, all the while fighting to shut out the droning of Ben Jessup's voice. It was no use. Even if he could disregard Jessup, he could not silence his own conscience. Those who said anticipation was worse than reality were as mad as May-butter. He had expected Julia would be upset if she ever learned the true reason they were at the Beechers', but nothing could have prepared him for the wrenching pain of watching her tender feelings for him dissolve before his very eyes.

It was her eyes he could not ignore.

Mick regarded Julia carefully, only too aware she deliberately kept her gaze from straying to his. Though her fingers obediently followed each of Jessup's directions, her eyes blazed with anger. Her shoulders were set with outrage and two spots of high color flamed in her cheeks like fire.

She was angry, she was stunned, and he knew she must be afraid, but still, she refused to surrender any shred of her dignity. Her anger fueled her determination and soon her long, slim fingers were moving over the locks effortlessly. When one finally popped open beneath the pressure of her pick, she sat back in her chair and threw Mick a triumphant look.

Mick forced himself to meet the look straight on, even managing to smile slightly. "Good." He stood and stretched. "It's time we were getting back." He clapped Jessup on the shoulder congenially. "Get these things packed away. We'll give you an hour's start."

Jessup grunted in assent and began to replace the locks in the large, wooden box. "Oh, one thing," he said, stopping and looking at Julia. "You've got to have your own set of picks. Here you go." Jessup tossed her a ring of slender steel picks.

"Now don't you let them Beechers catch you with those," he reminded her, his voice no gentler than the look in his eyes. "Put 'em somewheres where no one's likely to find 'em or it'll mean prison for you and likely for the rest of us." He hoisted the heavy box on his shoulder and left.

The sound of the closing door rumbled through the silence that filled the room. Julia stood but remained near the table, gazing at her hands linked in front of her.

It took more strength than Mick knew he possessed not to go to her. He wanted to drop to his knees before her, to take her hands between his own and smooth the look of worry from her face with soft, sweet words. He wanted to tame her erratic, anxious breaths, to still the fear that beat within her with tender embraces. He wanted to kiss her. Sweet Jesus, how he wanted to kiss her!

A shudder stormed through him, nearly upsetting his fragile mask of composure. Only the voice of pure reason could soothe the turbulence. It was better this way, the voice inside Mick's head reminded him. Better she should think him a thief than be put in danger by learning the full truth; better, and safer, for both of them.

To disguise his distress, Mick went to the bed and retrieved a small stack of parcels. In other circumstances, it would have been pleasing to offer them to Julia. Now, he hoped she would take them quickly and simply leave.

"I bought you a new pair of shoes." He held one parcel out to her.

Julia clasped her hands behind her back and stared at him.

Mick held up another parcel. "Printer's ink and a gelatin roller. That is what you needed for your fortune-telling, isn't it? And"— he held up one last package—"toffee."

It was too much. Julia glared at him. "And what do you expect me to do to earn my toffee? Is this an early reward for snatching the Beechers' jewels? Or is it the silver we're after?"

"Damn it, woman. You're as stubborn as a knotted bootlace. I don't expect you to do anything for the bloody toffee. I've brought it for you." He shoved it in her direction. "Here. It's yours."

Julia did not move. So furious she could not speak, she flashed a look of loathing at the parcel in Mick's hand.

Mick had not missed the look of disdain in her eyes. It was well deserved, he knew, and the realization made him angry, angry at her, but even more angry at himself.

"Damn!" Mick hurled the parcel of toffee at the far wall. "What is it now, Joan of Arc? Do I have to get down on one knee and beg you to accept my gifts? You were willing to accept more than just toffee from me before Jessup got here."

His words were as sharp as knives, and they hurt Julia not because of the way he said them, but because they were true. She had been willing to accept his affections this afternoon, that was undeniable.

Anguish dried her throat and strangled the words inside her. Didn't he understand? She wanted nothing more than a man who would ease her fears, a man who could help her forget her wretched life at the Beechers', a man who could wipe away her tears with his gentle touch. All the loneliness and longing of the past month rose within her, sharper and more painful than ever. For a few hours this afternoon, she thought Mick O'Donnell was that man.

She faced him, her voice low, her anger barely controlled. "Before Ben Jessup got here, I didn't know you were a common criminal."

Mick stalked to the bed and back again, his boots beating a tattoo against the bare floor. "I asked you to leave."

"You asked me—"

"I asked you to leave because I didn't want you to know. I didn't want you to be a part of it. Here." He dug into his pocket and shoved a handful of bank notes at her. "Take it. Go."

Julia swallowed the lump rising in her throat and eyed the money in his hand as if it were a poisonous snake, fully coiled and about to strike. "I won't take your money." She turned and retrieved her coat, punching her arms into both sleeves before she went to the door.

"I won't use money you've stolen from other people. Not even to leave. I will earn my own money. Honestly. And you can be sure I'll leave as soon as is humanly possible. After that, I would like very much to never see you again."

She spun from him, yanked the door open, and fled into the corridor.

Curse the man! Julia told herself she did not care if the Beechers discovered Mick was a thief. She did not care if the police apprehended him and kept him locked away for the rest of his life. She did not care if the devil himself came to claim him and he burned in the fires of Perdition for all eternity.

But if she did not care, why was she crying?

Chapter 6

"IMAGINE an old stick like Mrs. Beecher bein' interested in somethin' what's as excitin' as contactin' the dead." Daisy shook her head in wonder, her eyes sparkling with the exhilaration of delicious gossip. "A séance! Imagine the Beechers havin' a séance!"

"Hmph." Julia grunted her indifference and tugged her blanket over her head. It was at least an hour before sunrise and she was not in the mood for either Daisy's unrelenting chatter or her company. She wanted nothing more than to go back to sleep.

At least while she was asleep, she could forget the gentle look in Mick's eyes, the tenderness that turned to ice when Ben Jessup arrived at the Red Lion yesterday. Asleep, she could banish the memory of Mick's honeyed words, his delicate touch, the nearly imperceptible brush of his lips that was so satisfying, and yet so tantalizing it made her ache for more. At least while she was asleep, she could pretend he had not been revealed as a thief, and a fraud, and a liar.

"Oh, I almost forgot." Daisy's voice broke through Julia's thoughts. "These was on the floor outside your door."

With a sigh, Julia emerged from beneath the bedclothes. Daisy had brought a candle into the room, and it flickered wildly in the drafty attic. Julia focused her eyes in the dim light, staring with disbelief at the parcels Daisy held up for her inspection. There were three of them, and one of them was split, as if it had been flung against a wall. Julia bolted upright.

"Take them away," she said, scooting as far back from the offending parcels as possible.

"Take them away?" Daisy squinted at Julia, mystified. "S'lp me Bob, I don't know what you're thinkin'. Why ever would you want to get rid of 'em? I don't know who left 'em, but look." She turned the smallest parcel over in her hands. "This one's tore open. It's toffee. Lordy! I ain't had nothin' that tasty in months."

With a flick of her hands, Julia rejected the sweets. "You take them."

A delighted smile brightened Daisy's face. "Don't need to ask me twice. What about these others?"

"I . . . I don't know." Julia turned away, refusing to look at the other two gifts. "Just leave them over there," she decided, motioning toward the end of her bed.

With a shrug, Daisy discarded the parcels and hugged the package of toffee to her ample bosom. "Ain't this plummy," she said. "Toffee at five in the mornin'!" She looked at Julia and the smile vanished from her face. "What's happened to your eyes?" she asked, genuine concern warming her voice. "You're all red and puffed like you been cryin'."

"Nothing's wrong." Julia knuckled her eyes with her fists. "It's just that it's very early and I didn't get back until late last night and my head aches and—"

"Don't tell me you didn't have a nice time yesterday?" Daisy's mouth dropped open. She leaned over and gave Julia's arm a reassuring pat. "You poor dear. I was certain you would. That's the only reason I helped get you to St. Ives. I figured you was due some fun."

"I know." Julia smiled feebly. "It isn't that at all. It's . . ." Her voice trailed away. She looked over at Daisy. Her long hair was caught up in a braid at the back of her head and her face, fresh and freckled, looked as innocent as a child's. Daisy was sweet, uncomplicated, naïve, and very young. How would she react to what Julia was about to tell her?

Julia took a deep breath. "We've got to leave here as soon as we can," she said.

"Leave here?" Daisy's eyes widened. "You're touched in the head, and no mistake. Why ever would we want to leave a place as fine as this?"

Julia twisted her blanket over in her fingers. "I found out something about Mick," she said, trying to break the news as gently as she could, but finding it harder than she imagined to put her newfound knowledge into words. "He's not . . . he's not really what we think he is."

The peal of laughter that erupted from Daisy was loud enough to wake the dead. Clutching her sides, she buried her face in the bed in a desperate attempt to control her fit of humor. When she settled down enough to speak, she sat up and wiped tears from her eyes.

"He's finally told you."

"Told me?" Julia looked at the girl in wonderment and her voice broke with disbelief. "You mean, you knew? You know? You're one of them?"

"As are we all." Daisy nodded her head in affirmation. "Well, not all. Not that prig Mrs. Harrison, the house-keeper, or Cook. But Jessup's in on it with us. And Rose. All of us what met there in London and came here together."

"And it doesn't bother you?"

"Bother me? Why ever should it bother me when we've got a scheme like this, as grand as fivepence?"

Julia could barely make the offending words leave her throat. "You're here to rob the house. You're thieves and that doesn't bother you?"

"Shh." Daisy held one finger to her lips. "Not so loud. Somebody might hear. Why do you think we was so anxious to fill Annie's place? It's key to the plan to have someone you can trust in the mistress's rooms. That's where most of the jewels is kept and sometimes some of the actual, too. You know, the money. We're on the game, you see, and that means we're here for some serious thievin'."

"But it isn't a game." Julia grabbed for Daisy's arm and held her tight, hoping to talk some sense into her. "You could be caught and put into prison."

Daisy's face took on a dignity far beyond her years. "You ain't never lived on the streets, have you?" she asked. "'Course you ain't. I could tell that from the day you comed along. I growed up on the streets. Prison couldn't be no worse." Daisy smiled wearily. "No, it don't bother me none. This is my chance to get somethin' for myself." She screwed up her face and studied Julia for a moment, her head cocked. "You ain't thinkin' of backin' out on us, are you?"

"I . . ." Julia hesitated. She could not trust Daisy, that much was clear. Last night, she had decided to leave the Beechers as soon as she possibly could. It would take another two months' wages before she had enough for train fair to London and a little to live on once she got there. She had hoped to take Daisy and Rose with her. Now, she would simply have to go alone.

"Of course I won't back out on you," she assured Daisy, hoping the lie didn't sound too forced. "I was more concerned about you and Rose than about myself. But as long as you know what you've gotten into . . ."

Daisy grinned. "'Course we know. Me and Rose have been doin' this sort of thing for years. It's the second time . . . no . . . it's the third time we've worked with Mick. He's always gotten us into the best sorts of houses. Why, last summer, we was workin' in a house where members of Parliament came and went, all la-di-da. Imagine that! Workin' in a place like that and thievin' right under their noses and they never noticed. That Mick! He's a grand one!''

Mick was a grand one, that much was certain. A grand imposter. Julia punched her pillow in an effort to keep her agitation from showing.

"Tommy-rot!" She looked down her nose at Daisy. "You needn't tell me anything about Mick. Nothing Mick O'Donnell says or does is of the least bit of interest to me."

Daisy nodded, but there was a sly, disbelieving smile on her face. She bounced off the bed, the package of toffee still clutched to her breast. "It's gettin' light. You'd better be up and about. Though it ain't hardly heard of for a lady's maid to serve, I hear you'll be helpin' out at the séance. We'll be busy as bees in a treacle-pot, you can be sure of that."

Julia tossed off her blanket and rose from the bed. She crossed the room to retrieve her clothes, slipped out of her nightgown, and began dressing. "Did you say the séance is this week?"

The excitement of the séance glowed in Daisy's face again. "That's right. They're to have all sorts of folks here for the weekend, so Mrs. Harrison says. High-steppers, all of them. And a real . . . real . . . what do you call them, them what contacts the dead and reads minds and all like that?"

"A medium."

"Medium. That's it. Do somethin' with your eyes, love. They're as red as roses."

Julia went to her washstand and splashed cold water on her face.

"You'd best be feelin' better fast, headache or none," Daisy warned. "I've heard the missus is in quite a fret about it all. She'll have you runnin' faster than ever and I daresay those two dragons what she has for daughters will, too. There will be young men comin' and sure as eggs is eggs, Miss Regina and Miss Louise will be lookin' to impress 'em.'' Daisy snickered and gave Julia a broad and knowing wink.

''Have you ever! Those girls look at men the way beggars look at a feast of food. Even Mick ain't safe. I've seen them eye him like an apple ripe for pickin'. If the missus ever knowed, she'd have a royal you-know-what.''

Julia finished buttoning her dress and tied her starched white apron around her waist. ''If you're suggesting I might be the least bit interested in what Mick O'Donnell does with Miss Regina or Miss Louise or anyone else in this cursed household . . .''

Without finishing the thought, she sailed out of the room and down the stairs.

THERE wasn't much time.

His hands steady, his mind seemingly on nothing more than filling the glasses, Mick scanned the crowd of well-dressed aristocrats gathered for after-dinner sherry in the Beechers' drawing room.

They were all here, every one of the politically prominent guests he'd expected to see. The only question was, which of them was the courier?

If backbone was the only criterion the British government used to determine who would serve it, more than half the men in the room could easily be eliminated. Mick tossed a small look of disdain at the crowd. Spineless as snails, most of them, more interested in preserving their own skins than in serving their country.

But this scheme required no courage. He was looking for the man, not with the most bravado, but with the most cunning. There was shrewdness behind this plan, and the person clever enough to have devised it would certainly not be fool enough to give himself away.

Freddy Halliday.

Mick's gaze wandered around the room, instinctively searching for the one man who came to mind. ''Think of the devil, and there he be.'' He whispered the words to himself, his eyes narrowed, his thoughts not on serving the guests, but on the young gentleman lounging near the fireplace.

If Halliday felt the heat of Mick's gaze, he pretended not to notice. He tossed down the remainder of the glass of sherry in his hand and continued his conversation with a yellow-haired beauty in a low-cut gown.

Mick took a deep breath and forced his gaze back to the tray of empty glasses waiting to be filled, deliberately ignoring the fact that Julia was the one who would be serving them. She stood before him, her gaze fixed upon the silver tray in her hands, her lips set into a tight line that spoke her displeasure more eloquently than any words.

Damn. It was bad enough Mick could not eat or sleep or work without the memory of what he'd done to Julia intruding on his thoughts, now he had Freddy Halliday to worry about. He needed Halliday's interference as much as a dog needed a side-pocket.

But whether he liked it or not, Halliday was here. The plan that had been put in motion in London more than four moths ago was moving toward completion. And from now on, only one thing was certain. There wasn't much time.

THERE wasn't much time.

Julia pulled back her shoulders, forcing herself to wait patiently while Mick filled each glass on her tray. All the while, she was careful to keep her eyes averted from his. If she did not, she was certain he would see the spark of apprehension there, the mix of expectant exhilaration and fear on her face.

Julia was leaving the Beechers and she was leaving tonight.

Where the outrageous notion came from was nearly as baffling as how she would find the courage to carry it out. She dared a look at Mick, so absorbed in pouring the sherry he did not give her as much as a glance, and she knew none of it mattered; not her lack of money, nor the perils of traveling alone, not the inevitable hardships that awaited her in London nor the struggle for survival she was certain to face.

At the beginning of the week, she'd convinced herself not to leave until she saved sufficient funds. But by the time Friday came, she was certain she could never wait that long, not when every chance meeting with Mick, every stony look he gave her, shattered her heart.

In the past week, they had not spoken more than a dozen words to each other. She had seen Mick at meals, passed him in the halls, encountered him on the stairs. Each time, he looked beyond her or offered an abrupt "Good morning." Julia pretended to be only too pleased to return the courtesy. She wondered how good an actress she was. Did he see through her thin pretense? If he did, if he cared, he did not show it.

Julia swallowed the lump of regret in her throat. In spite of her firm resolve to remain calm and detached, she could not look at Mick and remain indifferent.

For a few short hours earlier this week, she thought he would be a vital part of her future. Now she knew it was best to dismiss him as a regrettable piece of her past. Soon, she could begin to forget him. Though the thought filled her with icy despair, she held on to it, firmly refusing to yield to emotions that were as painful as they were futile.

There wasn't much time left. That, at least, was a comfort. As soon as the entertainment began, she would withdraw to the kitchen. If Cook was still awake, she would plead a headache, or better still, a female ailment. No one would dare question her then. The rest was easy. She would hurry up the back stairs, collect her things, and slip out of the house. By the time anyone missed her, she would be well on her way to Redruth.

Julia felt the first prickles of panic intensify. She circulated through the crowd serving the sherry, forcing herself to disregard the fluttering in her stomach.

When Mrs. Beecher finally signaled her daughters to begin the music, Julia set her tray on the nearest table and wiped her damp palms on the skirt of her gown. In only a few minutes, she told herself, she would put her plan into action, and once she began, there would be no time for nervousness or second thoughts.

The Beecher daughters had chosen a selection of songs from *H.M.S. Pinafore,* Miss Regina at the piano and Miss Louise singing. They were lovely songs, Julia thought, songs that could not easily be mangled by anyone, no matter how poor the talent.

She was wrong. Louise's voice was as shrill as a train whistle, and Regina's playing, lackluster and heavy-handed. The disharmony of their tunes reverberated off the crystal chandeliers, rocketed off the damask-papered walls, and ricocheted back at their bewildered audience with all the subtlety of cannon fire.

Julia cringed. A second later, Mick caught her eye. He poked his chin in the direction of a tray of dirty glasses, silently commanding her to take them away.

Julia breathed a prayer of thanksgiving. Without knowing it, Mick had played into her plan. She picked up the tray and hurried from the room.

The kitchen was blessedly quiet. Julia paused, her back against the door, and squinted into the darkness. A lamp had been left burning near the sink; the rest of the huge room was lost in shadow. There was no one around, but from the amount of dirty glasses on the table, she knew there wasn't much time before the maids who were serving in the drawing room would be back to wash up. Without another look around, she bolted up the back stairs.

By the time she reached her room in the attic, Julia was out of breath. With trembling fingers, she struck a match to light her single candle, and by its feeble light, she pulled her portmanteau from beneath the bed. She dashed to the wardrobe and grabbed for her clothes.

Less than five minutes later she was back in the kitchen. At the bottom of the stairs, she stopped, cocking her head to listen. The only sounds she heard were coming from the drawing room, the music still painfully apparent from the other side of the baize door. Hoisting her suitcase into her right hand, Julia crept across the room.

The brass doorknob was cold against her sweaty palm. She twisted it, but the handle slipped beneath her fingers. She wiped her hand against her coat and tried again. This time, the door yielded to her pull. Julia closed her eyes and thanked whatever fates were guiding her. Because of his duties at the dinner party, Mick had not yet locked up for the night. At least she didn't have to worry about locating and stealing a key, or, she thought wryly, about picking the lock herself.

A cool, sweet breath of outside air brushed Julia's cheek. She pulled the door open wider and stepped closer to the threshold. There she stopped.

Something was moving in the deep shadows to her left, beyond the halo of light from the gas lamp. Julia peered over her shoulder, but she could see nothing. Slowly, she turned from the door and tried to penetrate the surrounding gloom, her eyes darting left, then right. She jumped at a small, muffled noise coming from the direction of the stairway. Though it was almost imperceptible, the sound made the hair on the back of Julia's neck stand on end. She forced herself to think, calming her ruffled nerves with mindless reassurances.

It was probably nothing, she told herself. It was probably just the wind, or a creaking floorboard, or the cat. But the wind wasn't blowing, and floorboards in brand-new houses didn't creak, and even if the Beechers had a cat, she was sure it wouldn't chuckle.

Curious, Julia stepped closer to the darkened stairway. If

she turned and ran, if she left the house without knowing who was watching her, she was certain to worry about being followed. That was intolerable. She refused to be haunted by fear, real or imagined.

The next second, all logical thought scattered like snowflakes before a howling winter wind. Julia sucked in a tight, uncomfortable breath and held it, as a hand clamped down on her shoulder.

Chapter 7

PANIC numbing every muscle, Julia stood motionless. The seconds dragged by in slow, maddening succession. When she could stand the tension no longer, she swallowed hard and spun to face her assailant.

In her anxiety, she had envisioned every possibility: Mick, his anger provoked, his eyes blazing; Cook, rolling pin raised, sure she'd discovered a burglar; even Mrs. Beecher, outraged at the one maid impertinent enough to leave the drawing room.

She had not expected this.

The young gentleman with his hand clamped on her shoulder was one of the Beechers' guests. He was no taller than Julia, and for a moment, his dark eyes stared directly into hers, mirroring her own surprise. Then, his hold on her loosened and his eyes brightened with amusement.

"Frightfully sorry to have startled you," he said. His voice was finely rounded, with the refined, precise accent of a man educated at the best public schools. "I've lost my way back to the drawing room. When I heard someone near the door, I felt it only right to investigate."

Julia moistened her lips with the tip of her tongue. She had planned for this emergency, she reminded herself. She had thought out exactly what she'd say in the event of being discovered. It was a wonderful story, all about a sickly aunt, a desperate letter, and a train that could not be missed. Try as she might to speak them, the words would not come.

The young gentleman lifted his eyebrows, his curiosity obviously piqued, his enjoyment apparent. There was a delighted glimmer in his dark eyes and the corners of his well-shaped mouth rose into a good-natured grin.

"I say! I seem to have frightened the words right out of you." He gave her a quick, friendly nod. "Freddy Halliday, at your service, miss. Can I get you something? A glass of water?"

This time Julia found her voice. "No." She rejected his offer instantly. "I . . . I wasn't . . . that is, I mean, I was . . ."

Halliday glanced at Julia's suitcase, still lying near the door. He stepped back, his head to one side, and inspected her carefully, his discerning look missing neither the outdoor boots she was wearing, nor her coat. His lips pursed, he gave her a knowing wink.

"I must admit, I had to get away from that music, too," he said lightly. "But I hadn't thought of actually leaving. By Jove, I think you've come up with the best solution."

Julia stared at him, too bewildered to answer.

Halliday leaned closer. "Mrs. Beecher would be appalled if she knew you were that desperate to get away from Miss Louise's golden voice. Or is it Miss Regina's musicianship you're escaping?" He grinned. "It only proves that even music can be a dangerous thing in the wrong hands."

As if in support of his statement, they heard a discordant sound float in from the drawing room, the unmistakable clink of a wrongly played note.

In spite of herself, Julia could not contain a smile. "Miss Regina definitely has the wrong hands," she said. " 'How sour sweet music is.' "

Halliday's face sobered and he eyed her, suddenly more interested than amused. "You don't talk like a maid," he said. "Most maids couldn't quote Shakespeare if their lives depended on it."

Julia returned his frank gaze, studying him as openly as he was assessing her. But she did not answer. She could not think of a response neutral enough to appease the questioning in his eyes or to satisfy the curiosity that colored his voice.

"Perhaps you're not really a maid." Halliday's words echoed back at her through the darkness, his tone still casual, but the words underpinned with speculation. "Perhaps that's why you've decided to leave?"

This time she had to answer. Julia opened her mouth, ready to challenge him.

Halliday did not give her the chance. He fixed her with a steady look. "You'd best go while you can," he said. "You'll be sacked before you've had the chance to walk out if anyone finds us here. It doesn't look right, does it? A girl as attractive as you and a gentlemen she hardly knows standing close together in the dark. And you with your suitcase close at hand. Tell me, my dear, who is it you're waiting for?"

Julia found her voice, denying the insinuation as quickly as she could. "I'm not waiting for anyone. Or anything," she said. "I'm simply leaving. I don't like it here."

"It's a shame." Halliday stepped nearer. He skimmed a leisurely glance from the top of Julia's head to the tip of her chin and back again, pausing long enough to give careful consideration to her eyes and her mouth. "I was hoping to get to know you better. I've been watching you since I arrived this afternoon. You're not like the others. Not like a servant at all. I knew that from the moment I saw you."

As he spoke, he leaned toward her. The movement was sudden, and so unexpected Julia did not have time to react. Before she could move away, Halliday brought his mouth down on hers. It was a quick kiss, and so impersonal it did little more than astonish Julia. She stiffened and a small noise of surprise escaped her.

Halliday was delighted by her reaction. He backed away and stroked his chocolate-colored hair, a huge smile brightening his face. "That's proved it," he crowed, as happy as a schoolboy. "You even kiss like a gentlewoman. As cold as a glacier and just as stiff."

"Cold?" Outrage rose in Julia's throat, strangling her. "Tommy-rot! How dare you, sir? I didn't expect a gentleman—"

"I knew it the minute I saw you this afternoon," Halliday continued, ignoring her protests. "You're not like the rest of them. You're better quality, better breeding. So tell me, my blue-blooded lady's maid, why are you playing servant in a household like this?"

"I'm not playing anything. Not anymore." Angry and tired of Halliday's foolishness, Julia turned to the door and picked up her portmanteau. "That's why I'm leaving."

"But you were playing." It was not a question. Halliday took a small step forward, his voice as smooth as expensive brandy. "You were playing, weren't you? And now it isn't fun any longer. Someone's ruined it for you. Who was it? Those two horrible Beecher girls? Or the lady of the castle herself, our dear hostess? Or could it be, perhaps, that you're running away from Mick O'Donnell?"

The mention of Mick's name hit her with all the force of a physical blow. Every muscle tensed, every instinct signaling her to be wary, Julia set her portmanteau on the floor and slowly turned to face Freddy Halliday.

"What do you know about Mick O'Donnell?"

Halliday stroked his top lip with the tip of one finger. "I know there's been many a girl led astray by that handsome Irish devil," he replied. "And I know he's no gentleman, as much as he wishes he were. If he's taken advantage of you in any way . . ."

Julia bristled at his unspoken accusation. "Are you implying—"

"I'm implying nothing. Merely pointing out the obvious. A pretty girl like you needs to be careful. Careful of men like Mick O'Donnell. And very careful of going off alone in the middle of the night." He paused, giving her time to consider his warning. "Wouldn't it be better to wait? You can talk to Mrs. Beecher tomorrow, have her make suitable traveling arrangements. If you're afraid, I'll come with you, help you explain things."

"No." Julia shook off the momentary, paralyzing effects of her apprehension. "You don't understand. If I don't leave soon, I might not have a chance to leave at all." She heard the final, grinding strains of "Little Buttercup" coming from the drawing room and she knew the entertainment would soon be over. When it was, Mick would surely come to see where she'd disappeared to with the sherry glasses.

"I've got to leave now," she told Halliday, urgency vibrating in her voice. "I don't want to wait until morning. I don't want to talk to Mrs. Beecher. I just want to disappear before anyone knows I've gone."

"I could help."

His offer brought Julia up short. This time, she knew it was more than instinct that cautioned her to be careful. This was logic, pure and simple. Young gentlemen did not offer to assist housemaids, not without expecting something in return.

"Why would you help me?" she asked. "What is it you want?"

Halliday's face was serious. "I only want you to tell me what's wrong. I know you're afraid and I think I know why. Tell me about it and I promise I'll help you."

"Tell me what you think you know."

Halliday laughed. "I was right," he said. "You're no

maid. No girl from the lower classes would dare challenge a gentleman.''

Julia did not respond. She studied Freddy Halliday from beneath her lashes. He was looking for information, and he wanted it badly. That much was certain. What did a young swell like Halliday know about Mick O'Donnell? Why did he care? Julia folded her arms across her chest and stared at him, unsmiling.

''Very well.'' Halliday surrendered, both hands thrown up in a friendly gesture of resignation. ''I'll tell you everything I know. You tell me if I'm right.'' He glanced over his shoulder. ''Mick O'Donnell is not a butler. He is an immoral, depraved, dangerous thief. He's here as part of a wider conspiracy. You may be involved. You may be trying to escape it. Am I right so far?''

Julia was too surprised to answer. She stared at Halliday, her mouth open.

''O'Donnell's done this kind of thing before,'' Halliday continued. ''He finds himself a few trusted confederates, they obtain false references, and they rob their unsuspecting employers. This time there are a couple of maids in on the scheme with him, as well as an outside man called Ben Jessup. You needn't say a word. I can tell by the look on your face that my information is correct.''

''How do you know?'' Julia whispered.

Halliday smiled broadly. ''Finding things out is the easy part. The hard part is putting what you've found to good use. I simply spent a few productive minutes with Ben Jessup this afternoon.''

As desperately as she tried to control it, Julia could not quell the anger that rose within her. Ben Jessup, who was supposedly Mick's ally, Ben Jessup who had been so careful to teach her everything he knew about lock picking, Ben Jessup had betrayed them all.

''Jessup told you that?'' She could not keep the outrage from her voice. ''In exchange for what?''

Halliday considered her question, a look of open admiration on his face. "You know Jessup well enough, don't you? It didn't take much to get him to talk. A few shillings, a few promises."

In spite of her resolve to forget Mick and everything associated with him, Julia could not help but feel curious. "Why?" she asked. "Why do you want to know? Will you tell the police? Or Scotland Yard?"

Halliday moved closer and lowered his voice. "I am Scotland Yard. I've been after Mick O'Donnell for a long time. Believe me, I won't forget those who help apprehend him. Anything you can tell me . . ."

Julia stepped back. "If you've talked to Jessup, why are you asking me questions as well?"

"I need a credible witness," Halliday said matter-of-factly. "Jessup's too unreliable to be of any use to me in court. But a girl like you, well-bred, educated, honest, you know what's right and you wouldn't be afraid to stand up in court and tell it. You're the kind of witness I need. Together, we can put Mick O'Donnell away for so long, he'll never bother you again."

Confused, Julia turned away. Through a swirl of disordered thoughts, she tried to sort through the deluge of startling information just thrown at her.

Freddy Halliday was from Scotland Yard. That was the most important thing she'd learned, and perhaps the most surprising. She supposed she should be thankful. More than thankful, she should be grateful. In exchange for information, he would help her leave the Beechers, where every corner of every precisely arranged room, every moment of every perfectly organized day, reminded her of a man she knew it would be better to forget.

She told herself she owed nothing but contempt to Mick. He had lied to her. He had taken advantage of her desperate situation to involve her in something both illegal and immoral. He had done everything in his power to entangle her in a conspiracy so disgraceful it made her shudder to think about it.

Though she tried to stop them, tears sprang to Julia's eyes. After all this time of keeping her dreadful secret, it would be such a relief to tell someone. "I took the place of one of the girls," she explained, her voice choked with tears. "She ran off, you see, and they needed someone quickly. I never dreamed—"

"No, a nice girl like you never would."

Halliday's voice had softened. Wiping a tear from her cheek, Julia turned back to him and found him smiling, much the way a master smiles at an obedient dog. The resemblance made her uncomfortable. To conceal her uneasiness, Julia sniffed loudly and waited while Halliday fished in his pocket for a handkerchief and offered it to her.

He watched her dry her tears. "Go ahead," he crooned, his voice tight with excitement. "Tell me the rest. I can see you're afraid of Mick O'Donnell and you have every right to be. He's got a well-deserved reputation for being vicious. Just tell me everything you know, my dear, and I'll make sure you'll be safe. I give you my word. I've wired London. They're sending men down on the first train tomorrow. I've got enough information to arrest O'Donnell. With your help, I'll put him behind bars for the rest of his life."

Julia watched the fire of righteous fervor grow in Freddy Halliday's eyes. It did not take her long to make up her mind.

She told herself what she was about to do was for Daisy and Rose. But she knew she was lying, even to herself. It was not the girls she was thinking of. It was Mick's face she saw flash before her eyes, Mick's voice she heard, Mick's touch she felt. She could denounce Mick O'Donnell to the world, but she could no longer deny her feelings to herself.

"Tell me," Halliday said. "Tell me all about it."

Julia looked at him guilelessly. "I don't know what you're talking about," she said.

It was Halliday's turn to be surprised. "But you said—"

"I never said a thing. You're the one who came in here repeating Ben Jessup's ridiculous accusations. Really, Mr. Halliday, if you think you can believe a man like Jessup! I daresay, he would have told you the moon was made of green cheese if he thought it could earn him a shilling."

A sudden, icy contempt flashed in Halliday's eyes. "Are you telling me he made it all up?"

Julia shrugged. "Perhaps he did, perhaps he didn't. I'm telling you I don't know anything about it. I don't know anything about thieves or schemes or plans and I am certainly not afraid of Mick O'Donnell. As far as I can tell, he's as harmless as he is witless and—"

"Excuse me, Mr. Halliday, sir."

At the sound of Mick's voice, Julia jumped and spun around. He was standing with his back to the baize door, looking as calm and unruffled as he had all evening, his eyes fixed on Freddy Halliday. How long he had been there, how much he had heard, she did not know.

Silence filled the room. It pressed against Julia, as palpable as a touch, and amplified the furious pounding of her heart. Suddenly, she realized she could no longer hear music coming from the drawing room.

Julia's gaze darted from Mick to Halliday. The two men stared across the vast kitchen at each other, their eyes locked, their heads high, their backs arrow-straight. Like primitive warriors preparing for mortal combat, they challenged each other in silence. Both their faces were unreadable, but Julia detected the twitch of a small muscle at the base of Halliday's jaw. Whether he trembled with surprise, anxiety, or impatience, she did not know.

The moment stretched into two, then three. Finally, Mick bowed slightly at the waist.

"I'm sorry to bother you, Mr. Halliday," he said, his voice level. "But Miss Regina is looking for you, sir. She asks if you would be so kind as to accompany her into the dining room for coffee.''

Halliday straightened his jacket, tugged at his white bow tie, and cleared his throat. "Of course," he answered. "I shall go directly in." Without another look at either Mick or Julia, he left the room.

With the tip of her boot, Julia slid her suitcase further into the shadows. Once Halliday was out of the room, she darted toward the baize door. "Mick—"

"You haven't even started the bloody glasses," Mick growled, his voice so loud, Julia was sure even Freddy Halliday could hear it outside in the corridor. Mick's gaze was not on Julia, but on the tray of sherry glasses sitting, unwashed, in the center of the table. "You'd best get to work, girl. They'll be in the dining room in a minute, and if I know this crowd, they'll be wanting more sherry."

"But Mick, I need to talk to you."

Mick looked from the dirty glasses to Julia. With one frosty glance, he took in everything from her boots, to her coat, to the curl of her hair that had come loose when Freddy Halliday kissed her. For once, his careful scrutiny did not unsettle her. Absently, she pushed the unruly lock of hair out of her eyes, too concerned with her own crucial news to care what Mick was thinking.

"I have to talk to you. Now," she repeated, her voice stronger, more demanding.

Though his face remained impassive, his eyes burned. "Right now, the sherry glasses are more important than anything you've got to tell me." Mick punched the baize door open with one fist, then stopped and turned back to Julia, his hand still on the door. "We'll talk in the morning.''

Julia watched him retreat into the corridor. She grumbled to herself, pulled off her coat, and rolled up her sleeves. kicking the leg of the nearest chair for good measure. "In the morning," she muttered, "it will be too late."

Chapter 8

"Too late. Too late." Julia paced the length of her bedroom, mumbling to herself. "Curse the man for his Irish arrogance. If only he'd listened to me." At the far end of the room, she peered out the window. Though the full moon lit the surrounding countryside nearly as bright as day, morning was still more than four hours away. If she waited to talk to Mick then, it would be too late.

"That insolent, hardheaded . . ." Words failed her and Julia muffled a screech of frustration and pounded the windowsill with her fist. "Curse you, Mick O'Donnell. You're going to get yourself arrested in the morning."

Julia took a deep breath, fighting to calm her jangled nerves. She'd spent the better part of the night searching for solutions. Over and over again, she'd asked herself what she could do to help Mick. Over and over again, only one answer presented itself.

She had no delusions. Besides being dangerous, what she was about to do was insane. Only five weeks ago, no one could have convinced her she would risk her reputation and perhaps her freedom to warn a thief he was about to be captured. But five weeks ago, she was not the same person she was tonight. Five weeks ago, she had not met Mick.

Julia paused for a moment, the memory of their time alone together in St. Ives warming her against the night's chill, and she knew she would have to try, no matter what the risk. The vivid memory of Mick's lips brushing hers drove out all thoughts of danger and made her plan, despite its madness, seem not only probable, but possible.

It would be difficult to find her way to Mick's rooms in the dark. She knew the butler's private suite lay at the back of the house behind the kitchen, but it was strictly and understandably off limits to the female servants, and Julia had never been there.

"Tommy-rot!" She shook off her misgivings and, without another thought for the consequences, marched to the door and opened it.

Once in the kitchen, Julia stopped and took a close look at every corner, her startling encounter with Freddy Halliday earlier in the evening still fresh in her mind. The kitchen was empty. The rising moon sent bright light streaming through the windows on the far wall, and by its radiance, she navigated the sharp turn that led down a short corridor to Mick's rooms.

Outside his door, she leaned her ear on the smooth oak panel, but she heard nothing. As quietly as she could, Julia turned the doorknob and slipped inside.

She breathed a sigh of relief. Mick had not drawn his curtains. His parlor was nearly as bright as day. Briefly, she glanced around the room. There was the requisite desk and chair in front of the windows, a fireplace along the far wall, a sofa set before it. Everything was immaculate and orderly. But there were no photographs, no pictures, no personal mementos to mark the room with the singular character of its occupant. It was as stark as a monk's cell and just as cheerless.

The melancholy emptiness of the room overwhelmed her. Julia wondered what sort of man kept his nature neatly concealed, even in private. The next moment, she told herself it did not matter. She was here neither to gain understanding nor to pass judgment. She was here to save Mick's life.

From the next room, she heard the sound of rhythmic breathing and nodded with satisfaction. She had found Mick O'Donnell. He was fast asleep.

Spurred by her desperation and anxious to get back to her own room before she was discovered, Julia moved as quickly as she could. She hurried into Mick's bedroom and knelt beside the bed.

In the silvery light that poured through the open windows, she saw that Mick's blankets were pushed below his knees. He was not wearing a nightshirt. He was not wearing anything at all.

Julia stiffened, momentarily flustered. But in spite of her embarrassment, she was unable to tear her gaze away from him. His hair tumbled over his forehead, softening his features, but even in repose, the muscles of Mick's shoulders and arms seemed taut, rippling with barely controlled power. His bare chest shone like sculpted marble in the incandescent glow of the moonlight. It was smooth and completely free of hair and Julia watched, fascinated, as it rose and fell to the measured tempo of Mick's breathing. He looked splendid, like the statue of a sleeping god, except he needed a fig leaf. A large fig leaf.

Julia felt her cheeks flame.

She forced herself to focus on his face, swallowed her mortification, and poked at his arm. "Mick," she whispered.

He did not respond.

"Mick." This time, she nudged him harder.

"Hm." It was, at least, a response.

Julia grabbed his arm. For a moment, she did nothing else. Though the night air was cool, his skin was warm beneath her fingers. A tiny thrill of excitement coursed through her veins and froze her hand in place. The next moment, she reminded herself of her urgent mission. She shook him. "Mick."

Mick's eyelids fluttered open, then closed again and a smile touched the corners of his mouth. "Sure and it's dreaming I must be," he whispered, his voice hoarse with sleep. "Can't trick me. Had this dream before. You'll be gone when I open my eyes."

Asleep or not, Julia lost patience with him. She shook him with both hands and ordered him to wake up.

Half in a daze, Mick rolled to his side and reached out one hand. He ran it up what felt like an arm to what was almost certainly a shoulder. He caressed the shoulder. The crisp fabric of a housedress crinkled beneath his fingers. Saint Bridget and Saint Joseph! This dream was even more disturbing than the others. This time, he swore he could feel the warmth radiating from her.

He grinned, turning over the interesting possibilities in his mind. Another tentative touch. This time, he was certain he felt the silky texture of her hair. He wound his fingers through the luxurious knot coiled at the back of her head, savoring the feel of the soft curls against his skin.

"I'm telling myself it can't be true," he said, still reluctant to open his eyes. "But I'm thinking you're real." One blue eye popped open. "Can it be my prayers have been answered?"

"It all depends what you've been praying for," Julia said, her irritation spilling into her voice. "If your prayers included Scotland Yard, you may be getting your wish sooner than you think."

This time both his eyes drifted open. Mick raised himself on one elbow. "What in the name of the saints and angels . . . ?"

If it wasn't for the invigorating chill of the night wind on his skin, he would have sworn he was still asleep. Julia looked like a vision, an apparition no more corporeal than the shimmering light itself. Moonlight turned the feathery wisps of her hair into a halo and accented the ivory glow of her face. Her eyes were pools of darkness, sparkling with reflected moonlight; her mouth was a moist temptation that invited tasting.

He edged closer, the cobwebs just beginning to clear from his sleep-numbed mind, and moved his hand from her hair to her cheek, outlining her silvery silhouette with his thumb. Her skin was satiny beneath his fingers, and when he skimmed his thumb to her eyes, her eyelashes dipped and brushed it.

Holy Mother! This was too marvelous not to be genuine. She was not a dream. She was real. And she was in his bedroom.

Suddenly, Mick was completely awake. He blinked to focus his eyes. He had been right about one thing, the silvery light made her look like a goddess. He wondered how much of his own eagerness the treacherous moonlight had revealed.

Tentatively, he glanced down at his own body, hoping his physical reaction to Julia's presence was not as noticeable as he feared. Mick's eyes widened and he grabbed for his blanket. He pulled it up to his nose and glared at Julia from beneath it.

In spite of her annoyance, Julia grinned. She had not expected modesty to be one of Mick's virtues. "I told you I needed to talk to you," she said, her voice softened by a surge of affection.

"So you decided to do it in the middle of the night? Are you daft, girl? If anyone finds you here—"

"Which they undoubtedly will, if you don't keep your voice down."

Mick slid himself up, half sitting, and ruffled his hair. His lips thinned with irritation, but when he spoke it was in a whisper. "If anyone finds you here, we'll both be sacked."

"That is a chance we'll have to take. I need to tell you about Freddy Halliday."

The oath Mick grumbled was by far the foulest thing Julia had ever heard. She sat back on her heels and frowned. "Really, Mick O'Donnell, if you insist on being profane—"

"Saints protect me!" Mick shook his head in wonder. "I wake up to find a woman in my bedroom spouting nonsense, and now she's lecturing me about my language. I'll have you know, my fine and fancy lady—"

"Whatever you'll have me know can wait. Can't you stop prattling long enough to listen to me? Freddy Halliday—"

"—is the most unscrupulous, nastiest whoreson you're ever likely to meet."

"He said the same thing about you."

"He did? The bastard." Mick snorted, but there was a look of satisfaction on his face. "The devil take his Saxon arrogance." Mick struggled to sit up, all the while keeping the blanket tucked discreetly around his body. He stood, fumbled in the dark for his trousers, and disappeared into the parlor.

Barely able to control her anxiety, Julia rose and walked the length of Mick's room.

A minute later, Mick was back, his trousers on. He rifled in his wardrobe for a shirt and slipped that on, too.

"I suppose Halliday told you what a villain I am," Mick said, and Julia detected a small note of perverse pleasure in his voice. "He would say that, the no good, son-of-a—"

"Mick!" Julia fought to keep her voice low. "I didn't come here to talk about Freddy Halliday's shortcomings."

Mick stalked over to her, buttoning his shirt. He looked at her, his eyes burning with indignation. "I suppose he tried to kiss you."

Julia stared at him, her mouth open. "What on earth difference does it make?" she said, her voice shrill with disbelief.

"Well, did he?" Mick glared at her and waited for an answer.

"Yes."

"Yes, what? He tried to kiss you? Or he kissed you?"

"He kissed me."

"Damn!" For a second, Mick turned away. Just as quickly, he spun to face her again. "And you let him?"

"I didn't let him do anything. He did it, that's all. I wasn't expecting it and I certainly didn't encourage it." Julia tossed her head and eyed him defiantly. "I would no more encourage Freddy Halliday than I would encourage you."

Without another word, Mick stalked back to his wardrobe and fished along the floor for his boots. In the darkness, Julia could no longer see his face, but she was certain she heard him chuckle.

She clamped her mouth shut and dug her fingernails into the palms of her hands, certain she would scream with frustration if she did not distract herself. Mick finished with his boots, found a candle and struck a match. He set flame to wick.

All the wild emotion gone from him, Mick sat on the bed and patted the spot beside him.

"Now," he said, "stop your blathering and get on with it. What is it you need that can't wait until morning?"

"Me? Blathering?" Julia refused the seat. She stood staring down at Mick, her anger renewed by his incredible audacity. "I have never blathered in all my life. And if you insist—"

"I insist you forget your damned English superiority and sit down. Tell me what happened."

With a supreme effort, Julia pushed her anger aside. Dropping onto the bed, she faced Mick.

"How do you know about Halliday?" she asked.

"Know what? About him being the biggest bastard this side of—"

"Don't start again." Julia sighed with exasperation.

"How did you know Freddy Halliday was looking for you?"

Mick shrugged. "We've crossed paths before. I suppose he told you he was from Scotland Yard?"

"That's right."

"That smarmy little beggar wouldn't know Scotland Yard if his mother was the charlady there and he was born in the cellar."

"Then who is he?"

"Who?" Mick lifted one eyebrow, looking at her uncertainly. "Bah! That hardly matters. What did you tell him?"

"I didn't need to tell him anything. Jessup took care of that."

Mick slammed one fist down on his knee. "Damn the man! He's been dissatisfied since our last job. Thought he didn't get his fair share. I should have left him behind." Though the look in his eyes said Mick would never forgive Jessup's treachery, he dismissed the outside watchman with a wave of his hand, sucked in a deep breath, and let it out again slowly. "How much does Halliday know?"

"He knows you and Daisy and Rose are here to rob the house. He wasn't sure about me."

"And what did he want from you?"

"He said he needed a reliable witness," Julia explained. "He said I looked like the type of girl who would be believed in court."

"I've heard that story before," Mick replied with irony. "What's he willing to give you in return for your testimony?"

"He said he'd help me get away from here."

Mick sat quietly, looking not at Julia, but at some unseen, faraway thing. Then, his mind made up, he turned to her. "That's all well and good, then. What did you tell him?"

Taken aback by his assumption that she'd given in to Freddy Halliday's temptations, Julia stared at him. "I . . . I told him I didn't know what he was talking about."

"You did?" Intense astonishment touched Mick's face. "You did that? For me?"

"For you. For Rose. For Daisy. What difference does it make?" Julia rose from the bed and went to stand near the window, away from Mick's distinctly unsettling closeness. "The important thing is, Halliday's got men coming down from London in the morning. He says they're going to arrest you."

Julia expected Mick to be surprised. He only nodded. "Then he does believe Jessup's given him enough to go on. It'll never hold up in court, of course. No judge and jury would ever believe Ben Jessup. But Halliday's no fool, as much as he likes to act like one. He knows if he detains me . . ." Mick's brow creased, his words trailed away as he sat deep in thought.

"Well, we'll have to outsmart the bastard, won't we?" Mick sprang from the bed. "Go upstairs—quietly—and get Rose and Daisy," he said. "Halliday knows they're a part of this, we can't leave them here." He knelt on the floor, yanked away the braided rug beside his bed, and began to fiddle with the floorboards. A second later, one of the boards gave way under the pressure of his hands. He flipped it up, reached beneath it and pulled out a revolver.

Aside from parades and military exhibitions, Julia had never seen a gun, and never this close. Its silver barrel shone in the candlelight, but even the yellow glow of the fire did little to warm the cold steel. It looked sinister and the familiar way Mick handled it sent shivers down her spine. "What do you plan on doing with that?" she asked, her mouth dry, her voice quavering.

"Never you mind. Just do as you're told. Tell the girls we'll have to move tonight, not tomorrow. Go on now," he said, waving her toward the door. "Get the girls and get out of here. I've got business in Mr. Beecher's study."

"Mick!" Julia could not believe what she was hearing. She stepped toward him, her hands out in appeal. "I didn't tell you about the trap so you'd rob the house tonight. That's not what I meant at all. I thought . . . I thought perhaps you'd just leave, quickly, before anyone found out. I thought if you had a second chance . . ."

"Are you trying to save my soul?" Mick crossed the room to her. Gently, he pressed a kiss to the top of her head. He held her at arm's length, the look in his blue eyes unbearably tender. "Because if you are, I think it's only fair to tell you, I don't have one." He chucked her under the chin with his forefinger. "Now, get your things together and get out of here."

"I'm not going."

"What?" Mick stared at her in disbelief. "What do you mean you're not going?"

"Just what I said. I'll get Daisy and Rose for you, and you can be sure I won't raise the alarm. But I won't leave. That's as good as confessing my guilt."

"You are daft." Mick slid the gun into the waistband at the back of his trousers. "You believed Halliday, didn't you? Damn you upper-class English. You think because someone's got a pretty face and a roll of money bigger than Russia, you can trust them with your life."

"But I told Halliday I didn't want his help," Julia protested. "I told him I didn't know anything about you or what you planned to do."

"You'll stand no more chance than a cat in hell without claws. Every servant Halliday's ever questioned has ended up in the dock. He'll prosecute you, my fine and fancy lady. I promise you that. If for no other reason than to get even with you for not cooperating."

Julia felt her courage waver. "What shall I do?"

Mick blew out the candle and, grabbing her elbow, led Julia into his parlor. "Get the girls and get down here as fast as you can," he told her. "Don't wait for me."

"Don't wait?" Julia grabbed for the sleeve of Mick's jacket and held on tight. "You're not coming?"

He put his hand over hers where it rested on his sleeve. "It's better if we're not found together," he whispered, his voice tight, as if he were struggling with some powerful emotion. "Daisy and Rose will take you as far as London. When you get there, see a man in Battersea Lane by the name of Finnegan."

"Mick, I—"

"Enough." With one finger under her chin, he delicately closed her mouth. "Enough, *acushla.*"

Stroking the curve of her neck, Mick cupped her chin and stood silently, looking down at Julia.

He would never see her again.

The thought caused a painful ache deep within his body where only a short time ago he had felt the delicious tug of desire. He would never see her again, and he could neither tell her nor explain, but only pray she would get as far from here as fast as she could and avoid being caught in the deadly tide of events he was about to unleash.

She was watching him carefully, a question in her dark eyes. Mick forced a smile and shrugged away her concern. "Perhaps another time," he said.

His piece spoken, he should have turned around and walked away. It was the wise, the prudent thing to do. But try as he might, Mick could not convince his body of either the wisdom or the sensibility of his own advice. If he was never to see her again, he would at least leave with the taste of her on his lips.

Damning his logic one moment, his conscience the next, Mick bent and kissed her.

Julia was too surprised to respond. For a second, she stood perfectly still, her arms at her sides, her eyes drifting closed, coaxed shut by the smooth and subtle feel of his mouth against hers.

What started as a kiss of excruciating gentleness deepened with each beat of Julia's heart. For all Mick's nonchalance, there was more in his kiss than simple leave-taking. His body trembled, whether he knew it or not, and his lips signaled a certain potent desperation that was more meaningful than words. He was not saying they would meet another time. He was saying good-bye.

Julia brought her hands to Mick's arms and slid them up to his shoulders, drawing herself nearer and returning his firm, moist kisses with an intensity born of despair. A month ago, she might have tried to control her response. Tonight, she knew she could not.

Butler or thief, fugitive or felon, Mick O'Donnell was as essential to her as the air that strained in her lungs, as vital a part of her being as the blood that pounded its heat through her veins. She knew that now, as certainly as she knew the pain of hopeless longing that spiraled through her and caused her pulse to throb in her ears.

As abruptly as he'd begun, Mick pulled away from her, struggling for control. Julia swallowed hard and fought to force her cantering heartbeat into some semblance of normalcy. For a long moment, Mick studied her in silence. Then his face cracked into an enormous smile that sparkled his delight in the moonlight.

"Mother of mercy! If I knew you were going to react like that, I would have kissed you a long time ago." He pulled a rough workingman's cap from his pocket and clapped it on his head. The glimmer in his eyes stilled and he leaned toward her for one final, fleeting kiss.

"Good-bye, Julia."

Without another word, he nudged her into the corridor and on toward the servants' stairway.

Before she started up the back stairs, Julia caught one final glimpse of Mick, his shoulders steady as he disappeared through the baize door and on into the front of the house.

There was no time to worry about him. With each step, each furious beat of her heart, Julia told herself her anxiety was useless. The thought brought little comfort. Every instinct screamed its warning. Mick was marching into inescapable danger. And there was nothing she could do to stop him.

Julia dashed to her bedroom to retrieve her mother's photograph from her suitcase before she roused Daisy and Rose. She waited as patiently as she could while they hurried to dress. In less than ten minutes, they were in the kitchen again.

At the bottom of the stairs, Julia paused, tempted to go looking for Mick. She hurried across the kitchen and her hand was on the baize door when she heard a shout. Behind her, Daisy and Rose gasped with alarm. Julia stiffened, her head cocked. The noises were coming from the first floor.

A disturbing memory lodged itself in her mind and, try as she might, she could not be rid of it. Mick, with a gun tucked neatly into his trousers. Mick, on his way to Mr. Beecher's study. She squeezed her eyes shut and fought to drive the image from her mind, but it remained, clear and disquieting. The alarm had been raised somewhere upstairs, near Mr. Beecher's study.

Julia looked from Daisy to Rose. She did not hesitate. "Come on." She ran to the back door and, opening it, fled into the garden. "We've got to get as far away from here as we can. Do you know the stone fairy ring on the moor?"

Both girls nodded in response.

"We'll meet there," Julia said. "But not right away. Hide in the thicket of trees beyond the lawn. Wait until it quiets down. They're not expecting help until morning. If we run quickly . . ." She swung open the garden gate and shoved Daisy and Rose out ahead of her.

Glancing back at the house one last time, Julia dashed onto the lawn. There she stopped.

Like a row of lead soldiers they stood, shoulder to shoulder, an army of constables, their trim blue uniforms dark and forbidding in the silvery light.

Julia's gaze darted along the unyielding line, searching

for any signs of a vulnerable spot where she could slip
through and escape. It was no use. They were already
leading the other two girls away, and they could see her as
clearly in the moonlight as if it were day.

From somewhere to her right, a stout, white-haired man
advanced on her and took her elbow. He cleared his throat
and looked to the ground, as if he were embarrassed to be
involved with apprehending women. "No need to be
afeared, little one," he said.

Her panic and fright brought with them an incredible
flood of recklessness. Julia stuck out her lower lip. "I'm not
afraid of anything."

"You should be."

At the sound of a new voice that came from the deep
shadows along the garden wall, Julia's heart stopped.

A second later, Freddy Halliday stepped into the open.
"You should be," he repeated. Instantly, he was surrounded
by six sturdy constables. He took a step toward Julia,
signaling the white-haired man to return to his comrades.

"I almost believed you this evening." Halliday's voice
was as smooth as a well-oiled machine. It dripped amusement. "I can see I'm not quite the judge of character I
thought myself to be. And as you can see"—he dipped his
head toward the phalanx of police—"I wasn't entirely
honest with you, either." He leaned nearer, his eyes as hard
and cold as his voice was warm. "You won't mind coming
to where we have the others detained, will you?"

Unable to control her reaction, Julia winced.

Halliday chuckled. "No. We haven't got O'Donnell
yet," he said in answer to her troubled expression. "But we
will. Don't worry. We will." He smiled and, raising Julia's
wrists, clamped on a pair of manacles.

Chapter 9

"DAMNED, bloody sheep!"

With the tip of a long shepherd's staff, Mick prodded at the mass of woolly animals all around him.

"Filthy creatures!" He wrinkled his nose and side-stepped an ancient, hobbling ram which seemed especially intent on getting wound between his legs and knocking him over.

Just a short way to go. He cheered himself with the thought, convinced beyond a doubt he'd chosen correctly when he refused to become a farmer like his father and four older brothers.

Ahead of him, the town of Redruth was coming alive in the early morning light. Already, the road teemed with farmers and tradesmen taking their wares to the train station and on into the larger market towns along the rail line.

What's another farmer in a crowd such as that? Mick smiled to himself as he steered the flock around the village square and headed toward the station. He hoped another farmer would cause no more notice than one more bee in a busy hive.

The next second, Mick snorted with derision, astounded by his own simplicity. "It's a guffoon I am, to be sure," he reprimanded himself under his breath. For hope was the refuge of the helpless, and he was surprised to even hear the

word in his own vocabulary. Hope would do little to assure
the success of this scheme, and it would do nothing to save
Julia. No, he could not merely hope this would work, he had
to be sure.

Mick tossed the staff from his left hand into his right, and
urged one errant member of the flock closer to the others.
He patted the left-hand side of his jacket. The familiar feel
of the revolver in his pocket brought a rueful smile to his
face. There was no hope like the security of a sidearm, he
had learned that much from his years with the Fenians.

And if he had denounced violence? For a moment, his
conscience rose to reproach him. He had rejected violence,
he assured himself—violence for the cause of independence, violence for political aims, and personal ambitions,
and reasons of honor, and pride, and loyalty. But love was
another thing altogether.

Darting a glance up and down the platform, Mick paused
before the train station. They were here, just as he'd
anticipated, a small detachment of constables stomping their
feet against the morning chill, their prisoners hunched
beside them.

Mick scanned the group and his heart skipped a beat.
Even from this far away, he could see there were only three
prisoners. None of them was tall, none was dark. Julia was
not here.

For a minute, Mick had no more time to consider the
problem. Two of the largest ewes were involved in a noisy
dispute over a lamb and he stepped between them to force
them apart, cursing under his breath. When the ruckus
finally settled, he hurried the flock toward a makeshift
animal enclosure just down the platform from where passengers awaited the London train.

Out of the corner of his eye, he caught the flash of an all
too familiar smile. Across the road, Freddy Halliday
emerged from the local inn, his hand solicitously on Julia's

elbow, a grin on his face as bright and large as the rising sun.

"As pleased as a dog with two tails," Mick grumbled under his breath. He had borrowed a large-brimmed straw hat from the same farmer who had been convinced to loan him his flock in exchange for a five-pound note. Now, he tugged the hat over his eyes, bowed his shoulders to conceal his height, and guided the sheep into the pen, all the while carefully watching Julia.

She looked exhausted. There were dark smudges beneath her eyes and the pretty pink flush that usually stained her cheeks was gone, erased by anxiety, and replaced with a waxen pallor. Though her shoulders were back, her chin high and steady, he could tell the effort cost her dearly. She held her mouth too rigid, and her hands were clasped at her waist at an unnatural angle and held so tight, her knuckles were white.

There was something about the peculiar twist of her hands that made Mick take a closer look. Like a kettle at the boil, his temper soared and he grasped the shepherd's staff until he heard it snap.

Julia was manacled.

"Damn you, Freddy Halliday." Mick's anger blinded him to reason and he stepped toward the road, stopping only when he met resistance in the form of the ancient ram with the faltering gait.

He took a deep breath and muttered an oath when the old sheep stomped on his foot. "Better to wait, boyo." He whispered the warning to himself, shaking off the pain in his foot and struggling to control his temper. "Better to wait."

Mick jostled the rest of the flock into the pen. When they were all inside, he swung the gate shut and leaned against the fence, his shoulders back, his hat over his eyes, looking for all the world as if he hadn't a worry and not caring a damned, bloody fig that he'd left the gate unlocked.

*   *   *

JULIA sucked in a deep swallow of chill, damp air and shifted the weight of her manacled wrists from her waist to her side. Even propped against her hip, the irons were heavy. They clutched at her wrists like the claws of a vicious animal, savage and relentless. Already, what little skin she could see on either edge of the bulky manacles was red and raw. The moist, cold air stung the abrasions, nearly as painful as the ache of despondency that pressed like a leaden weight on her heart and strangled her breathing.

Freddy Halliday did little to help. He had been amiable, almost to the point of fawning over her, insisting even on buying her breakfast at the local inn while Rose, Daisy, and Ben Jessup at the other end of the platform ate yesterday's bread and cold tea.

Halliday's affability did little to soothe Julia's fears. For just beneath his graciousness, she sensed a sinister purpose. His conversation was sprinkled with questions and strewn with veiled accusations designed to shake her faith in Mick. Afraid of saying too much, afraid she might betray him, Julia had said nothing at all.

That didn't seem to bother Halliday. He strolled beside her, as chipper as a bird in nesting season, one hand attentively beneath her elbow, guiding her through the station and on to where they would wait for the London train.

At the farthest end of the station where an open field bordered the bustling village, a makeshift animal pen had been constructed. Julia watched a strapping man dressed in sturdy, homespun clothing hurry a flock of sheep inside.

He prodded his sizable herd along, not cajoling them as she had seen other shepherds do, but nudging them on impatiently until they were all corralled. When they were, he closed the gate behind them and turned to lean against the fence, his broad shoulders thrown back, his long legs stuck out in front of him.

Julia sighed. Images of the sheep shut in their enclosure crowded into her thoughts, reminding her she was on her way to certain imprisonment.

As if reading her mind, Halliday leaned toward her. "You could be a free woman when we arrive in London." He smiled at her, his eyes as brown and benign as a cow's.

Julia looked away.

Halliday's hand tightened on her elbow. "You really can be a stubborn little chit, can't you?" His voice was perilous, the words bitten off and hurled at her with such severity, she recoiled as if she'd been struck. Julia turned to find him watching her, the look in his eyes suddenly as chilling as the morning air.

"I've tried to be patient." Even enraged, Halliday could not slough off the manners of a gentleman. He bowed slightly from the waist, as if to apologize for his hasty words, but his eyes lost nothing of the malevolence that shone like fire beneath their amber surface.

"I've tried," he said again, his voice constricted, tight with the effort of control. "But it seems you will not listen to reason. Will you at least listen to the truth?"

When Julia did not answer, Halliday snickered. There was no delight in his laugh, and the sound sent a shiver up Julia's spine.

He nodded. "I might have known you'd be obstinate. A girl with your background can hardly help it, can she? After all, when you're the only heir of Margaret Barrie . . . "

Julia's head came up and she stared at Freddy Halliday, too stunned to speak.

A slow smile spread across his face. "Yes. I know. Ben Jessup told me that, too, and I wired London last night to find out more. I understand you've been missing from your grandmother's home for quite some time. What will the dear old thing say when she learns you've been arrested?"

"She won't say a thing. She doesn't care. And if you think you can use her to make me talk—"

"Nonsense! You've been reading far too many dreadful novels, my dear." Halliday brushed a speck from the front of his coat. "I hardly think I'm the type who would threaten your sweet old white-haired grandmother in order to get information from you. I merely wished to point out that a girl from your decidely privileged background should be more discriminating. Defend O'Donnell if you like. Lie for him. Steal for him. But I think you should know, he hasn't told you the truth."

Halliday bent closer, his face level with Julia's, his gaze holding hers so she could not look away.

"You have no idea what you're involved in," he said. "You see, O'Donnell isn't a thief. Did he tell you that? Or did he let you believe he was one of them?"

"Of course he isn't a thief." For one brief moment, relief flooded through Julia and she let out a breath she had not realized she was holding. "I've been telling you that all morning. He's not a thief, he's a—"

"He's a traitor."

Halliday's words crashed into her, shocking her into numbness. Unable to find the words that would erase the allegation and all it implied, Julia kept her silence.

"They'll hang him." Halliday purred at her, his eyelids heavy and halfclosed with satisfaction like a lover's. "They'll hang him when he's caught."

Julia felt Halliday's spite encircle her, a rope around her own throat. It closed on her neck, strangling her until her mouth was dry and the air caught in her lungs strained against her ribs. She brought her hands to her waist and pressed her fists against her heart, fighting to control the wild, jagged beat that sent blood crashing into her ears.

The rushing noise inside her head was answered by a different, throbbing beat. A low, steady rumble echoed through the village at the same time the platform began to vibrate, proclaiming the iron presence of the London-bound train.

Julia released a ragged breath, drew in another, and let it out slowly. In the distance, she heard the train whistle once to announce itself, clear and shrill in the morning air. Nearer each second, it whistled again, but this time the crystalline, distinct signal sounded different. It took her a moment to realize why.

There were other sounds mingled with the whistle—the sounds of sheep bleating in terror as the train came closer and closer. She glanced toward the sheep pen at the far end of the station and blinked in amazement. The shepherd who had been tending the flock was nowhere to be seen and his sheep were escaping. They raced through the open gate onto the platform, their eyes rolling in their heads with terror and the exhilaration of freedom.

"God bless it!" A farmer standing nearby hurled down his basket of cabbages and ran toward the sheep. "In there. In there." He waved his hands at the terrified animals, trying to get them back in their pen. He was joined by most of the other country folk who waited for the train and who clearly saw the potential for disaster if the sheep escaped onto the tracks.

Their efforts were of little use. The sheep raced down the platform, scattering the waiting passengers, their frightened cries drowning out the noise of the approaching train.

The flock came nearer, and Julia saw from the flash of alarm in Halliday's eyes that he recognized their own danger. He caught Julia by the arm and hauled her toward the station. The entrance was blocked by a crush of passengers fighting their way inside. He dismissed the commotion with a grumbled curse and pulled Julia farther down the platform. There, he found a dark, narrow passageway between the station and another stone building next to it. He dodged inside and pulled Julia in after him.

Julia leaned against the cold stone wall and fought to catch her breath. Halliday's hand was still on her arm and she was grateful for it now. She was about to thank him when she heard an odd, muffled thump behind her.

She turned just in time to see Halliday's face pale. He gave her one look of surprise before he crumpled to her feet.

The next second, a hand darted out of the darkness. It spun Julia around and forced a wet, sweet-smelling rag over her mouth and nose.

A curious buzzing noise began in Julia's head. She fought to get free, but without the help of her hands, her efforts were in vain. She tried to stay alert, but the cloying odor on the rag seemed to muddle her senses. Her eyes drifted shut. Blackness engulfed her and she felt herself falling into oblivion.

"DAMNED, bloody sheep!"

Julia's eyelids fluttered open. For a moment, she stared in wonder at the emptiness around her. There were no walls that she could see, no pictures, no furniture, no ceiling. She was lying on her back, surrounded by a gray void.

Try as she might to untangle her puzzling surroundings, her brain sharply refused. Her head felt as if it were stuffed with woolen rags, her eyes as if they'd been weighted with bricks. She closed them, wanting only to drift again into nothingness.

"Damned, bloody sheep! Filthy creatures."

This time, the voice penetrated her drugged mind enough for her to recognize it.

"Mick!" Her words were raspy and muffled, as if her own voice came from very far away.

Julia tried to sit up. She was as limp as wilted summer flowers. Slumping back against the softness beneath her, she turned her head, straining for a glimpse of Mick.

"You impossible, horrible man." She whispered the words, hearing the relief in her voice and feeling a weak smile tug at her lips.

Mick laughed in response and she saw him stalk across her line of vision.

He dragged a roughly made, homespun shirt over his head and hurled it in the corner before he stopped and looked down at her, his bare chest shining like polished marble in a stab of sunlight that came from somewhere to his right.

''Is that all the thanks I get for rescuing you?'' His expression did not mirror his words. Though his voice was raised in mock outrage, his mouth was tipped into a smile and his eyes sparkled with delight.

''Rescue.'' A wave of fatigue assailed Julia and she closed her eyes, lay back and smiled, contentment washing over her like warm water. She sank into sleep and dreamed of Mick O'Donnell, standing half naked over her, a self-satisfied smile on his face.

Chapter 10

IT wasn't a dream.

Julia's eyes popped open and the first thing she saw was Mick, seated on a rug spread out next to her bed. He was reading a small book bound in blue leather, a pair of spectacles perched on his nose. The farmer's clothes were gone. He was dressed again as he had been their last night at the Beechers', in dark tweed trousers and a white shirt. His cloth cap and jacket were hanging from the back of a nearby chair.

She gazed around the room, taking in their strange surroundings. The sunshine she'd seen earlier was gone. The room was lit only by candles; one candlestick was on the small, square table next to the chair, another closer to the bed. Their light sent eerie shadows flickering against the walls, walls that looked as if they were hewn from solid rock.

"Where in the world are we?"

She did not realize she'd voiced the question until Mick glanced up. He studied her over the wire frames of his eyeglasses and smiled.

"In a cave on the moor. Do you like it?" He swept the room with a proprietary gesture.

"A cave." Julia repeated the words, her voice rough, the lassitude just beginning to clear from her head.

"We should be safe enough here for tonight." Mick pulled off his spectacles and set them on the ground. "It's about time you're up," he said. "I thought perhaps I'd given you too much ether and I'd have nought left of you but your body to bury."

"Ether?" Julia repeated the word in a disbelieving whisper. She tried to raise herself on her elbows, but her hands were still manacled. Rolling to her side, she glared at Mick. "Why, you appalling Irishman. I ought to—"

"I'm glad to see you're feeling like your own self again." A twinkle in his eye, Mick bounced to his feet and helped her sit up. When she was settled, he went to the table and poured a glass of water. He sat down beside her and raised the glass to her lips.

"Here," he said. "This will make you feel better." He watched her take two small sips and nodded with satisfaction. "I'm sorry about the ether. I couldn't risk you making a fuss. And knowing you . . ." He shook his head, a wry smile on his face.

Julia pursed her lips. "You didn't have to drug me. I would've been quite reasonable." Mick was sitting very close, his left arm touching her right, his thigh against hers. In spite of his nearness, Julia shivered. "I would have done anything to get away from Freddy Halliday. He said the most awful things about you, Mick. He said you're a traitor."

Julia thought Mick would be angry. She expected him to denounce Halliday, to rant and rave and explode into a torrent of invective. He did not. He did not do anything. He merely sat, his hands gripping the water glass, his gaze on the far wall.

His silence spoke louder than words. Julia turned to him, her head to one side. "I was right. In St. Ives, I was right. You are a Fenian."

"No." The answer was quick and so impassioned, it made her flinch. "No." With one hand, Mick slashed the air in a conclusive, unequivocal gesture, his movement so abrupt, the glass fell out of his hands and crashed onto the ground. There was anger trapped in the rigid muscles of his jaw and neck, bitterness captured in the fists he held close to his sides, passion released, then controlled again, in the shudder that racked his body and ended in a hard breath held tight behind a face as unreadable as stone.

He turned to her, his voice edged with raw emotion. "The Fenians are pledged to Irish independence, it's true. But they will use any means to get it. They are not opposed to violence, or murder. No." He shook his head, the action both definitive and filled with regret. "There are others besides the Fenians."

"Parnell." Like a fresh, cool wind blowing away a fog, his words penetrated her drug-numbed mind. The simple truth was written on Mick's face. "You said you supported Charles Parnell. But you told me he was an honest man, a good man. Would he have you betray your country?"

"Your country." Mick bounded from the bed, and spun to face her, his eyes blazing. "Your country. Not mine. Before you pass judgment, you'd best consider. I'll wager a rump of beef and a dozen of claret that Halliday's definition of a traitor and mine are not entirely the same."

This was a new thought and it brought with it a glimmer of hope that beckoned to Julia like fire in the dark.

"You mean he lied?"

"I mean he's looking at it from a Saxon's viewpoint." Too agitated to stand still, Mick paced from one end of the tiny cave to the next. Stopping at his jacket, he pulled a small, flat parcel from the pocket.

"This is what Halliday considers the work of a traitor," he said, holding the papers up for her to see. "Letters. Letters that do not belong to him nor to anyone else in the British government."

"And do they belong to you?"

Mick's eyebrows snapped together and he considered her

question. "No," he answered after a moment. "They do not. But that doesn't mean—"

"Why do you have any more right to them than Freddy Halliday?" Julia challenged him with as much dignity as could be mustered by a woman in manacles.

"Bedad! You're as tough as old boots when you think someone's done wrong." Mick's face brightened and he let out a laugh that echoed back at them from the stone walls, cheerful and admiring.

The next second, his face sobered. He dropped to the bed and turned to face her, gently placing both his hands over hers. There was no apology, no rationalization in his voice, or in his eyes. His words were precise, his gaze level. "The letters belong to the Chief, to Parnell. They were written to him by his mistress."

Mick's explanation did little more than confuse Julia. She looked at him expectantly. "And?"

"And Halliday's after them, the spalpeen." Mick's top lip curved with distaste. "He's planning on releasing these letters to the newspapers."

"Tommy-rot!" Julia tossed her head. "What possible business is it of anyone's that Mr. Parnell has a mistress?"

"I'm forgetting you're not a political person." Mick smiled slightly and patted Julia's hands. "These letters are from Katherine O'Shea," he explained. "Mrs. Katherine O'Shea. She's a married lady, you see, and an English-woman. When the public finds out the Chief's been carrying on with another man's wife, his reputation will be in shambles. And his political influence? That'll end quicker than hell would scorch a feather."

Julia wrinkled her forehead, certain there must be some sense to what Mick was saying. Somehow, the logic of it all eluded her. "Why does Freddy Halliday care?" she asked.

"He probably doesn't. Not for himself. No more than Mr. Beecher cared, and he's the man who's been keeper of the letters these past few months. Ever since they were stolen from the Chief's home.'' Mick shrugged off Mr. Beecher as if he were nothing more than a bad memory. ''It's those Halliday works for who would like to see the Chief ruined.''

Julia felt his response settle in her stomach, a weight as cold and hard as ice. ''My government.'' She spoke the words with certainty, her voice no louder than a whisper.

''Your government.'' Mick wound his fingers through hers and looked down at her. ''Politics is a dirty game. Right now, those who want to see Ireland stay a slave to England have the upper hand. They'll do anything to destroy Parnell, and if they do, they'll bring the hope of Irish independence down with him.''

Julia drew in a deep breath and let it out slowly. ''You risked your life.'' She looked up at Mick, tears brimming in her eyes. ''You risked your life to save Parnell.''

''No.'' A sudden, fleeting smile lightened the solemnity of Mick's face. ''Not for Parnell. For Ireland. That's why I've got to get these letters back to the Chief.''

''Get them back?'' Julia looked at him, puzzled. ''Why don't you burn them? Or throw them into the ocean? Then no one would ever find them and Mr. Parnell would no longer be threatened. And if he and this woman never wrote each other again—''

''There's more wisdom in a woman's words than in all the talk of politicians.'' Mick brushed a wayward strand of hair from Julia's face. ''The Chief's a born leader, and the right man to bring Ireland its freedom,'' he said. ''But he's the type who would believe your spiritualist malarkey. Superstitious as all hell. He thinks it would be bad luck to destroy the letters. And as for never writing the woman again.'' Mick snickered, but there was more forbearance than amusement in the sound. ''The Chief's a grand man, but when it comes to Mrs. O'Shea, he should think with his head, not with his—''

He caught himself in time and blushed, the color spreading up his neck and across his face with alarming speed.

Julia hardly noticed. Her eyes were half closed, her lips pursed in thought. "Then what we've got to do is get the letters back to Parnell as quickly as we can. Am I right?" she asked.

"You are not." Mick dismissed the idea instantly. "I've got to get the letters to London. Not you. You don't need to be found with them, or with me." He rose from the bed and tucked the letters back into his jacket pocket.

"But, Mick—"

"No."

"But, Mick, don't you see? If Freddy Halliday finds you, he's sure to find the letters. You'll have them in your pocket—a very unoriginal hiding place, I might add—or you'll tuck them in your boot or some other such spot. Even if Halliday doesn't find them at once, all he needs to do is search you. He'd have them in a matter of minutes and you—"

"Holy Mother!" Mick stalked to the bed and stood staring down at her, his eyebrows raised with wonder. "Are you suggesting—"

"That I carry the letters for you. Yes." Julia nodded earnestly. "That's exactly what I'm suggesting."

"By all that's sacred. I can't believe it. I'm hearing it, but I can't believe it." As Mick spoke, his face grew redder and redder. "You don't think I'd let you—"

"But why not?" Julia breezed on, firmly ignoring his mounting irritation. "It's the most logical decision. At least I'd have the sense to hide the letters somewhere Halliday wouldn't find them. I daresay, even he wouldn't have the cheek to search me."

"I'll go hopping to hell and pump thunder!" This time, Mick could not control his temper. He spun away from her, tramped to the other side of the cave and came back, looking more than ever like a lion pacing its cage. "The hell you will." He glowered at her, his eyes flashing. "Why do you think I tried to get you to leave? Back in St. Ives, why do you think I wanted you to leave? I wanted you free of this. I didn't want you to be implicated. I didn't want you to be caught and tried as a burglar. Or worse.''

He dropped to the bed, his words ringing back at them from the stone walls. "They'll hang me if I'm caught," he said.

Julia clicked her tongue, as much to hide her discomfort at the words as to reject them. "They certainly wouldn't hang a man for stealing a few letters.''

"No. Not for the letters. But there are other things . . ." Mick looked away, his jaw tight with emotion. "That is a choice I made when I pledged myself to the cause of Irish freedom," he said, turning back to her. "But I won't put you at risk.''

Too affected by the hint of tender emotion in Mick's eyes to abide it in silence, Julia swallowed hard and forced a ringing note of bravado into her voice. "I can certainly take care of myself." To emphasize her point, she hopped to her feet.

The room pitched and swayed. With both her manacled hands, Julia grabbed for the nearby chair. It was not as close as it seemed. Clutching at nothing more than air, she felt the room give one final lurch, and found herself falling to the ground.

Mick was beside her in an instant. He locked his arms around her, pulling her up and propping her against him. Julia leaned back, her eyes closed, grateful for his shoulder and the feel of his hands, strong and reassuring, at her waist.

Saints and angels, the woman felt good in his arms! Mick sucked in a sharp breath, not as surprised as he was flustered. Somehow, he knew she would fit against him, snug and comfortable like this. Somehow, before she ever leaned back, eyes closed, her head on his shoulder, he knew she would be soft, and warm, and so exquisitely feminine, his heart ached with affection at the same time his body reacted to the undeniable pull of desire.

He hadn't been prepared for the overwhelming certainty of the feeling, and now, it made his heart throb like a steam engine, the sound of it thumping in his ears with desperate strength. He had not been prepared for the feeling, nor for the obvious logic of the voice inside his head that cautioned him to be careful.

Not for himself. There was no warning strong enough or reasonable enough to save a heart that had been lost in the bleak confines of a sun-speckled dry-cleaning room. No. He had to be wise, and cautious, and careful, not for himself, but for her.

It had been safe enough to kiss her when they said their good-byes at the Beechers'. That night, he thought he would never see her again. But tonight? Tonight, they were trespassing into dangerous territory, and he was sure he could not explore it without risking both her honor and her innocence.

That was a gift that had to be given, not stolen or, worse, beguiled. That was a gift only she could bestow, and he silently pledged he would not persuade or cajole her more than she permitted.

It would not be easy. Mick tightened his hold on Julia's waist, savoring the feel of the crisp fabric of her gown and the tempting hint of her hipbones beneath it. By the saints, it would not be easy!

After a second, Julia's eyelids fluttered open. She looked up at Mick, her face no more than a few inches from his, her mouth so close, he could feel the warmth of her breath and see the tempting flick of her tongue as she slid it between her teeth to wet her lips.

He braced himself against the sight and settled her on her feet. "Yes," he said, smiling down at her. "I see you can take care of yourself." He watched her carefully, making sure she was not about to swoon again. Satisfied the ether had left her nothing more than a touch wonky, he shook his head and smiled.

"You're as plucky a heart as you are foolish." Almost afraid of the answer she would give, he lowered his voice and asked, "Why would you do that for me? Why would you offer to carry the Chief's letters?"

For a moment, Julia did not reply. She could not. The gentle look in Mick's eyes took her breath, and her words, away. Her mouth was suddenly dry, and she knew, though it was just as powerful, the sensation had nothing to do with ether. This drug was more remarkable; its effects, she suspected, more lasting. Suddenly she no longer felt like sleeping. Her head cleared and she blinked, lifting her chin, her gaze as ingenuous as Mick's was tender. "Why did you come back to Redruth for me?" she asked him.

Mick left her question unanswered. He stared at her for a long, quiet moment, his eyes warmed by the candlelight. He pointed to the manacles. "Let's see about getting these darbies off, shall we? I'm thinking we have some things to settle between us."

Julia pulled her gaze from his and looked down at the torturous manacles. "I don't see how we can."

"I tried while you were asleep and had the devil's own time of it." Mick looked around the room. "There must be something we could use to pry them."

A distant memory made its way through the confusion in Julia's brain. Her head shot up and she smiled. "I have my lockpicks!"

"You do? Good girl." Mick patted her arm. "Where?"

Julia eyes widened with mortification. "Ben Jessup told me to keep them somewhere where the Beechers would never find them," she said. She swallowed hard. "So I've got them tied around my waist. Beneath my petticoat."

"Beneath your petticoat." Mick's mouth curved into a smile. "Well, lift up your gown then, woman," he said, his gaze roving from her waist to her ankles and back again. "And let's have a look at those lockpicks."

Julia shot him as haughty as look as she could manage. "I

certainly will not. Not while you're watching. Leave the room.''

"I—"

"I said, leave the room. I won't do it while you're here ogling me like a farmer buying a sheep.''

Mick gave her one last look of exasperation and headed out of the cave, mumbling, "Don't talk to me about sheep.''

Julia waited until he was well outside before she lifted her gown.

Though she had never planned to use them, she was terrified the Beechers or their housekeeper would inspect her room and find the set of lockpicks. She had made a belt out of a strip of flannel from her cleaning basket and tied the ring of picks to it. She reached for the belt and sighed. The belt was still there, but the lockpicks were gone.

"What's taking so long?'' Mick's voice floated in from outside.

"One more minute.''

Her manacled hands were clumsy. She grappled with the belt's stubborn, twisted knot, fighting to slide it farther to the front where she could see it better. It was then she realized where the picks had gone. They had shifted to the backside of the belt, and they were firmly caught there, tangled in the lace on her pantaloons.

Julia groaned. With her hands bound, she could never manage to untangle the picks on her own. She stomped her foot in frustration.

"Having trouble?'' Mick poked his head around the corner, his eyes curious, amused.

"No.'' Julia dropped her skirt, refusing to meet Mick's eyes. "Yes,'' she grumbled, exasperated. "The lockpicks are tangled. In the back. I can't reach them.''

"Oh.''

She looked up to find Mick staring at her.

There was a devilish smile on his face, a smile that turned her heart and caused it to clatter against her ribs. In spite of herself, she answered with a smile of her own. "You're a rogue, Mick O'Donnell."

"Perhaps." Mick gave her a knowing look. "But perhaps it's a rogue you really want."

He did not wait for an answer, or a confession. He merely took her hands and led her closer to the light. He settled himself on the floor behind her. "Right, then. Now lift your gown."

Julia swallowed hard and hoisted her skirt. It took a little longer to gather the courage to lift her petticoats. For a moment after she did, there was total silence. Finally, she could stand the tension no longer. She strained to look over her shoulder.

Mick was on his knees, regarding her backside with meticulous attention.

"Well?" she asked.

"Well," he said, his voice unsteady, "they're tangled right enough. I'll have to . . ." Tentatively, Mick touched the ring of lockpicks where it had installed itself firmly within the lace trimming that decorated her pantaloons.

"Sweet Jesus!" The words escaped him like a sigh, and he sat back on his heels, his eyes closed.

"Won't you be able to do it?" Julia asked, barely controlling the anxiety in her voice. "Is it worse than you thought?"

Mick raised his head. "Oh no," he said, smiling up at her, his eyes sparkling. "It's much better than I thought."

Julia blinked in bewilderment. A second later, understanding flooded through her and she turned away as quickly as she could, sure that if she did not, he would see the red-hot blush she felt shooting up her neck and staining her cheeks.

She forced herself to stand quietly while Mick worked, keenly aware of the feel of his hands as they moved through the layers of muslin and lace.

To mask her agitation, she struggled for something to say. "Are you almost done?"

"Almost." His voice was muffled. "Just a little more. This one's loose. And this. There! Got 'em." Julia felt him loosen the knot and heard the soft, satisfying sound of the lockpicks jingling in his hands.

As quickly as she could, she fluffed her skirt into place and knelt in front of him, her hands flat against her knees, the skirt of her gown spread around her. She drew in a ragged breath to try and relieve the swell of tension caused by his touch.

"I'd try the extractor," she said, pointing to one of the picks.

Mick tossed her a look. "You'd try the extractor and would get nowhere. I've had some little experience with Her Majesty's bracelets. I know it's the circular we want." He chose the pick and bent over her hands with it. A minute later, a gruff curse escaped his lips and he looked at her from the corner of his eye. "The extractor it is." He let out a long sigh and reached for the pick she'd suggested.

He was not as skilled a picklock as Ben Jessup and the procedure took more than ten minutes, with Mick cursing and grumbling the entire time. Finally, he chuckled triumphantly and pulled off the manacles.

His good humor did not last long. The raw skin of Julia's wrists caught Mick's eyes and he bent closer, mumbling an especially foul curse. "Mother of God! That damned Freddy Halliday. Look what he's done to you."

"It's not that bad." Julia pulled her sleeves down over her hands to hide the wounds. But before she could move away, Mick caught her hands in his, and drew back the stiff black fabric. Without a word, he moved his fingers over hers, gently drifting over the painful abrasions, chafing at her wrist to encourage circulation. His touch was remarkably strong, yet amazingly delicate, a balm as soothing as any poultice.

After a minute, he turned her hands palms up, and ran one finger down the center of her left hand. "Your poor hands," he said, his voice filled with regret. "They were so soft and white that day we met. Look at them now." His face twisted into a pained expression as he studied the red, dry patches and the deep cracks, souvenirs of the harsh soap and cleaning fluids she used at the Beechers'.

"Remember the day you told my future from my hand?" he asked, looking up at her. "What does it say in your own hand? What does it say about me?"

"It doesn't say anything," Julia answered. "Not really. You know that. It's all a lot of tommy-rot." She raised her right hand, the palm out to him. "See? It isn't different from any other hand."

Mick did not reply. He simply sat across from her, gazing at her with a mixture of devotion and desire that set her soul aflame. After what seemed a very long time, he reached one large, square-tipped finger toward her. Slowly, he slid it up and around her thumb.

Julia watched the progress of his finger, stunned by the intimacy of such a seemingly innocent gesture, spellbound by his touch. After the thumb, he skimmed the next finger, and the next.

When he was done, Mick edged nearer and outlined each of her fingers with his lips, his kiss following the path sketched by his hand. With each lingering climb, each achingly slow descent, Julia trembled. The touch of his lips raced through her bloodstream and left her breathless.

Mick nuzzled his face into her hand before he grazed a kiss from the center of her palm to the tip of her ring finger and planted soft kisses on each of her injured wristbones. He bestowed another kiss on the inside of her elbow and yet another on her shoulder, until his face was level with hers, his lips beckoning, his eyes bright with unspoken invitation.

Julia watched his face, mesmerized by the passion she saw flashing like hot summer lightning in his eyes. She leaned toward him, gliding her hands up his arms to his shoulders, and lifted her mouth to receive his kiss.

Mick's hands followed their own path, up her arms, to her shoulders, over her back. He flattened them against her spine and drew her nearer. "I'm sorry," he whispered, his eyes brimming with regret. "I promised myself this wouldn't happen."

Julia stiffened. "Sorry?"

Mick loosened his hold and, with both hands, ran his thumbs along the high arch of her cheekbones. "Not about you. Not about . . . not about us." His mouth tilted up on one side, a look that might have been a smile if it did not contain a note of measureless sadness. "I'm sorry about all this." His gaze roved the tiny cave before it settled again on Julia's face. "This wasn't the way I wanted it to be for you. Not in some godforsaken cave in the middle of nowhere, with Freddy Halliday hot on our tails."

"I don't care."

The simple declaration caught Mick off guard. For a second, he seemed too surprised to speak. He recovered with a start and shook his head, his voice filled with skepticism. "You don't know what you're saying," he said, still trying to reason with her and with himself. "You may not care tonight. But tomorrow . . . we have no future, Julia. You have no future, not with a man with a price on his head. There isn't a tomorrow for us."

"Then we have only tonight."

Mick did not reply. There was no need. His chest rose and fell to the erratic rhythm of his breathing and, for just a moment, Julia thought it was the glint of candlelight she saw reflected in his eyes. It did not take her long to realize she was mistaken. This was a deeper fire, a hotter flame. Her own primitive desires flickered in response to the devastating heat. Flickered, caught, and flamed.

Reaching over her head, she pulled a pin from her hair

and smoothed the liberated curl over her shoulder. "I want you to love me, Mick."

A glimmer of affection sparkled in the depths of Mick's blue eyes. He coiled the loosened curl around his finger. "Do you know what you're asking, *acushla*? Do you know what it's like when a man and woman come together?"

Watching the yearning grow in Mick's eyes, Julia drew out another pin, and then another. "You can teach me," she said.

Chapter 11

SHE looked like a fairy queen. How the image came to his mind, Mick did not know. Yet somehow, it suited Julia. She looked like one of the Good People of the ancient legends, her dark hair tumbled around her shoulders, her eyes glowing and mysterious. She should be wearing flowers in her hair, he decided, running his hands through its softness. She should be crowned with flowers and dressed in a gossamer gown that bared each delicious curve.

He allowed his hands to wander where his thoughts had led, down the length of her neck, across the line of her collarbone. Would she disappear like one of the fairy folk if his touch was too quick, too brazen?

Watching her carefully to gauge her reaction, Mick inched closer and ran one hand along the curve of her breast. She did not vanish, or shrink away, and he ventured another, firmer touch. Even through the layers of her clothing, he felt her respond, her nipples hardening until they felt like small, round gemstones beneath his fingers.

Mick smiled, excited as much by the feel of her as by the look of absolute delight on Julia's face. Her eyes drifted closed, and she caught her bottom lip between her teeth, purring like a contented cat.

With one finger, Mick outlined each breast in turn. "Does that feel nice?"

Too delighted to speak, Julia simply murmured some unintelligible response and snuggled closer.

"Do you want more?"

She opened her eyes. "I want you to kiss me," she said simply.

Mick chuckled. "That's what I like. A woman who knows her own mind."

He brought his mouth to hers slowly, prolonging the anticipation until Julia felt she would shatter with the thrill of expectation.

His lips were gentle and exploratory, searching and learning as sure as his hands were learning the curves of her body. When he felt her relax in his arms, he deepened the kiss and nudged her mouth open with his tongue.

It was an astonishing sensation, a secret shared as only lovers could, and Julia did not resist it. She gave herself to the feeling, memorizing the taste, and the touch, and the texture of him, returning kiss for kiss. Slowly, she inched her hands up his arms to his shoulders, tickling the short, prickly hairs on the back of his neck.

Mick shivered beneath the feathery brush of her fingers and a low, satisfied sound escaped Julia's throat. He was as sensitive to her touch as she was to his. The awareness deepened her desire. She swirled her hands across his broad shoulders and down to his chest.

Mick broke away, fighting for breath. "Bold as brass, that's what you are!"

"Is that bad?" Julia frowned at him, but there was more temptation than remorse in her eyes.

"Oh, no." Mick planted a kiss on the tip of her nose and sat back to admire her. "That's very, very good."

She had no idea how seductive she looked, he would wager a month's income on that. She hadn't a clue how ripe and red her lips were, nor how her eyes were glazed with desire, a desire made all the more alluring because it was so innocent and so reckless. Her longing reflected in the flush of her cheeks and caused her breath to come in short, shallow gasps that pressed her breasts against the fitted bodice of her gown. He'd bet a stiver and more she didn't know what she was doing to his insides. Already, he felt as if he would burst from wanting her. "We need to take this slowly." Mick took a deep breath and spoke the words out loud, not sure which of them needed more convincing. "We have all night and—"

Julia wasn't listening. She hopped to her feet and looked down at him, a half-smile of expectation glowing on her face. "Help me out of my gown."

"Help you . . . ?" Mick sat back on his heels. "Woman, I'm thinking you don't need any help."

"Very well." Before he could protest further, Julia unfastened the top button at the front of her dress. Still kneeling, Mick could see little besides a small patch of pink at the base of her neck. Somehow, that did not matter. The tiny hint of skin was more alluring than every inch of naked flesh he had ever seen. He watched, fascinated, as she unfastened the second button, and the third.

But it was neither her artless enticement nor her physical flawlessness that sent his desire soaring. It was the unmistakable look of delight that glowed in Julia's face, the implicit faith that shone in her eyes. She trusted him. The thought filled Mick with warmth far beyond that which could be explained by his physical excitement.

It was hard to maintain such sparkling rationality when she peeled her sleeves from her arms, and Mick swallowed hard. Against the unyielding dreariness of her black dress, her bare arms and shoulders looked as soft and pink as flower petals. Her underthings were pale ivory and they gleamed, almost phosphorescent, in the dim light of the candles.

Her dress slipped over her hips and floated to the floor. Julia stepped out of it and kicked it aside. She had not realized until now how very awkward it could be to undress in front of a man. How did you remove your boots without looking a complete fool? And your stockings? Sudden embarrassment sent heat flaming into her cheeks.

Seeing her discomfort, Mick raised himself on his knees and took her hand.

"How is it a fine and fancy lady like yourself knows so very much about pleasing a man?" he asked, looking up at her.

"Am I pleasing you? You don't think . . . you don't think I'm a ridiculous simpleton with no more in my brain than—"

"There's plenty and to spare in your brain." Though his words had the ring of truth, it was obvious Mick's thoughts were far from contemplating Julia's intellect. He carefully untied the bow that held her petticoats tight around her waist and slid them down her hips.

"How do you do it?" he asked, whirling his fingers over her stomach and down to where an intriguing dark shadow showed beneath her thin linen pantaloons. "I'm certain they didn't teach you seduction at that fine boarding school of yours."

The warmth in his voice banished Julia's self-consciousness. She smiled down at Mick, her fingers twined at the back of his head. "You taught me that," she explained.

"Me?" He sat back, studying her. "I'm sure I would have remembered saying—"

"You never said a word. You never had to." Julia dropped to the ground across from him, her hands still wound in his hair. "I could see it all in your eyes."

"Now you're reading my eyes as well as my hands?" With one hand on either side of her face, Mick captured her gaze with his own, a look so filled with yearning it burned itself on her heart. "What does that look tell you?" he asked.

"That look . . ." Julia forced her words past the ball of emotion in her throat that caused her voice to quaver. "That look tells me exactly why you came back to Redruth for me.''

"That it does." Mick leaned toward her and brushed a kiss against her lips before he fixed his eyes on her again. "And that look?"

"That look tells me you know exactly why I offered to carry Mr. Parnell's letters for you."

"Right again." The corners of Mick's mouth lifted, the smile traveling all the way from his lips to his eyes. Gently, he sketched the line of Julia's jaw with his thumbs, from the tips of her ears to her chin. His hands coasted down the curve of her neck, drifted across her bare shoulders. He nudged aside the expensive lace that edged her corset and, with one finger, skimmed the top of each breast in turn. Nodding solemnly, he carefully regarded the intriguing play of light and shadow there before his gaze returned to hers.

"And that look?" he asked.

His enjoyment was contagious, his candor, disarming. Julia smiled and pretended to ponder the question. "Ah, that look," she finally said. "That look tells me you'd like to help me take off the rest of my clothes. Am I right again?"

"Again." Mick brushed a kiss between her breasts. "And again." He placed another at the top of her right breast. "And again." He bestowed yet another kiss on her left breast. "I would be more than happy to help you out of your clothes."

He brought his mouth down on hers, one hand braced against her back while, with the other, he traced the contours of her body, down her arm to her waist, over the smooth curve of her hip, along the length of one leg. Without bothering to lift his head to see what he was doing, he grappled with the knot on her left boot.

"Damn!" The oath escaped him with good-natured zeal. He brushed her lips with his once more before he reluctantly pulled away. He fingered the bootlace. "Tight as can be."

Julia sat up. "I'll do it."

"No." With one hand he pressed her back until she was leaning against the bed. He straddled her legs. "I'll do it."

The knot was not nearly as stubborn as the one in her flannel belt. In less than a minute he had it undone. He slipped the boot from her foot and massaged her ankles before trailing his fingers up her leg. "Long and slender, like a cat's elbow." He looked up at her, his eyebrows raised, his eyes glowing with pleasure. He paused at the top of her stocking only long enough to hook it over his fingers and pull it off before he began work on the other boot.

Julia tipped back her head and sighed. His touch sang through her veins, as light as champagne bubbles and just as intoxicating. It caused a curious and quite delicious tingling that vibrated through her like harp strings brought to life beneath the fingers of a master musician.

When he was finished with her boots and stockings, Mick leaned closer. "There's a tie on your corset as well," he said, studying the object with a hint of trepidation in his eyes. "Are you women all held together with ribbons and strings?"

"Ribbons and strings. Whalebone and cotton." Julia shrugged and sighed. "You never know what you may find underneath."

"Oh, but I think I do." Without another second's hesitation, Mick snatched one end of the blue ribbon that fastened the front of her corset. He untied the bow and murmured a low, pleasant sound as his hands moved down the row of hooks and eyelets. When the corset was loosened, he sat back, watching carefully as he parted the fabric and pulled it away from her body.

"I was right, you see." He grazed one breast with his palm, learning its shape and softness before he moved to the other. "I knew exactly what I'd find underneath. Perfection." He dipped his head, his tongue following the path his hands had established, while with his hands, he skimmed off her pantaloons.

The feeling was too sweet; the sensation, too maddening to bear. Julia twisted beneath the touch of Mick's mouth and reached for his shirt.

Mick sat up and playfully swatted her hands away. "I can do that. I'll simply blow out the candles and . . ."

Julia was more amused than bewildered. "Don't blow out the candles. You've seen me. Now I want to see you." She ran her hands along the front of his shirt, unfastening the button at his neck.

He did not give her time to move to the next button. Mick hopped to his feet and stood staring down at her, suddenly looking as abashed as a schoolboy. "It's the candles, you see. I'm not used to getting undressed with the lights. When you're the *gosoon*, the youngest, and you share a room with four brothers and six sisters . . ."

He looked away, his face pink, his hands clenching and unclenching anxiously.

His embarrassment melted Julia's heart. Before he could move a step further, she raised herself to her knees and, with one breath, blew out the candles.

After a moment, her eyes adjusted to the inky blackness and Julia distinguished Mick's shape outlined against the doorway, his figure backlit by moonlight that made the moor outside nearly as bright as day.

Though the blackness was hardly complete, it seemed to be refuge enough to dissolve some of Mick's uneasiness. "It wasn't the boys, of course," he said by way of explanation. "But all those girls . . ." He sighed and she watched him move to the chair and sit down. "I've never been comfortable—"

Julia did not give him time to finish. Feeling her way along the ground, she scooted to the chair and kissed him. She nestled closer, running her hands up the front of his shirt, unfastening his buttons. "I didn't know you had sisters. Tell me about them."

She heard Mick swallow a large gulp of air. "Saints and

angels! Let's not talk about my sisters. Not now." He cupped her breasts in his hands and kneaded his thumbs across her nipples. The feel of her bare skin was enough to cause the remainder of his mortification to disintegrate. "I don't want to talk about them or think about them," he whispered, skimming her breasts with the tip of his tongue. "I only want to think about you."

"Good." Julia tugged off his shirt and tossed it over her shoulder. Scattering a long line of kisses across his chest, she dipped her hand along the front of his trousers.

"It's a great deal like picking a lock, isn't it?" she asked.

"It is?" Mick laughed, genuine amusement warming his voice. "Now that's one way I haven't heard it described."

"Well, yes, don't you see?" Julia traced a path up to his chest and down again, teasing, at the same time her voice sounded impossibly sensible.

"It's like what Ben Jessup said that day he taught me to pick locks. If you can't see it with your eyes, you've got to see it with your fingers. And if you won't let me see with my eyes . . ." She continued her massage, unfastening another button each time her hand returned to his trousers and murmuring a small sound of pleasure in response to the delectable feel of him.

Mick sat back, his eyes closed, his body reacting to every fleeting stroke. "Woman, you're a witch," he said. "I'll be drunk as Ballyhana in a minute, just from the touch of you." He ruffled his hands in her hair, spreading it through his fingers. "You'd best be careful or you'll have me so bewitched I won't have the strength to carry you to our bed."

"Then I'd best be careful." She affected his brogue, her hands stopping their delicious swirl, her voice shaded with anticipation.

Mick peered into the darkness. Julia was sitting on the ground, looking up at him. Looking at him, and waiting.

Like mirrors, her dark eyes glittered with moonlight and threw back reflections of his own growing desire.

He rose to his feet, discarded the rest of his clothing, and lifted her into his arms.

She felt good against him, so soft and warm in spite of the night's chill. Before he moved toward the bed, he had to taste her again. Mick tightened his hold, his mouth finding hers in the dark. The kiss was not nearly long enough to convey all that was in his heart. He outlined her lips with his tongue, swearing he would remedy that when they got to bed.

Mick took one step toward the camp bed in the corner. His foot smashed into the leg of the chair and he barked out a curse. Try as she might, Julia could not contain her laughter. By the time they made their way to the bed, Mick was laughing, too. He set Julia down and knelt over her and she pressed her hands against him, savoring the vibration as the laughter rumbled through his chest.

As one, their laughter stopped. Mick braced himself with his arms, far enough away so their bodies did not touch, yet close enough to watch the emotion in her eyes.

"Have you changed your mind?" he asked.

With one finger, Julia touched the scar at his hairline. "About you?"

"About me. About this. If it isn't something you want—"

Julia brought her mouth up to his, devouring his doubts. Mick smiled to himself and deepened the kiss. This was the kiss he promised himself when he stood in the dark cradling her in his arms, and he continued it as long as he was able, his body aching with the need for her, a hunger whetted all the more by the feel of her naked flesh pressed against his.

He pulled himself away, his voice warm in her ear and dreamy with desire.

"In Ireland, we have a proverb. 'In every land, hardness is in the north of it.' " He kissed her forehead. " "Softness is in the south.' " He nestled his hand into the warmth between her thighs. " 'Industry is in the east,' " he continued, brushing a kiss against her left breast. " 'And fire and inspiration in the west.' " He moved his mouth against her right breast. "You are the fire and the inspiration," he said. "My fire and inspiration."

His touch started a fire of its own. Julia sucked in a small noise when Mick nudged her legs apart and settled over her. He eased himself inside her, watching her face for any sign of discomfort or reluctance, and smiled when, instead of hesitation, he saw only eagerness and sweet surprise there.

He set a slow tempo, letting her adjust to the feel of him, relishing the softness and warmth that sent waves of pleasure rushing through his body like electric shocks.

"Is it all right, *acushla*?" When he spoke, his voice was rough and irregular.

"All right?" Julia breathed the words back at him. "It's perfectly splendid!"

Instinctively, she moved her hips against his, the rhythm of their silent lovers' dance increasing until all sense of time and place was lost to her, all but the feel of him in her arms, the taste of him on her lips, the exquisite sense of hunger and satisfaction, longing and fulfillment, contentment and reckless passion that fused into one emotion so astonishing, she could not begin to understand it.

She heard Mick groan, a murmur that sounded her name. He moved against her harder and faster, his body tensed with the same craving that reverberated through her, a tension released in a rush of ecstacy so overwhelming, it left her trembling and exhausted.

Mick lowered himself to the thin sliver of empty bed next to her, one arm draped around her. He was slick and warm, and Julia ran her hands down his back and up to his hair, curiously comforted by the sprinkle of dampness at his hairline.

She smiled when she heard Mick sigh. "Are you that tired?" she asked.

"No. But it's a blessing that's over with."

"A blessing?" Julia raised herself on her elbows, her voice tinged with disbelief. "You insolent Irishman, I—"

Mick's hearty laughter stopped her. "That's right. A blessing." He pressed her back with a lingering kiss, his hands wandering across the plain of her stomach and up to her breasts. "For now we can begin all over again."

THEY had rested little during the night, yet the fatigue did not show on Mick's face. He slept as soundly as a child, contentment and satisfaction smoothing away all traces of passion. Julia propped herself on one elbow and looked down at him, returning the small, tender smile that even at rest played its way around his lips.

He looked more like a sleeping cherub than a man who had introduced her to unimagined delights only a few hours earlier. The memory of their shared pleasure danced through her veins and, for one moment, she considered waking him.

That was impossible. Impossible and unwise. She knew it, even as the thought entered her mind, and she scolded herself for being so easily distracted.

Julia edged her way from beneath the protective circle of Mick's arm and slipped off the bed. She did not light the candles. Instead, she groped for her clothes in the half-darkness and finished dressing as quickly as she could, her eyes on Mick. Once, he stirred restlessly and called her name, and Julia froze, her breath caught in her lungs.

But he did not awaken. His breathing evened into a soft snore.

Before she could change her mind, Julia forced herself to move. Mick's coat was still dangling from the back of the chair and she darted to it and reached into his right-hand pocket.

Charles Parnell's letters were not there, but Mick's roll of

bank notes was. With trembling fingers, Julia counted out
ten pounds. Silently, she reprimanded herself for feeling as
guilty as she did. If she was to travel all the way to London,
she would need money, she told herself. Still, a sense of
foreboding sat on her shoulders like a physical weight that
could not be shaken.

The letters were in Mick's left pocket. Julia drew them
out solemnly. The packet was smaller than she remembered,
and she balanced it in her hands, amazed that one man's life,
another's reputation, and an entire nation's freedom depended on nothing more than these few folded pieces of
paper.

Without another look at the letters, Julia unbuttoned the
front of her dress and tucked the package inside.

She took a deep breath and balled her hands into fists,
trying to steady herself. Her gaze moved from Mick to the
doorway of the cave and the moor beyond, but try as she
might, she could not bring herself to leave so abruptly.

Kneeling next to the bed, she brushed back the unruly
lock of golden hair that had tumbled over Mick's forehead
and studied his face, committing every inch of it to memory.
A rush of affection surged through her at the same time a
stab of regret shattered her heart and turned her blood to ice
water.

She would miss him.

Julia dashed away the tears that threatened to cloud her
vision and silently promised herself the separation would
not be forever. She would find him again, she vowed,
somehow she would find him again. But for today, for now,
with the threat of certain discovery and imprisonment
hanging over him, this was the only way.

Mick would be furious when he woke and discovered that
she'd taken it upon herself to deliver the letters to Charles
Parnell in London. That was certain. But even before he had
made love to her last night, she had been sincere in her
offer. It was far less dangerous for her to carry the damning

letters, far less likely that the authorities would be looking for a woman. She wouldn't—she couldn't—let Mick risk his life to return the letters when there was such a simple solution to the problem.

And if she was jeopardizing her own safety? That was a chance she would have to take, she told herself pointedly. She was willing to risk everything for the protection of the man she loved.

Gently, softly, she brushed a kiss on Mick's forehead and whispered in his ear.

"Good-bye, Mick."

Chapter 12

"Mr. Finnegan, please."

"Finnegan, did you say?" The behemoth of a woman who had answered the kitchen door wiped her hands on her starched white apron and gave Julia a curious look. Her green eyes narrowed like those of a cat waiting to pounce on its supper. "Which Finnegan is it you might be wantin'?"

"I'm sorry. I don't know. I was told only Finnegan." Julia's voice faltered and she added hopefully, "I was sent by a friend."

"Mustn't be Sean, then." A man who had apparently been listening from behind the half-opened door came out from his hiding place and barked a harsh laugh that ended in a sputtering cough. "Sean Finnegan didn't have no friends."

"That's no way to speak," the woman upbraided him, wagging one meaty finger in his direction. "There are those who would disagree with you."

"And those who wouldn't." The man turned and headed through the kitchen, a jug of whisky slung over his shoulder.

"You'll have to excuse Peadar," the lady said. She shook her head cheerlessly and watched the man disappear into the next room. "There are those who can't put aside differences, even . . ." As if remembering Julia's presence, she broke off her mumbled remarks with a click of her tongue and turned her attention back to the girl at her door.

Her massive pink arms were crossed over her enormous bosom and she eyed Julia warily, examining everything from her hair to her boots. "You say you were sent by friends?"

"A friend. Yes. That's right." Beneath the probing scrutiny of those shrewd green eyes, Julia was suddenly aware of the layer of dust and grime that had settled on her dress. She brushed at it ineffectually and polished the toes of her boots, rubbing each of them in turn against her stockings.

Two weeks of travel had done little for her appearance, she was certain of that, but the lady at the door of the Battersea Lane house didn't seem to notice. The woman's gaze settled neither on Julia's tousled hair nor on the dirt caked to her clothes. She looked instead directly into Julia's eyes.

"And what friend would that be?" she asked.

"His name . . ." Somehow, speaking the name proved to be far more painful than Julia anticipated. She forced the words past the ball of loneliness and longing in her throat. "His name is Mick O'Donnell," she said, rushing through her speech. "He said when I got to London—"

The woman put one finger to her lips and glanced over her shoulder as if to be sure no one was listening. Her own voice fell so that it could not be overheard. "O'Donnell? Mick O'Donnell, did you say?" As unexpectedly as the sun appearing from behind a bank of thunderclouds, the woman's face lit with a tremendous grin. The transformation was as sudden as it was complete. She held out immense hands to Julia and her face changed from forbidding to congenial, her eyes sparkling like pebbles in a clear stream, her cheeks flushing nearly as bright and as red as her hair.

"Why didn't you say so?" She tugged Julia into the house and closed the door behind her, but not before she shot one last look up and down the street. "If you're a friend of Mick's, you're welcome and no doubt, though I'm sorry to say, Sean can't tell you that himself. Poor lad.'' She mumbled what sounded like a prayer. ''Ah, but that's no matter now. For now, you look to need a cup of tea and a place to rest your bones.''

There was a man sitting in one of the room's two wooden chairs and the woman shooed him out the door and offered the seat to Julia. Still talking, she turned to put the kettle on the cook stove.

''There's a good deal going on here,'' she said over her shoulder. ''You'll have to forgive the commotion. You understand.'' Suddenly the color drained from the woman's face and she dropped into the chair across from Julia's, her elbows propped against the scrubbed wooden table.

''But you don't understand, do you?'' the woman asked. ''I'm carryin' on like the fool I am and you haven't a notion what's happenin'.'' The woman took a deep breath. ''Let me start again. My name's Kate Malloy. I live down the road. I've come over to do for Teague these next few days. Until things settle again.''

Julia stared at the woman wordlessly, too bewildered by her unending chatter to begin to comprehend much of what she was saying. She smiled feebly and confessed her confusion. ''I don't understand. Do what? For whom?''

''There I go again, prattlin' on so as no one can follow a word I'm saying. They're all in my head, you see,'' Kate said, hurrying to remove the kettle from the fire when it started to boil. She poured a tiny measure of tea leaves into a chipped pot and sloshed the boiling water in on top of them. ''All the words are in my head just the way I want to say them, but they don't always come out right.''

She set a cup of watery tea in front of Julia. ''It's Sean Finnegan you've come lookin' for, I'm thinkin','' Kate said. She bent her head closer to Julia's. ''He was a particular friend of Mick's. They were boys together back in Ireland, and the best of friends before . . . before they had their differences between them. But even so, Mick never trusted no one like he trusted Sean, and if Mick sent you, I'm thinkin' it's Sean he wanted you to see. There is a special reason you're here . . . ?'' Kate's voice trailed away. She was clearly uncomfortable asking the question and just as clearly curious to know the answer.

How much could she explain? Stalling for time, Julia sipped at the bitter tea and thought through the problem again. As it had so many times these past two weeks, her dilemma whirled through her mind, but she was no closer to a solution now than she had been before.

When Mick had suggested she see Mr. Finnegan in Battersea Lane, he had obviously meant her to take refuge here while he worked at returning Charles Parnell's letters. He had no idea Julia would be carrying the letters herself, or that she would be looking for Sean Finnegan, not to hide here with him, but simply to stop and obtain advice on how to accomplish her real mission—finding Charles Stewart Parnell.

Could she trust Kate Malloy with her story?

As Mick had been quick to point out, Julia was not politically astute, but she knew enough of deception and betrayal to understand not everyone could be trusted implicitly. Her grandmother had taught her that much, and if she needed a further reminder, she only had to recall Mr. Weems, the man who had taken her money on the London train, or Ben Jessup, who had betrayed his friends and still been arrested, all for what little luxury could be purchased with a few shillings.

Not everyone was honest, or as friendly as they seemed, and as much as Julia would have liked to trust the jovial woman sitting across from her, she knew she could not risk the security of Charles Parnell's letters, and more importantly Mick's safety, on the uncertain integrity of strangers.

She shrugged, hiding her apprehension beneath a pretended layer of naïveté. "It was Sean Finnegan Mick asked me to see," Julia said, smiling sweetly at the older woman.

"I'm sorry, I wouldn't feel comfortable talking to anyone but him. If you could just take me to him."

For a second, Kate's face darkened with some unreadable emotion. Julia supposed it must be annoyance; annoyance at her mulish insistence on talking to Scan and Sean alone; annoyance at a stranger—and an English one at that—disturbing the family at what appeared to be a very busy time. But as quickly as it came, the flash of emotion disappeared and Kate laughed out loud.

"Leave it to Mick to take up with an Englishwoman, and a stubborn one besides." She rose from the chair and motioned Julia to follow her. "If you insist on seeing Sean . . ."

Kate pushed open the kitchen door and they were met by a babble of voices coming from the parlor across the passageway. From where she stood behind the formidable Kate, Julia could see only a portion of the tiny parlor.

She apparently had interrupted a celebration of some sort. The room was filled with people and layered with a haze of shag tobacco smoke so thick, Julia could barely see through it. What she could see only confirmed her suspicions—men and women in drab working clothes crowded onto the threadbare furniture, packed the well-scrubbed floor, and stood two and three deep against the walls. A bottle of whisky passed from hand to hand and from somewhere deep in the shadows of the far corner came the sounds of a lusty folk tune, sung, not well, but with great enthusiasm.

A self-satisfied twinkle in her eyes, Kate stepped aside and ushered Julia into the room with a flourish. "There you go. There's Sean for you."

For a few long minutes Julia could do no more than stare. She should have suspected, she told herself over and over. She should have known. The people. The noise. The evasive answers and veiled references from Kate. She should have known. If only she'd been listening more attentively and thinking a little less of Mick. Now she found herself the center of attention in the small parlor where family, friends, and neighbors were holding Sean Finnegan's wake.

Her mouth opened and closed wordlessly and Julia gaped at the body laid out on a table against the far wall. The plain wooden coffin was surrounded by candles that cast a soft flush over Sean's still features. He was a young man, no older than Mick she supposed, and as dark as Mick was fair. His hands rested peacefully on his chest, prayer beads wound through his fingers. His hair was combed neatly back to reveal a strong, handsome face. There was an ugly gash close to Sean's hairline and still angry-looking blue bruises along his right temple and below one eye. The wounds were poorly concealed by rice powder, but their meaning was unmistakable. Sean Finnegan had died a sudden, violent death.

As Julia entered the room, a small group of women hurried to the casket. For a few, uncomfortable minutes, the room was filled with the sounds of their grief. The women wrung their hands and wailed their misery, speaking in turn their words of praise for Sean Finnegan.

Then, as suddenly as it started, the keening stopped. The mourners returned to their seats and the chatter of conversation began again. Sean Finnegan might not have been there at all.

Julia's appearance, too, and her obvious embarrassment, were enough to interest the crowd, but only for a while. As quickly as their collective curiosity had been piqued, it was dispelled by a wave of Kate's hand. She knew their visitor, her gesture seemed to say; it was acceptable for Julia to be there.

"I'm sorry." Kate chuckled good-naturedly and steered Julia to a chair in the corner. "I couldn't help myself. It was a wicked thing to do to you, to be sure, but worth it. You should have seen your face!"

Julia looked at her doubtfully. "I don't know what to say. Won't they be upset?" she asked. With one hand, she swept the room with a feeble gesture, while with the other, she fanned away the sudden heat that flamed in her face. "Haven't we disturbed them? Dear God, I'd never presume to disrupt a family's mourning!"

Kate laughed and patted Julia's arm reassuringly. "Don't worry. Most of them aren't sober enough to care, and the ones that aren't on the drunk don't mind another soul here to pay respect."

From across the room, someone called Kate's name and she waded through the crowd and bent her head, speaking quietly to a man whose drooping shoulders and weathered, sorrowful face seemed particularly out of place in the spirited gathering.

Julia sat back, grateful for a few minutes' respite to try and digest the startling turn of events.

Because she knew Mick trusted him, she had expected Sean Finnegan to help her return Charles Parnell's letters. As she looked across the room at the handsome figure surrounded by flickering candlelight, despair settled on her, as chilling as the dead man's silent face. Sean Finnegan could not help her now.

It looked as if Mick had been right all along. The thought was as painful as the sting of smoke that filled Julia's lungs when she tried to take a deep breath. She had no business carrying the incriminating letters. She was not clever enough, or resourceful enough, or shrewd enough, and now she could only hope to be lucky enough to find an ally to guide her and pray that her recklessness had not served to endanger Mick even more.

Someone nudged her shoulder and startled Julia out of her thoughts. A young man stood next to her chair, blinking down at her, a whisky bottle in his hands.

Julia started at him mutely, unsure of what was expected of her. It was Kate who came to her rescue.

Watching from across the room, Kate gave her an encouraging wink and quickly pantomimed tipping back the bottle. "Take a drink." She mouthed the words. "And pass it on."

Julia gave the young man an uncertain smile and accepted the bottle. She turned it over in her hands, trying to will the confusion from her mind as she studied the swirl of amber liquid inside, longing to find some consolation, not in the liquor, but in the warmth left by the touch of so many hands.

She closed her eyes and took a drink. The whisky was cheap and strong. It burned its way down the back of her throat and into her stomach. As quickly as she could, Julia passed the bottle on and coughed behind her hand. She leaned back in her chair, the warmth of the liquor dulling the edges of her exhaustion, numbing her despair. Julia closed her eyes.

When she felt a tug on her sleeve, she expected to see the young man with the whisky bottle again. One drink had been more than enough. Already, her head was spinning, muddled from the liquor, the lack of light, and the absence of fresh air. She sat up, a polite refusal ready on her lips, and started with surprise.

There was a middle-aged man looking down at her, his eyes dark and distant. He poked his head toward the door. "You're wanted," he said, his voice no more friendly than his look.

Not understanding, but hardly in a position to challenge the man, Julia simply nodded. She looked for Kate, hoping the older woman would make some sense of the unexpected summons. She was gone.

Stretching the fatigue from her shoulders, Julia followed the man out of the room. Outside, two young men stood like sentinels on either side of the kitchen door. Her escort took his place beside them, stopping only long enough to call inside, "I've got her here."

He was answered by another muffled voice, the door swung open, and Julia stepped into the kitchen.

A single lamp had been lit on the wall. In its feeble light,

Julia could see that the table where she and Kate had shared an amiable few minutes had been moved to the center of the room. Someone had brought in more chairs and each was occupied. There were six of them—six sober-eyed men, their elbows on the table, their hands folded in front of them, their eyes square on Julia.

They did not ask her to sit.

The man directly across from her was the first to speak. He tossed a look over his shoulder. "She says you're Saxon."

Julia followed his gaze. Kate was standing in the deeper shadows near the cook stove. The sight of the older woman calmed her anxiety, but only for a moment. Something about the worried look in Kate's eyes made her uneasy.

Julia held her jaw rigid, looking down at the group of men with as much boldness as she could muster.

"That's correct," she answered. "I am English." She scanned the group slowly, giving each man a measured look.

"She says you comed here lookin' for Sean."

"I was told to ask for him. Yes."

"Who told you?"

At the question, Julia saw Kate stiffen. Kate's look was steady but she gave a small, almost imperceptible shake of her head that told Julia to be careful.

Julia smiled. "His name is hardly important," she said. "Our business was . . . er . . . private." She tried to force herself to blush prettily, the way she'd seen her friend Harriet Lloyd do when an attractive young man was flirting with her. She wasn't sure the flush was successful, but the slight, quavering catch in her voice was enough to embarrass one or two of the men at the table. They dropped their gazes.

Her strategy was not effective enough to fool them all. One man, younger and burlier than the others, stood so quickly, his chair tipped and fell to the floor. "We're in no mood for women's games," he said, stalking over to her, his blue eyes flashing his impatience. "You were asked a question and we expect you to answer. Who was it sent you to see Sean? Was it the Saxons, tryin' for information? Or was it that turncoat bastard, Mick O'Donnell?"

The malevolence with which the man spoke Mick's name was enough to warn Julia to tread carefully.

She gave him as vacuous a look as she could manage. "I have no idea what you're talking about," she said.

"Bah!" The man raised his hand and Julia tensed, preparing for the blow. Before he could strike, the kitchen door flew open and the old man Julia had seen talking to Kate earlier burst into the room.

"Jackanapes!" The man was small and wiry, but he pushed the brawny young man aside as if he were a child. "What's wrong with you, Owen? Comin' to a house in mournin' and actin' no better than a madman." Gently but firmly, the old man took Julia's arm and ushered her to stand with Kate in the corner. He turned back to the men at the table, effectively shielding Julia from them with his own body.

"It does Sean no honor to have you actin' this way while he's laid out in the next room."

"It does Sean no honor to have such as that here." The man named Owen gave Julia a sour look. "What's an Englishwoman to do with Sean? That's what we should like to know, Teague. Or maybe I should be askin' what Sean had to do with the English, or with Mick O'Donnell."

Where it came from, Julia never knew, but Teague grabbed a sturdy blackthorn walking stick from somewhere in the shadows and brandished it like a pikestaff. "If you've questions to ask about my son's loyalty, ask them to my face, Owen, not creepin' behind my back." He raised the cudgel over his head and Owen backed away. "Out of here! Out of here now, all of you. You're the ones who got him killed, you and your kind, and you won't come questionin' Sean, or Sean's friends, or Sean's decency here, not in the house where he's lyin' cold and his aunts and sisters still cryin' over the body."

Teague glared at them, his breathing harsh but his hands rock steady. One by one, the men at the table rose and shuffled out the back door. Owen was the last to move. He walked to the door and stopped, his hand on the knob. His lips twisted over teeth as gray and pointed as a wolf's, he turned and glared at Julia. "I'll see you again, Englishwoman."

The door banged shut and Julia let out a long, shuddering sigh.

"There, there." Kate patted her hand and led her to the nearest chair. "They're no more than fools. Pay them no mind. They didn't mean a word of it, I'm thinkin'. They're just upset. That's all. What with Sean dyin' so sudden like." Her voice trailed away and Julia knew instinctively that not even Kate believed her own prattle.

Julia's gaze never left the door. "Who are they?" she asked.

"Jackasses." Teague thumped a glass of whisky on the table in front of her and motioned her to drink it. "All of it," he advised. "Fast."

Julia watched her host curiously. Though his eyes still glowed with the remnants of his outrage, his face and his voice were as calm as if he had just come from a proper afternoon tea. She smiled weakly in response to his well-meant invitation and sipped at the whisky in her glass until it was gone.

"There." Teague nodded in silent approval when the glass was drained. "Now we can talk." He sat down next to her, his perceptive eyes assessing Julia with more than a bit of interest.

"Kate tells me you were sent by Mick O'Donnell." Unlike Owen, Teague spoke Mick's name in friendship, coloring the word with respect.

Julia nodded. "That's right." She folded her hands on

her lap. The whisky had warmed her stomach as soon as she swallowed it. Now the rush of comforting heat traveled all the way to her brain. She closed her eyes for a moment, composing herself. When she opened them again, Kate and Teague were both watching her carefully, waiting to hear her story.

"I was in service with Mick in Cornwall. He was working as a butler." She paused, expecting a barrage of questions. When there were none, she relaxed even more. If these people were not surprised by Mick's curious choice of occupations, perhaps they really did know him well. "He told me if I ever found my way to London, I would be safe with Sean." The sudden thought that she had never offered Teague her condolences made her stammer with embarrassment.

"I'm so very sorry." She placed one hand on Teague's arm where it rested on the table. "I had no idea."

Teague cleared his throat and looked away, and when he spoke his voice was husky with poorly concealed emotion. "Any friend of Mick's is welcome," he said. "And I won't ask what he's been about. It must be somethin' important or he wouldn't take the chance of sendin' you here. You know you were followed?"

The announcement struck Julia dumb and she stared at Teague in wonder. If she had been followed from Cornwall, she might be in a great deal more danger than she imagined. A sudden thought froze her blood in her veins. If she had been followed, was it because Mick had already been captured and the letters were not found on him?

"No," she finally said, her voice heavy with disbelief. "Not all the way from Cornwall. It isn't possible. That's why it took me two weeks to get here. I walked part of the way and took any number of trains. Why would anyone follow me?"

"I'm thinkin' you're the only one who can answer that for us." Teague lifted his grizzled eyebrows.

Her hands clenched in her lap, Julia drew in a deep breath. "I have some letters—"

Before Julia could get any further, Kate bounded from her chair and headed out of the room. "There's Father O'Connor, come to pray." With the kitchen door closed, Julia knew there was no way Kate could have heard the priest come in, but Teague bobbed his head, accepting her excuse and looked relieved to see her go.

The door banged shut behind her and the old man turned to Julia. "Kate's a wise woman. She knows she'd not be able to hold her tongue if she heard somethin' interestin', especially somethin' to do with Mick and the likes of them he works for nowadays." He tilted his chin toward the door and the now departed Kate. "She's an especial admirer of the Chief. Wouldn't want no harm to come to him or to Mick from somethin' she was careless sayin'."

Her concern for Mick tightened Julia's throat. "I don't want any harm to come to them either," she said, her mouth dry in spite of Teague's whisky. "I took something from him, you see. I thought it would help keep Mick safe, but now . . . now I think I may have made a terrible mistake."

"The letters?" Teague's sorrowful eyes softened, both interested and understanding. "Letters from . . . ?"

Julia sighed, relieved at sharing the burden of her secret. "Letters from Katherine O'Shea," she admitted.

Teague's response was not what she expected. He sucked on his teeth, so deep in thought he might have forgotten she was there. After a few silent minutes he shook himself and raised his eyes to hers. "Then it's true what they say about Parnell and that woman. Foolish man." He shook his head mournfully. Still deep in thought, he poured another glass of whisky for Julia and one for himself. He finished his drink in one gulp and banged his empty glass against the table. "We need to get those letters back to the Chief before anyone finds them. Am I right?"

"That's what Mick wanted to do. I thought he'd be caught, and if they found the letters . . ." Julia shuddered and pushed the idea from her mind as quickly as she could. "I thought it would be safer for me to carry the letters back to Mr. Parnell. But if I've been followed—"

"If you've been followed, you have two problems and no doubt. Them that's followin' you must be workin' for the English."

Julia forced herself to speak, as afraid of Teague's answer as she was of not hearing it. "Do you think they have Mick?"

Teague patted her hand. "Can't say. They may. Or . . ." he held one hand up for silence when he saw she was about to object. "Or they may think they can find him through you."

The realization was too painful to bear. Julia silently cursed her own impetuosity. "I never thought of that. I wanted to help. I never thought . . ."

"There now." With a crooked smile and a small motion of his hand, Teague urged her to finish her drink. "We won't worry until we know there's somethin' to worry about. For now, we've got to make sure them letters is safe, from the Saxons and from Owen."

"Owen?" Reminded of the hostile group of men who had so recently departed, Julia looked toward the door. "Who are they?"

"Fenians." Teague ground the word through clenched teeth. "Murderin' devils! And now that they know you're here, they're bound to figure something's astir. That Owen Kane, he can smell trouble brewin'. I swear he can. He knows full well Mick wouldn't send someone round to Sean unless it was real serious. One of them must have heard Kate mention Mick's name when she was talkin' to me. There's no other reason Owen would be so suddenly interested in Mick's whereabouts." Teague poured himself another drink.

"Them Fenians would like nothing better than to get their hands on somethin' that would discredit the Chief. They don't believe there will ever be a free Ireland unless the price is paid in blood. They'd like to turn the country back to violence and civil war. That's their way, you see, the way of violence. It's a sad state of affairs when your only son . . ." Teague's voice broke.

"He was one of them," he explained, not bothering to wipe away the tears that suddenly cascaded down his cheeks. "Corrupted by their promises. Blinded by their lies. He was killed because of it, killed by the English who took him in for questionin' and beat him so as he never recovered."

Julia reached for Teague's hand and held it tight, as much to comfort the old man as to keep her own fears at bay. "Politics is a dirty game."

She had not realized she'd repeated Mick's warning out loud until Teague chuckled mirthlessly in response.

"You know Mick well enough," he said, squeezing her hand in silent thanks for the comfort of her touch. "And he's a bright lad. He was one of the Fenians. Did you know? Thank the Lord, he came to his senses years ago and joined up with Parnell. He tried to get Sean to do the same. If only Sean had listened." Teague wiped his mouth with the back of his hand and rose from his chair. "You have the letters with you now?" he asked. "You'll trust me with them?"

Julia hesitated, but only for a moment. "If Mick trusted you," she said, "I know I can, too."

"Good." The old man's jaw tightened and he looked out at some unseen, faraway thing, courage shining in his red-rimmed eyes. "We won't let the English get ahold of them letters," he said. "They'll ruin Parnell and we can't let that happen. But we can't let Owen and his lot have them, either. They killed my boy. As sure as God's in heaven, I'll never forget or forgive them that." He looked down at her and gave her a sad smile, his face changing from sorrowful to impish.

"I know you've probably got the letters in one of them places women hide things and I'm sure that's been fine these past weeks. But I'm thinkin' there's only one place they'll be really safe through the night." He winked at her and headed out the kitchen door. "You get them out and bring them to me in the parlor," he said. "And we'll have Sean do his final share for Irish freedom."

Chapter 13

"You look to need a bath and a bed."

Julia pulled her gaze from the flickering candles surrounding Sean Finnegan's coffin. Their dancing light had mesmerized her hours ago it seemed, and she blinked away the hypnotic effect, not sure if she'd been asleep or awake. She looked up at Kate.

"It's almost dawn," Kate said, her voice hushed. "They'll be comin' to take the body to the train station soon. He's bein' buried in Ireland, you know."

Julia knuckled her eyes and nodded. She knew well enough that Sean was being taken to Ireland for burial, Sean and the precious packet Teague had tucked into the young man's suit pocket.

"We'll get a message to those receivin' Sean's body," Teague had assured her. "By the time they get the letters out of his pocket and pass them to someone who can bring them back to London, we'll have the Saxons so confused, they won't know where the letters are or who's carryin' them."

Julia agreed, it was a perfect plan. If only . . .

She drew in a deep breath. Her back and arms were stiff and she stretched, hoping to drive the misgivings from her mind at the same time she tried to will the fatigue from her body.

If only she could dismiss the pall of foreboding that hung over her, as real and just as impossible to ignore as the ghastly wounds on Sean Finnegan's face that drew her gaze back to him time and again.

Julia admitted her apprehension at the same time she chided herself for it. Teague's plan was a good one, and she could only imagine how much it cost, both in pride and heartache, for a father who had for years grieved his son's politics, to have to disturb his body after his violent and untimely death.

"Are you awake?" Kate gave Julia a friendly nudge and looked around the room one last time, making sure all was ready for the arrival of the undertakers. Most of the mourners had gone home to sleep off the effects of Teague's potent liquor. They would be back when it was time to close the coffin and say the last prayers over the dead. For now, Kate scurried around the room, waking those who were left.

Julia yawned and rose from her chair. She and Kate had spent much of the night washing up, making sure there were enough glasses for whisky, enough plates and bowls and spoons for the thin stew Kate had thrown together from whatever was in Teague's larder. Still, there were glasses scattered on the tables and Julia gathered as many as she could hold to take them into the kitchen.

She would not presume to intrude on the family's grief during their final farewell to Sean. She would stay in the kitchen, she decided, until they left for the station. Pausing in front of the coffin, she wondered briefly how suitable it was for an Anglican to offer a prayer for a Catholic's soul. Just as quickly she dismissed her doubts. Dead was dead, Catholic or Protestant, Irish or English. Julia whispered her prayers: one for Sean, another for the successful return of the letters hidden in his left-hand breast pocket, a third for Mick.

The final words were barely past her lips when the parlor door banged open.

"Good morning." The greeting was quiet, the voice perfectly polite, yet the words froze Julia in place. She squeezed her eyes shut, too alarmed to turn around.

"Tommy-rot!" She gathered her wits after a moment and mumbled the word, even managing to give Sean a lame, embarrassed smile. It was early, Julia reassured herself. She was tired. She was letting her own anxieties create ghosts and goblins where she knew none could exist.

"We've come to express our condolences."

This time, there was no mistaking the voice. The words were precise, the vowels perfectly rounded, the accent as impeccable as a newly tailored suit worn by a member of the House of Lords.

"Freddy Halliday!" Julia spun to face the door, disbelief and fear crawling up her back like icy fingers.

Halliday was talking to Teague. He paused when he saw Julia, and for an instant, the hypocritical mask of polite gentility he wore fell away. His eyes hardened as they met hers, his mouth opened with astonishment. Slowly, as if he were evaluating the circumstances and finding them very much to his liking, his lips rose into a smile so self-assured, it made Julia's heart crash against her ribs. Halliday's eyes held hers briefly before he returned his attention to Teague.

Even from across the room Julia could sense Teague's anger. The old man curled and uncurled his fists, and though his body was rigid and his shoulders steady, his mouth was pulled into a thin-lipped scowl that would have warned a less formidable adversary to be wary.

His outrage had little effect on Halliday, who carefully finished a too polite and obviously practiced condolence speech and stepped back to admit three other men into the parlor. They were huge strapping fellows whose coarse features and cruel eyes caused Julia to instinctively back away, the glasses clutched in her arms like a fragile, brittle shield.

Halliday's gaze returned to Julia and his voice rose. "Imagine finding you here!" He beamed at her like an old lady who'd just discovered a particularly valuable object at a church jumble sale. He smiled at Teague. "I had no idea you had such a distinguished visitor."

The first moments of stunned surprise vanished and Teague found his voice. "The likes of you and your hired toughs have no business here, Halliday. This is a house of mournin'. And I won't tolerate you disturbin' it to ask your questions or make your senseless accusations."

"No, no, no." Halliday waved away Teague's objections. "That's not it at all. I'm not here to ask any questions. Not this time." He gave Julia a knowing look. "This time," he said, "I have all the answers, and it's only right—"

"Right?" Teague chewed up the word and spit it back at him. "Ain't nothin' right about you botherin' a family at a time such as this."

Halliday clicked his tongue. "It's no less appropriate than you having this young lady here." He motioned toward Julia and she saw Teague's eyes fill with sudden suspicion, but whether he was questioning Freddy Halliday's good intentions or her own remained a mystery.

A small crowd of newly arrived mourners had gathered in the passageway outside the parlor. Julia heard a muffled curse and Owen Kane pushed his way into the room, followed by the five other men who'd questioned her last night.

Owen eyed Halliday and his thugs with distaste, and for a moment, Julia felt relief sweep through her. Owen and his men were as dangerous in their own way as Freddy Halliday was in his, but at least they were Irish; at least they would be willing to defend their own people against Halliday's unwelcome intrusion.

Julia's relief changed to fear when Owen's exacting gaze came to rest on her and his lips curled with distaste. "She's Saxon, as are you, Halliday. And neither of you has any business grievin' for Sean."

Halliday brushed aside Owen's objections. "I think

you'll agree, Kane, Sean Finnegan and I are old chums. We had a number of dealings, just as I've had with you, and I wouldn't feel right if I didn't say my proper good-byes.'' He directed an ingenuous smile at Owen and his men. "I hope to do the same for all of you someday. Besides,'' he continued, gliding to Julia's side, "I should think you'd all be grateful for my arrival. How else would you have discovered that this girl you've taken into your hearts and homes is Julia Barrie.''

It was Owen who put words to the collective looks of disbelief and astonishment on the faces around them. He eyed Julia, loathing etched in every line of his face. "I trust you're no relation to that English harridan who threw us off our land and left us and our families to die along the roads like flies,'' he said. "You're no kin to Margaret Barrie, are you?''

At the mention of her grandmother's name, Julia blinked in astonishment and fought to form some reply, though her mind and mouth seemed suddenly detached one from the other. Desperately, she tried to think back, to remember if she had ever heard her grandmother say anything about owning land in Ireland.

Was it possible that Margaret Barrie had interests in Ireland? Certainly she had business holdings throughout the Empire. But these people were not talking about business. They were talking about the Irish tenant farms. They were accusing her grandmother of being one of the infamous landlords who forced their Irish tenants from their homes and pulled their cottages down before their eyes for failure to pay the exorbitant rents they demanded.

Denial sprang to Julia's lips. "It isn't so. She couldn't . . . she wouldn't . . .''

Her mind fought against the awful accusations, while in her heart, Julia felt a disturbing certainty that caused her words to strangle in her throat. In spite of her blind objections, she knew the awful truth. Her grandmother could. Her grandmother would.

It was no wonder Mick had mistrusted her when they met, no wonder he had questioned her motives, her loyalty, her honor. Her grandmother had driven so many of his people from their land. Her grandmother embodied the injustices Mick fought against. Her grandmother, and Freddy Halliday, and the others of their class and station, were the reason Mick's life hung in a precarious balance. Even now, Julia felt the balance shift, heartlessly tipped by those who, in their greed, oppressed millions, ruthlessly manipulated by men of power who opposed Mick and those others who were brave enough to struggle for freedom.

"It ain't true." It was Kate who came to Julia's defense, stepping out of the shadows near the far wall, her arms tight against her sides, her feet set and far apart as if she were preparing herself for combat.

Julia swallowed hard. "It is. All of it." She whispered the admission, refusing to meet the look of betrayal and disappointment in Kate's eyes. Her shoulders sagged and she would have crumpled to the floor if not for Teague. He scooped the dirty glasses from her arms and piled them on the nearest table before he wrapped one arm around Julia's shoulders.

"What's the matter with all of you?" The crowd was making hostile noises and Teague silenced them with one severe look. "What difference does it make where a person comes from or who his folk is? This girl came to us because she needed help. Much as what we all did when her grandmother and the other landlords drove us from our land. We helped each other then and I can't see there's any difference to us helpin' her now."

"Helping?" Owen's voice rose above the murmured approvals and protests. "Helping the likes of that? Your own wife died when you were driven from your home, Teague. Would you pardon the kin of her that evicted you?"

"It's her grandmother, not the girl, who's guilty." Teague clasped Julia's shoulder to reassure her and turned his attention back to Freddy Halliday, who had been all but forgotten in the furor. "You've done what you meant to do, Halliday. You've spread your poison and disturbed my boy's final rites." He waved one hand toward the door. "I think it's the undertakers I hear comin' up to the house, so if you'll leave us now, we can begin our service."

"Dear me!" Halliday shook his head, ignoring the priest and undertaker who walked into the room and stopped, astonished at the scene before them. "Did I say I was finished? There was one other thing." He held out his right hand. "I want the letters."

Teague snorted. "I don't know what you're talkin' about."

"Don't you?" Halliday's voice was as smooth as a well-honed knife. "Then perhaps your lovely visitor does?" He looked to Julia, who returned his look in stony silence. "No? Well, if that's how it's to be . . ." Halliday snapped his fingers, signaling for his three husky associates. They surrounded him, one at each shoulder while the third guarded his back. "We will search the house if we have to," he said.

"Search if you like." Teague tossed off the invitation. "But perhaps you'll have the decency to wait for Father O'Connor here to finish with his prayers. If you've no sense, at least have some respect for the dead."

"Ah, respect for the dead." Halliday drew out the words and, for the first time, his gaze rested on Sean's bruised face. "It would be a shame to disturb the dead, wouldn't it?" His gaze slid from Sean, to Julia, to Teague.

"You wouldn't." Teague ground the words between his teeth.

"Wouldn't I?" Casually, Halliday ran one finger along the edge of Sean's casket. With a glance at the watching crowd, he lowered his voice. "The ladies would be upset, I think, to see this overturned." His hand gripped the coffin, his knuckles white, his eyes hard with determination.

"No!" Where Julia found the courage to speak, she hardly knew. It didn't matter. All that mattered was that Sean's dignity be preserved. "No," she said again, impulsively moving between Halliday and the coffin. "You won't touch him."

For a moment, Halliday was too surprised to speak. He recovered his composure with a start, his expression a frightening combination of contemptuous amusement and white-hot anger.

"It seems Mick O'Donnell's talent for converting people to the Home Rule cause has not diminished," he said. "He's even got the granddaughter of Margaret Barrie believing she's a friend of the Irish people. How delightful." He laughed, but there was no humor in the sound.

"Very well, my dear. Anything you ask. A favor from one of the Queen's loyal subjects to another. But if you would have me do this for you, perhaps there's something you'd like to do for me?" Again, Halliday held out his hand, the palm flat and empty, waiting.

Julia felt Teague tense at her side and looked at him out of the corner of her eye. His disgust was nearly as tangible as his outrage. It caused the blood to drain from his face and made his every breath sharp and harsh. Teague's eyes were not on Freddy Halliday. He looked neither at the ruffians shifting from foot to foot like restless racehorses at the gate, nor at Owen Kane and his Fenians. He looked instead at Sean, and his wise, dark eyes filled with tears.

It was not the thought of Teague's heartbreak that prompted Julia to make up her mind, it was the sight of Sean's battered face. He had done enough for the cause of freedom; he had paid the ultimate price. No one had the right to ask more.

Julia reached her hand toward the casket and Teague made to stop her.

"No." She put his hand aside gently, her voice low, the firmness of it telling him she would brook no resistance. Just as gently, she reached inside the left-hand breast pocket of Sean's jacket and drew out Mrs. O'Shea's letters.

Firmly refusing to look at Teague or at any of the other pairs of eyes trained upon her, she handed the letters to Freddy Halliday.

"That's my girl." Halliday fairly purred, his voice so filled with satisfaction it made Julia's blood run cold. He turned to Teague, smiling like Mr. Carroll's Cheshire cat. "You see, all that was needed was a little less Irish temper and a little more English sense." Carefully, he tucked the precious bundle into his pocket and signaled to his men to clear a path to the door.

"I wouldn't have got that kind of cooperation from any of you Irish rabble," Halliday said, addressing the mourners with one sweeping, disparaging glance. "I daresay, you would've tried to stop me. And Father O'Connor here would have been deuced busy this week, saying requiems for you poor fools."

With that, Halliday headed to the door. As he was about to leave, he paused and turned, his gaze on Julia, his eyes bright with pleasure.

"By the by, m'dear, I do suppose you're wondering how I knew the letters were here. Process of elimination, really. I had you followed and I knew Mick O'Donnell didn't have the letters. Put those two facts together and the rest is simple."

He laughed when he saw Julia flinch and his next words rolled like honey off his lips. "If you think he'll come for you as he did in Redruth, think again. You're missing the most salient point. You see, I knew Mick O'Donnell didn't have the letters, because I have Mick O'Donnell."

With that, Freddy Halliday swept out the door.

* * *

"DAMN you, Margaret Barrie!" Julia stared into the fire flickering in the hearth, her hands clenched into fists on her lap.

"Bless you, child, you didn't know, did you?" Her lips pursed, her eyes half-closed, Kate shook her head as if trying to plumb the depths of human nature. "You was as surprised by the old lady's doings as we was at findin' out you was kin to her. The Lord do work in mysterious ways, that's for certain, just as Father O'Connor said at this morning's service for Sean. Imagine any of us ever thinkin' we'd be takin' in Margaret Barrie's granddaughter and givin' her a place to stay." Kate heaved an enormous sigh and leaned forward to pat Julia's arm. "It don't matter now who your people is," she said. "You'll be fine here with me."

"No." Julia forced her gaze from the fire and brushed a tear from her cheek. "I won't be fine," she said, her voice filled with stubborn resistance. "Not as long as they have Mick."

"Ah, that's it then, is it? I suspected as much." Without another word, Kate reached for a piece of bright pink fabric that lay beside her chair, a needle already threaded and stuck into it. For a long while, she looked at the cloth, studying the rows of neat stitches along one edge before she glanced up at Julia again.

"I don't think Mick would have wanted it any other way," she said, her voice low. "It was his decision after all—"

"His decision? To be captured?" Julia nearly laughed through her tears. "He'd never wish to be a prisoner of the British."

"No. Not wish it. But he came by it honorably, doin' his part for somethin' he believes is more important than his own freedom or his own life. Those he works for won't forget it."

Kate bent over her work. When she finished with a row of small, perfect stitches, she knotted the thread and snapped it off with her teeth. "Sure and it's a pleasure havin' a young person in the house again," Kate said, her own gaze traveling to the fire. "I've been alone since my husband died these ten years ago and my sons left for America." Kate's face reddened, her voice broke. "But . . . it's just that . . ." She looked away.

Julia could well imagine why Kate was uneasy.

Though Kate had been generous enough to invite Julia to come and stay in her home, it must have been uncomfortable for her to harbor not only an Englishwoman but the granddaughter of Margaret Barrie. The news was all through this poor Irish neighborhood even before they had left Teague's and walked the half-mile to Kate's modest flat. Julia wouldn't be surprised if some of Kate's more militant neighbors didn't take to shunning her like their compatriots at home did to those who cooperated with the British. Some, she knew, even practiced a strategy called boycotting—they not only declined to socialize with the collaborators, they refused to patronize their businesses as well.

Julia knew Kate made her living as a seamstress, and a sparse living it was, it seemed, by the look of Kate's home and the meager dinner she had served only an hour ago. She would not jeopardize Kate's livelihood. She could not, not when Kate had been so kind.

Julia cleared her throat. "I understand. I'll stay here tonight, if you'll be so kind as to let me, and in the morning—"

She was interrupted by Kate's burst of laughter. "You're a sweet thing to care," Kate said, wiping tears from her eyes. "But that's not what I meant at all. Curse Owen Kane and his Fenians. Let them tell all of London you're here if they like. No, no. That don't worry me as much as the money." Her face sobered, her sparkling green eyes dulled.

"I've barely got enough money for myself, I'm afraid. And not enough to keep another person here for more than a day or two." She held up the piece of fabric she was working on. "This is the talent the good Lord gave me to earn my living and it's all that stands between me and the workhouse. We'll need to find your talent if you're to stay here. What is it you're good at doing, Julia? What talent has the good Lord given you?"

Chapter 14

TEAGUE was right, he was a madman.

Annoyed, Mick leaned against the nearest lamppost. It was the devil admitting your friends saw your own character better than you did yourself.

He let out his breath in an aggravated puff and watched the steam from his mouth float away on the cold night air.

It was a madman he was, to be sure, and he only need remind himself where he was and what he was doing here to convince himself of the fact.

No one but a madman would be out here in the cold waiting for a woman. No one but a madman would be waiting for this particular woman, a woman who'd stolen from him, deceived him, caused him to be arrested, and nearly gotten him killed.

Gingerly, he ran the fingers of his left hand over his right arm. After two weeks, the bone was healing, but it still pained him enough to be a constant reminder of the whack he'd administered with more force than forethought. Damn, but that policeman had a hard head!

The attack had served its purpose. It had helped him escape from the authorities and spared him yet another extended visit to one of Her Majesty's prisons, but it had also proved beyond a doubt the accuracy of Teague's diagnosis.

Distracted by a shadowy movement across the road, Mick snapped out of his sullen meditations and watched as a tall, dark figure emerged from a nearby house.

Only a madman would allow his heart to skip a beat at the sight of her. Only a madman would yield to the all-to-familiar stirrings of desire that threatened to destroy the last vestiges of his self-control. Only a madman would be fool enough to follow her.

Muttering a curse that was both colorful and all-encompassing, Mick pulled up the collar of his coat, shoved his cap on his head, and headed off into the night after her.

THE Countess Madame Anastasia Marinna Krakowska, renowned clairvoyant, celebrated occultist, eminent trance medium, and indisputable possessor of the Sixth Sense, reached across the ink-black darkness. Praying her chair would not creak, she cautiously strained to reach the bowl of toffee she'd seen earlier set on the small mahogany table just this side of the fireplace.

All the while, she listened to the interminable discourse of Adelaide Bancroft, who sat across the table from her.

". . . and the children, of course. I've never had nearly the respect from the children that I deserve. No one appreciates me the way you did, Basil my darling. No one understands. That's why I had to ask you about this. It's so very important. You see . . ."

There! Madame Krakowska breathed a quiet sigh of relief. Her fingers grasped not one, but two of the tasty confections. As quickly and quietly as she could, she tucked one of them into the safety of her pocket. The other was her reward for a job well done. She maneuvered the sweet into the palm of her left hand. Keeping her eyes closed and being careful not to disturb the small slate tablet on the table in front of her, she popped the toffee into her mouth.

Silently, she thanked the spirits of the Other Side for preferring darkness to light. It would hardly be fitting for a medium to be found chewing toffee while one of her most regular and highest-paying customers communed with her dearly departed husband. But with the curtains drawn and the gas lamps off, the room was darker even than the night outside.

Madame Krakowska finished chewing her toffee, swallowed its delicious, sweet juice and spoke suddenly. "Enough!"

Adelaide jumped, her last words to dearest Basil cut short by her gasp of surprise.

As if waking from a deep, otherworldly trance, Madame Krakowska slowly opened her eyes and fluttered her long, dark lashes. "I have felt the passing of Basil Bancroft's spirit. He was here. In this room. He has left a message. You may turn up the lights."

Hoisting herself out of her chair, her pudgy arms quivering with excitement, Adelaide crossed the room. She turned up the nearest gas jet and hurried back, her gaze focused on the slate tablet set directly in the center of the table. The look of excitement faded from her face.

The tablet was blank.

Adelaide's lower lip quivered, her shoulders drooped. "You were wrong, Countess," she sighed.

A brief, sympathetic smile crossed Madame Krakowska's face. She shook her head. "I am seldom wrong when it comes to feeling the nearness of the spirits," she said, in her low, faintly accented voice. She looked around the room as if seeking the evidence of Basil Bancroft's presence. Nodding in answer to some unheard voice, she slid the tablet across the table until it lay directly in front of her. She closed her eyes and ran her hands back and forth across its surface.

"He was here," she said, more to herself than to the woman who waited breathlessly. Madame Krakowska opened her eyes, lifted the tablet, and pursing her lips, blew upon it gently. When she was done, she laid it down on the table and slumped against the back of her chair, exhausted.

Slowly, letter by letter, a ghostly white message appeared on the tablet. As each letter formed, Adelaide's eyes widened. Before the entire message had a chance to materialize, she grabbed for the slate.

"You've done it! Oh, my dearest Countess, you've done it," she shrieked. "You've contacted my Basil, my dearest, sweetest Basil." She pressed the slate to her bosom, then held it at arm's length and read aloud the words printed there in spectral letters.

"'Yes, Adelaide, do what you are considering. All is understood.'"

Adelaide's eyes filled with tears and she sniffed into her lace-edged handkerchief. "All is understood. Did you hear that, Countess? Basil says all is understood. What a relief. I was so very worried about redecorating his bedroom. I thought he might mind. He did so love to sit there and smoke his pipe before he passed to the Other Side."

Adelaide laid the slate on the table and gazed at it, a mixture of wonder and reverence on her fleshy face. "You are truly gifted," she said, reaching across the table to touch Madame Krakowska's hand reverently. "I examined this slate myself when you brought it with you tonight. I'm sure when I turned the lights on, there was nothing on it. And now . . ." Her words were lost in a gush of happy sobbing.

Madame Krakowska smiled self-consciously, trying to ignore the look of bliss on Adelaide's face. She failed miserably. Adelaide was her second customer of the night, and just as with the first, she felt the certain, gnawing twisting of guilt deep within her.

How could people be so foolish as to believe the spiritualist bunkum she dished out like so many pieces of fat apple tart? How could she be unconscionable enough to do it?

The answers were nearly as disturbing as the questions themselves. People believed her clairvoyant powers were real because they desperately wished to believe in them.

They trusted blindly in the existence of a force that allowed them to communicate with those—some lamented, some unlamented—whose deaths had affected their lives for better or for worse.

It was easy enough to gain a steady clientele of people willing to believe in the Other Side; easier still to find out the small details of their lives they believed to be private—births, marriages, deaths. Every shred of information she needed to further their belief in her psychic abilities was close at hand, carved on churchyard gravestones or scribbled in parish records.

As to why she continued to delude them . . .

This was the question that kept her awake at night, in the small hours of the morning when sleep refused to come and worries crowded around her like hungry animals circling for the kill.

She need only look to Kate to see the answer, only remember the bare larder, the modest meals. And if she wanted a further reminder, she need only remember the plan Teague had helped her formulate more than two months ago.

"When we have enough money," the old man had promised, "we'll go see that Halliday fellow. If he can't be reasoned with, perhaps he can be bribed."

Bribed, indeed. She knew Freddy Halliday could never be bribed. But perhaps someone else could be, someone who could leave a door unlocked, a prisoner unguarded.

The thought crept up on her as it always did, so quiet and unpretentious that it filled her with terror and blinded her to any purpose beyond it. By taking Mr. Parnell's letters, she had betrayed Mick, by turning them over to Freddy Halliday, she had destroyed his dreams of a free Ireland. This was all she could do for him now, and she swore she would not fail him.

When Adelaide Bancroft pressed a stack of coins into her hand, she backed toward the door, hoping to make as tactful a retreat as possible. She avoided looking at the coins, weighing them instead in the palm of her hand and determining that her time had not been misspent.

"You are a miracle worker!" Adelaide's watery brown eyes were filled with respect. "I owe you so very much and I know you don't usually accept favors. But please, Countess, just this once, stay for supper. I would so very much like for us to get better acquainted."

"How very kind." Madame Krakowska smiled sweetly, accepting her coat from the doe-eyed maidservant who stood near the door, and slipping it on as quickly as possible. "But tonight . . . ah, tonight the spirits were demanding and Madame Krakowska must return home to rest. Perhaps another time."

She stepped out the door and let out a long, heavy sigh. For tonight, she was finished playing the role of Madame Krakowska, and she relaxed, relieved to be done with the charade. She drew in a huge draught of acrid London air. At least for tonight, she could go back to being Julia Barrie.

THE fog swirled around her feet like water, ebbing and flowing in the eddying currents caused by the brisk, chill wind off the river. It made her look as if she were floating on a cloud, a wayward angel clothed head to toe in black, only her face shining pale and heavenly in the dim glow of the gas streetlights.

The image appealed to his poetic sense—what was left of it—and Mick smiled wryly, keeping to the shadows outside Adelaide Bancroft's house while he waited for Julia to descend the stone steps and begin her long walk home.

She might as well be an angel, he thought, his mood no more clement than the weather. She was just as unreachable as an angel; just as unapproachable and untouchable as the cherubs that soared across the ceiling of Father O'Connor's church. As unobtainable as heaven.

The awareness did little to improve his disposition and Mick massaged the stiffness in his right arm and reminded himself of the pledge he'd made when he escaped the British two weeks ago. He could see Julia, he could watch over her, but he could not risk contacting her. Her anonymity was as critical as his own.

"Damfoolishness!" He mumbled the words, his irritation rising beyond measure. Even a madman could endure only so much.

When Kate's flat was less than a half-mile away, a large dark shadow emerged from a nearby passageway and fell into step behind Julia.

Mick slowed his pace. There was no use calling unnecessary attention to himself by hurrying to get between the fellow and Julia, no use rushing when he could still see her.

In spite of his own rationalizations, he watched the shadow anxiously. There was something about the man's noiseless steps, something in the fitful starts and stops he made in response to Julia's every move that twisted inside Mick's gut like the painful remnants of a badly cooked meal.

Just ahead, the figure passed beneath a gaslight. As if Mick's own worst fears had materialized like phantoms from the surrounding mist, the shadow gained form, substance, and a name.

It had been years since he'd seen Owen Kane. Mick did not need to be reminded that Owen was as much to be feared as the British—perhaps more so—for Owen had once been a comrade in arms, and there was no hate as fierce or as abiding as that of enemies who had once been friends.

Mick quickened his stride, watching Owen carefully, following the man's every move until Julia went inside Kate's flat and the door shut behind her.

His hands stuffed into his pockets, Owen crossed the road and posted himself in the shadows against a nearby building, his gaze firmly and unyieldingly on Kate's door.

Mick dodged into the nearest cross street and paused where he could see but not be seen.

"The devil take it!" He shook his head, irritated and more than a little apprehensive. Things had been difficult enough when he thought it was only the British he need fear. Now the Fenians had been thrown into the soup pot and a problem that had once been perilous enough in itself had become complex and dangerous beyond imagining.

Mick settled himself on the wet ground, prepared to wait out the night if that's what Owen Kane would do. He didn't mind giving up a night's sleep for the sake of Julia's safety any more than he minded giving up his home and his family for the cause of Irish freedom.

He'd give all that and more, he told himself, keeping his eyes on Owen and firmly ignoring the cold that soaked through the greatcoat that had once belonged to Sean. He'd sacrifice his freedom and even his life. He'd sacrifice everything for the cause.

The thought brought him up short and he mumbled an oath and recast it in respect to a new insight that was as surprising as it was frank.

He would sacrifice everything—everything but Julia.

Chapter 15

"THERE'S a traitor here somewheres about and you're goin' to march over there as brazen as the bloody Queen's bloody color guard? You are a madman!"

Mick turned away, his mind already a million miles from Teague's kitchen, his thoughts as far as possible from the old man's admonitions.

"Are you listenin' to me, Patrick?" Teague's voice rose with exasperation, but it was neither his annoyance nor the authority in his voice that caused Mick to stalk back to the table. It was his choice of words.

"Pat Fitzgerald is dead." Mick dropped into the chair across from Teague's and gave the old man a level look, the muscles in his neck tight with irritation. "It isn't my name any longer and you'd be wise not to use it."

Teague met his look straight on, his own eyes screwed up against the light streaming in through the kitchen windows. "You may be able to hide from your past out there." He indicated the rest of the world with a tip of his head. "But you can't hide here among your own people."

Mick crossed his arms over his chest, wincing only slightly as his right arm protested with a sharp pain. "Pat Fitzgerald was a fool."

Teague considered the statement in silence. He poured another glass of the poteen he brewed and kept in a jug nearby to moisten his mouth during important conversations.

"Perhaps he was a fool," Teague said, rolling the powerful liquor over his tongue. "But just 'cause a man's a fool is no reason to deny he ever existed at all. Everyone has a right to mistakes, just as everyone has a right to a past. You'd accept that readily enough in another person, but you're forbiddin' both to yourself."

"If it wasn't for my foolishness—"

"If it wasn't for your foolishness Martin would still be alive." One side of Teague's mouth curled with exasperation. "Is that what you were goin' to say? Because if it is, I'll say now what I've said before, both in front of your face and behind it. It was no one's fault but Martin's he went with Owen Kane and his men that day four years ago. No one's fault but the Saxon's he got a bullet in the brain for his trouble."

"If he'd let me rot in prison and stayed home with my sister where he belonged—"

"If he left you in gaol and stayed at home where he belonged, he wouldn't have been the man we all were proud to call our friend." Teague jabbed a finger in Mick's direction to emphasize his point. "Your dear sister understood that better than you ever did. She's never blamed you for the death of her husband, no more than any of the others blamed you for those who died with him."

"Owen blames me."

Teague snorted. "Owen. I care nothing for what that Fenian scum says." He snapped his fingers and downed the rest of his drink. "Owen says he blames you because his brother John was killed along with Martin rescuin' you, but the God's truth of it is, he blames himself. From the minute Owen was put in charge of the thing, he had it so fouled up, it's a wonder any of you made it out alive. No. That's not at all why Owen wants your blood and you know that as well as I do. He's still smartin' from you leavin' his circle, still hurtin' 'cause you had the sense to renounce the Fenians and tried to get the others like Sean to do the same.''

"Which brings us right to where we started." Mick fingered the glass Teague shoved toward him, but he did not drink. "Owen Kane has been following Julia and she needs to be warned."

"And I said I'd do it."

"She won't listen to you." Too tense to remain still, Mick vaulted from his chair and stalked across the narrow kitchen. "You don't know this woman, Teague. She wouldn't listen to the Lord himself if he came down from Sinai with the message carved in stone. She's as willful as the devil and—"

"And you're in love with her and that means you're not thinkin' like a sane man would." Teague sat back and gave him a look so discerning, it made Mick distinctly uncomfortable. He was reminded of the shrewd and knowing glances he'd been given by Father McGill back home when, as a boy, he'd seen the priest in pubic after confessing his sins to him in private.

He buried his uneasiness beneath a thin veneer of anger. "Are you throwing my involvement with her in my face, because if you are—"

"I am not and you know me well enough for that." Teague leaned back, his head cocked to one side. "Loving's like fightin' to an Irishman. Either one will get him through the night. And it follows that now you've stopped fightin', you need to start lovin'."

"And if I love an Englishwoman?"

Teague dismissed the thought with a shrug. "That's Pat Fitzgerald talkin'," he said. "And you said it yourself, Pat Fitzgerald's dead. You will be, too, if you go takin' chances for the sake of the girl. Let me go see her, will you?"

"No." Mick sat down again, his hands clenched together on the table in front of him. "She won't listen. She won't understand. And every day she stays in London, she's in more danger. I'm sure Owen has something planned. I've got to get to her and warn her.''

''And risk bein' taken by Halliday and his damned Home Office lackeys, or worse still, by Owen and his Fenians? I've said it before, you're as mad as a March hare. One of 'em will find you out.''

''Not if I'm careful.''

Teague threw a look to the ceiling. ''How careful can you be? Have you been listenin' to me, or is your head so full of the girl you can't think of anything else? There's a traitor close by. A traitor who was friend enough to be at Sean's wake and see what we did with the Chief's letters. A traitor who sold us all out to the British. Do I need to remind you? That's one of the reasons we haven't let it be known you escaped. Holy Mother! If Owen knew you were free, he'd be beatin' down my door to get his hands around your neck. It's better they all think you're still locked away somewhere. Better still if Julia doesn't know about it. She'd try to see you. I know enough about the girl to know that. And if word gets out that you're in London—''

''It won't.'' As far as Mick was concerned, the discussion was over. He downed his poteen in one gulp, thumped his glass on the table, and motioned to Teague for a refill. ''It can't,'' he said, his jaw set. ''All our lives depend on it.''

HE'D been angrier than hell when he awoke in the tiny cave on the moor and found Julia gone. Angry at her, angry at himself, and now, waiting for her in the small, third-floor room at Hatchett's Hotel, Mick expected the anger to return, as devastating and dangerous as it had been that morning more than two months ago.

Perhaps that's why his heart was skipping like an unbridled colt in a spring meadow. Perhaps that's why he felt his stomach turn over each time he heard someone pass by in the corridor outside. Perhaps he was afraid of what he might say, what he might do, when he finally had to face her again. Perhaps . . .

Mick took a deep breath and mumbled a curse, vexed at his own ungovernable thoughts.

Perhaps he should worry less about what he'd say when Julia walked in and more about who might be following her.

Stalking to the windows, he pulled back the curtains. There was little to be seen except the fog rolling by in great long wisps, as pale and unearthly as a skeleton's fingers.

Mick cursed his luck with one breath, his discomfort with the next. It had been Teague's idea that he come disguised and he regretted his acquiescence to the suggestion more and more with each passing minute. The long, dark coat was one thing. He could live with that easily enough, especially on a night as miserable as this. But the hat pulled over his eyes, the muffler wound around the lower part of his face? He needed these as much as a cat needed a fifth leg.

He was about to yank the scarf off when he heard a knock on the hotel room door.

"Good evening."

He didn't need to turn around to know it was Julia. Her voice was as melodious as ever, even if she did insist on using that outlandish, invented accent.

The door creaked open further. "I am the Countess Madame Anastasia Marinna Krakowska," she said. "I received your telegram. You are interested in discussing something very important, yes?"

Whether it was anger or relief that paralyzed him, Mick did not know. He only knew he could not trust himself to speak. He waved one hand toward the small, round table across the room, and waited until he heard Julia's chair scrape against the bare floor. It was only then he turned around.

Teague had told him about the peculiar occupation Julia had chosen to help earn her keep. But in spite of the old man's warning, he was not prepared for the sight of her.

She had discarded her coat on the back of the sofa and Mick could see she was dressed in a dark-colored, patterned skirt. Her white blouse stood out, stark and colorless, in the dimly lit room, and the chains and amulets she wore around her neck sparkled with the reflected light of the fire that danced in the grate. Her hair was caught up in a multi-colored square of fabric so that it was pulled away from her face but hung loose at the back of her head, cascading over her shoulders like a slash of ebony ink, smooth and liquid and so dark, it looked to be one with the shadows.

She had told him once that she had Gypsy blood, but it was never more evident than now. Her cheeks were flushed from the cold, her breathing irregular from the long walk up to the room. There was a wildness about her, an odd, almost supernatural radiance that glowed in her face and burned from her eyes like the fire of hot coals.

There was no flash of recognition in those dark eyes as she looked at him, no moment of understanding. Mick felt a stab of disappointment at the same time he reprimanded himself for it. He was supposed to be in prison. Teague's plan to keep his escape a secret had obviously worked. Besides, he consoled himself, if his disguise was effective enough to deceive Julia, he could be sure it had been good enough to throw both Freddy Halliday and Owen Kane off his trail, at least for tonight.

He was a fool not to discard the preposterous disguise right then and there, a simpleton for not revealing himself before another moment passed. But try as he might, Mick could say nothing. The last time he had seen Julia, she was lying naked beside him, her lips red and wet from his kisses, her eyes so bright with yearning, they filled him with reckless desire. The memory caught in his throat as he looked at her, and caused his words to choke and die there.

This was not the first client who had tried to hide his identity, and Julia studied the cloaked and covered man who towered over her with little more than passing curiosity. It had been a long day and she had had her fill of crystal gazing. The sooner they completed the transaction, the sooner she could get to her bed.

She motioned to the chair opposite hers and waited for the man to be seated.

"It is a palm reading you want?"

The man nodded.

He had the manners of a billy goat and Julia was about to tell him as much when she remembered the very generous fee he'd promised in his telegram. "Very well. We will begin." She forced the displeasure from her voice and settled into her well-rehearsed palm-reading routine, hoping to calm herself and her subject with the meaningless ritual.

Placing her palms against the table, she closed her eyes and took a series of deep, steadying breaths. She held the last breath for a long time, expelling it with an extended, barely perceptible sigh.

Finally, she opened her eyes and, keeping her voice low, asked, "There is some special area of your life about which you would like advice? Business, perhaps? Your fortune with the horses?"

The man did not respond. Instead, he inclined his head as if commanding her to answer the question for herself.

With an effort, Julia kept her face impassive. Curse the man! He was going to make this difficult. Ladies were far easier to read than gentlemen. Like her childhood friend Harriet Lloyd, most ladies were concerned about one thing only—love. Gentlemen were inherently more skeptical and far more difficult to read successfully. Some were concerned with commerce, some with finance, still others wanted to know about their chances of success in the world of the arts or sciences.

What did this one want?

Julia studied the man across the table, trying to learn all she could from the vague hints provided by his appearance. Though his face was shadowed by the brim of his hat, she knew he was assessing her with equal interest. She glanced from the rough woolen scarf wound around his neck and face, to the shabby hat on his head, to his eyes, barely visible in the shadow of the large-brimmed hat. She did not need to look any further.

Instantly, as if a voice had whispered the answer in her ear, she knew why he was here.

"You have come about a woman," she told him.

From across the table, Julia heard his sharp intake of breath. She knew she had hit upon the correct reason for his summons and she rushed on, making the most of her advantage.

"Is it a certain woman?" she asked clinically, forcing all emotion from her voice. "Or is it just love—how do you English say it—romance? That is it. Is it romance you wish Madame Krakowska to tell you about?"

"A woman." He pronounced the words carefully, his eyes never leaving her face, his voice muffled almost beyond understanding by the scarf. "One particular woman."

"Then give your hand to Madame Krakowska and I will see what secrets it reveals about you and this one particular woman." Julia laid her hand on the table, palm up, and the man leaned closer and placed his right hand in hers.

It was a large hand, well-shaped and firm, a philosophic hand.

"You are one of life's philosophers, searching always for the truth," she said. "You have a strong sense of justice. Even so, your life line here"—she followed the long, deeply etched line with the tip of her left index finger—"shows that you are impulsive. See, it begins here"—she pointed—"below the Line of the Head. Spontaneity, unpredictability. These are things a lady might appreciate in romance, yes? Your Mount of Mars Positive here"—she pointed again—"shows you possess great courage, strength, and vigor. You have the capacity to endure . . ."

The words died on Julia's lips. She coughed politely and took up where she left off. "You possess great courage, strength . . ."

She stared at the hand cradled in hers, not seeing it at all, but seeing instead an attic dry-cleaning room, and Mick with his hand out to her, a smile on his face. She had accepted his hand, and told his fortune.

"Mick?" Julia started as if she'd seen a ghost. "What on earth are you doing here? You're supposed to be in prison!"

"It's good to see you again, too, my fine and fancy lady." Mick laughed, the simple candor of her astonishment and the look of happiness in her eyes filling him with pleasure and driving away his apprehension.

Slowly, he uncoiled the scarf from around his neck and dropped it in the center of the table. He tossed his hat on top of it and shrugged out of his coat before he gave Julia a lopsided smile. "Even if you do look as if you just stepped out of a carnival sideshow."

Her surprise was so complete, Julia could do no more than stare, her eyes swimming with tears of gladness and relief. "You really are here!" She grabbed for Mick's hand and held on as if to make sure he was real. "They said you were in gaol, but you're not. You're here and—"

"And you're getting all that cheap jewelry wet." Mick leaned forward and brushed the tears from her cheeks with his free hand, his eyes gleaming with the reflected light of the gas lamps that burned on either side of the fireplace. "It'll rust. Mark my words. You couldn't have paid more than a few shillings for the lot of it."

His smile was magic, his touch as soothing as the warmth of the fire. Julia ran her fingers up Mick's arm and squeezed it affectionately.

"Careful!" Mick jerked his arm away and worked it back and forth. He smiled self-consciously when a flash of distress darkened Julia's eyes.

"Just a souvenir of my last visit to one of Her Majesty's

fine prison establishments,'' he assured her with a careless wave of his hand. ''Nothing to be concerned about. I'll be fine. But you . . .''

He had warned himself to tread carefully, to guard his anger and his tongue, but the words rolled off his lips before he could stop them. ''It was a damned foolish thing you did, taking those letters.''

For a moment, Julia had deluded herself into believing he had forgotten her treachery. One look at the sudden spark in Mick's eyes told her he had not. The realization stung her into silence and brought heat flaming into her cheeks.

How many times these past months had she practiced her apology? How many times had she asked herself what she would change?

Julia turned the thought over again in her mind, examining it like a scientist examines an especially valuable specimen. She need only look at Mick to know the answer. It remained as clear as it had each time before when she pictured his face or remembered his touch. It was as deafening as the clattering of her heart, as obvious as the fire that shot desire through her veins.

If she could relive her past, if she could go back to that morning in the cave on the moor, she would still take the letters. Then, as now, she would do whatever she could for Mick.

Julia clutched her hands at her waist. ''I'm sorry,'' she said simply. ''I thought I was doing the right thing.'' She rose from the table and moved back a step, her voice gaining strength as she distanced herself from the unsettling displeasure in Mick's eyes. ''I wanted to help.''

''Help?'' Mick bolted to his feet, his expression as incredulous as the disbelief that sharpened his words. ''How in the name of the holy saints did you plan on helping by stealing those letters? You didn't have a cat's chance in hell of ever delivering them. Didn't I say you were too naïve when it came to politics? You may as well have taken the letters right out of the Chief's hands and given them to the newspapers.''

''But they haven't been in the newspapers, have they?'' A satisfied smile lightened Julia's expression. This was one argument he could not use to rebuke her and she wrapped it about herself like a coat of mail, confident of its strength. ''Freddy Halliday's had them two full months and still the letters haven't been printed.''

''That's because—''

''I know very well why they haven't been published.'' Julia lifted her chin. ''I may have been a political lamb when you met me, but I assure you I am more informed now.'' She fluffed her skirt and went to stand near the window.

''We've been watching the newspapers, of course, expecting to see the scandal proclaimed every day. I suppose you and Mr. Parnell have been doing the same?'' She looked to Mick for acknowledgment but did not wait for his answer.

''Of course, I don't have access to firsthand information as I'm sure you do. But from what I've been able to ascertain, the letters haven't been published because it isn't politically advantageous to do that right now. The next debate on the Home Rule question comes up in Parliament in six weeks. That's when the letters will be released, when they can do the most damage, both to Mr. Parnell and to the cause of Irish nationalism.'' She looked at Mick levelly. ''I may be naïve, but I think you'll agree, I have a grasp of the situation.''

''A grasp of the . . .'' Mick mumbled an oath and stuffed his hands into his pockets, treading back and forth in front of the fireplace. ''If you hadn't given the bloody letters to Halliday—''

''If I hadn't given him the letters, you surely would have.''

"Sweet saints above!" Mick's face flushed with anger. "I never would have—"

"You were captured." Julia stopped herself just short of stomping her foot to emphasize the point. "Don't you forget, Mick O'Donnell, it didn't take Freddy Halliday long to take your precious self into custody. He would have had the letters days earlier from you than he got them from me."

Mick stopped his frantic pacing long enough to glare at her. "Halliday wouldn't have arrested me at all if I hadn't been out over hell's half-acre looking for you. I could have been safe and well out of it. But no, like the guffoon I am, I decided finding you was worth giving Halliday a chance at my hide. So you see, it is your fault. As much as it was your fault handing those letters right to the man when he came looking for them."

This was too much and Julia groaned, her voice rising to meet Mick's. "I hardly had a choice, did I? He was about to search Sean."

"Sean was deader than Julius Caesar. He wouldn't have cared."

The memory brought an unexpected lump of emotion to Julia's throat, and she forced her words past it, her voice perilously calm. "No. Sean wouldn't have cared. But Teague would have. He would have cared desperately. And Halliday would have found the letters anyway."

His reply rumbling in his throat, Mick turned his back on Julia. Curse the woman! It was bad enough she looked bewitching as night, standing there with her head high and the passion of conviction glowing in her eyes like the hottest fires of hell. But worse still—she was right.

He pulled himself to a stop and faced her, pushing one hand through his hair. "I'm sorry," he said. "I didn't mean to . . . to . . . upset you. I've heard what they did to Sean. How he looked and . . ." He took a deep breath. "Hell, I would have done the same thing had I been there."

Such a blatant lie could not be excused. Julia gave Mick

an acerbic smile. "You would have knocked Freddy Halliday on the head with the nearest candlestick."

"And kicked up the devil's delight with those hired louts I heard he brought with him." Mick's eyes glowed with mischievous pleasure. "Sean liked nothing better than a good donnybrook. More's the pity he couldn't be there to help knock some sense into those Saxons' heads."

The thought sobered them and both their smiles faded. Mick cleared his throat and lowered his voice. "I didn't come here to argue with you," he said, "though I might have known we'd be at it like Kilkenny cats before the night was out. I needed to talk to you. You're in a great deal of danger."

"Tommy-rot!" Julia tossed her head. "If it's the fortune-telling you mean . . ." She tapped one finger against the beads and chains on her chest. "I'm not in any danger at all. My customers had always been perfect gentlemen and—"

"Owen Kane is following you."

Confused, Julia shook her head. "Why on earth would Owen Kane want to follow me around?" she asked. "I'm staying with Kate. Every Irishman this side of Dublin knows that."

Sudden apprehension crept into Julia's veins, as cold and heavy as the fog outside. She wrapped her arms around herself to chase away the chill. "Owen doesn't want me. He wants you. And if he followed me tonight—"

"I trust my disguise took care of that." Mick threw a look at the scarf and hat where they lay on the table. "Owen thinks you're seeing a client. That's all. We should be safe enough while we're here."

It was not the words Mick spoke that sounded a warning bell in Julia's brain. It was what he refused to say. She gave him a penetrating look.

"But you don't think you'll be safe once he learns you've escaped. Is that what you're trying to say?"

"I'm trying to say . . ." Mick shrugged helplessly, his

carefully chosen words lost beneath the potency of the concern that glimmered in Julia's eyes. "I'm trying to say . . ."

Recognizing defeat when he saw it, Mick gave up. He crossed the room in two quick strides and scooped Julia into his arms, tightening his hold until she was pressed against him. For a moment he could do no more. She was soft and warm, and his body responded instantly, his heart pounding inside his chest in perfect time to her own.

Not two months ago, he thought he would never hold her again. He had dreamed of her those long nights in his prison cell—dreamed of her velvety softness, of the flavor of her lips, of the exquisite taste of her breasts and her thighs. Mick sucked in a great draught of air and loosened his hold on Julia long enough to drag the patterned scarf from her head and wind his fingers through her hair. He drew her nearer and looked into her eyes.

"I'm trying to say you have to leave. Now. Tonight," he said, his voice rough with emotion. "I'm trying to say I don't want you hurt. I want you gone, just as I did that day in St. Ives. Not for myself. I'm no more afraid of Owen than I am of Freddy Halliday and his lot. But you need to get as far from it all as you can. You can't be involved."

"I'm already involved."

Her declaration fell like thunder between them. With a small noise of disgust, Mick jerked away. "It isn't your fight."

Julia rose to the challenge that reverberated in his voice. "Yes," she said. "It is. My fight as much as yours. Mine as much as Kate's, or Teague's, or Sean's. And I have as much right to see it out as any of you."

Mick held out his hands to her, hoping to explain. "You know about your grandmother. I didn't want you to know. I didn't think—"

"You didn't think I had the right to the truth." Though she felt no more shame in admitting her grandmother's wickedness, the thought of what Margaret Barrie had done to the hundreds of people who looked to her for protection still caused a wave of nausea to wash over Julia. She swallowed her disgust, and struggled to maintain her composure, ignoring Mick's outstretched hands.

"I have just as much right to my anger as you do to yours," she told him. "I've learned that much these past months. I've also learned that I owe these people something. I owe them something for what she did to them. That's why I'm not leaving."

"Saints and angels!" Mick spun away, infuriated. "I'm telling you you're in danger and you're standing there telling me you won't leave."

"Not until we've gotten the letters back." Julia smiled, satisfied she'd surprised him enough to take the words out of his mouth. "We have the chance of retrieving them as long as they haven't been printed. After they've been returned to Mr. Parnell, I promise I'll leave. I'll go wherever you ask me to go, but only after we have the letters."

"No!" Mick turned back to her, his voice as dangerous as his expression, and slashed his hand through the air in one conclusive gesture. "We've been through it all before. I won't let you risk yourself again."

His reasoning was too ridiculous and Julia nearly laughed. "You won't let me risk myself and yet you ask me to stand by and watch you risk being imprisoned or hanged? No. That isn't fair. And it isn't right."

"We're not talking right." Mick's eyes ignited with blue fire. "Is it right for one country to hold another hostage? To drain the lifeblood from the land and drive the people from their homes? None of it's right. Damn it! None of it's right, Julia. That doesn't mean you have to jeopardize your life!"

"But you would jeopardize yours."

"It's my country, and I'll die for it if I bloody well want to die for it."

"I will do anything I can to save you, to help you."

"You can't." Mick advanced on her until he was no more than two paces away. He pulled himself up to his full height and glowered down at her, his voice precise, underscoring each word. "You can't help me with the letters. You can't help me with anything."

Where Julia got the courage to resist the strength of his gaze and the ring of authority in his voice, she never knew. "You're trying to frighten me. You think I'll leave if I'm afraid for you, afraid for myself. It isn't that easy, is it, Mick? Sending me away may help to keep me safe, but it won't do a thing for you. Getting rid of Owen won't eliminate the danger in your life, neither will returning the letters to Mr. Parnell."

For a moment, her next thoughts refused to form into words. Suddenly exhausted, she looked at Mick, all her fervor spent until there was nothing left but her voice, small, and hushed, and terrified, a whisper against the darkness.

"You'll always be in danger, Mick. Always. I've stood face to face with that reality these past months. I've looked it in the eye, but it never changes. I know there will never be safety for you. Not until there is a free Ireland."

"Hell and damnation!" Mick kicked the nearest chair and sent it skittering across the floor. "You want to be a martyr? Well, I'll tell you, my fine and fancy lady, I don't need any martyrs for my cause. I've had enough and more of that for one lifetime."

Mick moved away and Julia grabbed for his sleeve, her voice rising against the look of stubborn resistance in his eyes. "I'm willing to fight for what we both believe in. I'm willing to die for it just as you are. Don't you understand?"

Without another word, Mick pulled his arm away and grabbed his coat from the chair. He stalked to the door, yanking it open and stepping out into the corridor before he looked back at her one last time.

"Yes," he said. "I do understand. That is why I'm sorry I love you."

Chapter 16

"What do you mean, she's missing?"

Mick looked at Kate anxiously, waiting for an explanation while he finished doing up his buttons and stuffed the tails of his shirt into his trousers. He'd spent most of the night drowning his sorrows in Teague's poteen and his brain was still blurry, but he was sober enough to recognize the signs of trouble when he saw them.

He saw them now.

Kate's usually ruddy complexion was colorless, her cheeks were tearstained; Teague's expression was as somber as the grave. He stood in the shadows along the far wall of the kitchen, his bushy brows dipped over his eyes like threatening thunderclouds.

Mick swallowed the taste of panic rising in his throat and forced himself to wait for Kate to speak again, sure that if he pressured her, he would get little more than the frantic, confused statement she'd blurted out as soon as he'd walked into the room. He hauled up his braces, snapping them over his shoulders while he watched Kate, his mouth curled into a questioning grimace, his eyes urging her to speak.

Kate opened her mouth, but the only sounds that emerged were sobs. She stared at Mick, speechless.

"Saints and . . ." Impatient, Mick whirled from Kate to Teague. "What's she saying?" he demanded. "What does she mean, Julia's missing?"

Teague pushed away from the wall and took a step toward Mick. "You're terrifyin' the woman! She can't speak if she's frightened, and you won't hear a word she has to say if you don't calm down," he said, his eyes glaring his warning.

"Besides"—Teague cast a look of reassurance at Kate and his voice tapered off—"I've told her not to tell you anything until you promise you won't blame her for what happened. Blame me if you want. I'm the one who told her it was you Julia was goin' out to meet last night."

"That's right." Kate spoke up, her voice hoarse from crying. She sniffed into the corner of her apron. "I fell asleep early last evenin' and I didn't hear Julia come in. But I wasn't concerned on account of because I knew you was the one she was with and I thought how wonderful it was for the both of you. I thought if you two were together . . ."

Kate's cheeks flared with two spots of deep red. "I figured you being young and carin' for each other the way you do . . ." She cleared her throat and looked away, taking a moment to compose herself before she spoke again.

"But then when Julia didn't come home for breakfast nor later on for tea, I began to worry. So I came over here. And Teague, he tells me you're still upstairs snorin' loud enough to wake the dead. He peeked in, Lord forgive him, and you was alone—"

"Julia didn't come home last night?" Apprehension drained the passion from Mick's voice and filled his viens with ice. When Kate did not answer, he looked over at Teague. "You're saying she didn't come home last night?"

Teague sat down at the table next to Kate and put one hand on her arm. "Kate wasn't too worried, like she said, not until she came here and found I hadn't seen Julia either."

Mick squeezed his eyes shut, Teague's words barely making their way past the rushing noise that filled his ears and pounded through his brain. "You don't know where she is?'' He looked at Kate dumbly, hoping the whole jumble was merely the result of the large amount of poteen he'd drunk in a short amount of time. He was blathering like a bosthoon, and he knew it, but he could not seem to control his tongue. "Julia didn't come home last night and you don't know where she is?"

"I told you I'm the one to blame!" Kate dissolved into tears.

"No." The sound of Mick's voice, dangerously soft, quieted her sobbing. He looked beyond Kate, beyond Teague. "No," he said again. "It isn't your fault. It's no one's fault but my own. I'm the one who got angry with her last night. I left her to come home alone and . . ."

Mick could not put words to the horrifying possibilities that invaded his thoughts. Turning around, he massaged his forehead with one hand, hoping to drive away his confusion, while at the same time he tried to think of a suitable course of action.

It was little use. His anger was so complete, his sense of guilt so overpowering, he could think of nothing beyond one essential certainty—he must find Julia.

Banishing his hesitation with one swift shake of his shoulders, Mick retrieved his boots from the oval carpet in front of the cook stove and moved toward the door.

"You can't go after her when you don't know where she's gone."

Teague's words froze him in place, his hand already on the knob.

"You're right." Mick acknowledged the admonition with a shrug. "But I've got to look. What if she's lost or hurt?"

"You know as well as me, she's been taken by Owen." Teague dared to give voice to the one thought Mick would not pronounce, as if refusing to speak the words could keep them from being real.

"Yes." Mick aimed a look at the closed door as if he

could see beyond it, and faced the terrifying truth. "It is bound to be Owen," he said, his voice no more than a growl deep within his throat. "And the bastard needs to be dealt with."

"You won't find him home. He's too smart for that." Teague watched Mick as he might have watched a hungry lion, hoping to gauge his reaction. "And even if Owen's there, you know she won't be with him. He's too smart for that, too."

"The devil you say!" Mick tossed his boots back onto the floor and dropped into the nearest chair, his fists on the table, his jaw so tight with anger and frustration, his muscles ached in protest. "I can't just sit here waiting, not knowing where she is or what's happened to her."

A timid rap on the door prevented him from saying anything else. Mick's gaze darted to Teague, and with a quick movement of one hand, he signaled for the older man to open the door with caution.

"Mr. Fitzgerald?"

Mick could not see their visitor, but the voice was unmistakably that of a child. He rose from his chair and elbowed Teague out of the doorway.

"I'm Mr. Fitzgerald," he said, looking down at the young boy who stood in the street outside. "Who wants me?"

The boy eyed Mick warily, shifting from foot to foot. "Not anyone, sir." he said. "Leastways not that I know of. I . . . I got this 'ere for you." He held out a small, square parcel.

For a moment, Mick could do no more than stare at the package clutched in the boy's dirty fingers. It was foolish to be paralyzed by the sight of nothing more than brown paper and string, and he reprimanded himself sharply as he fought to make his hand move toward the bundle. He reached for it and stopped just short of taking it.

"Who gave that to you?" he asked the boy, his hand poised above the parcel.

The boy defended himself instantly, his bottom lip protruding with outrage. "I didn't take it, if that's what you're saying. It was given to me by a man."

"A man you know?"

"Ain't never seen him before and 'ope to never see him again. Irish, he was."

"A big Irishman? As big as me?"

The boy took in Mick's size, his dark gaze traveling all the way from Mick's stockinged feet to the top of his tousled head. "As tall. Yes," he decided. "But broader, if you know what I mean, sir. Big. And as nasty-looking as sin."

"Owen." Mick whispered the name, confirming the fact to himself. Hope rushed through him and he leaned closer to the boy. "Where did you meet this man?"

"Down on Oxford Street, sir. Stopped me as me and my mates was walking along and gave me a whole shilling if I'd bring this 'ere parcel to you."

"Damn."

Teague read the look of discouragement on Mick's face. He shook his head. "All of London walks down Oxford Street at one time of day or another. Owen chose the boy, came out of the crowd—"

"—and disappeared right back into it." Mick finished the sentence for him, discouragement rounding his shoulders and snatching the optimism from his voice. "Did the man say anything? Anything at all?"

"Just that I should give this to you, sir. And where you lived." The boy cast a nervous glance up and down the road and mumbled beneath his breath. "Me mum'll have a fit if she finds out I been in a bog-lander neighborhood." Remembering himself, he looked again at Mick and poked the parcel toward him. "'Ere. Take it. It's yours."

Reluctantly, Mick accepted the package, weighing it carefully in his hands. He was still looking at it when

Teague waved the boy away and closed the door behind him.

"Come. Sit." The old man urged Mick back to the table.

Mick pulled away from his grasp, his gaze still on the package.

"Patrick Fitzgerald. That's what's written here on the front." He lifted the parcel so Kate and Teague could see it and gave them a sour smile. "Obviously from someone who knows me well."

Kate hopped from her seat, her enormous bosom heaving with agitation. "Open it. We must know—"

"Yes." Mick heard and agreed, but he did not move to unwrap the package. The box was covered in brown, inexpensive paper that crinkled in his hands like dead leaves. He turned it over with every intention of slipping his fingers beneath the yellowed string that fastened it, but found he could not.

"Teague?" He looked at the old man. "I don't have my eyeglasses. Would you open it?"

Without a word, Teague took the parcel and slit the string with a paring knife. He ripped away the paper. Inside the wrappings was a small box. Teague lifted the lid and pulled out a sheet of writing paper that had been folded and stuffed inside. He tilted the parcel toward Mick.

It was filled with gold chains and amulets.

For a long while, Mick could do no more than stare at the glittering contents of the box. Like a pirate's treasure trove, it winked and sparkled at him, mocking him with its beauty, taunting him by its seeming innocence. A box of cheap gold jewelry. It was nothing more. Yet Mick found himself crippled at the sight. He was so overcome by the display of the necklaces he had last seen on Julia, he could do little more than stare at it, his voice gone, his heart beating painful time to every pulse.

His hands did not shake as he reached for the parcel, and he wondered briefly at the thought, amazed that agitation so complete could be veiled so readily, that emotions too powerful to name could be cloaked beneath a veneer of control so fragile it would surely crack at any moment. Gently, Mick tipped the box and watched as the jewelry spilled into his hand like a golden waterfall.

He closed his fingers around it, the gold-painted metal cold against his hot palm. He tightened his hold and looked up at Teague. "Read the letter."

Teague cleared his throat. "It's from Owen sure enough. I don't need the villain's signature across the bottom to tell me that." He pointed, one finger trembling against the paper. "He mentions his brother John. Says this is in repayment. Damn the man!" Teague slammed the letter down on the table and flattened it with his fist. "He says Julia is with him and the only way you'll have her back is to come yourself and get her. He'll send another message tomorrow to tell you when and where. He wants you." The old man looked up at Mick, his eyes suddenly brimming with tears. "He wants you in exchange for Julia, or—"

"Or?" Mick's voice was as stony as the look he gave Teague.

"Or he says he'll send her back to you in pieces."

"Dear Lord!" Kate dropped back into her chair and buried her face in her hands.

"That's it then." Mick spoke more to himself than Teague, pulling his shoulders back and letting go the breath he'd been holding. "I'll be ready tomorrow."

Teague slapped the letter where it lay on the table, his voice rising with disbelief. "You're not going?"

"Of course I'm going." Mick dismissed the dumbfounded expression on Teague's face with a chuckle. "Me for Julia. It seems a fair enough trade."

"We're not talkin' fair and you know that as well as I do." Teague leapt from his chair, his reed-slim body shaking, his voice harsh with barely suppressed emotion. "We're talking about Owen Kane. We're taking about the

Fenians. They know no more about fair than Lucifer himself. You of all people should know that. You know what they done to my Sean, and what they would have done to your own life had you let them." Teague's voice broke, his shoulders rose and fell in rhythm with the deep sigh that racked his body. "Why not ask for help?"

"Help?" Mick spun away. "And who will help us, I wonder. The police? What's one less Irishman to them? Or a girl with no family and no social connections? They'd sooner watch us die in the street than bend to lend a helping hand."

"What about Parnell, then?" Teague's face lit with sudden inspiration. "The Chief respects you, and he's always said he'd do anything he could to help you along."

"This isn't a political question, Teague. If it was, I wouldn't hesitate to ask the Chief for help." Mick looked down at the golden jewelry laced between his fingers. "This is personal. Personal business between me and Owen Kane. And if it wasn't before today, it is now. He made it personal when he took Julia."

Teague stuck out his jaw, stubborn and determined. "And how do you plan on the two of you coming out of this alive?"

"I don't know yet." Mick admitted the truth. He ran the necklaces through his fingers and watched the gold-colored metal flash and twinkle. "I don't know," he conceded thoughtfully. "But I've got all the way until tomorrow to figure it out."

"And when tomorrow comes?"

Mick shrugged. "When tomorrow comes, I'd bloody well have a plan, or I'm going to get my head handed to me on a platter."

THE steady hiss of the room's single gas lamp was nearly lost beneath the sound of Teague's gentle snoring.

Mick shifted in his chair and cast a look over to where the

old man slept with his head on the kitchen table. He should send Teague up to bed, Mick thought, but it hardly seemed fair to disturb him.

After hours of discussion, hours of looking for a solution to the problem and getting nowhere, the old man deserved a rest.

A rest was exactly what Mick himself needed most; he required no one to tell him that. After spending half the night here, his legs were stiff and his arms ached. He stretched and downed the dregs of the coffee in his mug, grimacing as the bitter, ice-cold liquid hit the back of his throat.

His right arm felt as if it had been weighted down with lead, and Mick flexed it tentatively, wishing not for the first time that he'd found a less breakable weapon to assist him in his last escape attempt. No matter. He smiled in spite of himself. He supposed his freedom was worth the price of a shattered bone. He'd escaped from prison and—

"Holy Mother in heaven!" His chair was propped against the wall and Mick righted it and sat up. "Owen knows I've escaped from the British!"

His own voice came back to him in the dark, the astonishment that colored his words still reverberating through the room when Teague stirred and raised his head.

"What's that you say?" Teague rubbed his eyes and propped his elbows on the table, his head in his hands. "Did you say something about the Saxons?"

The thought was too new, the implications too astounding for Mick to explain it wholly. He bounded from his chair and went to fill his mug from the pot of coffee simmering on the cook stove. He downed half the cup and refilled it before he looked again at Teague. "How do you suppose Owen knows I've escaped from the British?"

Teague sat up, the significance of Mick's words beginning to make their way into his sleep-dulled brain. He sat quietly, waiting for Mick to explain.

"That's it." Mick pounded the air with his fist, striding to the other side of the room and back again. "We've been sitting here all night trying to figure what we could do to help Julia and it's been in front of our eyes the entire time." Draining his cup, he set it squarely in the center of the table and looked down at Teague.

"How does Owen know I'm here? Last he knew, I was a guest of Her Majesty. Now he's sending me letters and parcels to your house with never a question that he'd find me."

"Interesting." Teague turned the thought over in his mind. "You think there's an informer somewhere who's spread the word?"

"I'd bet certain money on it. A Fenian informer. Probably the same one who let Halliday know about the Chief's letters, and—"

"And a British informer feeding information to the Fenians." Teague sat up straight in his chair, his eyes lighting with awareness. "They're working together."

Mick snatched his coat from a nearby chair and shrugged into it.

"Where are you off to in the middle of the night?" Teague rose and groaned, massaging his back with one hand.

"I'm off to prove my theory. If I'm right . . ." He stopped at the door and threw Teague a look over his shoulder. "If I'm right, the informer is the one person who can help us get Julia back. And Lord help me, I'm certain I know who it is."

THE house was spacious, the parlor elegant. Even at this time of night, a fire burned in the grate, and Mick could only imagine the army of servants who must have been busy, day and night, meeting the needs of their employer.

He cast another glance around the room, this time ignoring the priceless porcelain, the expensive paintings, the ornate furnishings, and concentrating instead on the doors. It was always wise to get the lay of the land, he told himself; better still to know your options for escape.

There were two: the double doors he'd entered not five minutes ago and the French windows across the room. The doors led out into the passage and, from there, to the entryway and on to the front door. Not the safest escape route, Mick decided, visualizing again a legion of servants, some of whom he imagined were as brawny as the footman who had shown him in.

The French windows? Mick crossed the room and pushed aside the Nottingham lace curtains. It was far too dark to tell what was outside the windows and he made a mental note of it, reminding himself the night might be his safest retreat.

A commotion outside the door interrupted his inspection and he stationed himself, his back to the window, planting his feet and crossing his arms over his chest.

A second later, the parlor door burst open and his host stamped into the room, his face red with agitation, his voice raised in anger against the hapless footman who walked behind him, wringing his hands.

"What on earth made you admit someone at this hour?"

"Top of the mornin' to you." Mick greeted him with a smile, deliberately slipping into his heaviest brogue. "And how are you this fine mornin', Mr. Halliday?"

Chapter 17

IF nothing else, Freddy Halliday was an accomplished actor. The flash of surprise that widened his sleep-heavy eyes and transformed the aggravated scowl on his face into a look of utter astonishment lasted no more than a moment.

The next second, he collected himself, dismissing his servant with an imperious wave of one hand, masking his surprise beneath a layer of nonchalance so effortless, Mick could only shake his head in admiration.

Without a word, Halliday untied the sloppy knot in the sash of his blue satin smoking jacket. He retied it, his full concentration seemingly on the unmanageable sash, and did not look up again until he was satisfied it was perfect.

Giving the knot one last, careful tug, he greeted Mick with an indifferent nod and a small quirk of his eyebrows, and strolled over to the mahogany desk situated at the far end of the room. "You needn't bother with the amenities, O'Donnell." He popped open a rosewood box that stood at one corner of the desk, removed a plump cigar, and sniffed it appreciatively.

"You don't care any more how I am than I care how you are. What I do care about . . ." He lit the cigar and took a long, deep drag on it before he spoke again. "What I do care about is what the devil you're doing in my home." He blew a ring of smoke and watched it spin to the ceiling. "The servant who allowed you in will be sacked in the morning, of course.''

''Of course.'' Mick fought to keep his voice impassive, his words a mirror of Halliday's affected pleasantry. ''That is to be expected from a cold-hearted bastard such as yourself. But you really shouldn't be too hard on the man. I can be quite persuasive when it suits my needs.''

''Yes.'' Halliday smiled, slick and smooth as a snake. ''I imagine you can.'' He took another puff of his cigar. ''And what,'' he asked, looking directly at Mick for the first time, ''what exactly are those needs?''

''Ah, now that's the curious thing.'' Mick rocked back on his heels. ''It seems for once, my needs and yours are one and the same.''

''Are they?'' Halliday's interest was aroused, though he tried his best not to show it. He rounded the desk, his eyes dark with barely contained malice, his voice icy with contempt. ''And what is it, may I ask, that a wretched bog-trotter criminal like yourself and a gentleman like me could possibly have in common? We hardly move in the same social circles.''

''But our political circles are not all that different.''

Halliday paused, deep in thought, his brow furrowed, his smoldering cigar temporarily forgotten.

He was not a stupid man; neither was he naïve. One look at the luxury surrounding them told Mick as much. Freddy Halliday was a man who looked after himself, a man who planned each scheme, each systematic move by one tenet and one alone—how would it benefit him?

He was thinking as much now. Mick need only watch the play of caution and curiosity that shadowed Halliday's face to know it. He was considering Mick's statement, weighing it in his mind, and wondering, wondering always, what the advantages were for Freddy Halliday.

He might be selfish, but at least Halliday was not ashamed of his shortcomings. This time, he did not try to conceal his interest. He looked up at Mick and smiled. "Tell me more."

Mick nodded, pleased that he had won this first, preliminary round. "I've come about Owen Kane."

"Kane?" Halliday pulled in a deep swallow of cigar smoke and curled the word around his tongue along with it. "I know the name, of course, and I think I can picture the face. Big, gruff fellow. Bad reputation. Fenian, isn't he? One of your friend Sean Finnegan's mates, I believe."

"Sean's friend. Yes." Mick paused, hoping to gauge Halliday's reaction. "And yours as well."

If Halliday was surprised by the accusation, he did not show it. He stood perfectly still, his face impassive, as if it had been carved from stone. Only his eyes revealed any emotion. They sparked at Mick, the corners narrowing slightly, the thick, dark lashes lowered as if to conceal some secret hatred.

"Rubbish!" Halliday snapped into action, casting off the allegation with an elegant shrug of his shoulders, and tossing Mick an irritated look. "You are sorely lacking in taste or tact, O'Donnell. If you've come here at three in the morning to entertain me with fairy stories, I think you should know I'm not that easily amused."

He crossed the room and stopped near the fireplace, his hand on the bellrope. "You Irish are a simple race and, I must admit, it sometimes brightens my day to watch your foolish antics, but I believe I've had enough of your Gaelic tomfoolery for one night. If you'll be so kind as to stay put, I'll call my servants in and have them hold you until the police arrive."

"I don't think so." Mick voice pierced the space between them. "You don't want the police here. Not until you've found out what I know." Turning, Mick strolled to the other side of the room, carefully assessing their sumptuous surroundings. He paused in front of an especially valuable painting and glanced over his shoulder at Halliday. "Not," he said, "until you know what's in it for you."

"You have a point." Halliday's lips widened into an avaricious grin. He moved from the bellrope and flopped into the nearest chair, one arm draped casually over the back while with his other hand he stubbed out the remains of his cigar in the nearest crystal ashtray.

He did not offer a chair and Mick did not take one. Instead, he resumed his place near the windows, his chin raised, his gaze leveled at Halliday, trading candid appraisal for candid appraisal.

"Owen Kane told you the Chief's letters were in Sean Finnegan's casket."

"So?" Halliday waved away the charge. "What business is it of yours if he did? Perhaps Kane is more loyal to the Crown than you imagined. Perhaps, in exchange for a little English appreciation . . ."

"In exchange for a little English money is what you mean." Mick eyed Halliday with disgust. "He's in your pay. I've no doubt of that. And in return, he tells you all you want to know. He's sold out his country, sold out the Chief, even sold out the Fenians, though they're the ones he professes to support. All for the sake of a few pounds."

Halliday flicked a piece of lint from the leg of his silk pajamas. "I really don't see what that has to do with me. Kane's treachery is none of your business."

"But your own treachery is."

This indictment was too blunt to accept passively. Halliday bounded from his chair and came to stand before Mick, his face screwed into a mask of outrage and resentment. "What proof do you have—"

"All the proof I'm likely to require." Mick turned away. He did not need to look at Halliday any longer. He had seen the truth in that one brief flash of emotion, seen it as surely as if it had been proclaimed in gold letters for all to read. And if there was no proof? Mick dismissed the problem without another thought. Of course there was no proof. But Freddy Halliday didn't have to know it.

It was madness to try and deceive a man as crafty as Halliday. Mick was certain of that. It was madness to try and best him at his own game. It was greater madness still to walk into the arms of the enemy with nothing to protect you but the quickness of your own mind and the picture of the woman you loved blazing in your heart. Madness. All of it, madness. But he had never been more sure of himself.

Before a smile could crack the somber expression on his face, Mick pulled himself up to his full height and whirled back to face Halliday, his voice steady, the unwavering assurance in his eyes the perfect disguise for his deception. "Kane feeds you information, and you do the same for him," Mick said. "How else did he know I'd escaped from the police? I can go to your superiors with my story or . . ."

"Or?" Halliday's voice brightened. "What are you proposing? What is it you want?"

"There's only one thing I want." Mick forced the words past the swell of affection that tightened round his heart. "Julia," he said simply, refusing to back down from the insinuation that flashed in Halliday's eyes as he spoke her name. "I want Julia. And Owen Kane has her."

"Does he?" Halliday looked genuinely surprised. His discomfort vanished and he laughed out loud, his even white teeth sparkling with the light of the fire. "Does he really? And, let me guess, you want me to get her back for you. You want me to talk to Kane, to show him the error of his ways." When Mick did not respond, he breezed on.

"I could do that, of course. I must confess, the thought intrigues me. Freddy Halliday, the peacemaker. It has a nice ring to it, doesn't it?"

Still chuckling, Halliday crossed to the marble-topped sideboard and poured himself a glass of brandy. He raised it in a mock toast and downed it in one gulp, refilling it before he spoke again. "Why?" he asked. "Why is Kane holding Julia? Don't play me for a fool," he added quickly when Mick did not reply. "If you expect me to help, you owe me that much at least."

Mick bobbed his head, a curt motion that signaled his agreement. "Four years ago," he began, "I escaped from prison in Ireland."

"Tell me something new!" Halliday sipped his brandy and smiled, rolling his gaze to the ceiling. "I know all about that. I was in Ireland myself at the time. If I recall correctly, you were tried for freeing two prisoners sentenced to death. And sentenced to hang yourself for your trouble. The night before your scheduled execution, the prison was raided by your Fenian comrades. You were freed. There were three Irish losses: your own brother-in-law, Martin O'Hearn, was one of them." Halliday lifted his eyebrows, watching Mick. When Mick refused to give him the satisfaction of a reaction, he continued. "The second was a lad of fourteen whose name I do not recall, and the third was John . . ." Halliday's face lit with delight. "John Kane," he said. "I'd forgotten. So that is why Owen Kane is so intent on revenge. I should have suspected as much, but I confess, I haven't had the time to waste thinking about it." He finished his drink and plunked his glass on the closest table.

"So Kane wants your neck because of his brother's death." Halliday laughed, the sound of it like a banshee's cry. "And he's taken Julia because . . ." He looked to Mick for the answer.

"Because he knows I'll come for her." There was no emotion in Mick's voice, no feelings surging through him as he spoke the words, only the certainty that he would save her. No matter the cost, he would save her.

"Charming." With one hand, Halliday rubbed his chin. "Utterly charming. So you want me to talk to Kane, to save the dear girl. Why not just go yourself?" He looked at Mick, still smiling. "Or are you afraid?"

Mick refused to take the bait. He smiled, the lopsided, insolent smile that always seemed to drive the British to distraction. "No more afraid of him than I am of you," he answered. "Being afraid of a man and not trusting him are two different things. One comes from cowardice, the other from caution. I'm not afraid of anything Owen might do to me, but I am afraid Julia won't come out of this alive."

"So you're asking for my help." Halliday tipped his head back, thinking, his words nearly lost beneath the satisfied laugh that rumbled from his chest. "This is too incredible, really too incredible." He straightened and wiped the smile from his face. "She is a charming girl. A charming English girl. It would be a shame to see her hurt because you Irish rabble can't seem to get along with civilized people, or with each other. Where is Owen keeping her?"

This was one question Mick had not anticipated and it raised the hair on the back of his neck. It was an old battle instinct, an instinct that surely warned of danger.

"I don't know yet," Mick admitted with perfect honesty. "I won't know until tomorrow. After that, we can go together to get her. Once she's safe—"

"Well, now you've come to it! I've been waiting to hear your bargain. Yes? Once she's safe, what? What do I get in return for my influence over Owen Kane?"

Mick gave Halliday a fixed look, his shoulders rigid, his back as straight as an arrow. "When Julia's safe," he said, "you get me. I'll turn myself in. Quietly. And I'll not try to escape again. You'll have all the glory of bringing an Irish fugitive to justice and I . . ." He paused for a moment and sucked in a deep breath, feeding his confidence. "I will have the satisfaction of trading my life for Julia's."

HER lower lip between her teeth, Julia closed her eyes and tried to concentrate.

"What you can't see with your eyes, you've got to see with your fingers."

She repeated Ben Jessup's advice beneath her breath, bracing her hands against the big brass door lock, hoping the sounds of her scratching were taken for nothing more than the scramblings of the mice who shared her miserable quarters.

The wire scraped and slipped inside the lock. It caught the spring, hooked the tumblers, and slid out again, uselessly.

Julia sat back on her heels, scowling through the dark at the length of curved wire in her hands, fighting to keep the swell of hysteria wedged beneath her heart from invading the rest of her body and affecting her dexterity. It was hard enough to pick a lock with a real lockpick, impossible to do it with trembling fingers and a bent earring.

"Tommy-rot!" She reproached herself for giving up so easily and attacked the lock again though her hands ached, her fingers raw and bleeding from where the length of wire had bitten into her skin.

Carefully feeling through the dark, Julia straightened the piece of wire beneath her boot and reshaped it, curling the end over into as neat a fishhook as could be formed in the blackness. Taking a deep breath to steady herself, she inserted the wire into the lock and touched it to the spring. There was a small, clicking sound and the knob turned in Julia's hands.

How such a simple thing as an unlocked door could have filled her with such inestimable happiness was as perplexing as the rush of tears that cascaded down her cheeks. Julia wiped them away with the sleeve of her blouse and, still kneeling, swung the door open and peeked into the passageway outside.

"Goin' somewhere?" The sound of Owen Kane's voice brought her bolting to her feet. He materialized from the direction of the stairway, the bull's-eye lantern in his hand blinding Julia to all but its bright beam of light.

"Looks like I got here just in time." Before she could dash back into the room and bang the door shut behind her,

Owen had his hand on her arm. He pulled her toward the stairway. "If you were on your way downstairs, that suits my purposes just fine. You see, it seems you have two gentlemen callers."

"I TOLD you she was unharmed."

With a grunt, Owen propelled Julia into the downstairs parlor. She skittered across the bare floor, her boots slipping on the discarded pieces of paper and the scraps of garbage strewn over the floorboards. She righted herself, her hand against the wall, and stared in wonder at the figure outlined in the flickering light of the candles.

"Mick?" Though Julia knew her voice did not sound the name, she formed it with her lips, her mouth suddenly dry with wonder, and relief, and fear. She managed a feeble smile, a smile that quavered on her lips before it faded beneath the look of stony solemnity on Mick's face.

His stance matched his expression. He stood perfectly still facing the doorway—perfectly still and perfectly straight, his shoulders back and steady, his head as high and rigid as if he had been frozen in ice. Only the raindrops that glistened upon the shoulders of his coat moved. As if the ice had begun to melt, they winked at her in the pasty light before they slid across his chest and dribbled to the floor.

Mick looked to Owen Kane, his voice as cold as his expression. "You say she's well. What does she say?" His gaze traveled to Julia, brushing her from head to toe with a look that spoke of the fire beneath the ice. "How are you, Julia? Has this sod—"

"He hasn't touched me." Julia rubbed the soreness from her arm where Owen's fingers had dug into her skin, and tossed Owen the kind of haughty look she had learned to use to her best advantage at her grandmother's knee. "No more than to drag me about from room to room."

Some of the tension faded from Mick's face. "That's

good," he said, eyeing Owen with open hostility. "For if he had, I'd have his guts for garters."

Owen grumbled a response, his top lip twisted, his fists raised and ready for a fight.

"Gentlemen, gentlemen."

Before either man could move, Freddy Halliday stepped in from the outside passageway, an amused smile on his face. "Can't you Irish get along for a few moments? Fighting already and we haven't even gotten down to business."

"Business?" The word sent a chill to the pit of Julia's stomach. She looked from man to man. "What business do you three have together? You have no business—"

"No business together but you." Halliday finished the sentence for her. With a weary sigh, he crossed the room and dropped into one of the chairs near the bare wooden table. Sitting at the head of the table so he could take them all in with one glance, he stripped off his leather gloves, flexed his fingers, and smiled over at Julia. "You are the business tonight, my dear. And a very profitable one it should be." He looked at Owen, still standing between Julia and the door. "For all of us."

"Yes." Owen ran his tongue over his lips and rubbed his meaty hands together. "You can have the girl. Just as we agreed when you arrived." He poked his chin at Julia before he shifted his gaze to Mick. "And I get him. A very profitable night, indeed."

His statement curled around Julia's heart, a claw of fear that clutched her insides and sent her blood rushing through her veins with frightening speed.

She looked at Mick, hoping he was not a party to it all, praying there was some other explanation that would account for Owen's contented smile. Mick did not respond, but merely stared at her, his face devoid of all expression, his eyes bright and blue with regret.

The truth shone there in his eyes, and Julia fought against

it instinctively. "No!" She slammed her hand on the table to punctuate the word. "I will not allow my freedom to be bought. Not at that price. I don't know why you're here, Freddy Halliday, but if you are a gentleman, you will refuse to participate in this ridiculous exchange. Trading one life for another is immoral, it—"

"Violates all the British Empire stands for? Oh, please!" Halliday rolled his eyes. "None of us are that gullible. Not even you, my dear. Besides"—he slapped the tabletop and rose—"we'll not be trading anything tonight. Or anyone. No." He held up one hand for silence when Owen made to speak. "I'm sorry, Kane, old man, but I'm quite adamant about this. I'm taking Miss Barrie, just as we agreed, but I'm not leaving O'Donnell for you. He's too valuable. Far too valuable to waste just to keep you quiet."

"What!" Owen's face reddened and he stepped toward Halliday, his fists level with his chest. "You thievin' Saxon. I thought we made a bargain. This girl for him." He shot a look at Mick. "And you agreed. You agreed to take the girl in exchange for his blood."

Halliday laughed in response, and Julia shivered, suddenly more unnerved by his cheerfulness than she had ever been by his animosity. She could read nothing beyond his smile, nothing beyond the cool inspection he directed at Owen, and she looked to Mick, hoping to find some answers.

Mick shook his head as her gaze met his, motioning with one small movement of his hand for her to stay put, to stay quiet.

Halliday laughed again, his malice aimed at Owen. "You really didn't think I'd let you have your way in this, did you, Kane?"

With a mumbled curse and sweep of his left arm, Owen thrust Julia aside and headed straight for Freddy Halliday. He took no more than a step or two when he stopped. His face paled, his eye grew round with terror, his lips quivered, the thick stripe of perspiration that sprang to his top lip gleaming in the yellow light like a glossy moustache. Owen fell back, and the light of the candles glinted against the barrel of the revolver Halliday clutched in his right hand.

He waved the pistol in Mick's direction before he leveled it at Owen's chest. "You've gotten sloppy," he said, his voice as steady as the hand that held the gun. "You've gotten careless. You've let your own desire for revenge jeopardize everything we've worked for these past years. I can't allow it, Kane. I simply can't allow it."

"And you say the Irish are balmy!" Mick roared with laughter. He stood with one hand against the fireplace mantel, the other clasped to the front of his coat, as if the jest were far too hilarious to believe. "Stop acting the fool, Halliday. You've proved your point. You are the almighty Englishman," he pronounced with a sweeping gesture. "And Kane here is just a poor gomus. Fine. Good. Now let's have this over with, shall we? It's late." Mick yawned behind his hand. "It's late and you've won. Julia looks as tired as yesterday's breakfast and I'd not be opposed to laying my own head down on a nice, comfortable prison pillow right about now."

With each word he spoke, Mick took another step closer, skirting the table until he was no more than three paces from Halliday.

"You've won," he repeated, smiling down at the Englishman, and making another gesture with his hand. "You get me to parade before a properly outraged public. You keep Owen working for you, telling you every step the Fenians are about to take. You show Julia the error of her ways so she is accepted back into polite society. We all live happily ever after. Now put away the gun and let's get out of this rattrap. It smells like cheap whisky in here and there's nothing an Irishman hates more than cheap whisky—unless it's no whisky at all."

None of Mick's amusement was reflected on the faces of

the others in the room. Halliday continued to glare at Owen, his face scarlet with the flame of reflected candlelight. Owen continued to gape. Only Julia showed any signs of understanding. Her face radiant with comprehension, she followed Mick's hand signals and his gaze to the corridor.

Good. Mick smiled to himself. She knew what he was trying to do. She knew he wanted her to run outside while he kept Halliday and Owen busy. Under his breath, Mick whispered a litany of thanks to every saint he could remember, and promised those he couldn't recollect that he would pray to them later.

He made another small gesture with his hand, waving Julia toward the door. She watched him, her chin tight with determination, her cheeks flushed with courage. She watched him. And decisively shook her head.

Mick looked at her in wonder. No? What did the woman mean, no? No, she would not take the opportunity to escape? No, she would not take advantage of Mick's ridiculous prattling to run away as fast as she could?

No. The thought struck Mick somewhere between his heart and his stomach, and he fought to keep himself firmly in place though he longed to cross the room and shake some sense into the girl.

She was telling him she would not leave, pure and simple. He could read that much in the damned stubborn tilt of her chin, see it in the firm set of her shoulders, sense it in the thin, willful line of her mouth. Hell and damnation! She was telling him she would not escape. Not without him.

Mick cursed silently and reminded all the saints he'd prayed to earlier that they were falling down on their jobs. Miracles were their speciality, were they not? Well, he needed a miracle now. A miracle to knock some reasoning into Julia's head. A miracle to get them both out of here alive.

Before Mick could speak again, Owen's voice crackled through the room. "Is this any way to treat an old comrade?'' he asked Halliday. ''Wavin' a gun in my face when I've never done nothin' but what's right by you. I've earned you money, Halliday. Money for the information I've given you to sell and more money still for the weapons you've confiscated from the Fenians and sold yourself before the government could get ahold of 'em. You've a valuable ally in me, Halliday. A valuable friend.''

''Friend?'' Halliday snickered. ''Do you really think you're my friend, Irishman? We may have mutual interests. But we are hardly friends.''

''You're more my friend than you are his.'' Owen's voice was laden with the sting of Halliday's insult. He looked at Mick. ''He's done nothin' but work against you all these years, just as he's tryin' to do now. Motionin' to the girl behind your back. Urgin' her toward the door while we're busy fightin' among ourselves. There. I've told you that much. And that's the act of a friend for certain.''

As graceful as a dancer, Halliday backed away a step and turned, putting Mick again in his line of vision.

''He has been my enemy,'' Halliday said, jabbing the pistol in Mick's direction before he pointed it again at Owen. ''But you, Kane, you have been a fool. I've played my connection to you for all it's worth. You're useless to me now.''

''I demand my revenge! I demand his blood in return for the blood of my brother, John!'' Owen pulled back his shoulders and pointed toward Mick, his hand trembling. ''If he hadn't been stupid enough to be captured, we wouldn't have needed to put our own necks on the line to save him. He killed John as sure as I'm standing here.''

''I killed John.''

Freddy Halliday's statement stunned them all into silence.

''What are you saying?'' Owen was the first to recover. He spluttered at Halliday, his fleshy face filled with confusion. ''We worked together even then, you tellin' me the British plans, me givin' you as much as I could about the Fenians. Are you saying—''

"I'm saying John's death was meant to be a message. A message for you, Owen Kane. You obviously weren't paying attention, just as you obviously never stopped to think how your mission to rescue O'Donnell turned into such a disaster. Haven't you ever questioned how the soldiers knew you were coming? Haven't you ever wondered how they found out about your midnight raid?''

Owen was too shocked to speak. His mouth opened, but no more came out than an outraged snarl.

"I told them,'' Halliday said, pronouncing each word distinctly so Owen could not fail to hear and understand. "I betrayed your mission. I needed a favor from the commander of the British garrison, so I bought one. Bought it with the information you handed me on a silver platter.''

Halliday's fingers tightened on the revolver until his knuckles were white. "Didn't you ever wonder why John was killed and not you, though he stood right beside you?'' he asked. "It wasn't a random shot. That was my message for you. My message to tell you to behave yourself. And listen to everything I said. And never, never to let your personal interests take precedence over our business together. You didn't listen. You didn't understand. Tonight, you must pay the price.''

Owen's scream of protest was lost beneath the discharge of Halliday's revolver. It exploded through the room along with Owen's howl of anguish, so loud, Julia covered her ears and closed her eyes. When she dared open them again, Halliday was standing over Owen's body, carefully keeping the legs of his trousers away from the bright red stain that soaked the front of Owen's shirt just above his heart. He had already turned the gun on Mick.

Julia's stomach turned over inside her and she clutched her hands together at her waist, forcing her panic and disgust to the back of her mind. She must remain calm, she told herself, her gaze searching Mick's for comfort, but finding instead only caution. She shuddered when Halliday nudged Owen's body with the tip of his highly polished boot, and recoiled when he grinned, satisfied the man was dead.

There was little remorse on Halliday's face. "Nasty business," he said, stepping around the body. "But I think you'll agree, O'Donnell, something had to be done. The man was a nuisance and I'm well rid of him. But you . . . you have been so much more than a nuisance, I'm going to enjoy this immensely. And the real beauty of the whole scheme is that no one will care. What's two less Irishmen in the world? The police will find your bodies—eventually— and what happened will be obvious. Killed each other in a fight. You killed him with this," Halliday explained, waving the first pistol at Mick. "And he killed you with this." He pulled another, smaller gun from his pocket and deftly switched hands so he was holding it in his right hand. He clicked his tongue. "Typical Irish. They are such an uncivilized race."

There was no time to consider the consequences and Julia did not even try. She pushed past Halliday and stood in front of Mick, shielding him with her body. She heard him grumble behind her, felt his hands tighten round her waist ready to thrust her aside, but she planted her feet and held her ground.

"No!" she said, grinding the word between her teeth. "You will not touch him."

Mick took a step to the side and Julia countered it perfectly, keeping herself squarely between him and the barrel of Freddy Halliday's gun.

"Holy Mother of God!" Mick muttered. "If you think I need a woman to protect me—"

"It seems you do." Halliday laughed out loud. "Good heavens, but this has turned into a charming little domestic comedy. Really, my dear," he said to Julia, "your loving concern is touching, but I cannot let you sacrifice yourself. I have other plans for you. So if you'll simply step aside, we can rid ourselves of this troublesome Irishman and make our way to Yorkshire. It seems your grandmother has been looking for you.''

"Tommy-rot!" Julia gave Halliday a bitter look. "She no more wants to see me again than I want to see her."

"Oh, but she does. And when you find out why, perhaps you'll realize it isn't in your best interests to waste your life protecting Irish rabble. You see, my dear, you are a very rich woman. A very rich woman, indeed."

Without responding, Julia crossed her arms over her chest.

Halliday seemed unconcerned by her skepticism. "You remember, when you were first captured at the Beechers', I was very surprised to find out who you were. I did some investigating after your escape in Redruth and found out your grandmother has been looking for you. Seems there's a will . . ."

This time, Julia could not control her disbelief. "A will? If my grandmother has a will, I'm certain I'm no part of it."

"It isn't your grandmother's will," Halliday shot back. "It's Donald Barrie's will."

The mention of her father's name sent a shiver through Julia. As if he sensed her uneasiness, Mick brought his hands to her shoulders and settled them there. She did not move to shake them off.

"My father's been dead for twenty-one years," she said, hoping her voice did not betray the anguish she felt chipping away at her heart when she thought of him. "If he left a will, it was read then. There's nothing new you can tell me."

"That is where you're wrong." Halliday fought to school his impatience. He shifted the gun in his hand, settling his fingers more comfortably against the trigger. "I can tell you something you never knew," he purred, his words rushing between his teeth like the noise of steam pouring from an engine.

"I can tell you that when your grandfather died, he didn't leave his estate to your grandmother. Margaret Barrie was the trustee, nothing more. That is news to you. I can tell by the look in your eyes. When your grandfather died, he left his estate to your father. Your grandmother knew it, of course, though she wasn't about to tell anyone. She intended to turn everything over to your father once he was of age, but when he married your mother . . ." Halliday lifted his shoulders in an elegant little gesture of disdain designed to show just how unsuitable he thought the alliance.

"When Donald Barrie . . . died"—he stressed the word just enough for Julia to know he had learned the circumstances of her father's death—"when he died, your grandmother thought it was a moot subject. Donald was gone. The estate was hers. What she didn't know was that he made a will just before you were born. His solicitor's had it since, with strict instructions not to open it until your twenty-first birthday. Everything your grandfather left—the mills, the estates, the mines, all that money—everything, Julia, everything is yours."

Julia raised her head and looked him in the eye. "And if I refuse it? The money brings my grandmother far more pleasure than I ever did. Let her keep it."

Halliday chuckled. "She can't. It seems your father made one last provision. If you predeceased him, or refused the inheritance for any reason, all the money was to be left to an actors' charity in London. Imagine what the old lady thought when she found that out! No, no, my dear. Without you, your grandmother is penniless. Now that you are of age, she has no control over any of it. Not until—"

"Not until you bring Julia to her." Mick pulled Julia nearer, his hands sliding up and down her arms, offering comfort and courage. "What will the old lady do to her?"

he demanded. "Force her to turn over all of it to her? Threaten her? And then where's Julia's safety?"

"You tell the girl, O'Donnell. That's what I've been trying to point out all along. Your grandmother wants you back," Halliday said to Julia, "so you can sign all the assets over to her. Obviously once you do, the old lady will get rid of you in a moment. But if you don't sign the document your grandmother had drawn up, you simply assume responsibility for the family fortune . . ." He paused, giving her time to consider.

"Part of what you own is in Ireland," he said after he'd decided she'd had long enough to think. "Part of what you've inherited are the lands from which Teague Finnegan and the rest of them were evicted. There's a great deal of good you could do in Ireland with your newfound fortune, Julia. A great deal of good you could do for—"

"For you?" Julia reproached him. "Is that the arrangement you made with her? Were you to bring me back and share in my inheritance?"

Halliday's face darkened. "Why do you think I even agreed to help with this ridiculous, melodramatic rescue? If I bring you to your grandmother, she has promised me a sizable reward. If I help you gain control of what is rightly yours, why shouldn't you thank me just as she is willing to do? If not for me, you wouldn't even know about the money and the land."

Mick did not need to see Julia's face to know she was angry. He could feel her outrage in the tensed muscles of her shoulders, tell it from her abrupt intake of breath, read it in the sharp tilt of her head. He pulled her back against him, hoping to keep her safe, at least for the moment.

She would have none of it.

She moved a step closer to Freddy Halliday, ignoring the gun and looking him in the eye. "Why should I trust you?" she asked. "I've yet to hear you speak the truth."

Holy Mother! Mick groaned. He thought he was a poor

politician. At least he wasn't fool enough to insult a man holding a gun.

"Julia!" Mick tried to tug her back into the protective circle of his arms, but she stood her ground, looking more the untamed Gypsy than ever, her eyes ablaze, her cheeks aflame, her hair loose and wild around her shoulders.

She glared at Halliday. "Well? Tell me, Mr. Halliday, why should I trust you?"

Halliday obviously found the question both confusing and unexpected. He opened his mouth to answer, then snapped it shut again. For a moment, Mick was tempted to laugh. He looked less like a gentleman and more like a fish just netted and gasping for breath on the shore.

Mick had no more than a moment to consider Julia's challenge or Freddy Halliday's answer to it. Out of the corner of his eye, he caught sight of something in the passageway, something that moved like a phantom in the deep shadows just beyond the open doorway.

He was about to dismiss the sight as nothing more than a trick of his imagination, when he saw it again—a shifting of the shadows, a glint that flashed briefly in the light of the candles, as if something hard and lustrous was being tossed from hand to hand. If the specter made a sound, it was lost in the noise of Halliday's rough breathing.

The Englishman was still staring at Julia, so incensed by her impertinence, he could only gape, and wait for her to withdraw her challenge.

Mick might have known Julia would not give him the satisfaction. They stood toe to toe trading scowls, and Mick had another chance to look outside. For the briefest of seconds, the shadow moved into the light and Mick grumbled with annoyance. He had left strict instructions with Teague. He was not to be followed. Yet here was the old man outside the door, his sturdy blackthorn walking stick in his hands, waiting for Mick's signal to attack.

Try as he might, Mick could not stay irritated for long,

not when his and Julia's salvation rested in Teague's gnarled hands. He breathed a sigh of relief. Perhaps miracles came each in their own form and shape.

Mick realized Halliday could not have noticed Teague, his back was to the door, and if Julia saw him, she covered her surprise as deftly as a seasoned actress.

She pulled herself up to her full height. "Well?"

Halliday looked away. "You can't trust me," he said, sounding as petulant as a child who'd just had a favorite toy taken away. "But you can rely on the fact that I think first and foremost of one person—myself. If you sweeten the pot, guarantee me more than your grandmother has promised, I will work for you in this."

Julia nodded. "Then we shall leave for Yorkshire in the morning, but not until you promise that you will never bother the Irish again."

"I—"

She cut off Halliday's complaint before he had a chance to voice it. "I will provide you more than enough money," she assured him. "You will be able to live quite comfortably without your position at the Home Office."

Mick grumbled a curse. "What difference does it make? There will be more after him. They reproduce like vermin, these so-called patriots who build their bloody empire on the bones of our people."

Julia silenced him with a look. "That is a problem for another day. For tonight . . ." She turned again to Halliday. "For tonight, you will vow to let Mr. O'Donnell leave. Unharmed. And you will swear never to disturb him again."

For just a second, Halliday seemed about to object. He collected himself before the damning words were out of his mouth. "It's a shame," he said to Mick. "I had thought to cap my career tonight. How I wish I could have eliminated you like I did the others. O'Hearn, Kane, Finnegan . . ." He smiled. "You didn't know I was the one who killed Sean, did you? Perhaps if you did, you wouldn't have been so eager to work with me tonight. A brilliant career, all for nought. Ah well, I have my memories.''

"Here's something to remember, you murderin' Saxon. Here's something for my son, Sean.''

Teague Finnegan bolted into the room, his blackthorn stick raised above his head, his face twisted with hatred and the thirst of revenge.

With a cry of surprise, Halliday turned to face him, snatching Julia and holding her in front of him for protection. He slipped in the puddle of raindrops that had dripped from his coat, lost his footing, and fought to right himself, the gun dangerously close to Julia's head.

Mick did not hesitate. He grabbed Julia and threw her to the floor just as Halliday pulled the trigger. Teague's cry of vengeance and the report of the revolver fused into one sound of horror, and the bullet flew past, only inches from Julia's head. Still, Mick did not loosen his hold. He wrapped his arms tighter around Julia and crushed her to him, sheltering her from the torrent of blood that rained down when Teague's stick smashed into Halliday's head and shattered it like a melon.

Chapter 18

I⊤ was neither the feel of the cold rain on her face nor the howl of the brisk wind that finally roused Julia. It was the sound of Mick's voice.

"Just a short way to go, *acushla*," he whispered into her ear, his words as warm and gentle as a summer's day.

Too numb to answer, she nodded in reply, and smiled weakly in response to the grin that banished the solemnity from Mick's face. He pulled her closer, tucking her under his arm as if she'd been made to fit there, and urged her along the footpath.

She remembered little else of the journey—the lights of Hatchett's Hotel blinking at her like faded stars through the fog, the odd looks directed at them from the desk clerks when they came in out of the rain, the blessed sound of the hotel room door closing, its fastness securing them against the outside world.

Her hands extended toward the fire already burning in the grate, Julia sighed and dropped onto the sofa.

Mick was beside her in an instant. Somehow, though she didn't remember putting it on, she was wearing his coat, and he tugged it from her arms and tossed it onto the nearest chair.

"Are you all right? You've had a shock, for certain," he said, plucking strands of wet hair from her eyes and tucking them behind her ears. "I shouldn't have made you come away so quickly, but we couldn't stay there. We—"

"Teague?" As if waking from a deep and troubled sleep, Julia looked around, her eyes wide with worry. "Is Teague here? Is he . . ."

"Teague is well, but he isn't here." Mick chafed her hands between his. "He's gone to fetch Kate. I've told them to go to her sister's in Liverpool for a few weeks. They'll be safer there. But you—"

"I'm fine. Really." With a shudder, Julia banished the memories and sat up. "It's just that . . ."

She could not continue the thought. There were no words for the emotions that racketed through her, no phrases that could adequately express her horror, or her worry, or the feeling of overpowering relief that threatened to snatch away her breath and reduce her to tears. She did not try to speak. She fell, instead, into Mick's open arms and brought her mouth to his.

His kiss was as comforting as a balm, as soothing as fire on a cold day, like sunshine after a storm. It stilled her worries and cheered her heart.

Julia edged closer. Mick's skin was cold, but his mouth was warm. He flicked away the raindrops from around her lips with his tongue, pulling her to him until she was crushed against his chest.

"You're soaked." Julia drew away long enough to scold him. "You'll catch your death. Why did you let me have the coat?"

"I couldn't find your coat, so I gave you mine." Mick sat back, exasperated. "You're complaining about a coat when you were senseless enough to try and exchange your own life."

"Me?" Julia looked at him in wonder. "You were the one who came marching in there, prepared to trade yourself for me. You could have been killed. If you'd given me more time, everything would have been fine. I had the situation in hand. I had already picked the lock on the door and was on my way out when—''

Mick mumbled a word in Gaelic that Julia did not understand. Something told her it was just as well.

''Saints above!'' He jumped from the sofa and stood glaring down at her. ''We'd both be dead now if it weren't for Teague. What sort of madwoman are you, standing up to a man holding a gun?''

''He was holding the gun on you, not me.'' Julia rose to face him. ''No English gentleman would ever shoot a lady.''

''No English gentleman would ever— Holy Mary! You're as daft as they come.'' Mick shook his head, marveling at her simplicity. ''Freddy Halliday was no gentleman. And the only reason he didn't shoot you was because he wanted to get you back to your grandmother and earn himself a few pounds for his trouble. How you knew that—''

''I didn't.'' Annoyed beyond measure, Julia nearly screamed. She controlled her temper at the same time she fought to control the rush of tears that sprang to her eyes. ''I didn't know about the will, and I wouldn't have cared if I did.''

A sudden, desperate longing drained her irritation. Left in its wake was one crystalline realization, an awareness that choked her words and squeezed her heart with emotion nearly too powerful to speak. ''I only knew what I was feeling,'' she told him. ''That you were in trouble. That you needed help. That I couldn't live without you, Mick. That I wouldn't even want to try.''

''Saints and angels!'' All the bluster was gone from Mick. He whispered the oath beneath his breath, his words shaded with more relief than irritation. An uncertain smile playing around the corners of his mouth, he took one tentative step toward Julia. ''What are you saying?''

''I'm saying nothing else matters in all the world but you,

Mick O'Donnell.'' Julia stepped forward to meet him, so filled with certainty, she held her head high and straight, so overwhelmed with emotion, her voice trembled. "Not my grandmother's money, or my upbringing. Not who you are, or who you say you are. Not even Charles Stewart Parnell, or his letters, or Ireland.''

"I would still give my life for Ireland.'' Mick broke in, his voice rich with intensity, his face charged with stubborn insistence. The next second, his fervor quieted and he caught her hand in his and brought it to his chest. "I would still give my life for Ireland,'' he repeated, his voice suddenly as soft as the look in his eyes. "But my heart I give to you.''

Julia flattened her hand against his chest, and the strong steady beat of his heart vibrated through her fingertips. She closed her eyes, feeling each pulse and recognizing in it the echo of her own heart.

The time for talking was past. Mick slipped one arm around Julia's waist and pulled her closer, bending his head to cover her lips with his own. He felt her tremble, felt the eager response of her lips, the exquisite softness of her as she melted against him. His heart leapt at the same time his body responded to the compelling tug of desire.

Julia shivered and Mick stopped his hungry search of her mouth long enough to smile down at her.

"Oh, hell, I'm getting you all soggy.'' His smile turned into a grimace and he held her at arm's length long enough to assess the damage, deciding with another, much more suggestive smile that perhaps getting her wet was not such a bad thing.

The water soaking his shirt had saturated Julia's blouse. The fabric clung to each delicious curve, accentuating her waist, delineating her arms, outlining her breasts until he could see the roundness of her nipples beneath the delicate white fabric.

Mick sucked in a breath, struggling to steady himself. It

was no use. He abandoned all pretense of restraint, reaching for her and caressing first one breast, then the other.

"I thought I'd never hold you again." He pulled her into the shelter of his arms, his voice a silky whisper against the softness of her neck. "I feared I'd never kiss you or love you again and I nearly went mad from the thought." He trailed a line of kisses along her neck before he took her lips with his again.

There was no way to steady the whirling in her head, and Julia did not even try. She leaned against Mick, hoping to keep herself upright though the sensations caused by his lips threatened to destroy her equilibrium. His clothes were wet and very cold, and Julia smiled to herself, surprised that a feeling so decidedly uncomfortable could also be so reassuring and, at the same time, so strangely tantalizing.

The rough fabric of his shirt scraped against her dampened blouse, the sodden legs of his trousers soaked her gown when he lifted her against him, his thigh tucked between her legs.

It didn't matter. None of it mattered—not the wet or the cold. Nothing mattered but this time and this place and the feel of Mick's muscles, taut and hard beneath her fingers. His touch spread fire as he moved his hands over her body from her arms to her back, from her waist to her breasts.

If there was a world outside his arms, she did not know it. If there were sounds other than the harsh whispers of their own breaths, mingling as one, she would not have heard. Julia raked her fingers through Mick's hair, drops of water sliding over her hands like beads. She tightened her hold, her hips swaying in time to a primitive, inescapable rhythm.

He bent to move his mouth to her breast, nibbling her with teeth and tongue until she groaned with pleasure.

"Mick." Julia's voice was rough with need. She pulled at his shirt, fighting to undo his buttons though her legs felt as shaky as a newborn kitten's.

Mick took a step back, smiling down at her with a look

that glowed with delight, and happiness, and adoration. "Bold as brass. That's for certain. Do you remember when I told you as much?" He ran his hands from her shoulders to her breasts and stroked them with his thumbs, and his smile widened when she caught her lower lip in her teeth and sighed.

"Bold as brass." He chuckled. He kissed the tip of her nose and, wrapping one arm around her waist, led her to the bed.

"You never told me if your hand shows anything about me." Mick ran his tongue across Julia's palm and up to the tip of her longest finger.

Julia wriggled beneath the weight of his body and laughed, her voice as light and airy as the feeling of contentment that filled her insides with warmth. "I don't need to read my palm to know about you," she assured him, her eyes sparkling with delight.

Reclaiming her hand, she grazed it along Mick's arm and up to his shoulder. In spite of the early morning chill, his skin was slick with a fine sheen of perspiration and still hot from the exertion of their lovemaking. With her forefinger, she whisked a drop of sweat from near his collarbone and gave him a sly, tantalizing look. "I don't need spirits and the supernatural to tell me about you. I know all about you."

"Do you now?" Even through the early morning shadows, she knew he was grinning down at her and she returned the smile. When he slid away to lie next to her, she turned on her side. Ruffling her hands through his hair, she settled them around his neck, her fingers locked together.

"Oh, yes. I know you're still shy," she told him. "You absolutely refused to light the lamp when you got undressed last night. And I know you're gentle, and quite amusing, and a very, very good kisser."

Mick nodded solemnly. "That's me right enough."

"I know you like this." Julia sprinkled a line of light kisses up his neck and around his ear. "And this." She traced his lips with her tongue. "And this." She skimmed her hands down the slope of his spine, stroking his backside through the bedclothes and smiling to herself when he groaned.

Lulled into contentment, Mick closed his eyes. Julia lowered her voice until it was no more than a whisper. "I know you'd like me to help get your letters back."

"Bedad!" The smile on Mick's face dissolved and he flopped back on his pillow, his arms crossed over his chest. "You've learned that sure enough, haven't you?"

Julia plumped her own pillow and sat up, her knees bent, the blankets gathered around her. "I don't know what you mean," she insisted, fighting to keep a smile from her face.

"I mean you've learned the ways of a crafty woman. Distract me with kisses and other things . . ." He swatted Julia's hand away when it wandered over his abdomen. "Distract me, and then ask for something you know I can't give. It's disgraceful, that's what it is, and you'll come to no good by it, Julia Barrie."

"Indeed." Julia tossed her head. "You sound as cross as Mrs. Dean when I was a girl and she found I'd raided the larder. If you'd only let me help—"

"If I let you help, you'd be back in trouble as certain as I'm lying here." Mick's voice rose louder than he intended. He fought to control his temper. It was of little use. "Those who knew about your involvement with the letters have been gotten rid of," he reminded her, his words pointed and as biting as a well-honed knife. "Let's leave it at that."

Julia grumbled and looked away.

Damnation! Mick pursed his lips and muttered an oath. This was the wrong time for a barney, that was for certain, as certain as the fact that Julia thrived on being irrational, stubborn, and unreasonable.

As irrational as she was beautiful?

The thought materialized inside Mick's head, as unexpected and just as unnerving as the fabricated spirits he suspected Julia conjured at her séances. But before he could stop it, the question had established itself firmly in his mind, pestering him without end.

Out of the corner of his eye, Mick took a long look at Julia. She sat with her back against the bed board, her face illuminated by the morning light just beginning to filter through the draperies. Her lips were pinched, her arms straight at her sides, holding the blankets close against herself as if they could deflect his angry words.

Her lips were red and moist and still swollen from the intensity of his kisses. Her breasts pressed against the blankets with each quick, sharp breath she took. Her hair was loose, a waterfall of curls and ebony ringlets that cascaded around her shoulders and dipped over one side of her face, casting it into shadows nearly as mysterious and intriguing as her dark eyes.

Was she as irrational as she was beautiful?

Mick swore softly and turned his head away, purposely shutting out the sight of the woman at his side. It was bad enough his conscience pricked him for being too quick-tempered, worse still when he looked at her sitting there, offended, aggravated, but ever proud, and his heart melted like a candle left too long in the sun.

Try as he might, he could not block out the picture of her face, nor ignore the bewitching memory of her kiss. He turned back to her, smiling ruefully. There never was a woman more beautiful, he decided, savoring the sight of her. There never could be a woman more beautiful, just as there never could be one more clever, or more courageous, or more dear to his heart.

He rolled to his side and drummed his fingers up and down Julia's leg, trying to soothe and distract her.

"I've given the Chief my solemn assurance he'll have his letters back before a fortnight's over," Mick said, keeping his voice as even as he could manage. "That will be an end to this business, once and for all, and we can stop bickering about it and go on to bickering about something else."

He raised his eyebrows and smiled devilishly, but Julia did not respond to his attempts at humor. She picked at the blankets, her head thoughtfully to one side.

"How do you plan on getting the letters back?" she asked.

This, at least, was more to his liking. Mick sighed with relief. At least now Julia was being reasonable, logical. At least now she was asking his plans, not formulating her own.

"It's too late to go into service in the home where they're being kept," he told her. "We don't have much time before Parliament debates Home Rule again. As far as I can see, the best way to retrieve the letters is through a clever burglary."

"A burglary?" Julia shot him a look. "If you're caught—"

"If I'm caught . . . well." Mick shrugged. "I'd sooner die a prisoner than a coward."

Julia's face paled, her eyes widened, and Mick raised himself on his elbows long enough to plant a quick kiss on her lips. "I won't be caught," he promised. Stroking one finger across her cheek, he captured her gaze with his own. "I will be as careful as a cat and as quiet as a mouse, and I swear, I will come back to you."

Her expression did not lighten as he expected it would. Julia continued to consider the problem for a few long, quiet minutes. Finally, she tossed her hair over her shoulder and looked at Mick levelly.

"Where are the letters?" she asked.

"At a place the Saxons think I'll never find them, fools that they are. They've given them to the sister of one of the Home Office fellows. A lady named Ashcroft."

"Ashcroft?" Julia bolted upright, her eyes wide. "Dolly Ashcroft?"

"That's the one." A look that was a mixture of anxiety and curiosity crossed Mick's face. "You know her? Is she one of your fine and fancy friends?"

"No. We couldn't be that lucky. I don't know Dolly Ashcroft, but I know of her. She's—"

"She's Lord Darnell Whiteburn's sister." Mick plopped back on his pillow. "There's no more to it than that. She's a society lady, one of them more interested in parties and horseflesh than in anything that really matters in life."

"She's one of the country's leading advocates of spiritualism."

This was news to Mick. Julia could tell that much from his stunned expression. She smiled down at him, as pleased with herself as she was at his reaction.

It took no more than a moment for him to recover. His lips thinned and he eyed her cautiously. "How would you be knowing a thing like that?"

Julia threw him a look. "I am the great Madame Krakowska, am I not?" she asked, slipping into her Eastern European accent with ease. "It is my business to know these things." As quickly as she assumed it, she abandoned the accent. Her face lit with excitement and she scooted to her knees. "Mick, we could get her to invite me to conduct a séance. I know we could."

Before he could object, she rushed through her reasoning, both of her hands on one of Mick's arms, her eyes aglow. "I could conduct a séance. That would get us in the house. Then you could—"

"I don't think so." Mick shook his head. "There's no need for you to be involved."

"You said a clever burglary." Julia sat back on her heels and glared at him. "Well, Mick O'Donnell, this sounds as clever as any burglary I've heard tell of. You could get the letters while I keep everyone in the house distracted. You could—"

"I could do it all myself." The apprehension cleared

from Mick's face and he sat up. "You could teach me, couldn't you? You could teach me enough so that I could be invited in for a reading, or a séance, or whatever the hell you call it. Then, when it's over . . ." He paused, working through his plan in his mind, as serious and contemplative as Julia had ever seen him.

For a moment, she was tempted to laugh out loud. The idea that he could learn enough about fortune-telling in two weeks' time to deceive Dolly Ashcroft was as ridiculous as it was frightening. He would be found out, found out and certainly captured.

The thought cut through her as sharp and cold as a winter wind, and she shivered. "No." She watched the expression in Mick's eyes darken and hurried on before he could protest further. "You couldn't. You wouldn't know how. You wouldn't know what to do."

"You could show me." Mick sat up to face her, ignoring her protests, his voice ringing with confidence.

"No," Julia said again. She pounded her fist on the bed to emphasize her point. The sudden movement shifted the blankets and they slid from around her shoulders, baring her breasts to the morning light.

She did not move to cover herself. She straightened her back and snapped her eyes to Mick's, watching and waiting for his reaction.

Saints and angels! Mick sucked in an uneven breath and his gaze slid from Julia's eyes, to her mouth, to her throat, and drifted even farther.

If he didn't know better, he might have suspected the slip of the blankets was more accidental than intentional. If he didn't know better.

Mick felt an unwelcome smile tug at the corners of his mouth. In spite of the deep red blush of Julia's cheeks and the small, embarrassed gasp that came from her parted lips, he knew better. He'd been outfoxed by a woman who was brazen enough to take advantage of his masculine needs and shameless enough to blush and pretend it was all by accident.

The thought should have made him angry. Instead, it sent a tingle of desire coursing through Mick, a slow, steady stream of heat that started in his stomach and radiated outward, igniting his heart, drawing him into an aching desire too powerful to ignore.

"It seems I've been bested by a master." He nodded his head, conceding defeat, and pulled his gaze back up to Julia's lips, wondering, despite his annoyance, how they'd taste when they were this red and moist.

She accepted his surrender with a smile and flicked her tongue over her lips, inviting him nearer.

"There's a clever way to end an argument," he acknowledged, sliding closer and gliding one arm around her. "And you're as pleased as Punch to think you've won, aren't you?" He pulled her to him, one hand at her back while with the other he stroked her skin, following the trail of sunlight across her shoulders and down to her abdomen.

"We'll make a pact right here and now, Julia," he said, his mouth descending to follow the path his hand had established. "You will teach me your magic. And I, I will teach you mine."

I⊤ was magic.

Not the clever sleight of hand and inventive prestidigitation Julia espoused, but magic nonetheless. A truer, more mysterious magic— the undeniable witchcraft that could be caused only by a man and a woman.

Mick opened his eyes and tried to get a glimpse of Julia's face. She was sitting not two feet from him, her knees pressed against his, her two hands over both his own. But he couldn't see her, the room was far too dark.

Though he understood the advantages of learning her fortune-teller's tricks with the lights off, the way they would be performed, he found the dark disconcerting. In the dark, it was too easy to let his mind wander, to ignore the tedious mysteries of the spirit world and think, instead, of the much more tantalizing prospects of the flesh.

He pushed the thought to the back of his mind, trying to picture Julia's face as he had seen it the last time she'd performed this trick. Her eyes would be closed, as they had been then, he knew. Her lips would be parted, her cheeks flushed with excitement. As she pretended to fall deeper and deeper into a psychic trance, her breathing would quicken.

He didn't have to try and imagine that, he could hear the soft, sighing sounds, so like the small, satisfied noises that escaped her when they made love.

Try as he might, Mick could not shrug off that disturbing thought, and he wondered briefly if she could feel the tingling jolt of desire that quickened his pulse and sent a revealing flush of heat all the way from the pit of his stomach to the tips of his fingers. In his mind he envisioned the front of Julia's high-collared, peacock-blue gown rising and falling in cadence to the rhythm of her breathing. Rising and falling. Rising and falling. With each intake of breath, the swell of her breasts taut against the shimmering fabric.

"Mick!"

He jumped at the sound of her voice.

"You haven't been listening to a thing I've said. I asked you, are my knees against yours?"

"Oh, yes." Mick pulled himself back to the present, answering without hesitation, certain he could not mistake a sensation that was so seemingly innocent and, at the same time, so delightfully intimate.

"And my hands. Are both my hands on top of yours?"

"Yes." Again he answered instantly. With no more than a slight lift of his fingers, he could feel the brush of her skin. Taking a deep breath, he fought to ignore his body's response to her touch and tried to concentrate on the lesson. "As sure as the Creed," he told her. "Both your hands are over mine."

"That is where you're wrong." He heard her chuckle. "Let's try one more time." She pulled her hands away and Mick felt, rather than saw, her peer at him through the dark. "Are your eyes closed?"

Feeling as guilty as a child caught in some minor mischief, he squeezed his eyes shut and waited patiently while Julia settled her hands over his again.

He heard her take a deep breath. "There. Now, tell me. Are both my hands occupied? Are they both on top of yours?"

Mick raised his fingers a fraction of an inch. "Yes."

"Could I possibly be doing anything else with my hands?

Could I be manipulating a trumpet to fly around the room? Could I be rapping against a table or chair?''

''Not likely. Unless you have another hand. Or an accomplice concealed somewhere in the room who's doing the rapping for you.''

''You're much too distrusting.'' Julia giggled, and Mick found himself pulling a sour smile, as annoyed by her humor as he was by his own apparent witlessness. She kept telling him how simple this all was, yet he had to confess, he had never been so baffled.

As if that weren't enough, he was also confused about Julia. She'd put up a hellish fuss about all this when he'd first proposed the idea, fought him tooth and nail every step of the way, insisting he could never master her tricks well enough to perform them in public, demanding that he give up the plan and admit that it was foolhardy, reckless, and dangerous.

Until two days ago.

Two days ago, Julia began to act as if the whole idea was nothing more than a lark. The color that had deserted her cheeks when he proposed the scheme had come back. So had the spring in her step, the enchanting little smiles she cast his way when she thought he was not watching. She was like a storm at sea, like one of those hurricanes he'd heard they had in places hot and tropical—blustery one minute and scolding him to abandon the plan, as calm as a church picnic the next.

Even their nights in bed had changed. A week ago, each time they made love was as intense as if it were the last. She knew he was embarking on a dangerous mission, knew he was walking into what could very well be a Saxon trap, and every kiss, every caress resounded her fear, like a bell tolling the death knell.

But last night . . . last night had been more like that first night in the tiny cave on the moor: reckless, lively, rollicking.

It was as if Julia knew what he was going to ask of her, and was as pleased as she could possibly be about it. It was as if she could read his mind.

Mick dismissed the notion with an irritated grunt. A change of heart, a change of attitude. That's all it was. No more real than this clever playacting. It had nothing to do with the powers Julia pretended to have, and everything to do with skillful magic. Like the malarkey she was trying to pretend now, it was all designed and executed to confound his reasoning and keep his mind in a puzzle.

The next moment, Mick heard a distinct rap from somewhere on his left, and all his sensible reasonings went scattering like snowflakes in a blizzard.

"Saints above!" Mick's eyes popped open, and he was tempted to sign himself with a cross. Though he could still feel Julia's knees pressed against his, still feel the tantalizing touch of her fingers, he heard another rap. Instantly, it was followed by another.

Mick swallowed his fears along with the descriptive curse he was tempted to mutter. The realization that Julia had outsmarted him again only served to increase his annoyance. Forcing himself to keep his hands still, his breathing steady, as if the unexpected events did not bother him in the least, he squinted through the darkness, hoping for some hint of what Julia was up to.

It was impossible to see more than the outline of her shoulders and head, impossible to imagine where the mysterious spirit message being tapped out even now was coming from. He knew one thing only—there were no spirits here, just as there were no accomplices hiding about, tapping on the floors. The origin of the disturbance must be with Julia herself.

As quickly as he could, Mick darted his left hand from under Julia's and made a grab at the darkness. His aim was flawless, his efforts, rewarded. Julia's right hand was at her side, tapping on the nearest table, and he grabbed it and held on tight.

Julia dissolved into laughter. "You're not supposed to touch the medium." Playfully, she slapped his hand away. "You see, that's how it's done. I move my hands gradually until my one hand is centered over both of yours. Fortunately, I have large hands, and while you think they're both occupied, I'm rapping on the nearest table. It works every time. Like magic."

"Magic." Mick grumbled the word beneath his breath and rose from his seat. He turned up the nearest gas jet, more to calm his nerves than because he was eager for the light.

"Damn it. I just can't stay interested in all this mumbo-jumbo," he said. "I start out listening, and the next thing I know . . . well, it just doesn't make any sense. None of it."

Julia let out a long sigh. "You're the one who wanted to learn about séances. I'm trying to teach you." She sounded much more aggrieved than she looked. While her shoulders were back, her voice tinged with exasperation, there were two bright spots of color in her cheeks and a tiny smile that tickled the corners of her mouth, raising her cheeks and making her eyes look more than ever like a cat's.

Her enthusiasm only served to increase Mick's aggravation and heighten his frustration. He walked the length of Kate's parlor and back again, his lips thinned with displeasure, his eyes sparking with impatience. With one hand, he massaged the tension from the back of his neck. "You've been trying to teach me this entire week and I'm not any further along than I was at the beginning. Even when you tell me how it's done, I simply don't understand any of it. Damn!" The oath exploded from him and he stalked across the room and came back to sit in the chair across from hers.

He leaned forward and took her hands in his, all the turbulence gone, as if he had expelled it along with the last, heartfelt oath. The shadows molded his face, underscoring the sudden look of tenderness that softened his eyes and brought a small, sad smile to his lips. "You're as precious as life to me, Julia," he said. "I'd sooner take off my own hand than put you at risk. But . . ."

Julia tightened her hold on his hands. She had never seen him so uncertain and the change was distressing and startling. She wound her fingers through his. "What do you mean?"

"I mean . . ." Mick looked up at the ceiling before he brought his gaze to hers again. "I mean, I know I insisted on doing this, conducting the séance, that is. I know we've made all the arrangements and they're expecting that Professor . . . Professor whatever you called him when you wrote to Dolly Ashcroft."

"Professor Von Trask."

"Von . . . whatever." Mick dismissed the notion with a shake of his head. "I'm saying, Julia, that I just can't do it."

Julia felt the color drain from her face. She didn't imagine she could possibly look as guilty as she felt. But if she did not, why was Mick staring at her so intently? She moistened her lips with her tongue. "Are you asking me to conduct the séance?"

Mick raised her hands to his lips and pressed a kiss on each. "If there was any other way . . . if there was someone else . . . I can't bear the thought of what could happen to you. There's so much for you in the world, a rich woman like you."

"A rich woman like me!" Julia could not have been more surprised if he'd started speaking Chinese. She looked at Mick in wonder, her mouth open, ready to protest, but she couldn't manage to find the proper words. After a moment, her sputterings shaped themselves in half-lucid thoughts.

"You can't possibly think my grandmother . . . you can't imagine that my father's money . . . You can't possibly believe the money I've inherited has anything to do with this?'' Though she'd hoped her words were no more than a statement of fact, they formed themselves into a question, and she waited for Mick to respond.

He did not. He sat in silence for a moment before he rose from his chair and went to the fireplace, both his hands on the mantel, his arms stiff, his back to her. When he spoke, his voice was heavy with regret.

''I think a lady who was everything in the world shouldn't risk herself for—''

''For what?'' Julia was beside him instantly, her voice no louder than the gas jets that hissed on the wall, not because she did not long to shout the words at him, but because it was impossible to speak above a whisper with a terrifying anxiety squeezing the air from her lungs. ''For all the things you've worked so hard for? The things you've risked your life to make happen? For the things Sean and Martin died for?''

Mick spun to her. ''How do you know about Martin?''

Instantly, Julia went on the defensive. Refusing to back down, she looked Mick in the eye. ''Teague told me. He told me how you risked your own life to save two men who were sentenced to death. He told me you were captured and how Martin and some others came for you and that three of them were killed.''

''He had no right.'' Mick took ahold of her arms and looked into her eyes, his own eyes glistening with remorse. ''If I was a fool in the past, it is no business of yours, or Teague's, or anyone else's. I was young and I didn't have the sense God gave a snail. I thought violence could change things, but I was wrong. The only change violence brings about is more violence, and the only thing it feeds on is the blood of the innocent.''

''You were a Fenian.'' She held Mick's gaze, refusing to let him turn from her, though he stepped back and made as if to push her away. Seizing his hands, she held him in place. "Teague told me that, too. He told me you had enough of their violence and renounced them as terrorists. He said that once you worked with Owen Kane."

"Dear Lord in heaven! Has my entire life been laid out for all of London to examine?" Mick looked at her, his eyes burning. "Did he tell you that when Martin died my sister Mary was left with four little ones and not a way to bring in a penny for any of them?"

Julia forbade herself from stroking away the tension that set his shoulders in a firm, unyielding line. She forced herself to keep her distance though she ached to kiss away the shadow of terrible remembrance that darkened his face and turned the very air around them heavy and sour.

She struggled to keep her voice level though it threatened to break with emotion. "He told me how you've taken care of Mary and the children all these years. How you send them money when you can. He didn't need to tell me anything else. Nothing else matters. All that matters is that I love you."

Mick looked away. "Can you love a man whose friends died in saving him?"

"You would have done the same for them. You did, for the two men you rescued on their way to the gallows." She brought her hand to his face and smiled a little when she saw the rigid line of Mick's jaw relax.

"I know I can love a man who will never accept that one nation should be the unwilling subject of another," she said. She drew her fingers along his jaw and caressed his chin. "A man who will risk all to bring freedom to his people. I know I can love a man who may never accept the tragic deaths of his countrymen, but one who understands what drives them to make those sacrifices and is willing to do the same himself if that is what he is called to do."

Mick searched Julia's eyes, hoping to find there the same truth he heard ringing in her words. When he spoke, his voice was rough with emotion. "And do you think it's worth risking yourself for that sort of man?"

"I do."

Satisfied and relieved, he nodded. The next second, all his self-assurance vanished, and a fierce rush of color stained his cheeks. He licked his lips.

"There's one other thing . . ." Whatever was troubling Mick, he could not face her to admit it. He backed out of her embrace and turned away, pacing to the other side of the tiny parlor and back again before he found the courage to speak.

"I have not been truthful, Julia." He looked at her from beneath the lock of golden hair that had fallen over his forehead. "There is more you need to know."

Somehow, though the confession sounded foreboding enough, it did not strike Julia with apprehension. Mick looked more like a wayward child than a repentant man, and she smiled instinctively in response to the honesty that shone in his eyes like stars in a clear night sky.

"I've been here in England nearly four years," he said, "ever since I escaped that Irish prison where they were preparing for my hanging. Once I got here, I couldn't use my own name. It would have been foolish. Foolish and dangerous."

Julia took a step forward, her hands out to him. "A long while ago, you told me O'Donnell was as good as any other name. It was good enough then. It's good enough now."

"No." Warming to the understanding that sparkled in her eyes, Mick slipped his fingers through hers and pulled her nearer. "I owe you the truth. You of all people. I was ashamed, and I tried to forget by changing into someone else. You've shown me I can live with the man I was, because with you, I can finally live with the man I really am. My name is Patrick. Patrick O'Flaherty Fitzgerald."

Whatever reaction he had expected, it wasn't the one he got.

He watched the color drain from Julia's face, watched her lips part with unspoken surprise and a disbelief so real, he felt he could reach out and touch it.

"It can't be." She shook her head slowly, like a person waking from a particularly convoluted dream. "It isn't possible."

"I've no one to vouch for me." Mick smiled down at her, not understanding her amazement but finding it, somehow, delightfully ingenuous. "My mother and father, God rest their souls, aren't here. Teague could tell you—"

"Patrick O'Flaherty Fitzgerald." It was as if Julia were not listening. He saw the shiver that trembled in her shoulders, felt the ice that flowed into her fingers.

She chewed on her lower lip, her eyes wide. "It isn't possible, of course," he heard her mumble to herself. "It's a mistake, or some kind of game. That's it." Julia's gaze snapped to his. "You're teasing, aren't you?"

Confound it if he could understand the woman! Mick smiled in spite of himself. "There's no way you can know the name," he said. "I'm hardly famous, even if there are those who think me infamous. And I can't be playing a game because I don't know what in the blazes you're talking about."

"I'm talking about you. About your name." Finally, Julia seemed to regain her wits. She blinked past whatever shock had mesmerized her and looked at Mick carefully.

"Months ago," she said. "Months ago, I was telling fortunes for my friend Harriet Lloyd and the spirits predicted . . ." She caught herself, more staggered than ever at the turn of events. "I knew your name," she said, her voice filled with amazement. "Patrick O'Flaherty Fitzgerald. I'm sure of it. But how—?"

Mick laughed, hardly understanding but perfectly willing to accept this as another aspect of her mystifying personality. She would always be so. The thought cheered him. She would always be so, and he would always be at her side to savor it.

"Perhaps you really are psychic," he said, his voice just light enough that he might be teasing. "Perhaps, for once, you read your own future."

Julia blinked away the problem. "Perhaps," she agreed, her voice no more than a whisper, the look on her face clearly saying she would have to think upon the puzzle more.

Still grinning, Mick slid one arm around her waist. "So you knew I'd be coming, eh?" He kissed away the lines of bewilderment that circled her mouth and began to work on the tiny crinkles of confusion around her eyes. "Can you love me anyway?"

The touch of his lips was too exquisite, the feel of his hand flattened against her back, massaging away her worries, too enticing to ignore. She snuggled closer, instinctively responding to the humor that warmed his eyes and echoed in his voice.

"Can you love a woman who isn't nearly as rich as you think I am?" she asked.

Mick laughed. "I loved you when you didn't have a penny to jangle on a tombstone. Why shouldn't I love you now?" He bent to kiss her, his mouth as warm and soft as his caress.

A second later, he moved his lips from hers and looked down at her, his eyebrows raised, a gentle amusement gleaming in his eyes like sun on a blue summer sea. "What's that you said? What do you mean, not as rich as I think you are?"

Not sure of how he'd respond to her news, Julia moved back a step. "Remember two days ago when you went to wire Teague and Kate in Liverpool? I visited my father's solicitor while you were gone. I gave a great deal of my estate to my grandmother." She stopped her narrative to study his reaction. "Are you disappointed?"

Mick looked as bewildered as she must have when she discovered his real name. "Not disappointed," he admitted. "Just surprised."

"I've let her keep the home in Yorkshire," Julia continued. "And I've given her the mines in South Africa as well as those in Peru and Venezuela. She's always been more fond of commodities than she was of people. Perhaps all that precious metal will keep her warm and happy in her old age."

The smile had faded from Mick's face, not because he was dissatisfied, but, she suspected, because he felt an injustice had been done. His words confirmed her suspicions.

"So, the old harridan gets her way?"

"Hardly," Julia assured him. "I've given five thousand pounds to that actors' charity my father mentioned in his will. And I've kept the rest of the businesses. After all, if we are to administer our lands in Ireland equitably, we do need some sort of income."

This last statement brought the smile back to Mick's face. "You wouldn't let her keep them, would you?"

"Not after what those poor people have suffered at her hands. If we can go there, Mick, we can help them. I know we can. I've already drawn up a plan to sell the land. I won't give it away; I suspect my tenants are much too proud to take charity. But for a few pounds, over a payment period of a few years . . . Do you think they would accept that?"

Mick's kiss was his only response.

"You are as wise as you are beautiful," he said, raising his mouth from hers and looking deep into her eyes. "And I can already see that the Irish people will love you. They'll practically declare you a saint. Joan of Arc, just as I used to call you. As brave and as true and just as determined."

"Determined to get those letters back before we do anything else." Julia smoothed the skirt of her gown and went to sit in the nearest chair. There was business to discuss and she could hardly do it while Mick's lips were so enticingly close.

"I've thought it all out," she continued levelly. "I'll conduct the séance and you come to the Ashcroft house as my assistant. While I keep them amazed, you make off with the letters."

Mick crossed the room and dropped to the floor in front of her. He took her right hand in his and raised it to his lips. "Agreed," he said. "I might have known a long time ago, you'd get your way in this. You get your way in everything else. Only, tell me, how did you know?"

Julia swallowed hard. "Know what?" she asked, her voice as innocent as a babe's.

"Know I'd ask you to conduct the séance. That's why you've been so chipper, isn't it? It's beyond me how you knew. Unless it's those psychic powers of yours. I only decided this morning there was no other way, but you, you've known I'd ask these past two days."

"Well, yes." Julia hesitated, drawing in a deep breath to augment her courage. "You see," she said, "I wrote to Dolly Ashcroft. Two days ago. I offered my services at the séance seeing as Professor Von Trask could not attend."

"Could he not?" Though she expected to see exasperation in Mick's eyes, she saw instead only resignation. "I know I'm up against a woman as stubborn as any bloody-minded mule, but would you mind telling me how you convinced Dolly Ashcroft I wouldn't be there?"

"Simple," Julia admitted. "She had to invite me or disappoint all her guests. I couldn't let you walk in there and risk revealing yourself. And I couldn't think of any other way. I told her Professor Von Trask had been killed in a carriage accident."

"Killed!" Mick roared with laughter and, tightening his hold on her hand, pulled her to the floor beside him. "You are the most bullheaded, willful, single-minded woman I've ever met, Julia Barrie. And I absolutely adore you."

As quickly as the rumble of delight came, it stilled, and the look on Mick's face softened. Beyond caring, beyond concern, the blue depths of his eyes sparkled with emotion too deep to name, too profound to ignore. The smile faded from his face and he placed one hand on each of Julia's shoulders and pulled her to him, crushing her in an embrace both potent and powerful.

"What we're going to do is very dangerous," he told her, stroking her hair with his hand. "One or both of us may be captured. One or both of us may be killed."

Julia refused to listen. She stopped the terrifying truth from leaving Mick's mouth by moving her lips over his with such intensity that she took both his words and his breath away.

Smoothing the hair back from his forehead, Julia placed a tender kiss on the jagged scar that peeked from the thatch of his hair. "I'm not afraid, Mick," she whispered. She stopped short, the words barely out of her mouth. "It's a habit." She laughed. "Would you rather I call you Patrick?"

"Patrick." Mick rolled the syllables over his tongue, as unaccustomed to them as he was to the name of a stranger. "It sounds fine when you say it, *acushla*. As fine as any name there ever was."

A new thought entered Julia's mind, and she tossed him a look. "But I shan't use it."

Her pronouncement surprised him, and he sat back on his heels.

Julia was too moved by the look of bewilderment on his face not to relieve it. She reached for his hands and pressed them to her heart. "I will make a vow to you, here and now. I will call you Patrick again, but not until we have successfully finished our mission, not until we have returned Mr. Parnell's letters and we are together in Ireland."

Chapter 20

"JULIA?"

The voice was tiny, breathless, but it froze Julia in place. She stopped just inside the door of Dolly Ashcroft's morning room, her heart suddenly pounding against her chest like thunder, her pulse beating a penetrating rhythm in her ears.

For one, impulsive moment, she was tempted to turn to the anonymous woman—for it was surely a woman's voice— and give her a cold, detached stare. As quickly as the idea came, she discarded it. In spite of her false name and her accent, in spite of the patterned scarf that pulled her hair away from her face, the billowing sleeves of her blouse, and the boisterous pattern of her skirt that made her look the very picture of a Gypsy fortune-teller, someone had recognized her.

The thought was not reassuring. Their mission tonight depended on secrecy, and being luckless enough to meet an acquaintance was a prospect she and Mick had neither discussed nor expected.

Julia struggled to invent some plausible explanation for her presence at the same time she braced herself against whatever might await her. Affixing a smile to her face, she turned. Relief surged through her and the breath she'd been holding escaped along with a small squeal of astonishment.

"Harriet!"

The two women fell into each other's arms.

The excitement of seeing Harriet again made Julia forget her caution, but only for a second. Pulling away, she caught herself before another, surprised tumble of words could escape her lips. She glanced up and down the corridor. Only when she was certain no one had seen or overheard them, did she drag Harriet into the morning room and snap the door closed behind them.

"What on earth are you doing here?"

"Me?" Harriet giggled and hopped from foot to foot, barely containing her excitement. "Dolly Ashcroft is Reggie's aunt. Didn't you know? I'm living here now."

Her initial astonishment melted along with the buoyant feeling of assurance that had filled her since they left London this morning, and Julia felt the smile vanish from her face. As if it were no more substantial than the glimmer of moonlight rippling against the windows, her confidence wavered.

She turned and paced to the far wall and back again. "Is there anyone else here we know?" she asked.

Trying to fathom the meaning of Julia's sudden change of mood, Harriet shook her head. "I don't think so," she answered, her voice low and thoughtful.

"Not even Reggie?"

"Reggie!" Harriet jiggled her shoulders and made a noise that was almost an unladylike snort. "Reggie is in London."

The show of irritation was so quick, Julia did not have time to comment on it. The next second, Harriet scampered closer and grabbed for Julia's hands.

"But what are you doing here?" she asked. The obvious effort of thinking out the puzzle clouded Harriet's blue eyes.

She shook her head mournfully. "Dear Lord, Julia, I thought I'd never see you again. We heard the most dreadful story from your grandmother, but no one was able to confirm it. Reggie said I should mind my own business, but

I just couldn't believe you'd run off with some young man and not even tell me! I didn't want to believe what your grandmother said but then I supposed it had to be true because she was so terribly distressed and in such a state looking for you. And it was all so dreadful.''

Harriet's creamy skin paled and she eyed Julia up and down, from the jaunty gleam of her gold hoop earrings to the hem of her paisley skirt. "Oh, dear Julia, You didn't run off with a man, you went to find your Gypsy relatives. Or did they kidnap you?

"Are you their slave? Their thrall? I've read about such things. Awful people. White slavers who kidnap young women and—" Harriet's cheeks got very pink, her eyes grew round as saucers, and she fanned away her distress with one hand.

Julia couldn't help but laugh. "Don't be ridiculous!" She tugged Harriet to the nearest sofa and dropped into the seat next to her. "I'm the entertainment," she explained. "The medium who's come to tell fortunes tonight."

Harriet's bow-shaped lips opened into a perfect circle. She clapped her hands together. "How delightful! Only, they said it was someone else, didn't they? A Madame—"

"Krakowska. Madame Krakowska." Julia glided into the clairvoyant's accent with ease. "I will be conducting the séance this evening."

This was obviously too great a leap of logic for Harriet. Her straw-colored brows dipped into a vee. "You? You mean, you . . . ? Oh, I say!" Her eyes popped wide with awe. "You are Madame Krakowska? How jolly! Oh, Julia! What a marvelous lark!"

Julia laughed, giving her a knowing look. "You don't think it's frightfully common?"

For a second, the excitement on Harriet's pretty face stilled. "Well, yes. I suppose actually working for one's living is terribly vulgar," she admitted. As quickly as the moment of pensiveness came, it vanished and Harriet was laughing again. "But what fun! It's like those games we played when we were girls. How beastly exciting and romantic it all must be. You must tell me more. Tell me all about it."

"Not tonight." Julia's face sobered. She fixed Harriet with a level look. "Tonight, no one must know we're acquainted. It's very important no one know who I really am."

"Oh, I see." Harriet nodded until her golden curls quivered like a well-made aspic. "It's a secret, isn't it? Another element of your disguise. What jolly fun!" She giggled. "I shall quite enjoy being part of your game. How lucky you are to have such marvelous adventures . . ." Harriet's voice took on a wistfulness Julia had not heard in it since the early days of her courtship by Reggie Atwalter.

"Is something wrong?" Julia asked.

"Wrong? There shouldn't be." Harriet's words were punctuated by a cynical laugh. "I should be the happiest woman in England. I married the man I was wildly in love with. I'm having his child and—"

Julia's impulsive hug squeezed the rest of the sentence out of Harriet, but when she released her, Harriet did not smile.

"You're not happy." Even to her own ears, Julia's words sounded inadequate. She patted Harriet's arm. "Is there anything I can do?"

Again, Harriet laughed, a flimsy sound hardly convincing enough to deceive an old friend. She looked away. "No," she said, her voice very quiet and so unnaturally steady, it caused a flutter of apprehension to tremble through Julia. "There's nothing you can do. Not unless your fortune-teller's magic can dispose of Reggie's mistress."

There were no words to soothe a pain as grievous as this. Julia sat in silence, waiting for Harriet to collect herself and was unnerved when Harriet turned back to her, her expression as serene as a statue's, and just as emotionless.

"It was a fairy-tale wedding," she said, suddenly looking years older than the lighthearted girl Julia had known. "How I wished you could have been there! I suppose I was so busy with all the plans and preparations, I never noticed how Reggie's temperament had changed. Once our engagement became official, he wasn't nearly as attentive as he had been before, although he pretended well enough." Harriet expelled a mumble of disgust.

"Especially on our wedding night. But when I announced I was to have his child . . ." Harriet shrugged, a fainthearted, helpless gesture. "It's as if that's all he cared about, an heir. I suppose if it's a girl, he may come back to me, expecting his marital privileges. But if it's a boy . . ." Harriet's gaze fastened on the far wall and the docile blue eyes that had always been so pleasant hardened beyond measure. "If it's a boy, I suspect we shall never again live as man and wife."

"Harriet, don't." Her own voice unsteady, Julia reached for her friend. Harriet pulled away and turned a jaded eye on Julia.

"I don't cry about it anymore," she said, her dimpled chin raised in a pathetic look of defiance, her eyes filling with tears in spite of her words. "I have no love left. I hate Reggie Atwalter, just as I hate living here with Aunt Dolly. The woman's a shrew, and he's packed me up and sent me here to Kent to live with her so he can carry on freely in London. I'm to stay here until the baby is born. That's what Reggie has told me. But that's more than five months from now, Julia. Five months of not seeing anyone, or going anywhere, or having any friends at all to talk to. Five months, and I swear, by then I shall either be staring mad or dead."

THANK God for informers.

Mick hurried down the dimly lit corridor, counting the doors on either side as he went.

"One, two, three . . ."

Seventh one on the left, he reminded himself. The servant he'd paid for the information had been quite specific. The door to the study where the Chief's letters were being kept was the seventh one on the left.

It was fortunate there were always those who could be bought, for in a house this size, he might have looked for hours and not found the study. Passage intersected passage, stairways and landings and closed doorways were as abundant as bugs in a poor man's bed.

As he passed one of the doors, it swung open and a man and woman dashed into the corridor, laughing, arm in arm. They stopped short at the sight of Mick, their faces paling, then reddening, their hands flying off each other and down to their sides. The man smiled nervously.

"Nice evening, eh what, old chap?" He clapped Mick on the back and tried, unsuccessfully, to tuck his shirt back into his trousers.

Mick did not respond. He merely stared in silence.

The gentleman squinted at Mick. "I say, it's that fellow who came with the medium, the one who's supposed to conduct the séance this evening," he informed his companion. A look close to relief swept over his face. "Chap comes from some foreign place, speaks one of those rum exotic languages, so I'm told." He edged closer to Mick and raised his voice. "You not speak English, eh what?"

Mick smiled, and whispered another prayer of thanks, this time for Julia. She had been wise enough to realize his accent would give him away and had, on their arrival, informed one and all that her assistant spoke not one word of English.

Convinced Mick had not the least idea of what was going on, the man stepped back and sighed. "Can't abide these foreigners," he said, still smiling at Mick and bobbing his head heartily. "Shifty. Can't be trusted. But at least he won't be telling tales to your husband when he sees him downstairs, eh what, my dear?'' He laughed and turned his attention back to Mick.

"Out for stroll.'' He marched the fingers of his right hand across his left palm. "Fine evening, what?''

With that, he grabbed for the woman's arm and tugged her away. They sidled around Mick, obviously avoiding as much as possible contact with a man who not only had the bad manners to be a foreigner, but one who worked for a living besides.

When they had disappeared down the corridor, Mick mumbled an oath. Curse these aristocrats. How could his people expect justice from a nation of dilettantes, as ready to betray and deceive each other as they were to abuse the rights and privileges of the peoples they governed?

Shaking his head, he continued down the hallway, dismissing the encounter without another thought. For tonight, all that mattered was the letters. He would not attempt to retrieve them now, there wasn't time. For now, he was here merely to reconnoiter, to think where the letters might be hidden, if there was not a safe, and to find the best way to open it if there was.

Once Julia began tonight's séance . . .

Mick forced himself to ignore the shiver of apprehension that crawled up his spine.

Once Julia began her séance, all would be fine, he told himself. It had to be. He'd have more than enough time to come back to the study, more than enough time to fetch the letters and get back downstairs before the lights ever came on again. Julia had assured him as much, and her word was as good as gold. Better.

The thought calmed and consoled him. Julia's word was better than gold. It was gospel. He had enough confidence in her to know she would play her part and play it well.

All he had to do was find the letters.

Mick paused outside the seventh doorway and took a deep breath.

All he had to do was find the letters. And now was the time to begin.

He grabbed the doorknob and mumbled a curse.

The door to the study was locked.

"I'VE seen your assistant." Harriet sniffed into her silk handkerchief then tucked it demurely into the plunging neckline of her gown. "He was watching the men play billiards a while ago." She raised her eyes to Julia's. "Are you very much in love with him?"

Julia was as surprised by the question as she was by Harriet's unexpected insight. "Yes." She smiled, feeling surprisingly self-conscious at the admission. "Very much in love."

Harriet fluffed her skirts. "I should warn you. Warn you about the infidelities men are predisposed to. But I suspect you wouldn't listen. I never listened when you warned me about Reggie."

"I?" Julia gave her a doubtful look. "I never—"

"Not in your words, of course." Harriet continued as if Julia had never spoken. "You knew I'd pay you no mind. But I should have been suspicious. You were not enthusiastic about the match. You foresaw what was going to happen, didn't you?"

"I . . ." Julia hesitated.

"You knew. Certainly, you knew." Harriet stuck out her chin, as resolute as Julia had ever seen her. "I wish I could see into the future for you, know what awaits you and this man."

Harriet could not desire a peek into the future any more than Julia herself did. "You needn't worry," she said, hoping to calm Harriet's misgivings at the same time she fought to control her own. "After tonight . . . after tonight I'm certain we shall be quite happy. As certain of it as I have ever been of anything in my life. He's a wonderful man, Harriet."

"If only I had been as lucky." Harriet sighed. "I'm not jealous," she added quickly. "Only . . . only wistful, I suppose. Like the time three or four summers ago when George Winston asked you to picnic with him on the moor. And I was so frightfully in love with him. And even then, I wasn't envious of you, I just longed to be you for that one afternoon and know what it was like. I only wish . . ."

Harriet coughed behind her hand. "You know his uncle Whiteburn has obtained a position for Reggie at the Home Office?" She clasped her hands together on her lap, her knuckles white. "That's the reason he uses for keeping me here in the country. He says he's quite busy with his work in London, much too busy to properly take care of a wife and a family. But I know it isn't true. He stays there with his pretty . . . whore." Harriet's lower lip protruded, her cheeks paled nearly as white as the satin dress she was wearing. Surprisingly, the expression lasted no more than a moment. Just as suddenly, her eyes lit, as bright with the desire for revenge as they were with tears.

"Julia!" She flashed a sidelong glance at her friend and smiled. "If there was a spell you could cast, a spell to take away her beauty . . ."

The pitiful faith reflected in Harriet's face snatched away Julia's voice. She opened her mouth to respond, then found she could not. Laying one hand on Harriet's arm, she cleared her throat and began again.

"I can't," she said simply. She held on tighter when Harriet made to move away and fixed her with a look Harriet could neither ignore nor dismiss with a flippant toss of her head.

"You see, Harriet, it isn't genuine," Julia said, her voice low and firm enough so Harriet could not mistake the truth of her words. "None of it. Not the palm readings, or the planchette, or even the séances. It's just what you said earlier, a vulgar occupation, nothing more. A bag of cleverly performed conjurer's tricks. I don't have any special powers. I never did. I played fortune-teller at home because it was fun and it amused you so. I do it now because I need the money. It's tommy-rot. It isn't real. It never was."

"Oh, but it has to be!" Harriet sat up, her eyes suddenly wide and worried. She shook her head, as if trying to reason through a particularly baffling dilemma. "It has to be real, don't you see? If it isn't real . . . if you're not real . . ." She grasped Julia's hands in both of hers. "They're going to find out. Tonight."

When Harriet tried to say more, Julia silenced her with a delighted laugh. "They won't find out. I've got it all planned. I—"

Before she could finish the thought, the door clicked open and Mick walked into the room. He looked from Harriet to Julia, a question in his eyes.

"It's all right." Julia rose from her seat and wound her arm through Mick's. "This is Harriet," she told him. "Harriet Lloyd, my friend from home. She's living here with Dolly Ashcroft now."

"And . . ."

"And she knows we are here to conduct tonight's séance, and she knows she is to pretend she's never seen us before." Julia smiled over at Harriet. "She's only too delighted to help us in our little game."

With one smooth movement, Mick spun Julia around and marched her to the windows. He bent closer, his voice so low, only Julia could hear it. "I don't suppose she'd be too delighted to get us the key to the study, now would she?"

"It's locked?" Her question was superfluous. Julia could tell as much from the hard set of Mick's shoulders, the trace of disappointment that added lines around his eyes and pulled his lips into an irritated line.

"As tight as the devil." With one hand, Mick rubbed his chin and cast a glance over his shoulder to where Harriet sat. "Do you think she'd . . . ?" He raised his eyebrows quizzically.

"I'll take care of that." Julia smiled up at him.

Mick gave her a quick peck on the cheek. "You're as fine a woman as ever there was," he said. "Just be sure to do it soon. The gentlemen"—he gave the word a curious intonation—"have just about finished their game of billiards. We'll be called to perform shortly."

Julia nodded her understanding. She pulled away from Mick and turned on her heels, a smile on her face and a small note of pleading in her voice. "Harriet . . ."

Harriet had not moved from her place on the sofa. She sat as stiff as a stone except for the quick, shallow breaths that shuddered through her and the steady movement of her fingers working over and over themselves.

At the sound of her name, she bolted out of the chair and hurried across the room, her face shadowed with distress. "But Julia . . . you've got to let me tell you . . . it's Aunt Dolly, you see." Wringing her hands, Harriet looked at Julia and Mick, her face screwed into an expression that was painful and confused.

"I'm getting all turned about," she wailed. She flapped her hands and her eyes brimmed with tears. "Aunt Dolly is one of this country's chief supporters of spiritualism. I suspect you know that. But what you don't seem to know is that she's so sure what you do is real, she's accepted a challenge of sorts."

"A challenge?" Julia heard her own voice respond though the sound seemed to come from a long way off.

Harriet nodded furiously. "All the guests here tonight agree with Aunt Dolly's beliefs. Except one. She's invited Hannibal Mayhew to attend tonight's séance."

Mick saw Julia stiffen as Harriet spoke. He reached for Julia's hand and held it tight in one of his own. "And who is this Mayhew fellow?" he asked.

Julia forced her words to sound calmer than she felt. "Hannibal Mayhew is a writer," she said, struggling to hide the alarm she felt at hearing the name. "An American. He's a newspaper reporter for the *New York News*."

Harriet broke in before she had a chance to say any more. "He's touring England and the Continent studying spiritualism, writing positively scathing articles about the things he's seen. He agreed to attend tonight's party on one condition," she said, her voice rising until it was shrill. "He's told Aunt Dolly that no matter what it takes, no matter how clever you are, he will expose the medium at tonight's séance, and prove once and for all that there isn't any truth in spiritualism. Julia, he's come here to find you out."

Chapter 21

"IT's the devil's own luck." Mick murmured under his breath as the door closed behind Harriet. He strode from one side of the parlor to the other, his expression dark.

He pulled himself to a stop opposite Julia. "We'll cry off while we can. If we're fast, we can be out of here before they ever come looking for us to hold this fool-headed séance."

"We'll do no such thing." Julia fought to control her temper at the same time she struggled to keep her voice low.

Dolly Ashcroft's guests were filing into the music room even now, settling themselves for the evening's entertainment. She could hear their footsteps as they shuffled by outside the morning room door. There was no use letting strangers hear them quarrel, just as there was no use quarreling about something neither one of them could control or change.

"We can't leave now," she told Mick. "Someone would certainly see us. And even if they didn't, we can't walk away when we're so close to getting Mr. Parnell's letters back."

Mick regarded her skeptically. "And what about this Mayhew fellow?" he asked. "You heard what Harriet had to say. He's on a campaign, a bloody crusade to prove that mediums are nothing more than bogus magicians. That you take peoples' money and promise them information about the dead when you can't possibly know any more about it than the next man.''

One corner of Mick's mouth twisted into an expression that was not quite a smile. ''In case you need to be reminded, Madame Krakowska, the man is right.'' The flash of amusement was fleeting. The next second, Mick's face sobered and he looked down at her, concern and very real fear burning in his eyes. ''He's set to pounce on you, like a tiger with its claws out and its fangs bared. You heard Harriet, he'll do anything he can to prove himself right.''

''Then we mustn't give him the chance.'' Unable to endure the look of tenderness in Mick's eyes, Julia began to pace, repeating the pattern he had made from one side of the room to the other. ''I've simply got to be smarter than he is,'' she said. ''I've got to make it so that he doesn't find a single flaw in anything I do, not a single reason to try and stop the séance. At least not until you've made it back with the letters tucked neatly into your pocket.''

Mick crossed his arms over his chest and looked away. ''I'm not putting them in my pocket,'' he informed her, his voice heavy with begrudging resignation. ''The last time I did that, you were quick to point out—''

''The last time you did that, I stole them from you and ended up causing a terrible mull. I feel responsible, Mick, and I won't walk away when I can help repair the damage I've caused. I'm not leaving here without the letters.''

''I can come back for them later.'' Mick took two paces toward Julia and stopped. He knew getting too near was unwise. The closer he got, the better he could see her eyes, sparkling with obstinacy, her lips, moist and pouting, her chin, so stiff with unyielding resolve, that the sight tugged at his heart, while at the same time it threatened to fuel him with the same hardheaded foolishness and reckless courage that filled her.

''You can't. You heard what Harriet said.'' Julia waved her hand absently toward the chair Harriet had been seated in. "The original owners of the house were frightfully afraid of being burglarized. They had bars put across all the windows, including the study. There's only one way in, and that's the door."

"And do you think Harriet will get us the key to that door?"

Julia stopped her pacing and admitted the truth. "I don't know. She acted like she wanted to help, but . . . she doesn't understand. She couldn't. Even if I told her the whole truth. Politics, and loyalties, and patriotism—they're a world away from Harriet. Right now, the only thing she understands is that she wants to hurt Reggie as much as he's hurt her. Though she doesn't know what we want, I think she realizes that helping us will damage Reggie's family's reputation. But if she has the courage to carry it out . . ." Julia shrugged. "I simply don't know."

"And do you have the courage to go into that room and perform when there's a man there eager to show you for a fraud and a charlatan?" Mick took another step nearer, looking into her eyes. Even he was not sure what he wanted to find there. One part of him prayed she would be wise enough to admit defeat, to leave as quickly as she could and avoid what could be not only an ugly scene, but a dangerous one as well.

Another part of him hoped he would see no change in her stubborn courage, no concessions to fear, or panic, or weakness. It was that part of him that was satisfied.

Julia stepped forward and took Mick's hands in hers. "There's nothing Mayhew can do to me. Let him expose me as a fraud! The worst he can do is write some dreadful newspaper article telling the world about my trickery. That's not at all what I'm worried about. After tonight I'll never perform another séance. No. The only thing that bothers me," Julia confessed, "is that if Mayhew thinks anything is wrong, he'll demand that we stop the séance. And if you're not back in the room, it will surely arouse suspicions. If they go looking for you . . ." She squeezed her eyes shut and pressed Mick's hands tighter in her own.

"I've got to be smarter than Mayhew," she said, opening her eyes and looking up at Mick through a sudden haze of tears. "Your safety depends on it."

"My safety couldn't be in better hands." Mick smiled and, gathering her into his arms, pressed a kiss to her lips.

"How can I help but trust you with my body," he said, his lips still touching hers so that his words were more breath than sound. "I've already given you my heart and my soul."

For once, she could find no words to answer him. Julia raised her lips to Mick's and kissed him, memorizing the taste of his mouth, savoring the strength of his embrace as he slid his arms around her and pulled her closer.

He glided his lips from hers and along the line of her neck and whispered in her ear. "You do remember about leaving tonight, don't you?"

Julia couldn't help but laugh. She drew away from Mick, her hands locked behind his neck. "Yes, I remember," she said, though it was amazing she could remember anything at all with Mick's hands stroking her back and his lips so provocatively close.

"When the séance is over, I'm to leave by the front door." She repeated the instructions he'd given her that morning. "I'm to pass up all the other carriages and take the very last one. The cabman will be wearing a green feather in his cap. He'll take me to the train station. From there, I'll take the first train to Holyhead, and from there, the first mailpacket to Dublin. In the meantime, you'll return Mr. Parnell's letters to him in London. We'll meet in Wicklow in four days' time, at the cottage Teague's promised to have ready for us." Julia drew in a deep breath. "But even there you won't be safe, will you? Even in Ireland, there will be those who will try to hunt you down."

"They've got to figure out where I've gone to first."

Mick smiled away her objection. "And that will take them a good, long while. In the meantime, there is a certain fine and fancy lady I'll be spending my days with. And my nights." He tapped the tip of her nose with his finger. "You can stop worrying about Ireland."

"Only if you stop worrying about tonight. Only if you kiss me."

"Bold as—!" Both Mick's voice and the laugh that erupted from him were stopped by Julia's mouth. She kissed him long and soundly, a kiss she meant to be good-humored. It quickly became something else altogether.

In spite of her show of bravery, there was a thread of worry beneath Julia's cool composure, an uneasiness that turned her blood to ice and caused a shiver of fear to crawl up her back and snake through her shoulders. She never meant her misgivings to be telegraphed through her kiss, never meant for Mick to know that beneath her nonchalance, she was as frightened as she had ever been. Yet somehow he knew. She was certain of it.

She could feel it in the movement of his hands, taste it in the bittersweet touch of his lips. She would not disappoint him. She could not. Not when she owed him this and so much more.

The kiss was over all too soon, and when it was, Julia forced a smile to her lips. "Very well." She swiped her hands across her cheeks, hoping to dispel her misgivings at the same time she banished the tears that had sprung to her eyes.

"We'd better make sure there's nothing for Mayhew to be suspicious of. Here." She held out her hands, her arms stiff, her palms raised. "Help me get rid of these things."

Mick looked at her in wonder. "What in the name of the saints and angels are you talking about?" He studied the long, dark sleeves of her dress. They were edged in a wide flounce of lace, ruffles so extravagant, they nearly hid her hands. "I don't see anything there," he admitted.

Julia gave him a knowing look. As Mick watched in stunned silence, she flicked back the ecru lace trim and untied a heavy piece of string, exactly the color of the lace, from around her left wrist. Reaching into the sleeve of her gown, she pulled out a stiff, black-bound wire from inside her cuff. The wire was doubled and hooked at one end, and while Mick tried to puzzle through what it was for, Julia repeated the procedure with the other sleeve. She deposited both the wires beneath the cushion of the nearest chair.

"What in the world—?"

She laughed at the dumbfounded expression on Mick's face. "That's how I levitate tables," she explained. "When the lights go down, I slip my hands beneath the table." She demonstrated with an imaginary table, holding her palms flat, her arms out in front of her at waist level. "And I simply lift it."

"Holy Mother!" Mick shook his head. "Do you think Mayhew might look for something like that?"

"It's a common enough trick." Julia tapped her top lip with her index finger. "Let's see, what else might he have heard about?"

"How about that rapping?" Mick suggested. "The kind you showed me how to do?"

"That's nothing he can prove unless he catches me in the act. Do you suppose he'd have the cheek to ask one of the women to search me?"

Mick opened his mouth, aghast.

"It's been done, you know," Julia informed him, trying not to laugh at the genuinely appalled look on his face. "Though no one's ever had the effrontery to ask it of me. But I suppose it's better to be safe." Julia hoisted up her skirts and bent at the waist.

Except for the top of her head and her hands moving quickly and assuredly over something attached to her pantaloons near her right knee, there was little Mick could see. He dipped his head, hoping for a better look and watched while Julia slid a small metal object down her leg and held it up for his examination.

The sight of the small soapbox dangling from the kind of frilly suspender used by women to hold up their stockings appealed to Mick's sense of the ridiculous as well as to his discriminating taste in feminine charms. He laughed out loud.

He held out his hand for the little container and pressed against it with one finger. The lid was convex and it sprang back from the pressure of his touch with a hearty crack.

"Dear Lord, woman." Mick's eyes sparkled, more with admiration and astonishment than with annoyance. "I'll never again trust you, as long as I live. So that's how some of those other noises are made. You press against this thing with your knees, am I right? What other surprises did you have in store for those poor innocents waiting in the music room?"

Julia reached into her pocket. "I've got the telescopic rod I use to make the trumpet float around the room," she said, pulling out a short length of folded framing and showing it to Mick. "And the trumpet itself." The trumpet, as she called it, was no more than a flimsy piece of aluminium, cut in the shape of a musical instrument and coated with luminescent paint. It was light enough to drift above a crowd of awestruck spectators, flexible enough to fold into her pocket when the trick was through.

Julia tossed the rod into the fire that burned in the grate and, folding the trumpet neatly in two, tucked it beneath the Oriental rug at their feet.

She had just finished when the parlor door opened and Dolly Ashcroft poked her head into the room. Pleased that she had found what she was looking for, she hauled the door open all the way and sailed in.

"Countess!" Her chubby arms out in a welcoming gesture that was more practiced than it was genuine, Dolly turned an indulgent eye on the medium and her assistant.

"The servants have finally finished preparing the music room. We are ready for you now."

Julia bowed graciously. "We will be there directly. I must ready myself."

"Certainly." Dolly's emerald eyes sparkled, her cheeks glowed with the promised excitement of a night's entertainment complete with fortune-telling, mind-reading, and materializations. "Certainly." She breathed the word again, eyeing Julia with a look as close to reverence as any she had ever seen.

Dolly withdrew and Julia made to follow. Before she could, Mick plucked at her sleeve and held her in place.

"What does that leave you?" He fixed her with a look.

Julia ignored the question. She threw back her shoulders and headed toward the door.

This time, Mick could not contain his apprehension. All the guests were in the music room, there was no one outside in the corridor, and he dared to raise his voice. "I asked, how will you keep them occupied without that clever little bag of tricks of yours?"

This stopped Julia. At the doorway, she spun to face him, one hand against the carved wooden door, a smile on her face.

"I haven't the slightest idea," she said, and turning, she swept into the music room.

Chapter 22

Even blindfolded, Julia could feel Hannibal Mayhew's gaze on her. His scowl burned through the lady's kid glove positioned over her eyes and the length of silk tied at the back of her head to hold the glove in place.

Bother! Julia stifled an oath of annoyance. She would not let the man get the better of her.

Struggling to ignore the power of Mayhew's dark, piercing glare, Julia turned her head to where she knew the American was sitting. Two could play the game as easily as one, she thought, keeping her face impassive, her sightless gaze trained on the man.

She had no idea if her ploy was working, but she held her ground, refusing to turn away. Finally, she smiled to herself when she heard Mayhew's deep, rumbling baritone, slightly out of breath, slightly irritated.

"Let's get on with it."

She could picture Mayhew's face as he made the request. He was as round and fleshy as an overindulged harlot, and she suspected his jowls would be quivering the way they had when Dolly Ashcroft introduced them prior to the night's performance.

How suave and unctuous he had been then, bending over her hand, ushering her to her chair, plying her with polite and gracious questions about herself, her background, her experiences.

But the longer the mind-reading portion of her performance went on, and the more successful it was, the shorter was Mayhew's patience.

Time and again, Julia had provided answers to the secret messages the guests had written earlier in hopes of hearing news about loved ones who had gone to the Other Side. Time and again, she had held the sealed envelopes containing those messages to her forehead, run them through her fingers, and known exactly what was inside. Time and again, Hannibal Mayhew had clicked his tongue, and shifted heavily in his chair, and huffed and snorted and mumbled his disbelief and his opinion, none to subtly expressed, that what the Countess was doing might certainly be remarkable, but it was, in no way, mystical.

If Mayhew missed the patent challenge inherent in the blind, unnerving look Julia turned on him, Mick did not. As her assistant for this billet-reading session, he was not among those seated at the table. He was standing behind her, passing her the letters that had been written to the spirits. Waiting to hand her the next envelope, he poked her unobstrusively and cleared his throat.

Julia suspected his cough was not so much a warning to be prudent as it was a message that her scheme was working. Mayhew was apparently annoyed by her impudence. The thought cheered her, and Julia decided to get back to the task at hand. She motioned to her assistant for the next billet.

She felt Mick lean over her shoulder and draw another envelope from the pile in the center of the table. He slid it in front of her and she took just long enough to grope for it to convince those watching that she was, indeed, handicapped by the makeshift blindfold. When she at last grasped the envelope, she passed her left hand over it several times, then lifted it in her right hand and pressed it to her forehead.

"From this message, I am getting the vibration of a man," she said, her voice slow and thoughtful as if she had to grapple with the spirits for each and every word. "A man who passed over very suddenly. It was not expected. His name, it was Thomas."

"That is my message."

It did not take more than those few words for Julia to know who this billet had come from. It was Hannibal Mayhew who spoke and Julia cursed her luck. Of all the letters Mick could have chosen, why did it have to be this one? She dismissed the problem instantly, instructing herself to keep her mind on the performance and not bother with the consequences.

"Yes." She aimed a sleek smile in Mayhew's direction. "It is from you, Mr. Mayhew. I can feel your harmonic motions, the psychic vibrations of your hand. Do you recognize this Thomas?"

"I do."

Mayhew responded with even less good humor than he had shown earlier. His voice was brusque, exact, so cold and dispassionate, Julia was certain he would not easily answer questions or provide her with further information, in spite of her best efforts to draw him in. She decided not to even try.

Again she held the envelope to her forehead, her elbow on the table. "This Thomas," she said, "he was shot, was he not?"

"Shot, indeed."

She could not tell if there was confirmation or ridicule in Mayhew's statement. She pressed on.

"Yes. He was shot. Shot right here." Dramatically, Julia placed her hand over her heart. "Very sudden. Very tragic. There was a child as well? A child you are concerned about?"

"Yes." Though the others seated at the table gasped in awe at the Countess's pronouncement, Mayhew sounded as if he were no more surprised by it than he had been by any of the other revelations Julia had made during the performance. "Yes," he said again. "There was a child."

"Thomas wants you to know the child is healthy. He is

growing. He is being cared for by a lady, a lady who loves him very much." She moved the billet from her forehead. "This is what you wished to know?"

"It is."

This time, she could not mistake the challenge in Mayhew's voice. It was as obvious as the small snort of scorn that punctuated his last words. Julia sucked in a breath, fighting to keep her composure. She was rescued by Dolly Ashcroft.

"Unfortunately, that is all we have time for." Julia heard the scrape of Dolly's chair against the hardwood floor. "If we don't let the Countess rest for a few minutes, she will simply not have the strength to finish the rest of the evening. Ladies. Gentlemen."

Following Dolly's lead, the others pushed away from the table, and Julia felt Mick loosen the silken blindfold. She blinked into the bright light, steadying her emotions, and met the gaze of Hannibal Mayhew.

He had not moved from his seat.

"Quite a performance." Mayhew sat back in his chair. Despite the presence of the ladies, he pulled an immense cigar from his pocket and lit it. He hauled in a long breath of acrid smoke, expelled it in a ring over his head, and looked at Julia. "You seem to have successfully hoodwinked these people. I'll warn you. Never bring your act to the States. We aren't quite so gullible where I come from. You haven't been clever enough to fool me, Countess."

It was not the stinging exactness of his words that sent a quiver of anger through Julia. It was not even the shrewd and brutal look in his eyes. It was the way he spoke the name.

The mockery in his voice was hard enough for Julia to withstand; she knew it would be impossible for Mick. She swiveled in her chair, catching him just before he could signal with a look or gesture that he had understood full well the American's words. With a sweet smile and a meaningful quirk of her eyebrows, she motioned for him to get her a cup of tea.

That hazard out of the way, she smoothed a lock of her hair over her shoulder and regarded the newspaperman with as perplexed a look as she could muster.

"I do not know what you mean," she said. "Perhaps—"

"Perhaps you might consider putting a stop to this nonsense." Mayhew leaned closer, emphasizing his words with a stab of his cigar. The beads of perspiration on his forehead gleamed like lamp oil in the bright light of the crystal chandeliers.

"Washington Irving Bishop's Sealed Letter Reading." He spoke the words as if they themselves held some kind of magic. "That is what you call that particular trick, isn't it?" He tossed a look at the other guests, most of them milling around near the tea tables that had been set along the windows.

"And what those poor fools don't know is that psychic powers have nothing to do with your reading those billets. You're reading those letters when they're still on the table in front of you. Reading them quite clearly because when you pass your hand over the envelopes, you saturate them with colonial spirits. Wood alcohol. Probably kept in a little sponge in the palm of your left hand. It renders the envelopes transparent, doesn't it, Countess? Long enough for you to read the messages because you really aren't blinded by that silly glove. It's rigid enough for you to see a small portion of the table when you look down. You read the questions and do some mighty clever surmising to fill in the blanks. Let's see, what did mine say?" Mayhew twisted his fingers through his well-waxed moustache.

"'Thomas, who fired the shot? Where is the child?' I made that far too easy for you. And oh, by the way," Mayhew added almost as an afterthought, "there never was a Thomas."

He sat back, a well-contented smile on his fleshy face. "If you're willing to be reasonable and admit I've been right all along, call off the whole hocus-pocus right here and now and admit to these people you've misled them. I promise you, it will be far less embarrassing than me turning up the lights in the middle of your séance and catching you red-handed. It could get ugly, Countess. Especially when our charming hostess finds out she's been had. But if you insist . . ." Mayhew raised his massive shoulders in a gesture that promised more serious, sinister consequences.

Fingering the tiny alcohol-soaked sponge in her pocket, Julia fought to disregard the terrifying feelings of panic that churned her stomach. Mayhew could not stop the séance. He must not. She would not allow it.

She forced herself to laugh, a tiny, flustered giggle, and fluttered her eyelashes as she had seen Harriet do a thousand times before. "Washington Irving?" She gave the name the most curious pronunciation she could. "This is not familiar to me."

"Balderdash!" Mayhew could not be so easily misdirected, either by her affected innocence or her womanly wiles. As quickly as he relaxed, he sat up, his eyes gleaming, his displeasure barely contained.

"Your innocent posturings are no more convincing than that preposterous accent. I'd bet you a million to a bit of dirt you're from no place more exotic than the boardwalk of Coney Island."

Mayhew was baiting her, trying to draw her into giving herself away, and Julia knew it. The realization did not make listening to him any easier. Straining to keep her temper under control, she reminded herself of the danger over and over. He was waiting for her to make the first mistake. He was waiting for her to say something, do something that would give away her identity and expose her as a fraud.

She would not give him the pleasure.

With a small noise of disgust, Julia thrust her chair from the table and rose to her feet.

"You challenge powers you cannot possibly understand, Mr. Mayhew," she said, looking down at him. "When we begin the séance, perhaps you will come to believe that not all things in this world can be so easily explained, so easily dismissed.''

"Perhaps." Mayhew took a long drag on his cigar. "But perhaps you'll be the one who will really come to learn a lesson."

With as much dignity as she could manage, Julia left the table. Across the room, Mick was standing in a alcove which overlooked the Ashcrofts' massive gardens. She joined him there, accepting the cup of tea he had ready in his hands, turning to look, not at him, but at the garden glistening in the moonlight.

"Son of a . . ." Mick growled the words. "He was harassing you, no doubt. I wanted to—"

"Which is precisely why I sent you for a cup of tea." Julia sipped her tea, her gaze still on the windows. "He's waiting for us to make a mistake."

"Mistake. I ought to smash some manners into the lout's head. That would be no mistake."

For a moment, Julia feared Mick might make good on his threat. His reflection was clearly visible in the windows and she watched him fight with an anger nearly impossible to contain. "If he says one more word to you, I'll—"

"Did Harriet give you the key?"

The unanticipated question was enough to stop Mick's diatribe. As if he were doing nothing more than pointing out some object in the garden, he held out his left hand. Lying against his palm was a long brass key.

"Not two minutes ago," he said, tucking the key into his pocket. "As cool as a cucumber, she was. Like she'd been in the spying business all her life. That takes care of one problem." He looked over his shoulder to where Mayhew sat puffing his cigar. "What about the other?"

"There's nothing much we can do about Mayhew except keep him under control. You'll have to work quickly, I'm afraid. He knows the business, knows what I'm doing and how I'm doing it. I'm not sure how much time you'll have."

In the glass, she was certain she saw a fleeting shadow

darken Mick's expression. His golden brows dipped, his eyes darkened. She watched as he slid his left arm around her waist and drew her nearer.

"I've never in my life been afraid before," he said close to her ear. "I've gone to battle with the Saxons with a song on my lips. I've gone as far as the steps of the gallows with no more concern than I might have had on my way to church on a bright Sunday morning. But tonight, I'm afraid. I'm afraid for you, *acushla*, afraid we may never see each other again."

The words he spoke were too near the awful fears that simmered just below the surface of Julia's composure. She refused to listen to him, just as she refused to listen to the warnings of her own heart.

"I forbid you to say that." She clutched her hands together at her waist and pulled away, turning to face him.

The feelings mirrored in Mick's reflection in the window were nothing compared to the raw emotion etched on his face. He was far more worried even than he admitted, far more concerned for her safety, far more skeptical that this foolhardy mission could be carried to a successful completion. His blue eyes spoke the words his lips did not dare to form. His touch, fleeting, intimate, light against her sleeve, caused her heart to leap to her throat. Julia fought to contain a sob. "I will not let you say good-bye."

"I might have known." A rueful smile on his lips, Mick chuckled. The sound was hollow, like the whisper of a passing spirit. As if hearing the desperation in his own voice and refusing to heed it, Mick shook off his pessimism. "There's my fine and fancy lady." He tucked a wayward curl into the scarf that covered Julia's head. "Not good-bye, then, but Godspeed. I'll see you when the lights come on again. I'm only sorry there won't be time to kiss you until we're together in Wicklow. You don't suppose . . . ?" He turned just far enough to see the guests returning to their seats around the table.

"No." Julia couldn't help but smile. "I don't suppose they would take kindly to you kissing me now."

"Then let's get on with it, shall we?" He offered her his arm. "The sooner this is over with, the sooner we'll be together again."

Before they came too near the table, Hannibal Mayhew was out of his seat. He glided smoothly between Mick and Julia.

"My dear Countess." His voice was raised, attentive and courteous, but the smile Mayhew turned on Julia was akin to that a fox might give a chicken. "Come. Sit here. Next to me."

"Does death hold for us the promise of the same unfathomable gulf of blackness out of which we came at birth?"

Though Julia spoke no louder than a whisper, her voice could be heard clearly above the blanket of perfect silence that had descended on the room.

She looked to her right. Dolly Ashcroft sat, breathless, next to her, her immense bosom heaving like an Arctic iceberg on a choppy sea. On her left, Hannibal Mayhew struggled unsuccessfully to keep a cynical smile from his face, chuckling insolently even when the Countess turned a caustic eye in his direction.

Harriet and Mick were next to each other, directly across the table from her. How Mick had managed that bit of sleight of hand was a wonder, and Julia did not stop to question it, only to whisper a prayer of thanks for his foresight and his resourcefulness.

She allowed her gaze to touch Mick's, but only for a moment. Too affected by the look that met her there, she turned her eyes on Harriet.

As Mick had said earlier, Harriet was as cool as a cucumber. In spite of the promised excitement of the séance, her face was perfectly impassive, except for the one brief moment she allowed her gaze to move to Dolly's.

Then her blue eyes snapped with emotion too painful to name and her mouth thinned until it was no more than a pink slash against her pale face.

Julia gave little notice to the ten others seated around the table. They would play but a small role in the drama about to unfold, she reminded herself. They would be easy enough to mystify, easy enough to impress. For now, her chief dangers were in Dolly Ashcroft, who believed so fiercely, and in Hannibal Mayhew, who did not.

Julia pushed the thought to the back of her mind. For now, her principal worry was conducting a séance that would baffle and amaze both the believers and the nonbelievers. For now, that was all that mattered.

Taking a deep breath, she closed her eyes and spoke, intoning the familiar words. "Is the eternal future to be to us the same as was the eternal past?" she asked. "Is life but a temporary abode on a peak that is touched by the fingers of light for a day, while all around yawns an infinite, shoreless gulf of impenetrable darkness, from one side of which we appeared and to whose other side we hurry to meet our destiny?"

She opened her eyes and looked from person to person, her gaze resting on each until they squirmed uncomfortably in their seats.

"Ladies and gentlemen, I do not think so. I, the Countess Madame Anastasia Marinna Krakowska, will prove to you the existence of the Other World. The spirit world. There are no deceptions, no—what is the English word—tricks. No tricks. If Mr. Mayhew suspects I have wires in my sleeves or some sort of devices hidden in my pockets, perhaps he would wish to have my person searched?"

She turned a wide-eyed, innocent look on Mayhew.

Mayhew grumbled. "That won't be necessary," he conceded, having the good sense to pretend he was as mortified by the thought as the other guests obviously were.

"Very well." Julia nodded. "Then we will continue. You

must understand that spirits are composed of actual substance, formed by quintessential matter beyond the reach of our normal five senses. At birth, we assume temporary and perishable material forms, and when we are destroyed by physical death, the spirit remains.''

She paused, prolonging the tension.

''You will lay your hands on the table. Flat against the wood. The person next to you, he will place his hands—''

Mayhew did not wait for further instructions. With a small grunt of impatience, he plopped his right hand on top of Julia's left, pressing it against the table. His palm was hot and moist, his fingers pudgy and far too short and small to suit a man so large.

Julia nearly recoiled from the touch. Instead, she nodded, seemingly complimenting Mayhew on the quickness of his understanding. She watched while the rest of the guests imitated the action. Satisfied all was ready, she instructed the servants to leave the room, turning out the lights as they went.

When the lights went off, there was always that one moment of confusion, that one brief second when the guests pulled back, their hands flying off each others', their attention momentarily drawn away.

It was that one instant of chaos she was counting on.

Luckily, this audience was no different from others. As the lights were extinguished and the room was plunged into blackness, people twisted nervously in their chairs, ladies giggled, hands momentarily lost touch with other hands.

Julia moistened her lips. So far, all had gone as planned. She only hoped Mick had used the opportunity to do exactly as she'd taught him. Slowly, so that it went unnoticed, he should have slid his hand, and Harriet's beneath it, across the table toward the person seated on his left. After the moment's commotion when the guests touched again, she prayed the person next to Mick would have no idea his hand was no longer on the table.

Mayhew knew the scheme, she was certain of that. When the lights dimmed, he tightened his hold on her. She did not struggle against his sticky grip, but used the moment to slip the edge of her shoe beneath the nearest table leg.

With Mayhew holding her hand firmly against the table and her shoe wedged under the leg, she was ready. As soon as she set the mood, the table would conveniently tip. It was not nearly as frenzied or spectacular a movement as could have been caused with the wires she usually had in her sleeves. But it would do. It would have to. In the moment of excitement that followed, Mick could leave the room.

"We are surrounded here by spirits," Julia said in a husky whisper. "I feel them. There. Over Dolly Ashcroft's shoulder."

She heard Dolly twitter, nervous and so thrilled she could barely contain herself.

"They are there. Over the head of the woman named Harriet."

There was no response from Harriet, but Julia hardly expected one.

"They are everywhere around us. And now, I ask them to make their presence known!"

The table tipped violently, dancing beneath their hands as if it were alive.

A chorus of shrieks greeted the startling movement.

Julia drew in a tight breath, straining against the involuntary gasp that nearly left her lips.

For though she was poised and ready to carry through with her plan, the table had begun its sprightly gambol without the least assistance from her.

Chapter 23

GOD bless her!

His back to the music room door, Mick heaved a sigh of relief and smiled.

The woman was amazing as well as beautiful!

As quickly and quietly as he could, he raced up the staircase and along the corridor he'd scouted out earlier, all the while congratulating himself for being canny enough to fall in love with Julia.

She had the mind of a scholar, the craftiness of the best of thieves, and the body of an angel. Not a bad combination, that.

Still smiling, he stopped before the door to the study. The key Harriet had been so gracious to provide was in his pocket, and he fished it out and inserted it into the lock.

The door swung open.

So far, everything had gone as planned. Mick dismissed the flicker of apprehension that assailed him at the thought. So far, everything had gone as planned. That in itself should have been enough to make him nervous.

He stepped over the threshold and into the study, clicking the door closed behind him. Turning up the gas, Mick looked around. Like so many of the other studies and libraries he'd hunted through in the past four years, the room was unexceptional. Except for the books.

The entire far wall of the massive study was dominated by bookshelves. They rose to the ceiling, each inch of shelving crammed with leather-bound volumes that spilled onto the floors, the tables, even the huge desk that stood against the far wall of the room.

It was an amazing display, all the more surprising because Dolly Ashcroft did not seem the type who would be concerned with anything more intellectual than the gossip columns in the London newspapers.

"Damned aristocrats," Mick mumbled to himself and headed toward the desk. "Always trying to impress each other."

The minute he touched the uppermost drawer, he knew his search there would be useless. The desk drawers were unlocked; there was nothing here Dolly Ashcroft wished to keep secret.

Just to be safe, he made a cursory examination of the desk's contents. He found nothing. A quick inspection of the rest of the room proved no more successful. There was no safe, nothing hidden behind the paintings, or beneath the carpets, or inside the bric-a-brac that lined the mantel.

He turned his attention back to the books.

"Face it, boyo," he grumbled. "She's outsmarted you. That Ashcroft woman's tucked the Chief's letters into one of these bloody books."

"FOR the love of Mike!" Mick tossed another book onto the pile at his feet. "Of all the damned, troublesome things the woman could have done." He ruffled through the pages of the last book near the fireplace and turned his attention to a stack in front of the windows.

This pile proved no more fruitful.

"Damned Saxons!" He kicked at the stack nearest his feet and turned to scan the books that lined the shelves. There must be over a thousand of them, far too many to examine in one night.

If only he could use a little of Julia's magic.

The thought crowded out all others and Mick wondered how she was faring down in the music room. So far, everything must be going well. If it was not, he was certain he would have heard the noises of the guests' departure.

Magic.

The word came again to his mind, and he was reminded of Dolly Ashcroft's fascination with the subject.

Searching the books on the shelves, he found seven or eight grouped together, the titles of which left no doubt that the books were about magic and spiritualism.

Mediumism as Explained in the Context of Modern Europe proved no more successful than any of the other books he'd rifled through. Neither did *Belief in the Occult*. But unlike the others, these books were well-worn, the dog-eared pages and notes scrawled in the margins attesting to the fact that Dolly Ashcroft not only read them, but studied them as well.

He was halfway through *Notes on the Materializations of Ectoplasmic Beings* when something slipped out of it and fell to the floor.

"Sweet Mother of mercy!" Mick raised the packet in his hands and smiled. "And isn't it about time something went right?"

He had just tucked the Chief's letters inside his shirt and finished doing up his buttons when the door to the study snapped open.

IT was not so much a rapping as it was a thumping, a heavy, resonant knocking that pulsed through the table like a heartbeat.

Julia felt the vibrations travel through the wood to her fingertips, each rap rumbling through her as if it were more physical force than sound.

If she wondered still where the noises came from, she did not stop to consider it. It seemed her capacity to think clearly had escaped her when the table first began to move. It had completely abandoned her when the tapping sounds began.

Now, the room reverberated with the noise, each a duplicate of the pounding of her heart.

Along with her audience, she listened to every rap, counting out the taps to form letters, keeping track of the letters to make words. As each word was completed, she congratulated herself. Not because she had the least thing to do with the rat-a-tat that formed the words, but because she managed to keep her voice unruffled as she deciphered each ghostly missive.

"That, I believe, was a message for Mr. Mayhew," she said, as the last tap rebounded off the gold brocade walls and faded from their hearing. "It spelled 'believe,' did it not?" She turned in her chair, hoping to hear the slightest indication of wonder in Mayhew's reply.

"Believe!" Mayhew grunted the word back at her. "That's the most preposterous thing I've ever heard, young lady. And if you think you can—"

For a moment, Julia did not understand why his voice sounded suddenly as if he were being smothered. In the dark, she could just make out Mayhew's profile, and she followed his dumbfounded gape to where it was riveted on the far wall.

There, her own gaze stopped. Her mouth fell open, and though Julia did not join in the chorus of wonder and disbelief voiced by the rest of the audience, she was convinced it was not because she did not want to speak, but because she could not.

For not ten feet away, was a spirit.

It glowed like a shaft of moonlight, the wall behind it showing through so that it seemed more dream than substance. Neither man nor woman, grown-up or child, the apparition appeared to be as light as a cloud, as airy as marshfire. It trembled and took form, gliding slowly toward them, more than four feet from the ground.

The first moments of heart-stopping fear dissolved, leaving Julia feeling nothing but utter amazement. She had read of the trick. She'd even practiced it several times. But she had never had the nerve to try it herself; she had never seen it performed in public. And she had never dreamed it could have such an astonishing impact.

She heard Dolly Ashcroft fall back heavily in her chair, sobbing with shock and the exhilaration of seeing a lifelong dream brought to fulfillment. The lady next to Dolly had fainted straightaway, Julia was sure of that. She listened as the woman's husband fanned her frantically, urging her to consciousness. In fact, each person at the table seemed just as thunderstruck.

As the apparition swirled above their heads and began its slow and stately glide back to the far end of the room, Mayhew flung himself from his chair. The next second, the lights were on and the sight that met all their eyes stunned them into silence.

The spirit was still there, a piece of luminous painted fabric hanging limply from a fishing line attached to the end of a telescopic rod. Harriet Lloyd Atwalter was holding that rod.

There was not the least hint of guilt in Harriet's expression. She blinked into the bright lights like a myopic owl, her eyes wide, an immense and very smug smile lighting her face.

For an instant, her gaze met Julia's and her smile widened, like that of a student who had just impressed his favorite schoolmaster with his prowess.

Julia could not help but smile in return. She was, obviously, the only one who was amused.

Dolly Ashcroft's voice rose above the grumbles of disapproval coming from her guests.

"Harriet! How could you?"

"I told you it was nonsense." Mayhew cut through Dolly's appalled sputterings. "It's poppycock, all of it. Engineered, no doubt, by this imposter." He pointed an accusing finger in Julia's direction.

Julia sat up, a protest ready on her lips. Before she could speak a work, Harriet was out of her chair.

She cast the telescopic rod and the drooping spirit to the floor. "No," she said. "She had nothing to do with it. It was my idea. All my idea. I had it planned weeks ago, long before I knew the Countess would be conducting tonight's séance. I did it to strike back at you, Dolly. To make a mockery of your little gathering the way you have made a mockery of my marriage. And I surprised each and every one of you, didn't I?"

Though Dolly struggled to control her voice, the bright splotches of red that mottled her throat and the bulging shelf of her chest confirmed her outrage. She rose out of her chair like an island surfacing from the depths of a roiling sea and faced Harriet, her hands flat against the table.

"And do you dare to make light of all I believe in?" she demanded. "And to shame me in front of my guests?"

To Julia's surprise, Harriet held her ground. She tossed a defiant, remorseless look at her aunt.

"I can dare anything now," she said, her voice steady though a gleam of recklessness lit her eyes. "I can dare anything and do anything. Because now you know how much I hate you."

"Harriet—" It was Julia who spoke this time, her hand out to her friend.

Harriet paid her no mind.

"You can keep me locked up here in the middle of nowhere," Harriet continued, her voice high, her words spoken quickly as if they had festered far too long inside and could no longer be contained. "You and your nephew. You and my husband." She laughed, the sound of it so bitter it sent chills shooting through Julia's body.

"He stays in London, stays there with his mistress." Harriet flashed a look around the table in answer to the gasps of horror from the other guests and the indignant protests of Dolly.

"Surprised?" Tears streamed from Harriet's eyes and splattered against the bodice of her gown, marking it with her misery. "Or are you simply horrified? No more so than I. No more so than I was when I discovered Reggie Atwalter married me for my money and my money alone. He has that now, doesn't he, dear Aunt Dolly? He has it, and he shares it with you, and you keep me here, a prisoner. What's that you say?" Harriet looked in wide-eyed wonder at one of the woman guests.

"No gentleman would ever treat his wife so? No gentleman would ever abandon a woman who is having his child? No gentleman would ever—"

The words refused to come. A mournful sound halfway between a shriek and a sob filled the room and Harriet crumpled to the floor.

Julia was the first to move. She rounded the table, but before she could reach Harriet, she was jostled out of the way by Dolly, who cast her aside as being of no more importance than the servants who had arrived in response to Harriet's anguished scream.

She was pushed even further to the back of the crowd by the other guests, vultures all, who crowded around Harriet's prostrate body, their nostrils flared with the delicious scent of scandal.

Julia took the moment to look around. Mayhew was still against the wall, his face white, obviously more disturbed at witnessing real suffering than he had ever been in writing about it. The servants had gathered in a small circle close to the door, some of the younger girls crying despite their best efforts to show bravery.

In the excitement, no one but Julia noticed that Madame Krakowska's assistant was conspicuously absent.

Chapter 24

FOUR days.

He had promised to meet her in four days.

Julia held up one hand, shielding her eyes to look out over the gray-green sea.

Four days, and four more, and four more besides she had waited, and still, Mick had not come.

Sighing, she turned to walk the length of the seafront just down the hill from the cottage Teague had let for their use.

Four days, and four more, and four more besides. Julia felt her heart squeeze and fought against the melancholy that filled her at the thought, as real as the leaden Irish sky, as impossible to ignore as the implacable alliance of sand and waves that sucked at her feet and drenched the hem of her gown.

The tide would be in soon, she could tell, as much from the way the water lapped about her boots as from the circling of gulls, eager to find their dinners. The tide would be in soon, and another day of anticipation would turn into another lonely, desperate night of waiting.

There had been no sign of Mick at Dolly Ashcroft's after the ill-fated séance. No sign of him, no indication of where he was or where he might have gone, no suggestion from anyone that he had been discovered, or intercepted, or captured.

It was as if he had vanished when the lights in the music room had been turned off. Vanished forever.

Turning her back on the water, Julia trudged up the hill and on toward the tiny cottage. She'd stoked the peat fire before she came outdoors, and the smoke hung, a wafer of gray, just above the thatched roof. She took a deep breath, strangely comforted by the scent that had been so foreign only a short time ago. Now, the aroma of burning peat was as much a part of her existence as the salt smell of the air, the dark green carpet of forests and hills that softened the distant horizon, the aching in her heart.

She pulled herself to a stop, the thought stealing her breath and bringing a sting of tears to her eyes.

Tomorrow she would wire London again. She sought to comfort herself with the thought. Tomorrow she would travel up to Dublin and send another wire to Teague. Tomorrow she would talk to the men who sailed the mailpackets and hope for word of a tall, golden-haired man traveling alone. Tomorrow she would scour the newspapers for any mention of Mick's name. Surely if he had been arrested . . .

This thought was too much, and she pushed it from her mind. Surely if he had been arrested, Teague would have heard. Surely if he had been apprehended, the word would have come to her through the loyal network of Parnell supporters who had made her feel so welcome here in Wicklow. Surely someone, somewhere, would know something.

The tears that streamed from her eyes combined with the salt spray to make her cheeks wet and sticky. Julia swiped at them halfheartedly and pushed open the cottage door.

The fire guttered in the gush of air, flickering and fading before it righted itself. It was a mild evening, and she left the door open, hoping the rhythmic sound of the waves would calm and console her.

Sloughing off the rough homespun shawl she had bought from a local woman, she draped it over a chair.

"Good evening, my fine and fancy lady."

The voice was no louder than the crackle of the fire, and for a moment, Julia was sure she had imagined it.

She spun toward the door in time to see Mick emerge from behind it.

"And isn't that a shameless way to welcome me home." He rubbed at a spot on his head. "You need to be more careful opening doors. You nearly knocked me out." He grinned at her, his face shining with delight.

Julia knew she should answer him. Somehow, she knew she should run to him and throw her arms around him and laugh out loud. But she could do nothing.

She found herself rooted to the spot, paralyzed by a sense of relief so fierce and overpowering, she could no more move than she could stop the torrent of tears that cascaded down her cheeks or quiet the soft, ragged sobs that filled her throat and made every breath painful.

Mick took one step toward her, a tender smile lighting his face.

"I tried to get a message to you," he explained, his voice as soft as a whisper. "But there were these Home Office fellows on my tail, and I didn't want to take a chance they'd find out about you. Are you very angry?"

"Angry?" The sound rose from her, more of a wail than a word. "I waited and waited at Dolly Ashcroft's as long as I could, and you never came. And so I came here and I've waited all these days and . . ." Unable to deal with the emotion any longer, Julia burst into a rush of tears.

In two long strides, Mick was across the room. He folded her into his arms.

"It's sorry I am, *acushla,* but it couldn't be helped. I knew you'd be worried. Damn it! I didn't mean to make you cry." He trailed his thumbs across her cheeks, banishing her tears, and bent to place a sweet, warm kiss against her lips.

"I never did have the chance to tell you about the two randy aristocrats I met in the corridor when I was looking for Dolly Ashcroft's study, did I?" He smiled down at her, coaxing away her pain.

Julia sniffed and shook her head.

"Well, wouldn't you know it. I had just nipped the letters and stashed them away when who should show up in the study but those two. Seems they must have tried every other unlocked room and hadn't found a comfortable enough place. They . . . they . . ."

Mick blushed all the way from his neck to the roots of his hair.

"They were looking for a place to be intimate and I'm afraid they found it. I couldn't move from behind the desk or they would have noticed me in a moment."

By the time he'd finished this much of his story, Julia was laughing.

She raised her eyebrows and smiled up at Mick. "And did you stay in the study the whole time they were there?"

"Dear Mother of God, did I not." He shook his head, his wretchedness apparent in his expression. "It was the most awfulest thing. The way they spoke to each other! If I ever tell you your eyes are dark and limpid pools, promise me you'll slap me silly. And the things they did!" Mick pulled a face.

"I thought you couldn't see them!" She gave him a look of mock horror.

"I couldn't," Mick countered instantly. "But I could hear everything and that was bad enough. Who would've believed that stick of a woman would have had that much energy! And the old goat himself, he wasn't about to give up until well after you'd left. Once they were finally done and gone, the house was locked. I never did get out until the next morning. Sneaked out the scullery door behind the maid's back when she went to empty the slop buckets."

"And you went to London?"

"That I did. That's when those Home Office boys picked up my scent. I couldn't wire you with them following me, and I couldn't risk Teague's safety by going there. After all that, I found out the Chief wasn't even there. He'd gone to Paris for a meeting of the Home Rulists. I wasn't about to leave the letters in London for him, or trust them to anyone else. I followed him and finally caught up with him."

"And he has his letters back?" Julia heaved a huge sigh of relief, the weight that had been lying heavy on her heart all these months finally lifting.

"He does." Mick smiled down at her. "And he says to thank you, and that he's anxious to meet you. And that he hopes the two of us will be of service to him again if he should ever need us."

"And you told him . . . ?"

"I told him we will gladly serve Ireland. Both of us. Together."

Mick brought his hands up, one on either side of Julia's head, and tilted her face up to his.

"You look fine, Julia. As fine as you ever did. And the smell . . ." He bent far enough to breathe deep the scent that wreathed her hair. "You smell of peat and sea and salt. Dark Rosaleen. That's the name the Fenians use for Ireland. Dark Rosaleen." He tugged off the scarf she'd worn outside on her head and spread his fingers through her hair, smoothing it over her shoulders and across her breasts.

"You smell of Ireland, and you taste . . ." He bent to touch a trail of slow, gentle kisses along the line of her jaw. "You taste like the sea and the land and the air when the fog's just burned off and the world is fresh and green again. Like Ireland herself."

There were no words for the warmth that filled Julia's insides. No words that could ever express the feelings in her heart, the joy she felt when she looked up into Mick's eyes and saw there the reflection of her own love.

She wrapped her arms around his neck and brought her

mouth to his, reveling in the flavor of his lips against hers, basking in the warmth of his affection.

She moved a step back to better see his face. "Patrick. I said I'd call you that once we were here. Once we were free of all the lies and all the secrets. May I, Patrick?"

He lifted her in his arms and swung her around until her head spun and her legs felt as if they would not hold her.

"Yes!" His voice reverberated against the whitewashed walls. "Patrick O'Flaherty Fitzgerald. And proud of it I am. But right now I'm a bit more concerned with other things than just my name or my pride, and if you don't let me kiss you good and hard like I've been wanting to these past weeks . . ."

He did not wait for her answer, but pulled her to him and covered her lips with his own, his tongue nudging her lips apart, his hands beginning a slow exploration of each familiar and beloved curve.

Like the waves outside their door responding to the relentless pull of the moon, she caught the flame of the insistent rhythm, heartbeat against heartbeat, minds and souls and bodies in exquisite harmony.

"The bedroom," she breathed into his ear, "is up the stairs along the far wall."

A laugh rumbled through his chest. "And I," he said quite clearly, "can surely not wait until we get there. It's right here for it, my fine and fancy lady. Right here. Right now."

Julia threw back her head and laughed. She gave him a sly smile. "With the fire going and the lamps lit?"

"Yes." Patrick smiled down at her, his blue eyes reflecting the light of the fire, warming her body and soul. "With all the lamps lit."

Diamond Wildflower Romance

A breathtaking new line of spectacular novels set in the untamed frontier of the American West. Every month, Diamond Wildflower brings you new adventures where passionate men and women dare to embrace their boldest dreams. Finally, romances that capture the very spirit and passion of the wild frontier.

__*FRONTIER BRIDE* by Ann Carberry
1-55773-753-3/$4.99

__*CAPTIVE ANGEL* by Elaine Crawford
1-55773-766-5/$4.99

__*COLORADO TEMPEST* by Mary Lou Rich
1-55773-799-1/$4.99

__*GOLDEN FURY* by Deborah James
1-55773-811-4/$4.99

__*DESERT FLAME* by Anne Harmon
1-55773-824-6/$4.99

__*BANDIT'S KISS* by Mary Lou Rich
1-55773-842-4/$4.99

__*AUTUMN BLAZE* by Samantha Harte
1-55773-853-X/$4.99 (February 1993)

__*RIVER TEMPTRESS* by Elaine Crawford
1-55773-867-X/$4.99 (March 1993)

For Visa, MasterCard and American Express orders ($15 minimum) call: 1-800-631-8571

FOR MAIL ORDERS: CHECK BOOK(S). FILL OUT COUPON. SEND TO:

BERKLEY PUBLISHING GROUP
390 Murray Hill Pkwy., Dept. B
East Rutherford, NJ 07073

NAME_____

ADDRESS_____

CITY_____

STATE_____ZIP_____

PLEASE ALLOW 6 WEEKS FOR DELIVERY.
PRICES ARE SUBJECT TO CHANGE WITHOUT NOTICE.

POSTAGE AND HANDLING:
$1.75 for one book, 75¢ for each additional. Do not exceed $5.50.

BOOK TOTAL	$ _____
POSTAGE & HANDLING	$ _____
APPLICABLE SALES TAX	$ _____
(CA, NJ, NY, PA)	
TOTAL AMOUNT DUE	$ _____

PAYABLE IN US FUNDS.
(No cash orders accepted.)

406